FOR WHAT IT'S WORTH

FOR WHAT IT'S WORTH

KELLI MILLIGAN STAMMEN

J Merrill Publishing, Inc., Columbus 43207
www.JMerrill.pub

Library of Congress Control Number: 2020924736
ISBN-13: 978-1-950719-72-3 (Paperback)
ISBN-13: 978-1-950719-71-6 (eBook)

Title: For What It's Worth
Author: Kelli Milligan Stammen
Cover Artwork: Amanda Kolitsos

CHAPTERS

Note: Most chapter titles originate from songs of the 60s and 70s.

To say this work was a labor of love is to sell it short. So many people, places, hopes, fears, dreams, and realities in my life, and the lives of those I love and admire are wrapped up in this work.

Thank you to my family and friends, all who have helped flesh out this other baby of mine. My biggest love and gratitude go to my husband and children who inspire, test, and love me every day.

For what it's worth, I hope you laugh, cry, live and love the story of Jesse and Becca as much as I do.

PRELUDE

Late December 1968

Rain.

He was vaguely aware that it was raining, pouring, in fact.

Wave after wave of water fell off the trees above him, crashing down onto him in a relentless onslaught. He tried to open his eyes. Actually, he believed his eyes were open, but he couldn't see anything. As he lay flat on his back in mud and puddles, all he could do was feel. He could feel pain -- a sharp, searing pain radiating throughout the top of his body. The pain seemed to be coming straight from his heart.

He used all the strength he had left to raise his right hand, weakly attempting to swat at the rain. His stark white face was fixed in a pinched grimace. Giving up on making the rain go away, he tried to roll over from his back, trying to push himself up with his right hand. But he couldn't find the ground under him, and soon, with a sound somewhere between a sob and a primal moan, he gave up and let his hand slide back to the ground with a gentle thud.

Between the rain and the pain, he couldn't breathe. Taking a deep breath was impossible. Small, shallow breaths were all he could muster. He was waiting for the darkness to come, almost welcoming the numbness ahead. Almost.

Then he remembered he had legs. If only his legs...

"Move," he whispered weakly to no one, willing his body to do anything, *anything* he asked it to do. "Move..."

In that lucid moment, he realized the agony he felt from his chest up seemed to stop at his waist. He couldn't feel his legs. The numbness had started to creep up his body.

An overwhelming feeling of sadness and loss that he had never once associated with this moment in his life crushed against him. His tears started to mix with the downpour as both rolled down the sides of his face.

As he lay there for several minutes, body and soul broken, the rain started to let up, though he didn't realize it. What thoughts he could piece together all swirled around her -- knowing deep down that he'd never see her again. He yelled out more from emotional wreckage than physical pain, and yet the darkness still stubbornly refused to come.

Suddenly a wave of strength washed through him, and he forced his eyes open a crack. He could see the trees and the sun through the rain. He felt a swift, strong wind that seemed to drown out all other noise. The numbness started to seep into this chest as he raised his right hand again and slowly, clumsily fumbled with the drenched pocket of his shirt. After several attempts, he pulled out the soaked contents inside with shaking fingers.

He tried to focus on the faded photo, but his eyes wouldn't cooperate, and the small amount of strength he had seemed to run away as quickly as it had come.

His hand dropped with the picture against his chest, and his eyelids fell closed once again.

———

All she could clearly make out was the word "die."

She watched through a haze all the flurry of activity around her. She was there, but she wasn't there at the same time. Doctors, nurses, all of them running around, not listening to her, not letting her tell them what needed to happen. They weren't listening.

The nurse, the one who had been so kind, moved in front of her, took her hand, and gave her a gentle, sad smile. Becca began to panic in earnest.

"What?!" she demanded, her blue eyes wide and watery and her heart pounding so hard and loud in her ears she was certain everyone could hear it.

"It's time," the nurse said quietly.

"No!" Becca yelled, trying to jerk her hand away, but the nurse held firm. "No, it's not time!"

"Miss Schmidt..."

"No!" she whispered fiercely, now gripping the nurse's hands in both of hers, squeezing her so tight her knuckles turned white. "It can't be...not now!"

The other nurse came over, the one who had been so rude before. She had a syringe at the ready between her fingers. She was waiting for the first nurse to give her the order.

"Should we sedate her?" she asked in a cold, matter-of-fact voice.

"Wait, Gladys," the first nurse said, somewhat exasperated at her colleague, but her gaze never left Becca's.

"Miss Schmidt," she said, her heart breaking for the young woman before her. "I know this is...difficult...but..."

"You don't understand," Becca said desperately, searching the woman's eyes with a crazed look on her face. "He needs me...I...I need him..."

Gladys took another step toward Becca before the kind nurse put up her hand in a "stop" gesture to halt her, and then she motioned to the side of the room.

Becca could see Liz and Penny come into view through her tears. Tears were streaming down each of their faces. She vaguely thought she caught a glimpse of her mother, too, but knew at that point she must have been hallucinating.

"Becca...Rebecca," Liz whispered softly as she took her hand, and the nurse stepped back a moment.

"Don't let them do it," Becca begged, imploring first Liz, then Penny. "Don't let them take him away from me..."

"Becca," Penny choked out, stroking her hair. "He...he wouldn't want... it...this way. We have to let the doctors...do what's best..."

Liz nodded and cried harder as Becca's fingers clamped down on hers.

Becca started to tremble as she looked at her best friends; her last rays of hope...and the betrayal and despair she felt ran deep.

"How could you..." she said miserably, looking right at Penny, her breathing deep and ragged. With enormous strength, she grabbed Liz's hand and jerked her until they were face to face, causing Liz to gasp in pain.

"*How could you*?!" she growled at her, sweat beading around her temples now.

"Rebecca," Liz said sternly, tears spilling unchecked down her cheeks, trying to disengage her hand. "I'm sorry...I'm so sorry. Becca..."

Becca's nails scraped against her hand as her friend made one more attempt to pull away.

"Let go," Liz said a little more forcefully. "Becca, you have to let go!"

Liz snatched her hand away and started massaging it, both she and Penny sobbing now.

"I won't let you do it," Becca said, trying to move away from them. "I won't! I swear to God, I won't!"

"Gladys," the kind nurse said, quickly coming to the young woman's side and grabbing her arm, struggling to hold her still.

"Now!"

1

IDES OF MARCH

CRASHING RED-STRIPED, WOODEN PINS AND THE UNYIELDING THUD OF bowling balls beginning their journey down hardwood lanes served as exclamation points to the chatter filtering through the smoke-filled haze in the room.

Jesse pulled the last loop of his laces tight to secure his bowling shoes and sat up in the blue, plastic chairs lined along with the scoring table. He reached over to grab the last half of his cigarette out of the ashtray when he saw Penny trying to walk back to their spot while balancing a martini and three cans of beer through the crowd.

He stood and ran his fingers through his dark chestnut hair to brush back the bangs that had fallen too far down his forehead.

"Need some help?"

"Thanks," Penny said, handing him a beer can and the martini. "Martinis?"

Jesse set down the drinks and picked up his half-finished cigarette, taking a quick drag.

"Drink of the month," he said, squinting at Penny through the smoke of his exhale.

"Drink of the rich," Penny scoffed, lifting her curly, strawberry blond locks over one shoulder and walking to the scorer's table to begin writing in the names of the bowlers.

Jesse looked toward the crowd gathered around the 24-lane bowling alley entrance, one of the largest in the Village, and packed on this Friday night -- a league night.

"They better be here tonight," Penny said, a hint of agitation in her voice. "I don't want to pull ringers again."

She crossed her long, jean-clad legs and crossed her arms over her loose blouse, shooting Jesse an annoyed look.

"Yeah," Jesse said, shaking his head and sinking back into the plastic chairs.

He and Penny had formed a team the autumn before with his girlfriend and his roommate, Keith. They played in the mixed couples bowling league. They were there every Friday night, except for the month around the holidays when the tournaments went on hiatus.

"Ah...martini!" Felicia said, coming up from behind Jesse and pecking him on the cheek. "Thanks, babe."

Jesse just nodded and winced a little at his girlfriend -- she was covered in large costume jewelry and bright, loud bell--bottoms -- the latest fashion fad. He and Felicia had been together for almost five months now. Their relationship had started off fun -- something different for them both. He'd met her at one of the events he was often required to suffer through as business manager for the large NYC Plumbers and Pipefitters Union. She was the daughter of one of the long-time members of the Public Utilities Commission board. He was well on his way to being blitzed when she introduced herself to him at the fundraiser where they met. She was loaded by the time they'd stumbled back to his apartment later that night.

One thing led to another, and before he knew it, he had bagged an uptown girl, and she'd enjoyed "slumming it" with her boy toy in the Village. It had gone on longer than he expected it to, but for a long time, he was just as ambivalent as she was about breaking it off. They were having fun, and there weren't any strong feelings involved... until recently. About a month ago, Felicia started to get needy and possessive. Jesse was pretty much ready to end it then -- he didn't want the drama or strings -- but she kept hanging on, despite his best efforts to send split signals her way.

"Where *is* everybody?" Felicia asked, more loudly than she should have, even over the din of the noisy bowling alley. She took a sip of her martini and sat down next to Jesse, immediately leaning into him, spilling some of her drink on his jeans.

"They're coming," Joe answered, walking up to them from the other end of the building, rolling his eyes when he spotted Felicia draped over a mildly disgusted Jesse. "Just saw the Mister and Misses coming down the street."

Penny chuckled at that, putting down her little yellow pencil and picking up her cigarette from the ashtray, flicking the ash away. She smiled up at Joe, who smiled back before sitting down to put on his own bowling shoes.

It was just before the winter league hiatus when the empty apartment next to theirs, in the building where Jesse and Keith lived and their friend Joe crashed most of the time, became occupied again. Jesse and Keith knew a doctor owned the unit, and when Old Mrs. Redd died that November, they assumed he'd sell the place. The Village wasn't exactly where society's upper crust was eager to live these days. Instead, his daughter, Liz, moved in. She was fresh out of NYU and looking to make her mark in fashion. She was always decked out in the latest clogs and short skirt, polyester suits that hugged every curve. And she'd convinced her Dad to let her live in the apartment in the Village because the "vibe" was "exciting."

Keith practically salivated to the point of dehydration when they first met her on the weekend, she moved in. Jesse thought she was beautiful and completely out of Keith Murphy's league. It wasn't that Keith wasn't good-looking. He was tall with dark blond hair, deep blue eyes, and an easy smile, but he wasn't a "catch a fox" kind of guy. But Jesse sure dug watching his new neighbor, who clearly was born to flirt, turn his roommate into a pretzel by simply saying "hello" and batting her hazel eyes at him. That was until her pre-med boyfriend Elijah "Eli" Schmidt came along, heavy cardboard box in hand, and began shooting darts with his big brown eyes at both men. The dude wasn't bigger than them, but he made it clear Liz was his territory -- and even clearer that he wasn't thrilled two attractive, young bucks lived in the apartment next to her. He was even less amused when he met Joe the next day.

Yet, the new neighbors got to know each other as the calendar turned from '67 to '68. They got to know Eli, too, since he was at Liz's place, and not his graduate dorm room on campus, almost every night. He was there so often that Keith started calling them "the Mister and Misses" as a joke, and the nicknames stuck.

"What about the other two?" Penny asked, taking a drag and looking around.

Joe shrugged, glancing toward the front door when he spotted Eli and Liz making their way past the crowd at the entrance, which was thinning out as teams gathered at their assigned lanes. Eli gave the group a friendly wave as Liz smiled at them.

Despite the brush with intense jealousy that first weekend, the neighbors, along with Penny and sometimes Felicia, hung out almost every night. They all came from wildly different backgrounds, but their personalities mixed well. Once Keith knew how serious Eli and Liz were, he completely backed off and relaxed. Keith was funny in an obvious way, while his roommate was more subdued. Jesse could whip out a witty, sarcastic comment in a flash. Otherwise, it was sometimes hard to tell what was going on behind his piercing, pale blue eyes.

"Where's your roomie?" Penny asked, giving Liz a hug before she sat down to change her shoes.

"They're right behind us," Liz said, gesturing behind her with one hand as Eli bent down to pull her shoes off for her. She smiled sweetly at him. Seeing this, Joe rolled his eyes again at Jesse, but Jesse didn't see it. His mind was otherwise occupied, and his eyes were focused on the front entrance.

It had been a little over a month ago when a new member came to the group. Eli's younger sister, Rebecca, moved in with her best friend, Liz, just after Valentine's Day. In the few months, the neighbors had known each other they had heard about but never met the woman. All they knew was that she was wrapping up a media internship after graduating from Northwestern in Chicago in December. She'd just moved back to New York after securing a job in the news department of CBS television, working with popular newscaster Walter Cronkite. They knew she and Liz were tight, and Eli thought the sun rose and set on his sister...when it wasn't rising and setting on Liz, of course.

The Mister and Misses had been so excited about "Becca" coming to live with Liz that Jesse had become somewhat annoyed with both of them. He'd seen her picture and agreed with Keith and Joe that she was very attractive. Still, in the couple of days before her arrival, it was all anyone wanted to talk about. Jesse was left to wonder what on earth the big deal was about this particular woman.

And then he met her.

He'd come home from work late on the day of her arrival, expecting to be berated by everyone for missing dinner. Instead, Eli and Becca had been late getting to the apartment from their parents' house on

Long Island, and dinner was yet to be served when he strolled in the door...

"Jesse!" Liz said, standing as he entered the room. "There you are!"

"Sorry I'm late," he mumbled as he casually looked around the room, seeing no unfamiliar faces.

"Don't sweat it," Liz assured him. "Becca just got here."

"Are you...hiding her?" he asked, scanning the apartment again.

"She's in the other room," Eli said, setting down the last of the plates. "She'll be out in a minute."

Jesse nodded as Joe caught his eye and gave him a big, goofy smile. Jesse sat beside Keith at the table and had to shake his head when his roommate nonchalantly leaned over and whispered "stacked" in his ear and widened his eyes.

"Here she is," Liz said as Becca walked out of the spare bedroom. Liz walked over to her and put an arm around Becca, sweeping the woman's very long, very straight black hair over her shoulders in the process.

"Jesse," Liz said as Jesse immediately stood up from the kitchen table. "This is my dear, dear friend, and Eli's sister, Becca."

"It's so nice to meet you," Becca said, smiling and extending a hand to him. "Everyone's been giving me the low down on you."

Jesse's slow grin came over his face.

"Have they?" he said, returning her smile as he raised his hand to shake hers.

Her smile deepened as she took his hand and gazed boldly into his eyes. Jesse thought her hands were soft, but her grip was strong. Her smile was adorned with little dimples on each side of her cheeks as she looked up at him.

But...it was her eyes. Her eyes were completely mesmerizing, hypnotic almost, and the deepest yet brightest blue he'd ever seen...

"Over here," he heard Eli bellow across the bowling alley, waving his arms.

Jesse turned his head and craned his neck a little, not noticing how closely Felicia was watching him as she slowly sipped her martini. He spotted the pair walking arm and arm toward the rest of them. Keith had a wide smile on his face.

"Sorry! Sorry," he said quickly. "We got...distracted."

Becca shook her head at the bemused look on Penny's face, then clarified what her boyfriend meant after catching the death stare her brother was tossing in Keith's direction.

"Truth is, he had to take a wiz... again," she said, rolling her eyes at Keith. "It's been three times since we walked in the door."

"I had a lot of coffee," Keith said, attempting to defend himself, playfully pulling her to him and tickling her. "You try being up at 5 a.m. to open."

"I was awake at 4 a.m.," she said, playfully pushing him away. "Mr. Cronkite likes his coffee fresh."

"Mr. Cronkite isn't there 'til noon," he retorted.

"And 'that's the way it is,'" Becca joked, using Mr. Cronkite's signature sign-off phrase, which made Jesse chuckle.

"Ah, hum," Eli said, clearing his throat, ready to put an end to their teasing as quickly as possible. "You ready to bowl?"

"Yes, sir," Keith said a little too jovially as he tripped into a chair, crashing into Joe, bowling bag and all.

"Whoa," Joe said, catching him. "Easy there..."

"Sorry," Keith mumbled as he straightened up, reaching to get his bowling shoes out of his bag. Felicia made a loud noise of annoyance.

Jesse briefly looked over at her before lighting another cigarette. He took a deep drag and let it out, leaning back in his chair and looking first at Keith, then at Becca.

Becca's eyes met his, and she gave him a small smile before bending down and pulling out her own bowling equipment.

"OK," Joe said, standing and walking over to the top of the lane, bowling ball in hand. He glanced at their competition and smiled.

"Let's get it on!"

2

RING OF FIRE

"WANT A LIGHT?"

Becca halted her fruitless search for matches at the bowling alley bar and turned to Jesse, cigarette at the ready.

"Please," she said, putting it to her lips. He stepped to her and flicked open his lighter, brushing against her as he cradled the flame in his hands and moved closer. Jesse watched her face as she closed her eyes and gently sucked in. When her eyes opened again, she caught him staring at her.

"Thanks," she exhaled, smiling at him. He grinned back, and her heart quickened just a touch, just as it had the first time she'd laid eyes on him...

"Jesse," Liz said. "This is my dear, dear friend, and Eli's sister, Becca."

Becca watched as the man immediately stood and made his way over to her. He was tall, a little lanky but in a strong, lean sort of way -- and even from 15 feet away, she could tell his eyes were blue.

"It's so nice to meet you," Becca said, smiling and extending a hand to him. "Everyone's been giving me the low down on you."

A sweet, crooked grin came over his face as he put his hand out for hers.

"Have they?" he said, his warm hand fitting snugly into her grasp.

Then he smiled at her, and her breath nearly caught. Those eyes and...my God, that smile...

"All good," she said as she released his hand, her eyes never leaving his.

"Solid," he said with a little nod. "Heard a lot about you, too. Welcome to the building."

"Thanks."

She smiled again, and he grinned as a brief silence hung in the air.

"Are we ready to eat?" Joe finally said, looking longingly at the casserole at the other end of the table. "I'm kinda starving."

Jesse chuckled and moved to pull Becca's chair out for her.

"Wasting away before our very eyes," Keith said, nudging Joe with his elbow and making everyone laugh.

Becca grinned at Jesse as she sat down and whispered, "thank you."

He caught her eye again, and she felt almost like she couldn't tear her gaze away.

"You're welcome," he nodded and then took his seat at the other end of the table.

Though they still barely knew each other, she'd spent a lot of time with him and the whole group since that first meeting. She learned that Jesse had a dry sense of humor, which she completely appreciated. He was particularly close to Penny, who seemed sweet but dressed and spoke like a hippie. Their friendship was interesting to Becca since Penny appeared to be a total contrast to who Jesse seemed to be. Then there were Keith and Joe, who made up an eclectic version of the Three Musketeers with Jesse. Two of them, though, seemed to be open books.

Not Jesse. When he wasn't letting zingers fly, he was quiet, observational -- and just mysterious enough to make her curious about his story. She sensed that he deliberately kept a lot of himself close to the vest, just behind those gorgeous, pale blue eyes of his -- that contrasted with his thick, wavy brown hair and his alluring grin -- made him so very attractive.

She couldn't quite figure him out, and frankly, he wasn't hers to figure out anyway. Liz told her the night she moved in when she'd mentioned how good-looking he was, that he was taken. That came as no surprise. And the more she got to know his loud and overbearing girlfriend Felicia, the more she saw the woman was determined to keep him. Jesse didn't really seem too bothered by that, either.

So, a few days later, she turned her sights to an attentive Keith. He wasn't as good-looking as Jesse, but he was available and interested and...fun.

Keith was fun, and that's honestly what she needed at the moment. She'd spent all her time at Northwestern focusing on a career in broadcast news, something that was nearly impossible for a woman to break into. She'd been interested in becoming a journalist ever since she did a report on Nelly Bly in elementary school, and she wanted to be an on-air reporter. She wanted to be on the front lines of history at a time when so many big things seemed to be happening every single moment.

Stories seemed to be breaking all the time, and TV was at the forefront of bringing the message to the masses. As unrest was taking hold in the country, civil rights leader Martin Luther King Jr. had given what many called an imploring and impassioned speech in

Atlanta in February. Mr. Cronkite had just gotten back from Vietnam, reporting on the aftermath of the Tet Offensive. Americans were restless, and thousands of American soldiers and Vietnamese civilians had already been killed In Country.

These were changing times in the United States, but it was an exciting time to be working in the news business and at CBS. When she'd gotten an interview at the NYC world headquarters, she almost couldn't believe it, and she was determined to make her mark as a newswoman.

But instead of being a reporter, the job she ended up accepting was as a gopher. She'd spent the last six weeks getting coffee for Mrs. Beele, who was Mr. Cronkite's *secretary,* and asking "how high" when any person ahead of her in the newsroom pecking order told her to jump. And that was nearly everyone. She didn't mind paying her dues; it was just a little humiliating. Living with her parents for a few days, in the beginning, didn't help, either. Moving in with Liz, though, had been a godsend.

She immediately got along with the unique mix of people her brother and best friend had discussed with such enthusiasm over the last few months. So, when Keith asked her out three nights after she moved in, she thought, "what the hell?" He made her laugh, ended up being decent enough in the sack, and seemed to balance out her neurotic, driven style pretty well.

Yes, moving in with Liz turned out to be a lot of fun.

"Where's Keith?" Jesse asked, briefly glancing around as he put his lighter back in his jeans pocket.

"Not sure," Becca said as they turned to walk back over to their lane. "He's spent a lot of time on the john. Do you think he's sick or something?"

Jesse shrugged. He had his suspicions about what was making Keith seem off lately, but no proof.

"Felicia is always in the john, and she's not sick," he said, noting that his girlfriend had gone to "check her face" for the umpteenth time since the night started.

Becca giggled a little as they rejoined the group.

Jesse glanced at the scoreboard overhead. "You're up."

Becca looked up, then took a drag on her cigarette and let out a deep sigh.

"I need a strike," she mumbled.

"What's that now?" Jesse asked, a tease in his voice.

"I need a strike," Becca repeated, putting down her cigarette and heaving up her bowling ball.

"You're not throwin' a strike," Jesse said with a disbelieving chuckle as Joe shook his head, mouthing "no" in agreement with Jesse.

"What makes you think I won't throw a strike," she asked, cocking an eyebrow at him.

"I've been watching you bowl for a month," he countered. "You haven't thrown one yet."

"That doesn't mean I can't," she challenged.

"Not with your form," he shot back.

"And just what is wrong with my form, Wanger?" she teased, tossing her long black hair alluringly over her shoulder as she exaggerated the sound of his unfortunate last name.

Suddenly Jesse's tongue felt thick, and his cheeks turned a little pink. She smiled at him, knowing she'd gotten the upper hand in this flirty repartee they seemed to slip so easily into when they were around each other.

He quickly recovered, however, and sauntered over to her, his crooked grin firmly in place. Her smile faltered just a touch when a lock of hair fell down against his forehead. She found herself fighting the urge to run her fingers through it and push it back where it belonged.

"There's nothing wrong with your form, Schmidt," he said quietly, briefly running his eyes up and down her body, making her shiver. His grin widened.

"You just can't throw a strike."

She swallowed heavily. He was towering over her now, a mirthful look in his eyes.

"Maybe you should show me how it's done," she said with a seductive grin.

He raised his eyebrows and took a step back. Then he crushed out his cig.

"Come here," he said as he took her elbow, leading her to the top of the lane. She walked with him and stood, bowling ball at the ready.

"Take a step to the right," Jesse said, standing directly behind her.

"Why?"

"You can't throw it right down the middle," he explained. When she didn't move far enough, he placed both his hands on the hips of her jeans and moved her himself.

Then he leaned against her back and lowered his face to the side of her head, his lips by her ear.

"See that spot," he said quietly, pointing to a marking on the lane.

"Yeah," she breathed.

"Hit it," he said, breathing in her perfume through the smoke and haze surrounding them. She smelled like flowers -- like deep, crimson roses...

"Do you always hit the...right...spot?" she teased quietly.

She could feel him smile against her hair, and she looked back at him, grinning.

"Always, baby," he whispered, looking right into her eyes. She jumped a little as he tightened his left hand on her waist and ran his right hand under hers, helping cradle the bowling ball. She let out a brief, nervous giggle, then held her breath, turning to look back at the pins.

He drew her arm and the ball back behind him, his other hand sliding to her stomach, keeping her firmly in place against him to keep her balance.

"Don't release too early," he said against her hair. Then he brought her arm and the ball swiftly to the front of them, lifting them both above her head.

"And make sure you follow through."

Becca was nearly trembling now as she let out a long, shaky breath. She turned her head again and smirked at him. He winked at her, knowing he'd won this round in the little game they were playing, and took a couple steps backward.

"Let'r rip," he said, folding his arms across his chest.

Becca took a deep breath to try and still her racing heart. She let it out slowly as she took a couple strides, threw her arm back, and released the ball right where Jesse had told her to.

And lo and behold, she threw a strike.

Cheers erupted as Becca screamed excitedly, threw her hands in the air, and turned to Jesse. He slapped her hands in a double high-five then briefly pulled her to him, big smiles on both their faces.

"Woo!" Liz yelled, jumping from her seat to give Becca a hug, followed by Eli. Penny and Joe were both clapping as they walked over to congratulate their friend.

"What'd I miss?" Keith said as he suddenly reappeared, rushing down the couple steps from the back of the alley to join everyone.

The only member of the team not smiling stood about 10 feet away, slowly stirring her martini and watching her man grin like a fool -- at Becca.

3

THE TIMES THEY ARE A-CHANGIN'

JOE AND PENNY WERE CROWDING AROUND THE BAR WITH OTHER TEAM captains as the evening's final tally was discussed, and the next round of the tournament was seeded. Felicia had practically ordered Jesse to follow her outside when the game ended, and Keith had gone to pay their bar tab.

Liz glanced over her shoulder at Becca, sitting alone on the chairs at their lane. She and Eli had yet to purchase their own bowling shoes and were waiting in line to return the ones they'd rented. She turned to Eli and smiled sweetly.

"Can you take care of this on your own, honey?" she said, batting her lashes at him.

"Sure," he said, taking the rented bowling shoes she was holding from her. She kissed his cheek and quickly made a beeline for his sister.

"So...what was that?" Liz asked, wide-eyed, plopping down next to her friend.

"What?" Becca said with an innocent look as she pulled off her bowling shoes.

"You? Jesse?" Liz said, nodding her head toward the building's entrance. "She's giving him holy hell now, I'm sure."

Becca rolled her eyes at Liz, trying her best to hide her smile.

"I don't know what you're talking about," she said with a wave of her hand. "She shouldn't be mad at him. It was a bowling lesson. It was nothing."

"Nothing," Liz mocked, unconvinced.

Becca shrugged and pulled on her boots.

"Got a strike, didn't I?"

"You got a strike all right," Liz said in a low voice, spying Keith out of the corner of her eye. "Against a match."

Becca let out a little snort at Liz but otherwise didn't reply as she put her bowling shoes back in her bag. Keith smiled and sat next to her, patting her on the leg and reaching down to change his shoes. She saw Jesse enter her peripheral vision and sit heavily in the chairs across from her. She couldn't help but smile to herself. She liked Keith a lot, and even though Felicia could easily get on her nerves, she knew Jesse was with her.

But, man, did she dig flirting with him. It was too far out to resist, and she knew he enjoyed it as much as she did. It was innocent -- all in good fun -- even though sometimes she *did* feel like they got a little carried away. And that crooked little grin on his face could be so irresistible, and then occasionally, she felt like she couldn't breathe when he stood close to her...

"Where's Felicia?" Keith asked as they packed the last of their equipment away.

"Out front," Jesse said quickly, as he slammed his shoes into his bag and then Felicia's into hers.

"Everything OK?" Liz asked apprehensively.

"Yep," Jesse said, convincing no one as he quickly zipped up the bags. "Just peachy."

Liz looked at Eli, who had just returned from the shoe counter. He shrugged and shook his head.

"Cumulative score, folks," Penny said, waving the scorecard and walking back to the group with Joe. "We won by three pins!"

"Knew it was close," Joe said, smiling and high--fiving with Penny, then Eli and Liz.

"That's my girl's strike, right there," Keith said giddily, pulling Becca to him. Becca briefly hugged him back, then stole a glance at Jesse, grinning. He had a bowling bag in each hand and a smug look on his face.

"Who are we going up against next Friday?" Eli asked, then added with a laugh. "Blue Balls?"

Blue Balls was a team they'd gone up against several times in the last six months or so, and players on both teams had gotten to know each other pretty well.

"No, ah, they're out," Joe said, looking over the match-up bracket in his hand.

"Why?" Liz asked. "They have a...horrible name, but they're really good, aren't they?"

Joe was no longer smiling as he shared a glance with Eli, who quickly pursed his lips together, his own eyes finding Jesse's.

The smug grin fell from Jesse's face, and he cleared his throat, looking back at Joe, who took a deep breath.

"Mike and Dean got their...notices, and the team is...breaking up," Joe said, with a nod.

And just like that, the air was sucked right out of the room. The frivolity of the evening was replaced instantly by an overwhelming, unwavering feeling of dread. That dread -- that black cloud that hung over every man of a certain age hung over his friends and family -- was the draft and the ever-escalating "military action" in Vietnam. They couldn't escape it, not one of them, even in a bowling alley on a Friday night. The fear, the conflicting emotions, the people it intimately affected, it was forever being thrown in their faces everywhere they turned.

For a moment, no one said a word. Worry flashed in Liz's eyes as she looked at Eli and mumbled "oh" in response to Joe's answer. Silently Joe handed the bracket sheet to Penny, and his eyes caught hers for just a moment. Her eyes were flashing anger; his were asking her not to unleash it right now.

Becca squeezed Keith around the waist as he stared at the ground. She looked over at Jesse -- his expression was impossible to read, and his eyes were seemingly fixed on the ball return. A chill ran down her spine. She knew how bad the war was going. She knew more from working in the newsroom than she ever wanted to know. It was an interesting job until it hit close to home -- then it was personal. She glanced at Eli, grateful that his enrollment in med school gave him an automatic draft deferment. As far as she knew, Keith, Jesse, and Joe had no such protection.

Joe cleared his throat.

"We're against Pete's Oyster Palace next week," he said, breaking the tension.

"So, if we win, we get free shellfish for a year, right?" Jesse deadpanned, and everyone forced a laugh, trying to push past the moment.

"Anyone wanna get a drink?" Eli asked. Liz, Joe, Becca, and Keith nodded their agreement.

"No, no thanks," Penny said, picking up her bowling bag and cramming the paper she was holding into it.

"Penn..." Jesse said. He could feel her outburst coming on.

"No, ya know, no!" she said, rage springing to her eyes as she turned to Jesse. "I can't just 'go get a drink,' act like everything's normal when it's not. It's not!"

"What choice do we have, Penny?" Eli asked quietly.

"No choice!" Penny said loudly with tears in her eyes, looking from Jesse to Keith then Joe. "You and you and you, you have no choice but to fight in an unjust war if Big Brother comes calling!"

"Penny," Joe said sharply as her outburst caught the attention of some of the other people around them. "Now is not the time..."

"Don't try to shut me down, Joseph Ambrosio!" she yelled. "Now is the time. Now is the time!"

Becca was taken aback. She hadn't seen this side of her new friend before. She knew Penny attended anti-war rallies -- Keith had even accompanied her a few times. She didn't doubt that Penny had strong convictions, but until that moment, she just assumed those convictions only went so far. She evidently was mistaken because she was clearly the only member of the group surprised by Penny's words.

Jesse took a deep breath and put down the bowling bags he was holding. He walked over to his oldest friend and put his hands on her arms. Becca looked at them curiously, unsure why Penny seemed to immediately calm down when Jesse stood in front of her.

"Penny," he said gently. Penny looked at him, tears swimming in her eyes. She knew the look on his face. They'd done this, settle each other down, for a long time now.

"Don't even try, Jesse," she said, sticking her palm up in his face. "I gotta beat feet. I've got places to go."

He dropped his hands, and they looked at each other for a moment before she brushed into his shoulder as she walked past him. They all turned and watched her leave.

"Should we go after her?" Eli asked.

Jesse picked up the bowling bags and shook his head but didn't say anything.

"Who wants that drink?" Keith asked finally, smacking his hands together. "We need to pay the tab, right?"

"I thought you paid the tab?" Becca asked.

"Oh yeah, yeah, no," Keith said sheepishly. "I was gonna do that after, ah, now."

Becca looked at him, confused.

"Let's go," Eli said, taking Liz's hand. "Jesse?"

He shook his head again.

"Can't," he said, sighing and glancing quickly at Becca before addressing Eli. "Felicia is, ah, waiting for me outside."

Joe gave him a sympathetic smile as the rest of the group made their way to the bowling alley bar.

"Where in the hell have you been?!" Felicia hurled at him as soon as he walked out into the cool spring air. She was pacing under a humming streetlight at the edge of the parking lot.

"Getting the bags, finding out who we play next week," he said matter-of-factly. "Shit like that. Where did you think I was?"

"I don't know, you tell me," she yelled, stomping over to him, her clogs clicking loudly on the asphalt.

"Um, pretty sure I just did," he said, an edge of anger in his voice.

"Everything?" she said, getting right in his face. He met her eye-to-eye.

"What's that supposed to mean?" he asked, still tense from the encounter with Penny. If she was picking now to continue acting like a bitch toward him, she'd picked the wrong time.

"She's screwing Keith, you know," she said in that annoying, high-brow voice of hers. She narrowed her eyes at him. "Your roommate? Remember him?"

"What in the hell are you talking about?"

"Your little 'flirty girl," she said, putting her hands on her hips, her cache of bracelets making rattling noises in the process as she tossed her thick, muddy brown hair. "The great and mighty Miss Becca who you boys can't stop springing a woody over!"

He pulled back and just stared at her. Then he walked past her through the small parking lot and onto the sidewalk. Whatever it was between him and Becca boiled down to harmless banter, and Felicia made it sound like it was much more than that.

"She just loves throwing that mountain of hair around and batting those baby blues and making you into a pile of putty," she said, jogging a little to keep up with his determined strides toward his building. He was trying hard to keep his temper in check because one more word from her, and he'd have a hard time remembering you shouldn't hit a woman.

Suddenly her clogs went silent on the sidewalk.

"Jesse?" she yelled, her voice demanding now. "Jesse!"

He stopped and squeezed his eyes shut. Drama, strings -- damn, he hated that -- all of that. He turned to her, dropping the heavy bags and putting his hands on his hips.

"What the hell do you want from me?" he said disgustedly. "It was a goddamn bowling lesson. That's all it was."

"Respect, Jesse," she said, walking over to him. "I want your respect. You're mine, and you shouldn't be making a fool out of yourself with other women."

"I wasn't making..." he started, then stopped and threw his hands up in the air, backing away. "You know, forget it. I'm out."

He turned, picked up his bag, and started walking again. She glanced down at her bowling bag, grabbed it, and started following him, screaming at him.

"What do you mean 'you're out?'" she hollered. "We aren't done until I say we are."

He froze and turned to her. His glare was so icy she stepped back from him. Slowly he walked over to her, and she recoiled a little.

"We're finished," he said quietly, between clenched teeth, his face inches from hers.

"No...Jesse," she half-mumbled, somewhat desperate now, knowing she'd gone too far. "I'm sorry. OK, I'm sorry. Can't we just...talk about this?"

"About what?" he said, blinking his eyes, his face now emotion-free.

"About what?" she said, throwing down her bag. "I'm sorry, OK? I...I was just pissed off."

"Why?"

"Because," she said, hands on her hips and nose in the air. "You're mine."

"Really?" he said, looking at her stuck-up expression and getting agitated again. "And what would your father say about that?"

She crossed her arms and stomped her foot, looking away from him, over his shoulder.

"Exactly," he said after a moment. "I don't know what you have floating around in your head, but look...this was fun while it lasted, but the fun's over, you dig?"

She looked back at him, a stunned expression on her face.

"The fun is *not* over," she said dismissively, glaring at him. "We'd work this out if you'd just do what I say..."

"No, Felicia, we don't have a damn thing to work out," he said, gesturing between the two of them. "We both know this was never going anywhere. It was a good lay for a while, that's it."

She took a step back and then slapped him square across the jaw.

"Why don't you just say it?" she said, seething. "You want to break up with me and go after her!"

Jesse blinked several times and gingerly moved his jaw to make sure nothing was broken. He spat out the extra saliva that had formed against his swelling cheek.

But he said nothing.

"You are such an asshole," she whispered fiercely at him, trying to get a reaction out of him. "A...an emotionally unavailable asshole!"

She searched his face of stone, then watched as he slowly moved his bag from one hand to the other.

"I'll...I'll tell my Daddy," she said, trying anything she could now to bring out some emotion. Her father was a powerful man with ties to the union. He could pull some strings and make life miserable for anyone who hurt his daughter.

She folded her arms again in triumph as he looked at her, mildly surprised at that.

Then he actually let out a laugh.

"Tell him what?" he said, taking a step toward her. "How you got down and dirty, multiple times, I might add, with the union's hired help?"

The smug look on her face fell. He smirked at her as best he could through the pain.

"Bye, Felicia," he said.

With that, he turned around and headed in the direction of his apartment alone.

"Fine! Go!" she yelled a few seconds later, standing where he'd left her in the middle of the sidewalk. "I hope that bitch knows you're not worth it! You don't amount to shit, Jesse Wanger, you hear me?! You're not worth shit!"

He lowered his gaze in front of him, clenching his flaming jaw, not looking back.

And kept on walking.

4

TIME HAS COME TODAY

EARLY APRIL 1968

Becca stepped into the breakroom and let out a loud yawn, much to the amusement of her fellow newsroom gopher Malory. The two had started at CBS the same day and became fast friends, bonding over their "other duties as assigned" and dreaming of being "real" journalists one day.

"Late night catching up with you this afternoon?" Malory said with a smirk as she poured herself a cup of freshly brewed coffee.

"Yeah," Becca said with a little grin. "More than I expected."

"Fun having a new beau, isn't it?" Malory said, handing a second coffee to Becca. "How long have you been with Keith now?

Becca shrugged.

"I don't know. A month, month and a half?" she said, reaching for the cream. "Oh, hey, did you hear about Gina?"

Malory grimaced. "Yeah."

Becca shook her head. Gina had worked at CBS for about a year and a half and was an editorial assistant on the news desk. She oversaw scrolling through the B roll -- the raw footage that came into the newsroom from affiliates around the country and the world -- picking out the best film to use on the national newscast.

She was also unmarried and six months pregnant. There had been talk about her "situation" for a long time. Some of the older coworkers were appalled, while others were more supportive. However, what really mattered was whether Gina would continue in her role once she had a child to raise on her own.

Someone high up on the network food chain decided she wouldn't be and had fired her without cause that morning. Becca was sure it was done to send a message to any other single women in the corporation – Gina was good at her job.

"I'm surprised she wasn't more careful," Malory said, handing Becca a stirrer.

Becca nodded her head.

"I feel for her," she sighed. "She's so excited to be a mom. I think she's going to move in with her parents until Carl comes home."

If Carl comes home, she added silently. The baby's father had been deployed for the last four months on his second tour in Vietnam.

"Yeah," Malory said, tapping her stirrer on her coffee mug. "So, what's yours?"

"My what?" Becca asked.

"Birth control?" Malory said, then added with an eye-roll. "My fiancé likes the 'pull-out' method."

"Well, that's dangerous," Becca said, stirring in her cream then licking the coffee off the mini straw. "I'm on the Pill."

"Isn't *that* actually supposed to be dangerous?"

Becca shrugged.

"Not as dangerous as ending up pregnant 'without the benefit of marriage' as my mother would say," she said. "Today, I guess I can see why."

Malory nodded.

"I suppose we're close enough to our wedding for it not to matter too much, except for the gossip," she said. Malory and her fiancé Lou were set to marry in May. "My mother would die from the gossip alone, but I don't know...I'm ready for it."

"Really?" Becca said, cocking her head to one side.

"Yeah," she said. "I'm 26. I'm not getting any younger. I'm not a young 23-year-old whipper-snapper like you."

"Pfft," Becca said, with a wave of her hand.

"Don't you want to have kids someday?" Malory asked.

"Sure, I do," Becca said, nodding. "I'd love it, someday, but I have my career to establish before I even *think* about it. Then there's, ya know, finding the right man."

"Keith's not the right man?" Malory said with a bemused look, taking a sip of her coffee.

Becca squished up her face with a small smile then shrugged.

"Hmmm..."

"Oh, lay it on me!" Malory said, anxious to hear more.

"Becca!"

Becca whipped around and saw her co-worker John waving frantically at her from the break room doorway.

"What?!"

"Mrs. Beele is looking for you," he said breathlessly. "Come on, both of you. We're gonna need everybody!"

With that, he took off down the hall. Becca and Malory stared at each other for just a moment and then raced after him, leaving two cups of steaming coffee sitting on the table behind them.

Jesse was tired of looking at numbers.

He leaned back in his old desk chair and rubbed his eyes as the late afternoon sun beamed into his tiny, cluttered office at the union. He'd been pouring over the ledgers all day, preparing the quarterly statement, and getting the association's tax return ready for Uncle Sam.

He didn't love being the office manager for the union, but he had to put his associate degree to work somehow. The job had come along at just the right time three years ago. He was down to his last $10 and wondering what he would have to do to survive, let alone afford the place where he lived now. Luckily, he was very good with numbers, and the job came pretty easily to him.

He sat back up in his chair and ran a hand over his face, resting it under his chin, wincing a little from the remaining bruise Felicia had left almost two weeks before. Thankfully, she, and more importantly, her father, had left him alone.

Movement outside caught his eye as he glanced out the window, and he spotted Joe walking toward his office. Jesse smiled to himself. He was grateful for the job for another reason -- he'd met and became close friends with one Joseph Ambrosio.

Joe's father -- "Big Joe" -- was a union legend. He was one of the key people who helped make the union a powerful player in New York politics before Joe was even born. He had served in World War II and was a decorated veteran. Big Joe's shadow loomed large in Jesse's working world, so the first time he'd met Jesse's namesake, he was a bit intimidated. And he wasn't alone. People seemed to part in a crowded room to make way for Big Joe's son.

But once Jesse got up the courage to talk to Joe, he realized he was just like every other guy in his early 20s -- just trying to find his way. Like his father before him, he was a plumber. He was perfectly fine with that -- the politics of the union not interesting him in the least.

Joe was a simple person, really. Everything was black or white with him -- there were no shades of gray. There was right, and there was wrong, period. Jesse had learned that about him pretty quickly -- that and the fact that Joe worshipped his late father.

Big Joe had volunteered for service again during the Korean War. The conflict was only a few months shy of being over when the jeep he was riding in along the 38th Parallel was ambushed, and he was killed. He was buried with full military honors in the service section of a large Catholic cemetery in Queens in 1953. The youngest and only son in a house full of women, Joe was just 8 years old.

Jesse and Joe had formed quite a bond over the last couple of years, each of them silently acknowledging the other as the brother they never had. Joe gave Jesse a kind of stability. Jesse allowed Joe to let loose every once in a while, and crash on his couch when a night out prohibited him from heading back to his Momma's house in Queens.

Marking his place in the ledger book, Jesse closed it then stood to stretch as the old metal door to his office creaked open.

"Hey," Joe said. "Bad time?"

"Nah, just taking a breather," he said with a groan as he twisted his body from side to side. He motioned for Joe to sit down.

Joe sloughed off his heavy work bag full of plumbing supplies and pulled over an old, scratched-up wooden chair. He had a pensive look on his face as he briefly squinted at the sun out Jesse's window then sat down with a sigh.

"What's on your mind?" Jesse asked as he sat down, too.

"I had a job next to Vanhook's today and saw Gus outside," he said. "He told me Keith hasn't shown for two days."

Jesse furrowed his brow, then flicked the pen he'd been holding down on the desk. He leaned back in his chair.

"Shit," he sighed heavily. "Are you serious?"

Joe nodded.

"Gus said he's gonna lose his job if he doesn't show tomorrow," he said. "I'm surprised he hasn't canned his ass already."

He threw a disgusted look at Jesse, who nodded back at him.

"It's finally catching up to him, you know," Joe said, sitting back and flopping both his hands on the wooden armrests, shaking his head. "You *know* that."

"Yeah," Jesse said, running his hands through his hair. "Yeah, I know... I know. Dammit."

Joe folded his hands and sat up, cocking his head to the side.

"You think it's more than the drinking?" Joe asked.

"Yeah, it's more than the drinking," he answered with resignation, glaring at Joe.

"Weed? LSD?"

"At least," Jesse said, shaking his head. Damn. Damn. Damn, he thought. He and Keith had been roommates for two years. He knew Keith often drank too much, he knew where he hid all the extra flasks and when a binge was coming on. Jesse had learned all those kinds of signs years ago. But Keith's vices had never included drugs -- or compromised his ability to help pay the bills or the rent and keep his job as a line cook at Vanhook's -- until now.

"You think his girlfriend knows?" Joe asked.

Jesse shrugged. There was a good chance Becca didn't have a clue as to Keith's behavior. He'd kept it hidden pretty well from his roommate the entire first year they lived together, though Jesse admittedly had just let some things slide. As long as the rent checks still came on time, and Keith was otherwise a good roommate and decent-enough friend.

But Becca was smart, and a trained journalist for crying out loud, she probably would figure it out sooner or later.

Maybe it should be sooner, though, he thought.

Jesse sighed, picking up the pen again and twisting it between his fingers. He glanced at Joe.

"He still hasn't paid his half from last month," he admitted.

"What?" Joe said, anger and surprise flashing in his eyes. "He stiffed you on rent?"

Jesse nodded.

"Man," Joe said, "that ain't right. Did you talk to him?"

"Yeah," Jesse replied, suddenly looking wearier than his friend thought any 24-year-old should. "He said it was coming, which obviously is total bullshit."

Joe shook his head.

"You gotta have a 'come to Jesus' meeting with him, man," he said.

Jesse laughed a little at that.

"A 'come to Jesus' meeting?"

"Yeah, you know," Joe said, beginning to gesture with his hands. "A 'this shit is real, get your fucking act together' talking to."

Jesse laughed harder.

"And I'm sure that's *exactly* how Christ himself would phrase it."

Joe grinned back, then swiped an apple off Jesse's desk, taking a big bite out of it.

"Ya mind?" he asked, mouth full of Granny Smiths.

Still chuckling, Jesse shook his head as his office door creaked open once again. He looked up and saw the evening custodian -- a kind, black man in his early 60s named Abraham -- shuffle tentatively through the door.

"'Hello Misser Wanger," he said, his voice shaking, then he saw Joe, and his eyes got wider. "Misser Joe. I, I's sorry to interrupt..."

Joe shook his head, turning around in his chair as Jesse waved for Abraham to come in.

"Don't sweat it, Abe," Jesse said, with a look of concern. Abe looked upset and unusually anxious. "You OK, man?"

Abraham looked around nervously, but he didn't know where else to go. He couldn't leave work, and Mr. Wanger had always been nice to him, so he thought his office would be as safe a place as any.

"Abraham?" Jesse asked again, trying to get him to tell them what was going on.

The man thrust his hands deep into the pockets of his worn overalls and finally looked up at Jesse as big tears fell out of his eyes.

"They shot him, Misser Wanger," he said, his voice raspy, as he pulled a red handkerchief out of his pocket, "at his hotel in Memphis. I...I heard it on the bus radio, 'fore they turned it off..."

"Who?" Jesse asked, confused. "Who was shot?"

"Dr. King, sir," Abe said, voice cracking. "They shot Dr. King."

For a moment, Jesse just stared at Abe, not quite understanding what he'd just heard. Then his face fell as it dawned on him the significance of what had happened. He looked to Joe, who immediately stood up from his chair.

"Sit, Abe, please," Joe said quietly, motioning for Abraham to take his seat.

"No, sir..."

"Yes. Please."

Abe let out a quiet sob as he took the seat, putting his head in his shaking hands and quickly wiping at his eyes with his handkerchief. Joe put a hand on Abraham's shoulder and watched the man in sympathy as he wept.

Jesse slowly reached over with a grave face and turned on the radio, tuning it to a news station. He wondered just how much faster the world around them would continue to go straight to hell.

5

BAD MOON RISING

MID-APRIL 1968

"Where in the hell is he getting it?" Jesse asked wearily.

"How am I supposed to know?" Penny said, immediately on the defensive. "Just because I support the cause doesn't mean I'm high all the time. It's everywhere at the rallies, Jesse. It's not like you can miss it."

Jesse flicked his cigarette ash over the side of the building, leaning his elbows on the railing of the narrow fire escape balcony outside Liz's apartment. He'd had his "come to Jesus" meeting with Keith, and at least Keith had shown up for work, but that was about it. He still hadn't gotten any money from him.

"If he's not pulling his load, kick him out," Penny said, standing next to him. "He's pulled this shit before. It's not like it's the first time."

"First time he's not paid his half of the rent," Jesse said quickly, leaning over and looking down at the sidewalk.

Penny sighed, taking a drag on her cig. She looked sideways at her oldest friend.

"I didn't know that. Sorry."

"Yeah, well," Jesse said, shrugging, then adding more to himself than to her. "Maybe his ass will get drafted, and I won't have to worry about his shit anymore."

He immediately winced. He didn't really mean that, and he was, oh, so sorry he'd actually said it out loud to Penny -- especially after he'd spent the last 10 minutes trying to calm her down.

"Shipping him off to Vietnam to kill innocent women and children or be killed himself is the perfect way to solve *your* problem," she said hotly, smashing her cigarette out on the rail as she turned to face his profile, fully in War Protest Penny Mode. "If you can't see how wrong that is, let me tell you something..."

She kept talking as he momentarily dropped his head and closed his eyes. He'd heard it all before -- non-stop, it seemed like for the last several months -- and he wasn't in the mood to hear it again. He took a couple puffs, concentrating on the orange glow of the ash as he breathed in, then exhaled slowly, each time waiting patiently for her diatribe to end.

"....and...and you shouldn't joke ...what if...what if karma comes back to bite you in the ass!"

He turned to her then, with a bemused look on his face, and raised his eyebrows.

She stopped speaking for a moment, knowing what he was thinking. She pointed a finger threateningly at him.

"Don't you even say it..."

"Now, Penn..."

"I'm warning you," she said, still pointing at him. "You stop it right now!"

They stared each other down for a few moments, a multitude of past conversations and experiences flashing between them. Slowly he grinned at her, and she relaxed ever so slightly. He put out his cig.

"Only the good die young," he said with a smirk and a smoky exhale.

She glared at him.

"Then you oughta fuckin' live forever," she shot back at him, pushing his shoulder and turning back to the window to go inside.

He chuckled a little at that and then slowly climbed back through behind her.

"Man," Joe sighed, shaking his head in disbelief as he stood up from the couch in Liz's apartment. He walked over to the kitchen to grab another beer, shooting a glance at Penny and Jesse as they climbed back in from the fire escape.

Liz, Eli, Penny, Jesse, and Joe -- along with the rest of the country -- were glued to the TV. Riots continued to break out in big cities everywhere in the wake of Martin Luther King Jr.'s assassination. The evening programs were being interrupted for breaking news on a routine basis. Even the tension in the room between the friends was obvious. Eli and Liz were uncharacteristically quiet. Penny had gotten so riled up earlier that Jesse had grabbed her arm and yanked her toward the fire escape, saying it was a lovely evening for a smoke.

The news segued from the King riots to the Vietnam War dead, causing Eli to abruptly stand up, walk over to the TV, and snap the dial to "off."

"I think that's enough," he said quietly as Joe shot him a questioning look.

"Oh, and you would be the arbiter of that, wouldn't you?" Liz spat at him from her place on the couch.

"Liz..." he said as he watched her stand angrily, pull on her skirt and stomp off to the bathroom, practically running over Penny and Jesse in the process.

"What the hell was that?" Joe asked, gesturing toward the bathroom door.

Eli let out a long sigh just as the apartment's door flew open and Becca walked in.

"Howdy, Stranger," Jesse said with a little smile. "You live here?"

"Hey," Becca said wearily as she walked over to grab a Tab out of the fridge. She opened it quickly and took a big gulp.

"Got the night off, huh?" Eli said, a little pensively. Becca glared at him in the living room, then directed her answer to her friends in the kitchen.

"Yeah. I've only put in about 120 hours the last 10 days, so I guess they figured I was due," she said, taking another long drink of the soda.

"We ordered Chinese earlier, but there might be some left," Penny said as she opened the fridge.

"Don't sweat it," Becca said with a wave of her hand. "I just came back here to change. Keith's picking me up in 10."

Penny, Joe, and Jesse exchanged a look as Becca made her way over to her bedroom.

"Is he?" Jesse said a little loudly after her as he took a step toward the living room. She stopped and turned to look at him, eyebrow at an arch. He tried to sound nonchalant as he added. "What's happenin'?"

Becca shrugged.

"Some house party in the Bronx," she said as she disappeared into the bedroom and closed the door.

Jesse nodded at the closed door, silently cursing himself for not having found time to say anything to Becca about Keith. Of course, he hadn't seen much of her lately; none of them had. She had gotten a swift promotion at work after the assassination. She suddenly was at the station all day and night covering "riot central," as she called it. Miles and miles of film were coming in every day, and she was in charge of going through it all.

"Was that Becca?" Liz asked as she emerged from the bathroom, eyes rimmed red.

"Yeah," Jesse said, grabbing a beer out of the fridge. "She's...changing to go out with...Keith."

"Oh," Liz nodded. Eli took a step toward her and then froze when she threw a cold stare his way. She walked over to the couch.

"Liz," Penny asked, her eyes darting between the couple as she sat back down with Liz on the couch. "You OK?"

Liz smiled a little at Penny, then narrowed her eyes at Eli.

"Why don't you ask him..."

"What'd you do, man?" Joe asked, a hint of anger in his voice.

"I didn't do..." Eli said, then sighed again. "I...I haven't done anything...yet."

Joe and Jesse exchanged a confused glance as Becca came back out of the bedroom. Jesse almost gasped out loud. In the space of about three minutes, she'd changed from her work clothes into a blue floor--length, loosely hung sundress with clogs to match. Her hair was down out of its up-do. She looked every inch a dressed-up flower child, earthy and stunning.

Joe let out a low whistle, which made Becca roll her eyes. Jesse cleared his throat.

"So, ah, where is this party again?"

"In the Bronx, *Dad*," Becca said, giving him a grin. "I don't know. Keith knows the address. I gotta run. He'll be here in a few, and I gotta grab a cab."

"Listen, Becca," Jesse started. "Can I talk..."

"Don't you think you might want to know where you'll be going?" Eli interrupted.

Becca's attention fled from Jesse and went straight to her brother. Her face turned red, and there was such anger flashing in her eyes that even Joe took a step back.

"You!" she said, pointing a finger at Eli. "You! You don't get to tell me what to do, ya hear? I have been working my ass off, and I...I just wanna go out with my boyfriend and let loose for a while. Is that a crime? Is it?!"

Eli opened his mouth to speak, and she threw her hand up.

"Zip it, Eli," she said, then she glanced at Liz and almost lost what was left of her composure, seeing the devastated look on her best friend's face. She turned back to her brother. "I'm so mad at you...I...I..."

"I assume you talked to Mom," Eli said calmly before collapsing into a chair across the room.

"Hell yeah, I talked to Mom!" she said, raising her voice. "She called me...at work!"

"Whoa...what is going on?!" Joe asked, finally. Becca blinked back in surprise, looking around the room at the clueless faces around her.

"Oh, he hasn't told you?" Becca asked, voice strained. "Why...my big brother has decided to enlist!"

Liz let out a little sob as all eyes turned to Eli.

"That's right," Becca said, desperately trying to hold back her tears. "He could go back to school, keep his college deferment, but nnnooo, he's gonna go get himself killed in Vietnam!"

"Eli!" Penny gasped, face as red as Becca's as she jumped to her feet. "How could you? How could you volunteer to be a...a baby killer?"

"Penny," Joe said hotly, turning quickly to her and getting right in her face. "He is volunteering to serve his country! It's the greatest thing a man can do for his fellow man!"

"Stop, please stop," Liz said meekly as she slowly stood, on the verge of tears again. Becca moved over to Liz and pulled her into her arms for a moment. She pulled back, smoothing Liz's hair.

"I'm sorry," she whispered.

Liz smiled a little at her. "Don't sweat it. Now, split."

"Are you sure?"

Liz nodded.

"Go," she mouthed. Becca nodded, and with one more glare at her brother, she picked up a sweater sitting on the kitchen chair and quickly left the apartment.

Jesse's eyes followed her out the door, and he thought about making his feet do the same but decided to stay put and take in the bombshell Becca had left in her wake. Penny put her hands on her hips and faced Eli once again. Joe sat on the arm of the couch and put his arm around Liz's shoulder. Jesse slowly lowered his eyes to the floor, hands grasping the back of the couch, then turned to Eli.

"They...the Army needs medics," he said quietly from the beaded chair in the corner of the living room. "I'm...I'm not enlisting to...to... kill anyone. I want to help. They...they need people who are trained who can...help."

Joe nodded as Penny crossed her arms over her chest. Eli looked at Liz, who sat again, immobile on the couch, refusing to look at him.

"I've been thinking about it a long time," he continued. "I know...I don't know how I feel about all...of...everything, but I feel like if I stay here knowing I can help..."

He paused, looking first at Jesse then at Joe.

"My Dad served, ya know?" Eli added quietly. Joe nodded his understanding.

"Medics die, too," Liz whispered. Eli stood up then and walked over to her. He pulled her up against him, and she clung to him as big tears fell out of her eyes.

Penny restarted her protest. Joe started to argue with her again. Liz cried harder. Eli told them both to leave as Jesse silently walked back to the window, climbed outside, and worked a cigarette out of its pack, firing it up. He flicked the ash over the side of the rail and looked down below just in time to spot a cab stop in front of the building. He watched as first Becca, then Keith climbed in the back seat.

He stared after the cab as it drove away...a nauseous feeling settling into the pit of his stomach. He knew exactly how the kind of house party Keith was taking Becca to would play out. He'd seen them up-close a hundred times before. His heartbeat quickened just thinking about it.

When the cab was out of view, he took a deep drag on his cigarette, his eyes darting around in the darkness anxiously as his mind worked overtime.

A familiar feeling he remembered all too well took hold of him, and instinctively he knew what it meant. He worriedly rolled his cig between his fingertips, his eyes wide, staring at the moon above the city.

6

WAKE UP CALL

BECCA WOKE UP, HER EYES BLURRY, IN AN UNFAMILIAR BEDROOM WITH the smell of marijuana wafting through the air. She coughed a couple times as her eyes began to focus. Her head felt so heavy she was sure it was going to fall right off her shoulders.

"Hey, Sleeping Beauty," Keith said far too loudly for her liking as he quickly turned to her, his eyes wide in surprise. He was sitting on the edge of the bed, in his jeans and unbuttoned, long-sleeved dark blue shirt, clutching a small bag and some paper money. "You're awake!"

"Yeah," she moaned. She slowly propped herself up on her elbows, and the sheet she'd been covered with fell down to her stomach. She realized she was naked, and she grabbed at it clumsily. Keith quickly handed it to her with a little grin.

"That was quite a ride," he said with a smirk.

"Was it?" she asked quietly.

She couldn't remember much of what happened after she and Keith barricaded themselves in an upstairs bedroom at the far end of the hallway. The house party was in full swing when they got there and booze and drugs were everywhere. Keith immediately introduced her to a couple of his "friends," who looked her up and down so brazenly it made her glad she'd brought a sweater to tighten around herself.

To her surprise, Keith bought a large amount of marijuana from them, which she had never seen him do before. She wasn't oblivious to the fact that he smoked weed -- nearly everyone her age had at least tried it. It was the way he'd gone about it, the smoothness of the transaction that tipped her off that this wasn't the first time he'd bought it.

She had started to feel very uneasy about the whole night. She'd wanted to relax, sure. But she wasn't in for booze and drugs -- and what she was sure was an orgy happening in the basement -- if the sounds making their way up the staircase were any indication.

To calm her nerves, Keith had quickly gotten her several drinks. She downed three shots of Scotch, and it still wasn't making her feel any better about the atmosphere around them. She told Keith she wanted to leave; he suggested they get away from the crowd for a while, and they made their way to where they were now. There were three bedrooms, and two of them were otherwise occupied...

"Keith..." she started, looking around the bedroom. At least it looked like the tiny twin bed hadn't been used yet, and she took a seat on the top sheet, the Scotch finally making her head spin a little.

"Becca, relax, OK," Keith said as he lit up a doobie and took a drag. Then he handed her the bottle of Scotch he'd swiped from the kitchen on their way up the stairs. "Come on, just try to unwind."

She looked doubtfully at him but took another swig. Maybe she was being too uptight, but this house party just wasn't what she was banking on. A few drinks, music, dancing, maybe a conversation or two with new people, but not this. She wanted to relax, not be on guard the whole night.

"Can't we go someplace else?" she said as he knelt in front of her. "Please? This just isn't my scene..."

"Oh...come on, girl, we're just getting started," he smiled at her and handed her the doobie.

She scrunched up her nose.

"Ever tried it?" he said.

After a moment, she admitted that she hadn't, her face turning a little pink.

"Try it," he said, putting it to her lips.

The Scotch started hitting her harder, and she took a drag, choking on it as she exhaled the first time.

"It's OK," Keith said with a chuckle. "You'll get used to it..."

Before she knew it, he was kissing her neck as they shared the joint between them...and her head kept spinning...

"What time is it?" she asked as she pulled the sheet up to her chin. She hated the way she felt at that moment. Her head was pounding. She felt like she either was going to vomit or had possibly already done so. Somewhere in her mind, she could piece together snippets from before she passed out. There was more Scotch, more weed, and definitely more sex with Keith. She couldn't remember if it was good or bad sex -- it really could go either way with him -- but what got her the most was that she couldn't remember. She didn't like that. She didn't like feeling like that. She didn't like being out of control.

"Ah..." he said, fumbling for his watch in the darkness. "12:30."

"I was sleeping for two hours?!" she said hotly, clutching her forehead.

"I guess, about...yeah," he said, distractedly. "I just got up a couple minutes ago."

He stood up, bag and money in hand, and headed for the door.

"Where are you going?!" she asked, incredulous.

"I'll be back in a few," he said, anxious to get out the door, adding with a grin. "I'll bring you more Scotch."

"I don't want more...Keith!" she whispered fiercely as he closed the door behind him before she finished her sentence. Then he opened it again.

"Just...stay here," he said with a small smile, his bloodshot eyes darting down the hall. "I'll be back."

She stared wide-eyed through the dark room at the closed door, feeling the full force of her nakedness. She turned on a bedside lamp and started to reach for her dress. Then she heard a thump and a couple laughing drunkenly in the hallway close to her room. She jumped out of the bed and quickly locked the door, shivering as she did so.

She finally reached for her clothes with a racing heart and shaking hands and put them on again. Then she sat on the edge of the bed... and waited.

She was sober now. Sober and completely pissed off.

Keith had been gone for as long as she'd been asleep. It was impossible to know, but Becca was pretty sure he wasn't in the house anymore, or if he was, he'd found someone else to entertain him. For the last hour, she'd debated with herself whether she should stay and wait for him or just leave. She'd finally had enough.

Becca grabbed her small, beaded bag purse and quietly unlocked the bedroom door, poking her head out into the empty hallway. Music was still filtering up from downstairs, but there didn't seem to be much movement. She wanted to find a phone, so she could call a cab and get home. She wondered briefly if that's what Keith had done --

gone home. But to be honest, she didn't give a damn at that moment where her erstwhile boyfriend was; as far as she was concerned, he could catch the first fast train to Hell for apparently leaving her to fend for herself.

Passed out bodies were draped over chairs and lying on couches. She made her way to the kitchen, where one holdout couple ignored her as they gyrated on each other against the back door. She looked at them with disgust as she reached for the phone on the wall, searching for a phone book. She put the phone to her ear and realized there was no dial tone. She slammed the phone back in its cradle, earning a wasted glare from the woman against the door.

She had to get out of that house.

Becca hurried out of the kitchen, through the living room to the front door, never taking a breath the whole way. Her heart was hammering in her ears. She saw a lot of people -- drunk, drugged people who would feel like shit in the morning. But she didn't see Keith. She vaguely remembered seeing a payphone by a neighborhood corner store not too far from the house. She was determined to make it there, even if it was the middle of the night. She'd call a cab from there, and this nightmare of a night would be over.

Tears stung Becca's eyes as she finally hurried out of the house, heading in what she hoped was the direction of the store. She blinked them back. She'd be damned if she was going to cry over her own stupidity, even if she had been under a lot of stress. She'd spent the day -- the last few weeks -- pouring over riot footage and war footage. The images she saw just by doing her job had turned her stomach. Then, just when she thought she couldn't take anymore, her Mom called in hysterics to tell her of Eli's decision. It had been too much. She'd actually been looking forward to the party -- to relaxing just for a little while.

"Fool..." she said out loud, chastising herself.

Becca spotted the intersection not too far ahead. The streets were quiet, and there was no one out at almost 3 in the morning. A few cars passed by, but no cabs. She walked over to the phone booth and climbed inside, shutting the door securely behind her. She took a deep breath, even though the smell inside was laced with stale cigarette smoke and moldy air. Her head started to pound harder, and she almost felt like she was going to be sick. She looked around for the phone book that was supposed to be attached to the payphone. The chain dangled empty under the box -- the phone book nowhere in sight.

"No!" she said, clenching her fist and slamming it against the plastic of the booth door, her anxiety climbing. She opened the door a crack and took a couple deeper breaths, trying to calm herself down.

"Call information," she told herself. "Just call information..."

She reached into her purse to pull out her wallet and couldn't find it. She shifted her bag toward the low glow of the streetlight, trying to look inside. Panic instantly seized in her chest as she realized it wasn't there.

"No, no, no, no!" she screamed as she spilled the contents of the bag on the sidewalk just outside the folding door. No wallet. No ID. No money. She was sure that Keith had taken it -- all of it -- and left her purse behind.

Becca hung her head, feeling like she'd been kicked in the gut as tears finally streamed out of her tired eyes, and she slowly sank to the floor of the filthy phone booth. She slammed both hands down onto the concrete and felt a small, cold piece of metal. She picked it up. It was a dime – one very thin dime.

Becca sniffed up her tears and said a little prayer, praying the dime would work in the slot. She stood and picked up the phone, putting the dime in once, twice...on the third attempt, the payphone finally accepted it. She was shaking as she dialed, feeling like she was moments away from a total collapse. She held her breath as it started to ring, pulling her sweater closer around her shoulders. It rang only once.

"Hello?" he said.

"Jesse?" she said in a small, shaking voice. She cleared her throat, straightening her spine, trying to sound much more confident than she felt.

"Becca?" he asked, feeling his body both tense and relax at the same time. He was wide awake -- he had been all night. "Are you OK?"

She took a deep, ragged breath and swallowed hard, trying to sound calm as she answered.

"Yes," she said as tears filled her eyes again. "No. Um, I don't know. Keith...Keith isn't...there, is he?"

"No," Jesse replied as his heartbeat started to pound in his ears. "Isn't he with you?"

"No," she said, clearing her throat again, as a brief but heavy silence followed.

"Becca?" he finally asked. He could hear her breathing heavily on the other end of the line.

She closed her eyes, gripping the top of the telephone box with one hand, trying to keep her knees from buckling. She so hated to ask Jesse -- ask anyone -- to come to her rescue, but she really didn't know what else to do.

"Jesse, I...I need help," she whispered, rapidly blinking back her tears.

Jesse closed his eyes, a sudden fury building inside of him. He knew it. He knew when he watched them leave together in that cab, they were headed for disaster.

"Where are you?" Jesse said in as even a tone as he could muster.

"I don't know, somewhere in the Bronx, I...wait," she said, spotting the street signs at the corner. She gave him the names of the cross streets.

"Stay right there. I'll call a cab."

"Jesse, he...Keith took my wallet," she said, anger and desperation coming into her voice. "My money, my ID, everything!"

Jesse made a fist with one hand, shifting the speaker end of the phone below his chin with the other, and started to breathe heavily through his nose. If Keith had been standing in front of him at that moment, he would have been a dead man walking.

"Son of a bitch," he said to himself in a low growl.

He swallowed heavily, then brought the phone back to his lips and said as calmly as he could... "OK, you stay there; I'm coming to you. I'll come to get you. Stay right there. I'm leaving now."

"Jesse, I...I'm sorry to..."

"Don't apologize. You have nothing..." he interrupted quickly, then let out a heavy sigh. "You just...just stay there, Becca, do you hear me?"

"Yes," she whispered, nodding her head as a flood of relief came over her. "Yes, I...I'm not going anywhere. I...th...thank you."

She said goodbye and hung up the phone, her hands still shaking. Despite herself, she let out a small sob as she slowly knelt down to put the contents of her purse back together.

Jesse slammed the phone down, grabbed his jacket, and palm-slapped the back of his apartment door with all his might. Then he jerked it open with a throbbing hand, slamming it shut behind him, and took off running down the stairs into the dead of night.

7

GIMME SHELTER

JESSE SCANNED THE STREET SIGNS FROM THE BACK OF THE TAXI AS IT slowly rolled down one of the cross streets in the Bronx where Becca said she would be. The neighborhood they were entering now was run down. Not horribly shabby, but definitely not affluent. Some of the houses were vacant, some of them housed families, but some were clearly communes of one kind or another. Lots of young people living "the dream" together, he thought sarcastically.

"There it is," said the driver as Jesse's eyes fell on a blue sundress shimmering by a payphone in the bright moonlight. They were still a block away, and she had her back to them. As they came closer, Becca turned, still leaning against the phone booth, and gave a half-hearted wave as the cab pulled to a stop. She immediately looked down, tugging on the sleeves of her sweater, pulling it as tightly to her as she could.

The driver stopped the cab and started to roll down his window to yell for Becca.

"Hey," Jesse said, putting a hand on the man's shoulder. "Give me a minute?"

The cabbie shrugged.

"Meter keeps running, man."

"Yeah, I know...just," Jesse said irritably as he opened the door, "cool it a minute."

The cabbie shrugged again as Jesse closed the door behind him, shoved his hands in his jean pockets, and slowly walked toward Becca, his eyes never leaving her face. She looked pale and tired, and though he was absolutely sure she'd deny it, pretty damn scared.

Becca could tell by his expression that he wasn't happy as he made his way to her. He wasn't angry, she didn't think, but he had a scowl on his face. Of course, he was unhappy, she thought, who wouldn't be if they were jarred out of bed to take care of another man's girlfriend in the middle of the night -- when said girlfriend should have been fine taking care of herself.

Becca swallowed hard, trying to fight the tears of relief that stung her eyes and get control of herself. When she'd first seen him, her body had started to quiver, the adrenaline of the night starting to ebb quickly as overwhelming exhaustion immediately began to take over. She was grateful he was there, and she wasn't alone anymore.

"Hey," she said, giving him a small smile.

"Hey," he said, returning her smile with a little grin. "You free tonight or just walkin' the streets for fun?"

He'd meant it as a joke, something to lighten her mood, but given what she'd witnessed that night, it hit her the wrong way and her eyes immediately filled with hot, angry tears.

"I'm not a whore, Jesse," she choked out softly, looking from him to the cab and quickly attempting to move past him. He caught her arm.

"God, Becca, I'm sorry," he said, his face falling. "I'm sorry, it was just a joke. I...I didn't mean to...to say that you...dammit!"

She looked up at him then, and his eyes were soft and sincere, with no hint of a tease at all, like there usually was with him. There was even a bit of panic in his features. She took a deep breath and then stepped back from him, crossing her sweater over herself so tightly that one of the seams started to tear. Finally, she looked away from him and dropped her gaze to the sidewalk.

Jesse thought she looked defeated.

"What happened at that party?" he asked gently, his heart starting to race. "Where in the hell is Keith?"

She gulped to fight back the tears pooling in her eyes and looked off to his left, toward the cab, then she shook her head.

"I don't know," she whispered, as a couple teardrops escaped down her cheeks. She swallowed heavily again, still shaking her head. "I don't know, I don't know, I don't know..."

Arms still wrapped around herself, Becca's head dropped against Jesse's shoulder. Instinctively, he protectively put his arms around her and pulled her against his chest.

"Shhh," he said softly, stroking her hair with one hand and holding her securely against him with the other. He closed his eyes and rocked her a little from side to side. "Shh, shh, it's okay, everything's gonna be okay now."

She curled her fingers around the inside edges of his open denim jacket. She pushed her head under his chin, letting all the emotions built up inside of her finally come out -- work, Eli, Keith -- all of it soaking into his shirt through her tears. She felt disgustingly weak, yet it felt natural to let him hold her because he seemed so strong right then.

As Jesse cradled her against him, he couldn't help but wonder at the woman who had swept into his world and seemed almost larger than life -- impossibly beautiful, radiantly confident, bullishly decisive, completely controlled -- now feeling so slight, so small as she shook in his arms.

After a few moments, Jesse's eyes opened, and he looked at the cab driver, who was gesturing to his meter. He frowned at him but gave Becca a gentle squeeze, her crying all but stopped now. She was once again determined to get ahold of herself.

"Are you ready to go home?" he whispered.

Becca sniffed a couple times and then nodded her head as she stepped away from him. She felt a chill as their embrace broke, but then he ran his hands quickly up and down her arms and looked at her with questioning eyes, and she felt her strength slowly returning. She nodded again and wiped her eyes with her sweater sleeves.

"Yes," she said thickly, attempting to swallow the remainder of her tears. She even smiled a bit at him. "Let's go."

Becca pieced together the shards of broken memories from the evening. She relayed them to Jesse in the cab on the way to their building. She told him how uneasy she was, how she wanted to leave the house almost as soon as she got there, but Keith wanted to stay. All kinds of drugs and alcohol were out everywhere, on countertops, on end tables, on the floor. She told him she'd watched Keith buy weed and "stupidly" drank too much Scotch herself. As she filled Jesse in, she became much more animated. He watched as the fire in her that was lost at the phone booth came back with a vengeance.

It was after 4 a.m. when the cab dropped them off. Jesse paid the cab driver and opened the door for Becca. He'd been doing a slow burn ever since she started relaying the story to him and was most anxious to hear what she could remember next.

"So, what happened after you got away from...the rest of the party?" he asked, opening the door to the stairwell.

He heard her intake slowly, then she turned to him. More and more of the night was coming back to her, but it was all still pretty hazy.

"I'm not sure," she said, clearly angry with herself. "I guess I...I passed out."

Jesse closed his eyes and swallowed hard, a dozen unpleasant scenarios flashing through his mind. He closed the stairwell door again.

Becca leaned up against the mailboxes lining the wall in the darkened entryway and took a deep breath.

"I...we...Keith and I...we," she started, looking at the floor. "There was...ya know, um...sex. Uh, and a...we smoked some..."

"Weed," he asked non-pulsed. "Solo?"

"I...I think so," she said quickly, turning her head, her face turning red. "If he dropped LSD in it, I wouldn't know."

Jesse scoffed at that.

"You'd know."

She eyed him wearily.

"Then I don't wanna know," she said, putting a hand to her aching forehead, then she sighed. "It'll never happen again! It's all... just...disgusting..."

Jesse just nodded.

"Anyway, I...my...I wasn't thinking clearly by then and then...then I passed out." She looked away, shuddering.

Jesse was clenching and unclenching his fists at his sides, trying to keep his temper under control. Damn, this was all his fault. Well, it was Keith's fault, he knew that, but the whole night could have been avoided if he'd only made more of an effort to get to her and tell her about Keith's issues. She would have been informed, anyway, before leaving with him.

"Was Keith...with you the whole time?" he asked, tentatively.

"Yes. He...he said he was. He was there when I woke up, I..." she said, then furrowed her brow. Then she sighed deeply. "I think so. He was awake by then, and I guess, had gone through my purse...dammit! He's such an ass! A thief and an ass and a liar and I'm...I'm so, so stupid, God!"

He shook his head in silent protest to her last statement as she put her hands over her face and rubbed her temples. Then she dropped her arms to her sides and cocked her head, looking at him.

"I'm sorry," she said, smiling a little. "I never thanked you."

He certainly didn't feel like he deserved her thanks.

"Hey, don't sweat it, you don't have to thank me..." he started.

"Yes, yes I do," she said, putting a hand on his arm. "I'll make this up to you, I promise. I woke you in the middle of the night..."

"No, you didn't," he said with a sigh. "I was awake."

She looked at him curiously.

"Look, I...I should have...I wanted to tell you," he sighed again, shuffling his feet, and looking past her at the mailboxes. "Keith... Keith's been drinking...bingeing for a...for as long as I've known him."

Becca cocked her head to the side again, studying him.

"I figured you maybe knew that he did that," he said, gesturing with his hands, trying to explain himself. "But the weed, the...whatever other shit he's into...that's new. He hadn't...I don't think he'd been into any of that before he...I think it started at the rallies he's been going to."

"With Penny?" she said.

"Yes, but Penny isn't...that's not her scene."

"I see," she said, crossing her arms in front of her. He looked at her then and couldn't read the expression on her face.

He pointed both hands to his chest.

"This is my fault, Becca," he said, resignation in his voice. "If I'd warned you...maybe you wouldn't have gone with him and...and gone through what you did tonight."

She stared at him, searching his eyes. The expression on his face was stoic, and her heart started racing about what that could possibly mean. He thought this was his fault. He stayed up all night...for her?

"So...you were awake...worrying about me?" she finally asked quietly, her blue eyes softening as they looked into his.

That was not the question he was expecting. He was prepared for her to yell at him for not warning her about Keith, so her gentle voice threw him off. It felt intimate, too intimate, and it made him uncomfortable, so he stepped back from her. He swallowed hard.

"I don't...I mean...it would be my fault if..." he stammered.

A sad smile came over her face.

"You felt guilty then," she interrupted quickly, suddenly feeling very weary. She shook her head a little and cleared her throat. "I get it. OK. Look, Jesse, I'm a big girl. If anyone's to blame for this, it's me -- and Asshole. Not you. You dig?"

"I...yeah," he said, furrowing his brow. "Still..."

She pushed back from the mailboxes and opened the door to the stairwell, not waiting for him to finish.

"I'm tired," she said simply. He gave up talking then and followed her up the stairs.

When they arrived in their hallway, she turned to him, pointing to his apartment door.

"I guess," she said, clearing her throat. "I assume Keith's not there."

"Ah...he wasn't when I left," he replied as he opened the door. It was pitch black inside.

"Humph," Becca said, lowering her head and wrapping her arms around herself again. Then she cast one more glance into the dark apartment.

"Just as well," she said in a scratchy, tired voice. "I'll deal with him... sometime...maybe..."

Tears came to her eyes again as she looked away. She looked so sad. She may not have wanted him to feel guilty, but Jesse was mad at himself anyway -- and beyond furious with his roommate.

After a moment, she rallied, not letting any tears fall, and smiled a little.

"Thank you for bringing me home, Jesse. I'll see you later."

"Later," he nodded as he watched her walk a few paces and unlock her apartment door -- at least Keith hadn't taken her keys -- then walk in, shoulders slumped, closing the door behind her.

A deep sigh escaped his lips as he entered his place, flipped on the light, then ran his palms over his face. Then he stared at Keith's bedroom and started clenching and unclenching his fists at his sides once again.

He stumbled into the glass door once before opening it to the entryway. It was almost 6 a.m., and just a hint of the sunrise was starting to make its way over the horizon. Keith turned and closed the door -- his glassy eyes and scrambled brain not registering that it had already closed behind him.

"Where's Rebecca?"

Keith jumped and spun around, stumbling once again, trying to focus his eyes on the dark figure leaning up against the wall of mailboxes.

"Who's 'at?" Keith slurred, feebly putting his hands up in loose fists in front of his face. He watched as Jesse emerged from the shadows, arms crossed and a scowl on his face.

"Jess...?" he stumbled again, then smirked. "Dude..."

"Where is she?" Jesse hissed at him.

In a drug-addled haze, Keith looked at him in confusion, unsure what Jesse wanted to know.

"Who? What...Becca? She...ah...Becca's at...work?"

Jesse reached out and grabbed two fistfuls of Keith's shirt, dragging him until he had thrown him hard against the row of mailboxes behind them. Keith scrunched up his shoulders and yelped in pain as Jesse dug his knuckles into his chest.

"You son-of-a-bitch," Jesse growled at him, his face red, veins sticking out along his neck. "You took her there, then you left her there, left her at that...place, you motherfucker! You took her money -- you wasted piece of shit!"

Keith started to panic, small parts of the night flashing back to him.

"Jesse...I...shit...no...I..."

"Shut the fuck up," Jesse said, eyes blazing as he slammed Keith against the boxes again, so hard Keith's head slapped back against the smooth metal behind him, reverberating like a sledgehammer in the entryway. Keith put a shaky hand to the back of his head, looked at Jesse in terror, and suddenly started to sob like a baby.

Jesse relaxed his hold on Keith, then let go completely as the man's legs gave way, and he collapsed on his knees to the ground at Jesse's feet.

Jesse stepped back, breathing hard as he watched Keith fall apart on the floor. He took a deep breath, licking his lips.

"You don't pay rent? Fine! You like your liquor? Fine! But you leave a woman -- your girlfriend -- you...you take her to a place like that then leave...leave her there...alone...to get your next hit?! Bullshit. That's bullshit! If you...let anyone...hurt her or you, you..."

"No! I didn't...Jesse...Jesse, please," Keith begged in a small voice, looking up at him with a tear--stained face. "I'm sorry, I'm so sorry..."

"Don't!" Jesse spat down at him. "Don't tell me, you sorry son-of-a-bitch!"

For a moment, Jesse just stared down at him as Keith dropped his head, palms, and knees flat on the floor.

"What the fuck is wrong with you, man?" he asked hotly.

"I'm scared, Jesse," Keith choked out between sobs, still on all fours. Then he rocked back on his heels and looked imploringly at his roommate with wild eyes.

"Scared? Of what?!" Jesse demanded.

"The draft," he said, another sob tearing out of him. "Of dying, Jesse! Aren't you scared? They're just gonna take us, and we're all gonna die over there. Aren't you scared?!"

Jesse blinked and took another step back. Scared of dying? No, he wasn't scared of dying. Was he itching to be drafted? No, but he wasn't afraid of dying. Hell, he'd spent large portions of his life -- the parts he tried hard not to think about anymore -- wishing death would come. Honestly, he was surprised he'd lived this long.

No, the thought of dying never once had bothered him. But at least now he understood. It still didn't make it right. It still didn't make putting Becca in harm's way right. But he understood why Keith had buried himself in every illegal substance he could find. He didn't agree at all with Keith's coping method, but he understood the need to escape and feel numb. He understood that all too well.

Keith crossed his legs and sat down on the ground, head in his hands. Once Jesse had his breathing under control, he walked over to the stairwell, and one by one, threw sacks full of clothes in front of him, plus one suitcase. Keith looked at the bags as the Saturday sun started to light the entryway and pedestrian traffic started to pick up on the street outside. He didn't understand and shot Jesse a panicked, questioning look.

"You're going home," he said, his voice now at an even tone.

"What?"

"Your mom's waiting for you in Hoboken," Jesse explained.

"My Mom?" Keith said miserably.

"Yeah, I called her a half-hour ago. Your parents still give a fuck about you," Jesse said. "Go home and...get your head on straight. I'll send the rest of your shit later."

Keith scrambled to his feet, swaying a little. Jesse shot him a disgusted look.

"You really need to be outta my face. You need to be outta Becca's face," Jesse said, pointing at him, then at the door.

Keith stared at him for a moment, then shakily whispered, "I'm sorry." Jesse just looked at him, exasperated. Then Keith nodded, and with shaking hands, he picked up one of the bags. Jesse picked up the suitcase and dragged Keith outside to the curb. He flagged down a cab and pushed Keith into the back seat clutching a bag to his chest.

Jesse and the cab driver piled the rest of Keith's clothes into the trunk, and Jesse slammed the lid shut. He gave the cab driver the address to Keith's parents' house in New Jersey.

Before the cab took off, Jesse opened the back door one more time.

"When you sober up, you call and apologize to her, but don't you ever show your face around here again," Jesse said, with a warning stare that made Keith shiver. "You dig?"

Keith nodded slowly, attempting to focus on Jesse's withering look before Jesse slammed the door and pounded on the top of the taxi. The driver pulled into the relatively light weekend morning traffic as Jesse let out a deep breath. He shoved his hands in his pockets, dropped his head, and slowly made his way back inside the building.

8

THE ODD COUPLE

EARLY MAY 1968

"What in the hell is this?" Jesse asked, holding up a painting and shooting a confused look at Joe.

"It's the Last Supper, dude," he said, shaking his head. "You oughta go to church, man."

"It's...dogs," Jesse responded, still perplexed, putting the painting on the floor against the wall next to Joe's bedroom.

Keith had been gone for almost three weeks. Joe had taken a couple days off work to move in with Jesse at the beginning of the month. Heeding Jesse's warning, Keith had stayed away from their building and Becca. Jesse told everyone Keith had come back to the apartment while he was asleep and packed a bag, leaving a note that he was going to his parents' house. He insisted that was all he knew and that Keith sent for the rest of his stuff a few days later.

He wasn't sure they all bought the story, but he was sticking to it. Keith and his addictions were out of their lives, and, to Jesse, that was really all that mattered. Joe immediately offered to move in, to help with rent and get out of the house full of women he lived in. Once he was certain Keith was gone, Jesse had planned to ask Joe to move in with him anyway, so it worked out perfectly.

"I'm gonna run this down to the truck, then grab a soda at the store. Want one?" Joe asked, holding a box of folded-down boxes they'd already unpacked.

"Sure," Jesse nodded, heading into his bedroom to change out of his work clothes so he could help his new roommate move the rest of his stuff.

Joe opened the door just as Eli was coming up the landing.

"Howdy, neighbor," Joe said with a grin as he turned and made his way down the stairs.

"Hey," Eli said behind him. Joe had left the door open to his apartment, so Eli let himself in.

"Jesse?"

After a couple of seconds, Jesse opened the door to his bedroom, buttoning the top of his jeans, wearing just his undershirt.

"Hey, Eli."

"Moving day, huh?"

"Yep," Jesse said, with a clap and a smile. Then he watched as Eli shut the apartment door and turned a serious face to him. He gave him a quizzical look.

"I, ah, I dropped by Vanhook's today," Eli said, keeping his voice low.

"You did?" Jesse said, straightening his spine. "Did, ah, did you go to see...him?"

"I did."

Jesse just waited. He knew Becca had told everyone very little about what had happened at the party. All they knew was that she and Keith had fought -- she wanted to leave, he didn't, she ended up coming home in a cab without him, and he was gone without an explanation the next day. She left Jesse out of it entirely, and he was grateful for it. Becca's vague explanation alone was enough to send Eli into orbit. But Becca told him since Keith was gone, she wanted to just put it all behind her.

Eli, being her big brother, couldn't do that. So, he went across town to try to track Keith down at work. When Keith came out of the kitchen at Vanhook's and saw Becca's brother, he froze, then he just started blabbering. What he told Eli completely took him by surprise.

Eli walked over to the barstool by the counter and sat down, crossing his arms tight across his chest. Then a slow smile came over his face as he looked at Jesse in the living room.

"You sure scared the hell out of him," Eli said.

Jesse put his hands on his hips and briefly looked at the floor, then he looked up at Eli as he opened and closed his mouth, not exactly sure what to say.

"I'm not going to ask for details," Eli said quickly. "She's...safe and seems to be...over it, but I got the distinct impression from Keith that he really fucked up big time."

Jesse looked at Eli, then nodded.

"Yeah," he said seriously. "Yeah, he did."

Eli's face turned white a moment at the steely look on Jesse's face. He wanted to ask more questions but decided against it. It would only make him crazy. Becca was OK, and Jesse, it seemed, had ensured that she'd stay that way. He cleared his throat and stood, taking a step toward his friend.

"He was shaky, man," Eli said, eyeing Jesse carefully. "Said he thought you were gonna kill him."

Jesse stared back at him a beat before replying.

"Good," Jesse said, nodding again. Eli nodded back, then looked into his friend's eyes, a new respect for the man in front of him rising to the surface. And he began to really wonder about Jesse's feelings for his sister. There had been nothing overt in the way they'd acted around each other since the night she and Keith broke up, but there were a few little things.

After a few days, when Becca was less bummed out, the two fell right back into their pattern of non-stop banter. But Becca seemed just a touch more demure around Jesse now. And he seemed just a hair more protective of her. Liz had noticed it first, but Eli soon picked up on it. The dynamic appeared to be changing, and Eli wasn't opposed to it. Any man willing to scare the shit out of someone for hurting Becca was OK in his book.

But he wasn't about to say anything in case he was wrong. Plus, meddling in his sister's love life wasn't something he really had time for now. He'd enlisted in the Army and was set to leave for basic very soon.

Eli reached out and patted Jesse on the shoulder, seeming to be satisfied enough to put the conversation to rest. Jesse was visibly relieved that he wouldn't have to answer any more questions from him, so he grinned.

Eli grinned back, then looked around at the boxes on the floor.

"Need any help?"

"Nah," Jesse said, "Joe'll be back soon. We're almost done."

As if on cue, Joe returned with the sodas and was followed into the apartment by Becca.

She had her hair piled up high on her head, wrapped with a yellow scarf that matched the sharp, polyester skirt suit that highlighted her legs. She'd pulled the early shift in the newsroom all week, so she'd been up since 4 a.m. Jesse swallowed heavily as she gave him a slow smile, marveling at how she still looked fresh as a spring flower after 12 hours of work.

"Hey," she said to everyone, but her eyes never left Jesse. Blue jeans, white t-shirt, mildly disheveled hair, bare feet...if he didn't look just a little like James Dean...

"Hey," he said, with that sweet little grin on his face.

She smiled wider, and they held their gaze just a second longer than two people normally would before Joe handed Jesse the soda, thereby turning his attention to him.

"We're pretty much finished?" Joe asked it as a question.

"Your stuff, man," Jesse shrugged. "If you're done for the day, that's cool with me."

"Cool, cool," Joe said. "I gotta get the work truck back to the yard, then I'm meeting Trina for dinner."

"Trina, huh?" Jesse said, nudging his friend. "That's the third time in, what, a week?"

"Yeah, yeah," Joe said with a grin. "Can't last too much longer, but a man's gotta eat, and her Mom makes the best..."

"Wait," Becca said, with a little laugh, holding up her hand. "Didn't you just leave your Momma's cooking behind?"

"Yeah? So?" Joe asked, clearly not understanding the question.

Jesse and Eli exchanged a bemused look as Becca just shook her head.

"Nothing," she said, with a wave of her hand. "Just asking."

A little confused, Joe looked at her and then set down his soda and took off for the bathroom to take a shower.

"So...Liz's working late tonight, right?" Becca asked, turning to Eli. She hadn't spent any time alone with her brother since he'd decided to enlist, and she hoped to spend some time with him, even though she knew it would be difficult for them both.

"Yeah, I'm meeting her about 9 for dinner," Eli said, then added tentatively as he glanced at Becca. "I'm, ah, meeting with my recruitment officer at 7."

Becca glanced at him, her lips pursed, but she didn't say anything. Jesse just nodded and took another sip from his can. Eli glanced at his watch.

"I, ah, I got some stuff to do. I gotta split," he said, nodding to Jesse. He walked over to Becca and kissed her forehead. "See you later?"

"Yeah," she said quietly, looking into his eyes for a moment, then looking away. He smiled a little sadly at her then left the apartment.

They watched him go, then Becca turned to Jesse with a little downward grin. He did the same.

"So, you got big plans tonight?" she asked, glancing at the closed bathroom door as they heard the shower turn on. She hadn't felt up to going out socially for a few weeks now, not even to bowl on Friday nights, but she was itching to feel like an active human again. He cocked his head to the side and watched as she nervously played with the handles of her handbag. He bit back the sarcastic comment on the tip of his tongue, fighting the urge to tease her, and simply answered her question.

"Actually, there's a new film opening I sorta would like to see."

"Yeah?" she asked, her curiosity piqued. "Which one?"

"Oh, nothing you would be interested in," he said, with a wave of his hand. "Kind of a dark comedy sorta thing."

"I'm not saying I have any interest in going to a movie with you," she said, smirking at him. "I'm just asking which one."

"I see," he said, with an equal smirk. "OK, then it's 'The Odd Couple.'"

"Oh," she said, furrowing her brow. "Wait...is that the Neil Simon play, about the two divorced guys...?"

"Yeah," he said, nodding. "That's the one."

"Yeah," she said with a shrug. "That could be groovy, that is if you want company."

"Humm, let me think about that," he teased, grinning at her. He couldn't help it now.

"If you don't want me to go with you, you can call up Felicia," she said nonchalantly, a sparkle in her eyes. "Wonder if she's perfected that right hook by now?"

He glared at her, taking a couple steps closer to her, and she grinned up at him. She felt her heart start to race again. It took off just about every time he was close to her these days. She knew she liked him. She really liked him, and the fact that he'd helped her out that awful night a few weeks ago had only added to his allure. But if her experience with Keith had taught her anything, it was not to rush into another relationship -- no matter how damn attractive he was.

Suddenly, he was right in front of her, with that playful look that came into his eyes. Whenever they volleyed back and forth like this, she felt her resolve weaken just a bit.

"Go to the movie all by myself or with a smartass?" he pretended to shrug and contemplate, looking to the ceiling, drumming his fingers on his chin. "Decisions, decisions..."

"Candyass," she whispered as she playfully punched his chest. He smiled down at her, and she felt a flush from head to toe.

"OK, OK, that was a low blow," she conceded, and he arched his eyebrow. She rolled her eyes. "How about I make us dinner first, after I change, and we can go after we eat?"

"You can cook?" he asked, surprised.

"You doubt my abilities?" she asked, glaring at him, hand on her hip. "This is more than a pretty package, you know."

"Oh, I don't doubt that," he said, his mouth suddenly dry. She was looking at him sweetly now, but that challenge was back, just behind her eyes, the one that he was drawn to so much it nearly did him in.

For a moment, they just smiled at each other, only a foot or two apart from one another. The running water from the shower was serving as perfect background noise. Then it abruptly shut off, breaking the increasing tension in the room.

"Ah, listen, I'll pay for my ticket," she said, glancing at the bathroom door again and clearing her throat. "Actually, I'll pay for both tickets. I still owe you..."

"No," he said, after a moment, blinking to get his bearings once again. "You...you don't owe me anything, and I'm not about to let a woman pay her own way, even a 'modern' woman."

His soft grin made her heart skip a beat. She swallowed heavily, then gamely bantered back at him.

"How nineteenth-century of you, Wanger," she said, cocking her eyebrow at him, becoming a tease once again. He stepped back with a chuckle.

"Go change, Schmidt," he said as she smiled and made her way to the door. "Just let me know when the vittles are ready, woman."

"Ugh!" she said as she threw back her head and gracefully waltzed across the living room, her heels making little click-clacks on the hardwood.

His eyes never left her as she moved, not looking back at him, and heat started to rise through his body as he watched her walk out the door.

He shook his head, took another swig of his drink, and plopped down heavily into one of the living room chairs.

"Damn..." he whispered to himself, a little grin spread wide on his flushed face.

9

NOTHING BUT A HEARTACHE

"TV DINNERS?" HE SAID, COCKING AN EYEBROW. "REALLY?"

"Hey," she said, taking the aluminum trays out of the oven with little brown potholders and setting them down on pads on the kitchen table. "To cook, you have to shop, and we haven't been to the grocery in a week. You're lucky we had this."

"So very lucky," he said with a grin as he took a seat in Becca and Liz's kitchen. Becca had knocked on his door just 5 minutes earlier, having changed into blue pedal pushers with a simple, thin blue V--neck short--sleeve sweater to match. If it was possible, Jesse thought the combination brought out the shade in her eyes even more.

"Eli and I grew up on them," she said as she took her seat. "Mom had these fancy TV trays; we'd sit in front of the television and watch the evening news."

"Is that what made you want to be on the news?" Jesse asked.

Becca shrugged.

"I guess that was part of it," she said. "My Mom isn't, um, the best cook, so we'd be happy when it was "TV dinner night." When we were older, they added desserts to them, remember?"

Jesse just nodded.

"Eli and I always fought over who got the brownie one and, of course, my parents always took his side and..."

Becca stopped talking suddenly and looked at Jesse, then she cleared her throat and took a bite of Salisbury steak. He frowned but said nothing for a couple moments.

"Anyway," Becca finally said, quietly. "This is what we had in the freezer, so...I thought it was better than nothing."

Jesse studied her as she concentrated on her food. She didn't look up at him, and he knew she was thinking about Eli. He'd never had siblings, but he could tell that Becca and Eli were more than brother and sister; they were friends. Given how upset Becca had been when he first mentioned enlisting and how upset Eli was with Keith, he knew their bond was a strong one.

They ate in silence for a few minutes. He peeled back the film on his dessert.

"Well, the cranberry-crusted mush sure is...far out," he said with an exaggerated grimace, as he swirled his over-processed mashed potatoes into the watery gravy with his fork.

She giggled a little at that.

"Yeah," she said with a sad smile. Then she put down her fork and folded her arms in front of her.

"Wanna trade desserts?" he asked, trying to get her to smile again.

"I think they're the same thing," she said with a little grin, then she started to play with the edge of her napkin.

"You know, I'm...I'm proud of him," she said quietly. Jesse put down his fork, lacing his fingers together on the tabletop.

"I mean," she said, looking away, tears in her eyes. "I'm mad at him, but it's...it's a brave thing to volunteer to...help the country. I just...I just wish it wasn't...there...now."

Jesse nodded again, not really sure what to say. She picked up her fork once more, and Jesse followed suit. A somewhat uncomfortable silence hung in the air a while longer as they both finished their dinners.

"It's bad, isn't it?" he finally asked, scooping up some of the cranberry mush.

She shook her head.

"It's not good," she said.

"War never is."

"Especially this one," she said, a hint of anger in her voice. He cocked an eyebrow at her.

"Aren't you supposed to be objective?" he asked with a half-hearted grin.

"Not when people I care about are a part of it," she said, looking directly into his eyes. She held his gaze so long that he started to feel like he was drowning in those baby blues. Finally, he pulled his eyes away from hers a fraction, searching her face.

"That's when...when it's hard to stay...objective," she said, looking so softly at him that his body jerked ever so slightly. Did she mean him? She cared about him. No. That wasn't...no.

He was just so damn captivated by her. He'd known plenty of women, but there was something about her that just...he couldn't put his finger on it. She was as tough and beautiful as polished steel on the outside. Yet, she seemed to be pure sugar and salt-of-the-earth on the inside. He was so drawn to her and couldn't understand why. Why her? He'd always been able to keep people at arms-length, even Penny, who was arguably the best friend he'd ever had. But Becca...

He shook his head to break his gaze, clear his thoughts, and try to remember what they were talking about in the first place...Eli! They were talking about Eli and enlisting and objectivity.

"I...I can imagine it is hard to be objective," he said when he could form a coherent statement, then he glanced absently at his watch. He noticed the time. "We, ah, we probably should split if we want to see the earlier show..."

"Oh!" Becca said, looking at her own timepiece. "Right on."

"I'll help clean up," Jesse said, standing up.

"I've got it," Becca said, taking his cup and fork. "Just toss the tins. Swanson's easy cleanup."

She gave him a smile and reached to hand him her foil tray at the same time he reached for it. Their hands touched for a moment, and she felt a jolt of electricity shoot through her. He instantly backed away and let her hand the tray to him.

"Would you just take it to the trash bin?" she asked, opening the door for him.

"Sure thing," he said, walking past her with both trays and out into the hall.

She turned and walked over to the sink, taking a deep breath. She let it out slowly with a smile on her face.

"That's you and Joe in 20 years, you know?" Becca said, giving him a cheeky grin as they left the packed theater a few hours later. They began walking down the sidewalk back toward their building, which was a good 15 blocks away. It was a gorgeous May night, with barely a nip in the air. The sun had gone down. But the city streets held the warmth of the sunny day close to the ground. The movie had been a gas. She couldn't remember the last time she'd laughed so hard, and she'd never heard Jesse belly-laugh like he did at the antics of Oscar and Felix on the big screen. She found it infectious...and completely adorable.

Jesse glanced at her and chuckled at her roommate's comparison on the screen with him and Joe.

"Oh, I don't think so," he said. "Joe'll be married with a passel of Catholic children and probably more on the way by then."

She smiled at that.

"And what about you?" she asked.

"I won't have a passel of Catholic children, no," he said with a mild look of horror.

She giggled.

"Fair enough," she said. "Where do you think you'll be in 20 years?"

His mind went blank. Twenty years? He'd never once thought that far ahead. He shrugged, grabbing a pack of cigarettes out of his pocket.

"I have no idea."

"Oh, come on," she said, playfully punching his arm. "You must have some plan for the future?"

He pretended to think a minute, getting ready to light up the cig at his lips. He offered her one, and she squished up her nose. It'd be a long time before she felt like smoking anything again. He raised his eyebrows but pulled the cigarette away from his lips and put it back in the pack.

"You can..." she started.

"Nah, that's OK," he said with a little smile, which she returned.

"So...the future, Wanger?"

"I plan to bowl tomorrow night with you," he said with a grin. "You're back tomorrow, right?"

"Yeah," she said, smiling up at him. "Yeah, I feel like I'm in the land of the living again."

"Good," he nodded, briefly putting an arm around her shoulders as they walked stride for stride through an entertainment district in the Village. He gave her a gentle squeeze, and she graced him with a dazzling smile. He swallowed heavily and dropped his arm.

"That's, ah, that's all I've got for future plans," he said, his face turning a little pink as he stuffed his hands in his pockets.

"OK, then," she said, not satisfied with that answer, not knowing exactly why she wasn't satisfied with that answer. "Did you always want to be a business manager?"

He rolled his eyes.

"What is this, 20 questions?"

"Well, I *am* a reporter, you know," she teased, nudging him with her arm. "You knew that when you asked me to come with you tonight."

"Oh no," he said, as he stopped walking and turned to face her with a grin. "Now, just a minute there, missy. You invited yourself."

"I did not!" she turned to him, mild shock and mock anger on her face.

"Like hell you didn't!"

"That's not how I remember the conversation going," she said, as she crossed her arms, trying hard not to break into a fit of giggles. "I believe you offered to pay."

"Well, yeah, once you declared you were coming with me," he said, hands on his hips now, trying his best not to smile.

"No, see, you offered to pay. That's an invitation," she said, with a smirk on her face.

"Some reporter you are," he scoffed. "Can't keep your story straight."

"That's the way I see it," she said. "And that's the way it is."

"Oomph!" he laughed, throwing his head back at her boss's signature catchphrase. He smiled back at the huge smile on her face. She stomped her foot and cocked her hip to the side, signifying that the debate was over.

"I might need that cigarette after all," he said, shaking his head, a bemused look on his face. "Are you always this...stubborn?"

"I prefer to think I'm always right, but you can call it stubborn," she said, grinning. "And you never answered my question."

"Good God, woman, which one?!"

"Did you always want to be a business manager?"

He rolled his eyes with an exasperated sigh and started walking again. She wasn't about to let it drop, though. She'd cracked that steely, blue-eyed code just a touch, and she was bound and determined to blow it wide open. He had a story, she just knew it, and she wanted to know what it was. Who he was, deep inside, was a mystery to her, and she wanted to solve it? No, she needed to solve it. In the last few months, he'd somehow become very important to her. Even when she was dating Keith, Jesse held her attention. Yes, her heart jumped when he laid that sweet, slow smile on her, but it was more than that. It was deeper, somehow, and she wanted to understand it. She wanted to understand him.

"Well?" she asked, matching him step for step.

"I don't know, Becca," he said, stuffing his hands in his jean's pockets once again. "It's not, like, my dream job. Pays the bills."

"What is your dream job?"

"I don't have one."

"OK, when you were little, what did you want to be when you grew up? Did you dream about being a baseball player? The milkman? What?" she said, grinning at him.

But he didn't return her smile, her question cutting him right then in a way he didn't anticipate. What did he want to be when he grew up? What did he dream about when he was little?

He was never "little," and he sure as hell didn't dream. There was no dreaming when you lived a nightmare day-to-day, not really thinking you'd ever grow up -- or knowing if you really wanted to.

"Jesse?" she asked, smile off her face as she looked at the clouds that had taken over his. She swallowed hard. What had she said?

He glanced over at her, and his face softened. She was looking at him so innocently, wondering how she'd offended him, he was sure. He smiled a little, trying to put her at ease.

"Baseball player," he lied. "Just never panned out."

She grinned, but her eyes were still questioning him. She knew she'd struck a nerve somewhere. She reached out her left arm and laced it around his right elbow, leaning into him, catching his eye, and smiling, trying to offer some kind of apology for making him uncomfortable.

His heart started to pound, even as his brain began yelling at him to not let her get too close. Subconsciously, he pulled away, a little. But if she noticed, she pretended she didn't. She held firm onto him, and finally, he just let her linger there against him as they walked along, past a row of bars and nightclubs just coming alive with the late-night crowd.

Another block further down, they heard the mellow sounds of jazz and blues pouring out onto the sidewalk. It was a contrast to the smoky, dead bar traffic and pounding dance beats a block back. Jesse slowed and tried to make out the name on the sandwich chalkboard on the sidewalk next to the front door.

"Ever been here?" he asked, nodding toward the entrance.

"No," Becca said, shaking her head and peeking into the bar. She loved rhythm and blues, and whomever the vocalist was inside sounded great. The front door was opened to let in the night air, and she could see the soft glow of a blue light in the relative darkness, dotted by the flicker of lighters here and there as cigarettes were lit. The musicians were on a far corner stage, and a few couples were dancing on a makeshift dance floor.

He watched as she took in the scene before her, and he grinned.

"They usually have good singers who do lots of covers," he said. "Wanna cool it here for a little while?"

"Sure," she said with a smile. "I'm game if you are."

"Oh, I'm game," he said, with his crooked little grin.

He took his hands out of his pockets, and she dropped her arms to her sides. He put his right hand on the small of her back and guided her to the door.

"After you," he said, with a grand gesture of his left hand.

She grinned at him and nodded a "thank you." Both smiling, they made their way into the club.

10

YOU MAKE ME FEEL

"THERE'S AN OPEN TABLE IN THE BACK," ONE OF THE SERVERS SAID, smiling at Becca and Jesse as they walked into the club's lounge area. There were tables and little loveseats scattered about, everything cozy in the shadows of the room, which was larger than it looked from the outside. All eyes were on the four-piece band; some people swayed to the music in their seats while others glanced periodically at the couples on the crowded little dance floor.

Taking their cue from the server, they made their way to a back table in the corner. Jesse motioned for the same waiter to follow them.

"What can I get ya?" Jesse asked.

"Scotch," she said, automatically, then thought better of it. "Ah, no, wait...um, what are you having?"

"Just a brew," he said with a shrug.

"OK, that sounds fine," she said, giving him a nod as she took her seat.

"You sure?"

"I'm sure," she said, smiling at him.

The waiter came, and Jesse gave him the drink order. Becca surveyed the place. It had a relaxed, laid-back feel to it that she had to admit she loved. The woman on lead vocals was amazing -- she seemed to be channeling the great soul singers of the decade with ease. Becca leaned back in the chair and crossed her legs, sweeping her long hair over one shoulder as Jesse took the seat next to her.

"So, you come here often, sailor?" she said, a tease in her voice. Jesse chuckled and shrugged.

"Once in a while," he said, nodding toward the vocalist. "She's great, isn't she?"

"Yeah, what's her name?"

"Roberta somebody," he said. "Flood, Flake, something like that. She's outta D.C."

"Ah," she acknowledged as the server came back to serve their beer. They both were quiet, listening to Roberta sing the last few strains of Etta James's "At Last" while they sipped their drinks. When the polite applause died down, the band announced they were going to take a short break, giving patrons a chance to mix and mingle and talk.

"So, what position did you play?" Becca asked.

Jesse looked at her, confused for a moment, but gave her a little grin as he answered.

"Interested in my positions, are ya?" he said with a smirk, taking another sip of his beer. He could have sworn he saw her turn a little pink over the rim of his glass, even in the shadows of the corner table. He smiled into his beer.

Thrown for only a moment, she leaned in and ran her fingertips along his arm and threw him a seductive glance, causing Jesse's breath to hitch.

"In baseball, smartass," she said, a little grin of her own gracing her features.

"Oh," he said, remembering the white lie he told in their earlier conversation. "Yeah, um, catcher. The problem was I couldn't catch."

Becca smiled.

"Pretty sure that would be one of the requirements."

"Yeah," he said, taking another swig of his beer, trying to figure out a way to change the subject.

"How about you? Did you always dream of being a reporter?"

"No," she said, shaking her head. "But when I was little, I would always want to be in-the-know. I always wanted to know everyone's business. It used to drive Eli crazy. He could never keep anything from me. I would always snoop around and find out. Which, of course, meant he couldn't keep anything from my parents."

She smiled, and he chuckled.

"I used to get in trouble for being a tattle-tale," she continued. "Of course, Eli could do no wrong, so..."

"Parents playing favorites, huh?"

"Maybe I just perceived it that way," she shrugged. "He was the first-born and a boy, and I just kind of...came along later."

Jesse nodded.

"Do you have brothers or sisters?" she asked.

"No," he said quickly. "You and Eli seem pretty close now, though."

"Yeah, we are," she said, a sad look passing over her face, twisting a ring around her finger on top of the little table where they were seated. She cleared her throat. "That's why I couldn't...I couldn't tell him the whole story about...Keith. He'd have killed him if he found him..."

"Hey, no, I understand," Jesse said, nodding, not about to reveal what Eli had mentioned to him earlier in the day. "I know how to keep a secret."

She cocked her head to one side, studying him, thinking, 'I bet you do,' but she kept the comment to herself. He winked at her.

"Thanks," she said softly, with a gentle smile, then she added with a sigh, "not that it matters much. He's leaving soon anyway..."

Her voice trailed off, and she looked away at the empty stage. The musicians were just beginning to make their way back to their instruments. She picked up her beer glass and took a long drink. As she set it down again, she felt Jesse's warm hand slide over hers. He grinned softly at her and looked into her eyes.

"Just let the blues lose you for a while, you dig?" he said quietly, gently squeezing her hand.

Becca nodded, her face softening and her fingers curling around his as the band started to play once again. She held his gaze long enough that he started to feel a little uncomfortable.

"What?" he whispered with a little smile that made her heart flip-flop.

"Nothing," she said softly, even as she felt her skin flush from her chest up to her neck and face. She was glad it was pretty dark in this corner of the club.

"I'm just getting lost in...the...blues," she replied, her eyes never leaving his.

The grin left his face as they sat there, a mild instrumental number playing in the background, blue searching blue. Jesse felt a shiver from head to toe. No woman had ever had this effect on him -- certainly not from a simple look or a gentle touch. Her gentle touch, which was making his hand feel like it was crawling with hot coals he longed to stay buried in, was as unnerving as it was pleasant. But, damn, did it feel pleasant.

The music's tempo changed a touch, and Roberta took her place at the microphone, channeling Aretha Franklin as several couples took to the dance floor as the opening vocals of "(You Make Me Feel Like) A Natural Woman" began.

Jesse lifted her hand in his and raised his eyebrows.

She smiled softly and nodded toward the dance floor.

"It's pretty full."

He looked to his right and was about to turn his head to agree when she put her free hand over his and stood up. He looked up at her with a grin as she pulled his hand toward the corner wall behind their table.

"There's a little space here," she said, gesturing to the small space behind her. He slowly rose to his feet and walked around the tiny table, putting one hand on the small of her back and pulling her to him until she was almost flush against him.

"So, there is," he whispered with a grin, as that one lock of hair that always seemed to fall against his forehead landed there once again. She brought the hand he was still holding to her waist, urging him to bring his hands together behind her as she moved to run both her hands through his hair; a simple gesture she'd wanted to do so badly for months, putting his rogue locks back into place. She grinned up at him, and he slowly smiled back at her, running his hands over the top of her hips, bringing her closer to him.

He could feel her breath against his neck as she laid her head against his shoulder, his heart beating wildly in his chest. They were making rhythmic circles in the middle of their own little, corner dance floor, each of their bodies seeming to give off heat like a furnace. He started to breathe heavily as he dropped his head against hers and brushed his cheek a couple times gently against her hair. She lifted her face to him, her eyes half-closed. She licked her lips, her gaze dropping to his. Gently, slowly, almost tentatively, he bent down, and she caught his bottom lip between both of hers, kissing him softly.

She released him after only a moment. She tilted her head back just a fraction. She felt one of his hands slide up her back and bury itself in her hair at the base of her skull, pulling her back to him, brushing his bottom lip against her mouth stronger this time. She kissed him harder, and quickly his mouth was full-on hers, their lips furiously seeking the other's taste.

Their breathing rapidly became labored as Jesse gently pushed her against the wall as she pulled on his shoulders, lips still locked in a blazing kiss.

Jesse moved his hand most hidden by the dark corner up under her thin sweater, making her shudder when his long fingers touched her warm skin. He cupped her breast and began to run his thumb back and forth against the fabric of her bra. She gasped against his lips, breaking their kiss, feeling him come alive against her through his jeans. She gasped again.

"Jesse..." she breathed.

"Yeah?" he replied in barely a whisper, trying to capture her lips again. She kissed him softly as she gently pushed his shoulders.

"Jesse...I..." she started, looking into his now confused face. She kissed him again, wanting to reassure him. "I want...this. I want this, but I...I..."

"What?" he asked, still confused but now running his hand slowly down the side of her face, the gentleness of his touch making her eyes well-up.

"Can we...take it slow?" she whispered. "I...I've rushed into...things before and I...I'm just..."

She was shaking, looking at him worriedly, her breathing still heavy. She loved to tease him, but she didn't want to be a tease. She just wanted to make sure...she wanted to keep from getting hurt again. The way her body was responding to him, she knew her heart would follow so quickly it would be unbelievable. She was so drawn to him that it took everything she had to hold back, but she needed to somehow attempt to keep her heart safe and her head clear.

Jesse tried to slow his breathing as he looked at her. In that moment, she looked so vulnerable, just a touch like the woman he saw shivering at the phone booth that night, that he wasn't about to protest. He wasn't going to question her. So far, this had been the best night of his entire life -- and he wasn't going to ruin it by pushing too hard to make anything happen. He smiled at her, watching as she visibly relaxed. He nodded.

"Yeah," he said softly, nodding again and smiling in understanding. "Will you just...dance with me?"

The smile she gave him was so brilliant and so sincere it nearly took his breath away. She nodded and fell back against his chest. He moved her around slowly in small circles, closing his eyes and holding her tight against him.

"Hell of a kiss, though," he whispered after a moment as they swayed to the next slow song. He felt her giggle in his arms.

"I know," she whispered, pulling him closer to her.

###

Becca closed the apartment door behind her with a little grin. A kiss on the forehead? Really? She'd have gone for more than that. But he'd given her a mischievous smile and a wink and walked into his apartment.

Oh, what a night...for the first time in a long time, she felt excited butterflies filling her stomach. God, he was gorgeous and sweet and just a drop of too sexy to completely resist. She was so in trouble...

"Becca?"

She jumped and looked at the figure sitting on the couch in the dark apartment.

"Liz?" she asked, walking over to turn on a lamp on the end table. Liz shielded her eyes from the light and pulled an afghan closer to her. Becca sat down next to her.

"Oh, honey, what's the matter?" Becca asked. It was obvious Liz had been crying.

"Where were you?"

Becca couldn't hide her smile.

"Out...with Jesse."

"Oh," Liz breathed, giving her a sad smile. "Oh, that is...far out. Had a neat time, I bet, huh?"

"Yeah," Becca said, a dreamy look on her face.

"I'm...that's so...I'm happy for you, Becca," Liz said, her voice cracking. She wiped her eyes.

"Liz, what is it? What's wrong?" she said worriedly, trying to focus on her friend.

Liz took a couple deep breaths.

"Eli asked me to marry him."

"What?" Becca said, both surprised and confused. "Oh Lizzy, hon, that's wonderful...isn't it?"

"It should be," Liz said, quietly.

"Then what? What is..."

"He wants to get married...this weekend...at city hall," she said, grabbing a tissue.

"This weekend?!" Becca said with a disbelieving laugh. "That's not enough time to..."

Then she stopped and stared at Liz, the color draining from her face.

"May 9th," Liz whispered. Becca gasped.

"That's...that's barely a week..."

"I know," Liz said, anger in her voice and tears streaming down her face. "This time...next week...he'll...he'll belong to the army for four years, if...he...makes it that long."

She said the last words in an agonized whisper. Becca's eyes filled with tears as she pulled her brokenhearted friend to her and let her cry into her shoulder, loud and silent tears ricocheting around the quiet living room.

"Love is a bitch," she eventually heard Liz mumble brokenly between sobs.

Becca took a deep breath and held her tighter, blurry eyes staring unblinkingly across the room.

11

BLOOD RUNS COLD

"WELL, WELL, WELL, SOMEONE'S IN A SHINY, HAPPY PLACE," PENNY SAID cheekily as she walked over to Jesse at the bowling alley the following night.

Jesse took a puff on his cigarette.

"What makes you say that?" he asked, grinning through his exhale.

"I spotted you from over there," she said, nodding toward the entrance, "all alone with a smile on your face and, dare I say it, a spring in your step."

He rolled his eyes.

"A spring in my step?" he asked. "Maybe I'm just happy to see you."

"Right on," she said with a matching eye roll, putting down her bowling bag and smiling at him, "I hear there was a date..."

"Yeah?" he said, leaning back in his chair, arms outstretched, crossing a foot over one knee. "Who told you that?"

"A little birdie," she teased, slapping his leg down. "Dinner, a movie, and dancing, huh?"

He shrugged but couldn't keep himself from grinning.

"Did ya have fun?" she asked, digging out her bowling shoes.

"Yeah, it was all right," he said with another shrug, but now with a huge, uncontainable smile on his face. Penny was pretty sure she'd never seen him smile so bright.

"Just to be clear," she said as he took another drag and raised his eyebrows, "that feeling that you're feeling right now? That's called happ-i-ness."

He grinned at her one more time through his exhale, then quickly put out his cigarette as he saw Becca come into view. He batted the smoke away with his hand as she came closer, Eli and Liz behind her. She smiled at him.

"Hey," she said, with a twinkle in her eyes.

"Hey yourself," he grinned back as she took a seat beside him, pulling out her bowling shoes with a little smile on her face. It had been a long night with Liz as she listened to her unload about the huge fight she and Eli got into after he proposed.

Instead of going to sleep, Becca stayed awake most of the night, thinking about her brother and his now fiancé, of course. But also, about the night she'd had with Jesse. She'd never felt so attracted to someone in her whole life -- not just physically but mentally. Figuring him out had become an almost all-consuming brain exercise. He'd occupied her thoughts most of her long day at work, and she was so anxious to see him tonight she could hardly contain herself.

Then she met Eli and Liz back at the apartment before bowling, and her thoughts were interrupted yet again. The two weren't arguing now, but rather discussing a fragile compromise to the question of when to be married. They brought Becca into the discussion when she came home. The three of them ended up in tears at the kitchen table before noticing the time and leaving to meet the others at the bowling alley for the last games of the current tournament -- and Eli's last Friday night with the group before he left for the Army.

Eli nodded to Jesse as he and Liz sat in the blue plastic chairs opposite him and Becca. Jesse nodded back, then watched as Eli stole a glance at Penny, who was purposefully refusing to acknowledge his arrival on the scene. The tension when they were all together was a lot thicker now than it ever had been in the months they'd known each other.

Becca stashed her regular shoes in her bowling bag as a silence permeated over their little team. She gave Jesse a small smile, then stood and walked over to Penny, who he could tell was pretending to busy herself at the scoring table.

"Can you at least say 'hi' to him?" Becca asked softly.

Penny's head shot up, and she stared at nothing down the bowling lane in front of her, then she looked at Becca.

"No," she said quietly, stealing a glance at Eli a few feet away. "I don't agree with what he's signed up to do, and I don't have to act all nice to him before he does it."

"Penny, please," Becca implored. "I...I want to make tonight as...as carefree as possible for him..."

"Carefree?" Penny said a little too loudly, catching the whole group's attention over the crashing pins and thumping bowling balls. Jesse stood then, shoving his hands in his pockets, and walking over to Penny and Becca. Eli cleared his throat and told Liz he was going to rent their shoes. Liz, almost already in tears, just nodded.

Becca placed a hand on her hip, ready to defend Eli. No, she wasn't happy either, but if she and Liz could come to some peace with it in their minds, then she reasoned that Penny could, too.

"Look," Becca said as Jesse came up to them. "I'm not thrilled either, but he's leaving. My only brother is leaving, and..."

Her voice hitched, and Jesse put a hand on her shoulder. Penny's face softened just a little. Becca took a deep breath.

"He's doing what he thinks is the right thing to do," she said in a whisper. "He wants to help save lives, and...and that's the same whether he does it in New York or Vietnam or anywhere else the military decides to send him."

"Becca, I'm sorry," Penny said, more resolved now, even though her eyes were watery. "I can't agree with the support of this war in any context. I can't..."

"You don't have to agree," Becca interrupted, wiping a tear from her eyes. "Just please...please don't make it harder than it already is...for everyone."

Penny looked to Jesse, who raised his eyebrows at her as if to say, "can you do that?" After a moment's hesitation, Penny nodded, and Jesse let out a sigh of relief.

"Thank you," Liz said loudly, her voice thick with tears. The three turned their eyes to her, and she met their gazes with a tear-stained but stoic face. Penny frowned and moved to sit down next to Liz. She put her arms around her, giving her a gentle squeeze.

Becca turned and smiled at Jesse.

"Thank you," she whispered, wiping another tear away. He put a crooked finger under her chin and lifted her face to his.

"I didn't do anything," he said, wiping her last tear away with his thumb. "What else is going on?"

He could sense it. There was something off between Eli and Liz, and it was more than him just enlisting. Becca sighed and took his hand from under her chin and held it in hers.

"He asked her to marry him before he leaves," she said quietly as they walked hand-in-hand over to their chairs again.

"Oh," he said, nodding. "Did...she...say...no?"

"Not exactly," she said, her face turned away from him.

"When's he leaving?" he asked as he furrowed his brow.

Becca looked at him then, with big tears in her eyes.

"May 9th," she whispered.

"May 9th?" he said. "But, but that's..."

"A week," she nodded with a watery chuckle. "Yes, I'm well aware."

Jesse swallowed hard and studied Becca.

"Wow, that's really..." he started, then stopped, not knowing what else to say. Just then, Eli came back with two pairs of shoes and a tray full of drafts. He surveyed the sad faces in front of him, and his heart flipped. He looked at Penny, and she smiled just a little at him. He breathed deeply and sat down the shoes. Then he started passing out the beer.

"I figured I owed you a brew at least," he said, handing two beers to Jesse in anticipation of Joe joining them soon, "and I have a toast. Liz?"

She stood, walked over to him, and wrapped her arm around his waist, looking up at him with tears in her eyes but a small smile on her face.

"This woman here has agreed to marry me," he said, smiling down at Liz. "But she's making me wait because that's what women do, am I right, Jess?"

Eli was doing his best to be light-hearted, and his eyes were imploring Jesse to play along. Jesse nodded and raised his can a little higher.

"It's what they do best, chief," he said with a nod to Eli, whose face broke into a big, appreciative smile. He glanced down at Becca, who smirked back at him as Penny and Liz rolled their eyes.

"We are not going to be married at city hall," he said as if the idea was the worst thing he'd ever heard. Liz smiled through her tears and giggled. He hugged her to him. "In many, many months, enough months to plan a wedding..."

"We'll see," Liz piped up with a grin. Eli threw a quick glare down to her but grinned and continued, "when I get my first R&R..."

"In Hawaii!" Liz said excitedly. "His R&R can be in Hawaii, and whenever it is, that's when we're going to get married!"

"A luau on the beach," Eli said, raising his can in the air, "and you're all invited!"

"Well, here here," Jesse said as all the beer cans bounced together. "Congratulations."

"I don't know how we'll get to Hawaii, but, sure," Penny said, smiling despite herself.

"Details, details," Becca said with a laugh and a wink to her brother. Eli smiled at her, happy to have succeeded in making the night less solemn and more joyful.

After everyone took a swig, the call came over the intercom for bowlers to report to their lanes. Becca stood up to take a couple practice throws with Penny as Eli and Liz secured their bowling shoes. Jesse was scanning the entrance for Joe and finally saw him come into view.

"Hey," Jesse said, grinning widely at him and handing him the unopened beer. "Glad you made it. Your woman coming?"

"Ah...no," Joe said, nodding at the others and setting down the beer, then he looked back at Jesse. "Can I talk to you a minute?"

Jesse shot him a confused look as Joe walked past him, over to the wall by the bowling ball rack. He put down his bowling bag as Jesse came up to stand next to him.

"Looking for a new ball?" Jesse asked. "I thought you just bought one..."

"When's the last time you checked your mail?"

Jesse shrugged.

"I don't know, a couple days ago, why?"

Joe bent down and unzipped his bowling bag, pulling a couple slips of folded paper out of it. He handed them to Jesse.

"I went to my Mom's to pick up mine today," Joe said quietly. "Thank God she wasn't home or...I didn't even look at it until I got back to the building..."

Jesse stared at the nearly identical papers in his hands, his eyes scanning the same words over and over. Joe took a deep breath.

"I saw a bill or something sticking out of our box," he continued. "So, I opened it up, and...I...it was buried in the stack, at the bottom."

Jesse glanced at him then, his expression impossible for Joe to read. Joe sighed, glancing back at their lane. Becca, Penny, Eli, and Liz thankfully were now engrossed in their own conversation.

"I...I went through my mail from home and found mine," he said. "It came today."

Jesse squeezed his eyes closed, and Joe clapped him on the back.

"May 9th?" Jesse whispered.

Joe nodded.

"Yeah," Joe said, his voice shaking just a little.

"Eli leaves May 9th," Jesse said in a low voice.

Joe's head shot up from the letters, and his eyes met Jesse's.

"No," he breathed with a sorrowful look. Jesse just nodded in affirmation.

"Son-of-a-bitch," Joe whispered, hands on his hips.

Jesse looked down at the draft notices a few more moments before he slowly folded the papers back together and handed them to Joe, pointing to his bowling bag.

"Listen, ah," he said, clearing his throat. "Don't say anything about... this...tonight. You dig?"

He turned then and glanced in the direction of their friends. Becca's arm was around Eli, smiling up at him. Liz was at his other side while Penny moved over to the scoring table, lighting it up above the lane. Joe's eyes followed his, and he nodded.

"Yeah," he agreed. "Yeah, no sense in making tonight...worse, I guess."

"Don't make it worse than it already is..." Becca's words echoed in Jesse's mind.

"I can't...I can't believe it...the same goddamn day," Joe said, shaking his head in disbelief. "What a fucking coincidence."

Jesse nodded as Joe bent down and put the papers back in his bag. Just then, Becca looked in Jesse's direction and smiled brightly at him, waving him to her, her tears from earlier all but forgotten at that moment. He smiled back as best he could.

"You ready?" Joe asked, picking up his bowling bag again.

Jesse glanced at him, and Joe pursed his lips and took a step forward.

"Works out that it's our last night, I guess," Joe said as they slowly made their way back to the group.

"Yeah," Jesse said quietly, his eyes never leaving Becca as he swallowed back the bile that had risen into his throat.

"Dammit it all to hell," he whispered under his breath.

12

PRAY FOR US

THE BLACK AND WHITE FILM'S REFLECTION WAS MIRRORED IN BECCA'S eyes in the darkroom down the hall from the CBS News studio. Her trained eye stopped the b-roll in snippets as the seemingly never-ending footage from Vietnam rolled out in front of her.

She felt sick, literally sick. She'd had to take several breaks that day, sometimes just closing her eyes, sometimes stepping away to the corner of the room just to catch her breath. She felt like running away after her lunch break, but she didn't. She went back to the darkroom and resumed her job, which now she detested with every fiber of her being. The face of every young soldier morphed into Eli or Joe, but more often than not, it morphed into Jesse.

She was deeply concerned for her brother, of course. She was very concerned about Joe, too, but Jesse...it made her heart stop when the worst happening to him flashed in her mind. When she saw footage of a soldier on a stretcher, or a body bag being placed gently on a plane bound for home, that's when she couldn't breathe. That's when she headed to the dark corner to try to calm down again.

It just wasn't fair he was leaving. It was true that she'd only known him for a few months, but in those few months, he'd worked his way into her psyche, and if she was completely honest, into her heart. There was so much she didn't know about him, but there was something in her that felt this incredible desire to be close to him. He'd proved to be an incredible friend with everything that had happened with Keith and had pulled her out of her doldrums when she was ready to go out again.

And then there was their one night -- the movie, the club, the dancing, the kiss. That kiss on the dance floor she wished now she'd never stopped because now...now he was pushing her away. He was pushing everyone away.

It started Friday night at the bowling alley. When he and Joe rejoined the group at the start of the first game, she'd put her arm around Jesse, and he'd smiled down at her for only a moment before disengaging from her. He went to the bar and ordered one of several hard drinks he'd had that night. Despite trying to make everything lighthearted for a little while, he, Joe, and even Eli were bombed by the end of the night. She, Penny, and Liz had to practically drag them home. The whole experience was emotionally draining for everyone and very confusing for her.

For a brief moment that night, she and Jesse had a moment alone. That was when Eli and Liz had entered her apartment at the top of the landing, Penny had descended the stairs for home, and Joe had run to his bathroom. He put both his hands on the sides of her face, and she was sure he was going to kiss her. Instead, his sad, oh so sad, glassy eyes tried to focus on hers. He swayed to the right just a touch, and she braced his arms to help steady him...

"Jesse, what is it? What's...?" she whispered, worried about the sorrowful look on his face. *"What is it?"*

He shook his head. His breath was laced with all the liquor he'd consumed, and to her, he looked completely lost.

"Leaving..." he muttered. "All the leaving..."

She brushed his hair back off his forehead, looking at him with questioning eyes, but she thought she understood what he meant. Eli leaving just served to remind him and Joe that they could be called to duty, too. She was sure that was what was bothering him. It surprised her only because his demeanor was usually void of that kind of worry. But it made sense, complete sense that it would come to a-head right then.

She ran her hands up and down his arms, trying to soothe him. She felt him shudder beneath her touch.

"I know it's scary," she said quietly, gently, trying to reassure him. "But he'll...he'll be fine. We all will."

She gave him a small smile, but instead of making him feel better, his face seemed to fall further, and he dropped his hands to his sides. He tried to stand up a little straighter and clear his throat, which only made him cough hard. She reached for him, and he backed away, putting his hand against the wall behind him.

"Are you gonna be OK?" she asked, gesturing toward his door as she continued to step toward him.

He put one hand up and nodded. Then with one more intense look at her, he scooted his body along the wall to his door.

"Good...goodbye, Becca," he whispered.

"Good night, you mean?"

"Yeah..." he mumbled as he turned the doorknob and stumbled inside.

She stood alone in the middle of the hall, staring at his apartment, more confused than ever.

She wasn't confused anymore.

She didn't see him over the weekend. He and Joe weren't awake on Saturday when she, Liz, and a very hungover Eli headed out to Long Island for an all-day get-together with her extended family. The event wasn't called a going-away party for Eli, but that's what it was. Then she'd stayed the night at her parents because the Redds were throwing a family brunch for Eli and Liz on Sunday in celebration of their engagement.

She didn't mind spending as much time with her brother as she could before he left, even if spending that much time with her Mom was trying. The hardest part was wondering how Jesse was coping. She couldn't get him off her mind. She hadn't been able to get him off her mind for weeks, but now she was worried about him. She couldn't get the broken look on his face from Friday night out of her head.

After the brunch, she had to go to work and pull a 12-hour shift. She got back to the Village very late, and when she woke up Monday morning, Jesse had already left for work.

She had that day off, so she threw herself into cleaning the apartment to stave off her nerves. It was something she'd done for years, and it relaxed her.

But no amount of cleaning could have relaxed her enough to prepare her for what she would hear later that night.

Becca took a deep breath, her eyes blurry. She stopped the film strip and turned off the projector light, her face falling into her hands...

"What?!" Penny said, a strange sound in her high-pitched voice.

"That can't be," Liz said as she sat heavily in one of the kitchen chairs in her apartment. Eli stood behind her and put a hand on her shoulder. *"This can't be happening..."*

Joe cleared his throat.

"We...we received our notices in the mail on Friday," he said quietly, nodding at Jesse. *"We, both of us, have to show up for our physicals on Thursday, just like the enlisted men."*

"What time?" Eli asked.

"0800 at the Dresden Center," Joe said, slipping into military time. In some ways, being the son of a military man, he'd been preparing for this moment his whole life. Eli just nodded. It was the same time he was reporting -- 8 a.m.

Jesse was staring straight ahead, refusing to meet anyone's eyes. Becca's heart was racing as she stared at him, her face white as a ghost. Friday night made sense now. It all made sense now -- they knew they were leaving then.

"I knew it, I knew this was going to happen," Penny burst out. "This is wrong, all wrong!"

"For the love of God, Penny, please, just stop it!" Liz said, with uncharacteristic force, pounding her fist on the table.

Penny ignored her and moved to stand right in front of Jesse.

"You can run -- you should run," she said, eyeing him carefully. He stared her down with a stone look on his face.

"I'm not running...anywhere," he said, glancing at Joe. "This is what...what we've been called to do."

Joe nodded.

"How are you going to feel," she continued, right in his face, her emotions getting the best of her. "When they put that gun in your hands and send you into a village to kill..."

"Out!" Becca shouted, anger coursing through her veins. "Out, Penny! I want you out of my apartment right now!"

Everyone looked at Becca, who was seething, and Jesse swallowed hard.

"Baby killers," Penny whispered fiercely, looking between him and Joe. "You are just fodder for 'the man' -- they'll make you into baby killers!"

Tears started to stream down her face. She loved these men, especially Jesse, like a brother, and they were all going to leave and fight in that war in that place. It was too much for her.

"I won't stand by and watch you leave," she said hotly. Then she grabbed her bag and walked out the door...

"Becca?" Malory said, poking her head into the darkroom and interrupting the scene that had played out in Becca's head a hundred times since Monday night.

Becca cleared her throat and stood up off her stool, smoothing down her long skirt.

Malory gave her a sad smile.

"Thanks for covering for me," Becca said in a whisper. "I know you're busy with your wedding this weekend..."

"It's fine," Malory said, stepping to her and giving her colleague a hug. "I'm just sorry I have to cover for you. Where are you going to dinner?"

Becca cleared her throat again.

"Some Italian place...ah, Tony's," she said. "My brother picked it out. My Mom wanted to cook on his...last night...home, but...but he refused, thankfully."

She gave Malory a small smile. It was the last time the four Schmidts and Liz would be together as a family for a long time. Becca was expected to be there, but she didn't plan to stay there too long. She hadn't seen Jesse since the Monday evening bombshell. He'd made himself scarce when she was home. She was desperate to see him and had been trying to talk to him for two days without any luck.

She was determined to see him tonight. Their physicals were in the morning.

"Your notes here?" Malory said, glancing at the shorthand Becca had jotted down in the reporter's notebook by the projector.

"Yeah," she said. "I...I stopped at frame 531-A, I...I think."

"I'll take care of it," Malory said with a nod. She looked at her sad friend through the shadows and could see tears in her eyes. Malory felt so badly for her. She couldn't believe she was losing so many men so close to her to fight in the war all at the same time. She shook her head.

"Good luck and tell Eli...all of them...I'll pray for them," Malory said, with another little smile.

Becca stepped back and nodded. She mouthed, "thank you."

She turned and exited the darkroom, wiping her eyes as they adjusted to the bright artificial light before any tears could fall. She collected her things and, with a nod to her boss, walked out of the building and into the bright sun of the late afternoon.

It was going to be a beautiful evening, just like the one last week when she and Jesse...

And her eyes filled with tears again. As she walked the 10 or so blocks to Tony's, she took deep breaths along the way.

"Oh, pray for us, Malory," she said out loud to no one as tears made their way onto her cheeks, her arms braced around her tight. "We're all going to need it."

13

THE SOUND OF SILENCE

Jesse closed the ledger book, absently running his hand over the leather binding and looking out his office window.

The sun was beating in through the glass, making his cramped, small office stuffy on this late afternoon in May, but he felt a chill run down his spine despite the heat. He stared out onto the shabby structures surrounding the Pipefitters Union building, wondering fleetingly if it would be the last time he'd look out a window at the end of a workday.

He shook his head. He really should know better. Of course, it was the last time.

He'd spent this last day at work finishing training the person who would take his job when he left and taking care of a couple special accounting changes that needed to be made. Abraham had stopped by his office to timidly wish him well; his own son having been drafted right out of high school just three months earlier. His boss had checked in on him a couple times, but mostly everyone kept their heads down or gave him a sad nod.

And that was fine because he didn't want their pity. If they only knew what he knew -- that this was the way it was always going to go. This was where the path of his short life was always going to lead. It really was only a matter of time.

Jesse sighed in the quiet room. That feeling of hopelessness that had been such a part of his life for so long had ebbed away in the last few years as he'd started to build a new life for himself, one that, for a brief, shining moment, felt like it was within his reach. But that hopeless feeling was back now, with a vengeance.

God, he always knew it was too good to be true.

Over the last few days, he'd been able to, for the most part, put those feelings of contentment away where they belonged -- tucked far back in his mind. They were back there with a few other treasured memories he pulled out to get him through the worst days of the past. He hoped they would be enough to get him through the worst days of the future -- however long the future might be as he headed off to war.

He could easily forget the "things" -- it was the people he had to stop thinking about who made it hard. In the past, it had been a little simpler to leave people. Their...behavior towards him had made leaving them behind easier to accept. He'd play a trick on his mind. He'd picture their faces and picture himself walking away until their features were hazy, and the wall he built inside between him and them was strong. He'd tried the same tactic over the last few days, though not with Eli and Joe. They'd be "with him," so to speak. They'd all be in the same place, even if they never saw one another in the next year or so. And it wasn't so bad with Liz. She was a friend, but she was Eli's fiancé.

It was harder with Penny.

Penny meant the world to him, but she'd never forgive him for leaving, especially when she thought he could run away. He hadn't heard from her since Monday night, and he honestly never expected to see her again. Over the last couple of days, he'd started to accept that. She was just one more memory to save in the recesses of his mind, to pull out when he needed to escape his reality in Vietnam. At this point, he had his feelings for everyone pretty well contained -- his feelings for everyone except her.

He'd picture Becca's face and couldn't picture himself walking away. He pictured her face and could see only the anger and horror he saw when he finally looked at her Monday night. Her perfect mouth seemed to be shaped in a permanent "O" -- the shock never quite leaving her features when he and Joe had shared their news with everyone else.

To him, she looked just like she had the night he came to get her from that house party -- vulnerable and scared. He wanted to reach out and hold her right then, but what good would that have done? None. So, he decided then and there to start the process of shutting down. He decided then and there to put back up the walls around his heart he'd lived with for most of his life -- telling himself he didn't want or need anyone to care about him.

So, he added her to the vault of memories and decided he'd said his goodbye to her on Friday night, no matter how drunk he had been. He knew it was wrong on some level, but he had no intention of seeing her again before leaving after Monday night. She'd be mad at him, he knew that, but she would be OK.

He remembered being braced for days of tears and drama after Keith hurt her, but it never happened. She was sad, sure, but she got up every morning, went about her business, and got through it like a champion. She didn't let it stop her or affect her life.

He had no doubt she'd do the same now. She'd get over whatever spark had been between them. They hadn't known each other that long. Their burgeoning relationship hadn't been that serious, even though their attraction to one another was unlike anything he'd ever experienced. Still, he didn't doubt she'd be able to let it go when he left. She'd move on.

He wouldn't, but she would.

She was the most amazing woman he'd ever laid eyes on, and the fact that she'd felt something for him, too, was just the world's cruel way of toying with him. She was strong, determined, beautiful, passionate, steady -- everything he'd never dreamed one woman could be. Everything he never dreamed one woman he would somehow cross paths with would be.

But that was all it was -- a momentary crossing of paths. It wasn't ever meant to be more than that. Becca was a dream -- and, oh God, did he ever dream about her -- but she wasn't going to be his future. War was his future, and he had accepted that.

He just couldn't look into her eyes anymore. If he didn't see her again, he knew he'd be fine, eventually.

Luckily, circumstances had kept him from seeing her. She, Eli, and Liz were gone all weekend, giving Joe and Jesse a chance to pack without raising suspicions. Then, when they had to face the inevitable a couple days later, Eli unwittingly had helped keep them from each other again on Monday night. Pretty quickly after Penny stormed out, he suggested that the three men take a walk, and Jesse was grateful for it.

He didn't want to look at the sadness and pity in her eyes, yearning to tell her everything would be OK, giving her false hope. Because in his mind, that was absolutely the cruelest emotional manipulation one person could knowingly do to someone else -- give them false hope.

So, he, Eli, and Joe walked around the Village for a while before ending up at an all-night diner for coffee. When they sat down, Eli did his best to answer what questions he could about entering the Army and Vietnam...

"I've been told most of the fighting is there," Eli continued, mapping out for them what little he knew about what was happening. "In Country," as most people called the jungle of Vietnam. Jesse leaned back in their booth and took a sip of his coffee next to him. Joe leaned forward on the table, keeping his voice low even though barely anyone was at the diner at 2 a.m.

"There's no way to know exactly where we're going to be, is there?" Joe asked quietly. Eli shook his head, and Joe shrugged.

"I guess we'll find out tomorrow," he said. "Not that I would have a clue if they told me, I guess."

Eli hesitated before answering.

"No," he said. "You won't know until after basic, and even then..."

The three looked at each other, then down into their coffee. The reality of their situation began to sink in even further.

"After tomorrow, I guess it won't really matter anyway," Joe said.

Eli cleared his throat.

"You might not leave right away," he warned. "Some guys have been, but most have a day or two, some up to a week. It's all over the place."

Jesse's head shot up. A week?! No, it had to happen now. He was prepared... now. Another week and...and who knows what would happen.

"That'll give you a little time, Joe," Eli said pointedly to his friend.

Joe looked at him, confused.

"Time for what?"

Eli sat up a little straighter and leaned in.

"Time to apply for a deferment," Eli said, voice quiet again. "You're the only son of a man who...who died serving his country. You know there's a good chance you'd be granted a deferment, right? As the sole provider for your mother..."

Jesse and Joe looked at each other. Jesse had already made that argument to Joe over the weekend when the news was fresh and new, and Joe had already shot it down.

"What?" Eli said, looking between the two.

"He knows," Jesse said when Joe was quiet. "I already tried."

"Why wouldn't you?" Eli said, looking at Joe. "Your Mom's already lost her husband."

Joe studied Eli for a minute.

"Why did you enlist when you could have stayed in med school?" he countered. Eli looked away, then down at his mug once again. "My...Dad... my father would roll over in his grave if he knew I didn't serve when I was called upon, you know? I can't do that to...to him, to his memory. I can't do that to our country."

Eli just nodded his head.

"Yeah," he whispered.

"My Mom understands it," Joe continued, then cast a meaningful glance at Jesse. "And she's...she'll be fine."

Jesse nodded back to him.

They were all silent a moment before Eli cocked his head and nodded at Jesse.

"What about your folks?" Eli said, for the first time, genuinely curious about Jesse's parents. He'd never asked about them before, and Jesse had never offered.

Jesse's heart raced at the direct question, but he kept his cool and shrugged.

"They're dead," he said quickly. "So, they don't have much to say."

Joe shot him a look while Eli winced and mumbled an apology. Then he stood up.

"I'm gonna hit the john," he said, turning and heading to the bathroom.

Jesse tried to ignore Joe's questioning eyes.

"Why'd you say that?" Joe asked.

"Because...they are," Jesse said, motioning to the waitress behind the counter for their check.

"No, they're not," Joe said quietly.

Jesse looked at him sharply, and Joe sighed.

"They are to me, you dig?" Jesse hissed quietly. "Drop it, Joe..."

A loud train whistle interrupted his thoughts, and Jesse looked at his watch. It was time to go, so he stood up and ran his eyes over his little office. He picked up his bag, which carried his sparse personal items, and threw the keys on his desk. He flipped the lock on the doorknob and closed the room behind him. He descended the concrete steps to the sidewalk and slowly moved to the nearest subway station, only two blocks away.

He boarded the train bound for the Village. He glanced around the filthy confines of the New York City public transit system; its walls covered in all manner of graffiti. In large print, someone had scrawled "Hell is Real!" in big, bold red letters. Jesse sighed wearily.

"No shit," he mumbled to himself, then closed his eyes and laid his head against the glass as the train car rocked him side to side on his way home.

"You're all set, Mrs. Ambrosio," Jesse said after arriving back at his apartment just after 6 p.m. He found Joe and his good-hearted, old-world Italian Mom, Grace, at the front of the building. Joe had already loaded the last of the belongings they were keeping at her home into her car. Ironically, Joe hadn't even unpacked half the boxes he'd brought when he moved in with Jesse just a couple weeks earlier.

"I appreciate it, Jesse," Grace nodded, running her hand down Jesse's stubble cheek. He hadn't shaved since Friday. She gave him a little smack. "You're a good friend to my boy -- and his old mama."

"Ma!" Joe said, hugging his mother. "You're an Italian queen!"

"Ha," she mocked, looking lovingly at her only son. "Maybe 30 years ago, honey."

Jesse chuckled.

"Thanks for taking some of my stuff," he said. Grace shrugged.

"I got a big house and no people in it," she'd said, with that harsh Queens accent mixed with a hint of Italian. "Fill it up."

It wasn't entirely true. She had a parade of grandkids in and out every day, but the gesture was a nice one.

"I'll be in the car in a minute, Ma," Joe said. "I'm just gonna grab the last box."

Grace nodded, and with a wistful look at her son and his friend, she began walking back to her vehicle.

"So," Joe said as they walked up the steps to their apartment. "She's really all set?"

"Yeah," Jesse nodded. "The union is going to send 80-percent of your paycheck to her every month. They'll take care of her."

Joe patted him on the back as he made the turn on the landing and opened their door. Jesse glanced at the other apartment, and all was quiet. He knew Becca was at the Schmidts family dinner. He let out a sigh of relief. He planned to be at a bar about the time they got home and not come back until it was late enough everyone would be asleep.

They walked into their apartment, and Joe closed a box that still lay open on the kitchen counter.

"A couple of my brothers-in-law will stop by and pick the rest up before the super lists it," Joe said, shaking his head and looking around. "It's a great place. Hard to give up."

Jesse nodded once.

"Can't be helped," he said, convinced that even if he tried to find a way to keep the apartment, he would never see it again anyway. It was best that it belonged to someone else.

Joe stepped over to him.

"Listen, ah, thanks for everything," he said, his voice catching. "Thanks for making sure my Mom was taken care of."

Jesse shook his head, fighting off the sadness that enveloped him.

"Don't sweat it, man," he said, trying to sound unaffected, stoic. "I'll see you in the morning."

Joe shook his head before his watery eyes got the best of him, then he pulled a surprised Jesse in for a hug. Jesse briefly hugged him back.

When their embrace broke, Joe glanced at the telephone on the counter and looked Jesse right in the eye.

"Call your Mom, Jesse," he said sternly.

"Joe...no..." Jesse started.

"It might be the last time you talk to her," he said. "Maybe...maybe it'll be...different if she knows, if she knows you've been drafted."

No, it wouldn't, Jesse almost said. But Joe, everything- was-black-or-white Joe, would never understand that.

"Just do it, man," Joe said, scooting the phone closer to Jesse.

"See you tomorrow, Joe," Jesse said quietly, not even looking in the direction of the phone.

Joe sighed and picked up the box on the counter. Jesse followed him to the door.

"Bye, man," Jesse said, his voice shaking just a touch.

"Goodbye," Joe said quietly, and with one more glance in the apartment, he turned and started toward the steps.

Jesse closed the door behind him and leaned up against it. The silence in the room magnifying the sound of his heart pounding in his ears.

He took a deep breath, breaking out in a cold sweat as he stared at the telephone.

14

A WHITER SHADE OF PALE

As soon as he heard the first ring at the far end of the line, he nearly hung up the phone.

This wasn't a good idea.

He knew it wasn't a good idea.

He hadn't spoken to her in almost six years when she'd decided to leave the confines of her sad little existence and somehow managed to find her way to New York to track down her only child. Despite all odds, he'd graduated high school, and when she showed up at his door, he'd been completely dumbfounded. A very small part of him wondered if she had somehow found out he was graduating and came for the ceremony.

That theory was quickly debunked. It wasn't the reason that she was there at all.

She'd lost her source of income. His grandmother -- an emotional train-wreck of a woman -- had finally died, leaving his mother, Ivonne, to fend for herself. Ivonne was the product of a fling in France between a poor Canadian farmer-turned-soldier and the daughter of a poor French farmer at the end of World War I. The soldier brought home a war bride and went right back to being a poor farmer. Jesse's grandmother had never recovered and eventually established a love/hate relationship with her daughter.

But she let her come home and live rent-free in the farmhouse just northwest of Montreal, and with her mother gone, the money-well had run dry.

After not speaking to him for almost five years, she demanded Jesse come home and tend the family farm to support her. He refused. She threw an absolute fit, then left. The whole exchange lasted less than a half-hour.

That was the last day he even had the fleeting thought that she really gave a damn about him.

And still...

"Hello?"

Jesse swallowed hard.

"It's...it's Jesse," he choked out.

"Who?" came the slurred voice at the end of the phone.

"Your son."

He could hear ice cubes hitting the bottom of her glass through the static of the connection.

"Well, to what do I owe this honor?" Ivonne said with a bitter, sarcastic laugh. She was clearly already drunk. This late in the day she would be, Jesse remembered that well.

"I'm fine, Mother. How are you?" he retorted, just as sarcastically.

"Oh, life's just one party after another," she said, the weariness in her voice. "I'm divorced again."

He sighed heavily.

"I didn't know you...were...married," he said quietly.

"Why would you?" she said, anger evident in her tone. "You haven't called me in years, Jesse. For all I knew, you were dead."

He squeezed his eyes closed. Well, he soon might be, he thought.

"I wanted...I called to let you know..." he took a deep breath. "I've been drafted."

The silence at the end of the phone was deafening.

"What does that mean?" she finally said, still slurring her words.

"It means..." he started, anger building up inside of him despite his best effort to fight it. What the hell did she think it meant, for Christ's sake?! "It means I have to join the U.S. Army, and I'm probably going to Vietnam."

Ivonne was silent for a moment at the end of the line.

"I suppose you already told your father," she said, in that angry and defensive tone she always had in her voice when she felt like she was being slighted somehow.

Jesse briefly looked to the ceiling and then lowered his head to his palm. She hadn't changed, not even a little bit. He heard the clanking of more ice cubes falling into the glass, which he knew would quickly be followed by Kentucky bourbon. It was her drink of choice. It had been forever.

"Haven't talked to him in eight years," he said evenly. "I'm not going to now."

"You want to come home?" she asked, somewhat pensively. He could hear the bourbon pouring into her glass.

"No," he said, without a moment's hesitation.

She let out a cackling laugh -- half crying, half laughing.

"Of course not," she said belligerently. "All these people, these... these hippies are coming to Canada, but not my son. See, this is why I never wanted a boy. They die in wars. You'd rather die than spend time with your mother. Well, that's fine. That's just fine, Jesse..."

Despite himself, Jesse's eyes filled with tears, and he wished to God he'd never picked up the phone and called Canada in the first place. He quickly swallowed them down. He'd stopped crying over his mother a long time ago.

"I just wanted you to know," he said quietly, preparing to hang up the phone.

"Well, thanks for calling with that happy news," she whispered fiercely before taking a long drink. She was breathing heavily, and Jesse could picture her clearly. She was a beautiful woman but with sullen features and smudged mascara and a drink, always a drink, to her lips. The way she looked when he was 18 was how she looked now; he was sure of it. He'd seen her once in 11 years, and she hadn't changed. She never would.

"I shouldn't have..." he started, then stopped. He wasn't going to apologize to her. "I thought you might want to know, that's all."

"Now I know," Ivonne said, knocking her drink against the phone. She didn't say another word.

"Goodbye, Ivonne," he said, fighting back more tears her silence evoked in him.

"Bye, Jesse," she said before she slammed down the phone.

———

Becca glanced at her watch as the last of the plates were cleared away at their table at Tony's.

"Grab us another, will ya, honey?" her dad, John, said to the waitress, gesturing to her with the empty bottle of red wine in the middle of the table.

"Of course, sir, right away," the woman said with a smile. Becca let out an audible moan.

"Are you OK, dear?" her mother, Wilma, asked in such a way that Becca understood she had better answer in the affirmative.

Becca just nodded, glancing at her watch again. Ten hours. They were all leaving in ten hours, and she still hadn't talked to Jesse.

"Liz says your friend Joe is at home tonight at his mother's house?" Wilma asked Eli, taking a sip of Pepsi, while Liz nodded.

"Yeah," Eli said. "She lives in Queens."

Wilma nodded.

"Did your friend, what's his name...Jesse go home to be with his family, too?" John asked.

"Um, no," Eli said, casting a sideways glance at his sister. "I, um, I found out the other night that his, ah, his parents are deceased."

"Oh," Wilma said, putting a hand to her chest. "Does he have no family in town? Brothers or sisters?"

Becca's heart sped up ten-fold. His parents were dead? How did she not know his parents were dead? Suddenly she realized that they'd never had a chance to talk about his parents, to ask about his family. They'd never had a chance to talk about much of anything. Silently she cursed to herself. It was so cruel. She wanted more time with him. She needed more time with him.

All through dinner, she kept getting chills when she thought about him, and she didn't know why, except that she was desperate to see him, desperate to know if he was OK. Now, knowing he was completely alone on the night before he could be shipped off to war...

"Becca?" Liz asked, giving her a quizzical look.

"What?" she snapped, having been pulled swiftly back into the conversation.

Liz looked at the other confused faces at the table before her eyes found her friend's again.

"Does he?"

"Does he?" Becca asked, blinking. "Does who? What?"

"Does Jesse have any brothers or sisters?"

Becca remembered their conversation at the blues club the week before and at least knew that heartbreaking answer.

"No," she said quietly. "No, he doesn't."

"Oh, that poor boy," Wilma said, shaking her head sadly.

Suddenly Becca stood up, and four sets of eyes were on her. She tried to smile a little.

"I have to go to the powder room. Please excuse me," she said as she stepped away from the table. Her throat felt thick, and she started taking big gulps of air as she made her way to the bathroom, Liz on her heels.

"Becca?" she said when they reached the door. Becca swung it open and barreled inside, Liz following her.

"Rebecca!" Liz said, grabbing her arm. "Are you OK?"

Becca took a couple breaths as deeply as she could.

"I've gotta split," she said, clutching the vanity and looking at a worried Liz in the reflection of the bathroom mirror. Becca's cheeks were flushed, and her eyes were wide. "He's alone. He's all alone."

"Who?" Liz said, furrowing her brow.

"Jesse!" Becca answered miserably, turning to face her friend. "I've got to see him before...I have to see him, Liz. I have to go."

"But what about Eli?" Liz said, somewhat indignant.

Becca looked at her and looked down for a moment.

"I love my brother, I do, I really, really do," Becca said, her voice breaking. "But, Liz, I...Jesse, he...he means more to me than...he's done more for me than... than you know. I have to...I have to go find him. Now. Please?"

Liz studied Becca closely for a moment. She couldn't recall ever seeing the look on her face that she saw now. Her usually controlled best friend was clearly in a panic.

"OK, OK, honey, go," she said, nodding in at least partial understanding. "I'll...I'll back you up, whatever you need."

Becca gave her a relieved smile and hugged her. Liz rubbed her arm, and they both left the restroom and headed back to the table. Becca looked at Eli.

"I'm sorry, I'm not feeling too well," Becca said, looking apologetically at her brother. "I'm so sorry. I think I should go."

"What's the matter?" Wilma said, bristling.

"She...she has a headache," Liz said, bracing Becca's shoulders. "Like the ones she had when she was little, remember?"

Becca looked gratefully to Liz. She used to get horrible migraines when she was younger. She was thankful that Liz remembered them because she was having trouble explaining why she had to rush off from the family dinner.

"Do you want us to take you?" John asked, concerned.

"No...no, I'll make it home," she looked at her brother again, tears in her eyes. "Eli..."

"Go," he said, standing and coming to her. He pulled her into a hug.

"There's a good chance I'll be home another day or two," he whispered, smoothing down her hair. "Love you, sis."

Becca squeezed him then reached up to kiss his cheek.

"You, too," she whispered, her voice thick. She glanced at her parents and Liz one more time before hurrying out of the restaurant.

———

It had been years since he'd felt as miserable and alone as he did right then.

The sense of déjà vu was overwhelming.

Suddenly he was 13 again. He was being told he was leaving. He was being told he had no choice, to man up and pack his bags.

He'd hated where he was then, but he was even more frightened about where he was going. Not surprisingly, his mother wasn't fighting for him. His father didn't really care what he was thinking or feeling either. He had to go, and that was that.

The phone call with Ivonne had thrown him off balance, and he was still shaking. Now, he'd also lost track of time as the past had come rushing back to him in a deafening stampede. His head was swimming. Now he was scurrying to pack up and get out of the apartment as quickly as possible.

He figured if he found a bar close to the Dresden Center, he could just pass out at its doorway after the final call. He guessed Joe or Eli or someone else would find him and make sure he made into the building by 8 a.m. -- or not, he really didn't give a damn.

He was in his bedroom when he heard the front door to the apartment open. Jesse didn't want to see a soul, but he guessed it was Joe coming back for something he'd forgotten.

"What do you need, Joe?" he said, walking out. Then he stopped dead in his tracks.

"Becca..." he whispered.

"Hey," she said gently. He looked completely disheveled, lost. It was clear he hadn't shaved in days. His hair fell in askew waves around his face, making his blue eyes stand out more than ever before. She started walking towards him, her heart racing and breaking at the sight of him.

He swallowed hard and ran a shaking hand through his hair. She was a vision. Loose blouse, long skirt, her hair pulled back at the top but cascading over her shoulders. Her big, bright blue eyes were shining at him.

"Why are you here?" he asked, his voice low, as he took a step back, looking anywhere but at her.

"Why am I..." she countered, confused. "Jesse, I haven't seen you since Monday. Don't you think I wanted to... to see you before..."

"What about Eli?" he said, looking for an out. "Shouldn't you be spending time with him?"

"I've spent time with him," she said, eyeing him closely. He backed away again, trying to put physical space between them. She could tell he was attempting to keep her at a distance. His body language was defensive like he was insulating himself from something, though she wasn't entirely sure what. She wanted to comfort him.

"Joe...Joe's out in Queens," Jesse mumbled. "He's meeting us tomorrow morning..."

"I know all that," she said, trying hard to hold onto her patience. "I want to spend time with you. I know...I know you're alone, and I thought..."

"I don't want your pity," he said quickly, with a flash of anger in his voice and dark clouds hanging over his features.

She didn't know what happened to bring that look of devastation over his face, but it nearly took her breath away. Why wouldn't he let her comfort him? She so wanted to comfort him...

"Look, don't waste time on me," he said dismissively. "I didn't even know you until, what, three months ago?"

It was her turn to take a step back from him.

"What does that matter?" she said, getting angry herself. "Jesse..."

"No, look, no!" he said. The pain in his eyes as they finally met hers made her heart constrict. "This is the way it is, you dig? This is it. If I die over there, no one should give a shit, Becca."

Her eyes filled with tears.

"But..." she started weakly.

"Like your boss says, 'that's the way it is,'" he interrupted with a strangled chuckle.

He turned away then and walked back into his bedroom, fighting the tears in his eyes as he continued to pack his things. He wanted desperately for her to go away. Right then, he wished he'd never met her in the first place. She'd fueled his fantasies, made him believe a happy future was possible when he knew -- he knew -- it was all bullshit. That wasn't going to happen to someone like him -- someone who was a mistake to begin with -- someone who "wasn't worth it," as Felicia had once screamed at him. Someone who was born so he could "die in a war," as his loving mother just told him. Well, the universe was taking care of that now, wasn't it?

Somewhere under the hurt, he knew she wasn't to blame for the way he was feeling right then. Still, if he'd never met Becca, he never would have forgotten that living a long, happy life was never in the cards for him.

Becca stared at his back in the other room. She wanted to run to him and throw her arms around him and make his hurt go away. Instead, she backed toward the door, her own emotions threatening to drown her in the middle of his living room, the walls he put up around himself now so high she wasn't sure she could scale them.

"I...I will give a shit, Jesse," she said just loud enough for him to hear, her hands finding the doorknob behind her. He stopped packing and stood up straight, making a mild attempt to glance back at her. She waited a moment, but when he didn't turn around, she closed the door behind her and hurried over to her apartment, tears beginning to stream down her face.

When she'd left, he turned and looked blankly at the closed door, his heart pounding hard in his chest. He heard her apartment door shut behind her. He hesitated -- his head trying to keep his feet planted in the middle of his bedroom. His heart pushed him forward, though, and haltingly he walked over to the front door, pressing his forehead hard against its cool, metal surface. His hand massaged the doorknob. His desire for the comfort he sought from her engaged in a raging battle with his desire to keep her at arms-length at all costs. He squeezed his eyes closed.

Finally, when he couldn't fight it anymore, he turned the knob and swung open the door.

15

ANGEL OF THE MORNING

BECCA SLAMMED THE APARTMENT DOOR SHUT AND RACED OVER TO THE couch, gripping her hands on the back of it until her knuckles were sore.

The darkness of the room fit her mood as more tears swam in her eyes. It was a nightmare -- the last few days had been an absolute nightmare. The draft. The war. The goddamn war. The pain.

His pain.

She couldn't take it. He was pushing her away just when she knew he needed someone. He needed her the most.

She took a deep, ragged breath, willing her heart to settle down. She wanted the look in his eyes to leave her mind -- the words he'd said erased from her memory.

If I die over there, no one should give a shit...

A sob escaped her as she moved slowly from her spot behind the couch, tears once again streaming down her face. How had it come to this? How had he become so important to her so quickly?

Why was her heart crying out for him?

She didn't understand it. She didn't understand him -- all she knew was he was hurting, and he was leaving. They were all leaving.

"So much leaving..." he'd said in his drunken state on Friday night.

Her breath hitched, and her shoulders started to shake as she made her way toward her bedroom. All of it -- all of it -- was killing her.

Suddenly she heard the apartment door open swiftly, then slam behind her. She jumped, turning around in her bedroom doorway, quickly wiping the tears from her eyes.

"I don't want your pity," he said in the same tone he had before, same shadows clouding his features.

She took a couple steps toward him, furious, her emotions taking over every move she made.

"I don't want to give you pity," she spat out at him, devastation coursing through her, blue eyes blazing. Then she added in a fierce whisper. "I want to give you me..."

And just like that, the clouds ran away from his face. A look of confusion replaced it with something akin to shocked relief. Something like taking a painkiller. Something that made him look, and feel, like a man again.

He didn't say a word as he took long, determined strides over to her. He grabbed her face, pulled her hard against him, and kissed her raw. Strong, fast, slow, endless...all the while backing her into her bedroom. She pulled on him, pulled his sleeves, his arms, his hips, his hair, anything she could to get him into that room and closer to her.

Closer -- to take him in, all of him, to take all of his pain into her -- to make her own pain go away.

Her legs hit the side of the bed, and she fell back, their lips attacking each other -- not missing one touch. She pulled and pulled until she ripped the buttons off his shirt and tore it away from him. He roughly pulled her loose, pilgrim blouse over her head in one motion, changed direction, and pulled her skirt and panties down in the next. She tugged and pushed down his jeans and underwear -- he kicked them off then hovered over her, heat radiating from every inch of him. Her arms were thrown over her head as his wild eyes briefly raked her body before locking with hers again.

"Jesse..." she breathed, raising her hands to grip his shoulders.

"Don't speak," he whispered in a hoarse plea. "Don't make it real."

Through sheer force of will, he hesitated, waiting for her to answer him, bracing himself just above her. His arms extended as he gripped the edge of the mattress at either side of her naked hips. His breathing was labored.

She was breathing rapidly. His body took up all the space surrounding her while his kiss lingered in the spaces of her mind. None of it seemed real. All of it felt like a fantasy.

Instantly she understood that he was begging her to keep it that way. Keep it a fantasy -- keep it a dream. Keep it something he could hold onto when he was being shot at in a jungle far away.

Keep it hungry -- pure passion -- nothing more.

She ran her hands up his neck, through his thick hair. Pulling him forcefully to her, she complied -- not willing or able to control her need and desire for him any longer. Anything he wanted tonight -- anything he needed from her right now was his. Anything.

Anything...

He let out a shuddery breath as he ran his hands up her sides and pushed her bra away from her breasts, kneading them between his fingers. With his help, she pulled it over her head and dropped it to the floor behind her. His lips moved over her like he was starving. First, one breast, then the other, tasting all of her as he moved to reach every part of her body he could find—his rough whiskers leaving trails of burning flesh behind as he made his way lower...lower.

She shrieked as she felt his mouth on her and pushed his head down against her, moaning -- stars shooting out from behind her eyes. Their deep groans and high-pitched gasps were filling the empty space of her bedroom like a heartbroken symphony.

Becca bucked her hips and pulled on his hair, her body aching in pleasure. Suddenly he was over her again, kissing her mouth with a ferocity she'd never known -- with a desperation that she knew was coming from somewhere deep inside of him.

She pulled on his arms, and he fell on top of her. She let his weight linger there for just a moment before she used all the strength she had to make him turn over onto his back. She stole a glance into his eyes. He looked back at her through the dim, artificial light that filtered in from the window. He looked drugged -- desire and lust swimming in the blue.

"Bec...Rebecca..." he breathed raggedly before she stopped him with another kiss. She tasted herself on his lips as he deepened the kiss, clutching the back of her head to him with both hands. When they broke for air, she swallowed the lump in her throat and gave him a little grin. He grinned back in that crooked way he had the first night they met. She pressed her lips to his stubbled jaw, blinking back the tears that sprang to her eyes as he started to moan in her ear.

She tried to force back the emotional onslaught. It was crashing over her in waves as she started kissing him like he'd kissed her -- lower and lower until her lips wrapped around him. She closed her eyes as his arms shot up behind him, grabbing onto the headboard of her bed with such force that his entire body jerked violently. He hollered out, a deep, deep exhale layered with a sound of profound relief.

She continued as he writhed beneath her. Moments later, she let him go, flipping her hair back and taking a deep breath, ready and willing to start again. Then in what felt to her like one swift motion -- he dragged her against him, turned her to her back, pushed her legs apart, and dove into her.

She clutched her body around him, pulling him as tightly to her as she could, digging her fingertips into his flesh, grinding her hips against him. She wanted him closer...closer.

Despite her best efforts to fight it, his name tore out of her in a deep, gurgling moan as he started to move fast and rough in her -- every part of him pressed to her.

Every part of him was coming apart in her.

She threw her head back as hot tears finally streamed down her temples into her hair. To hide them, she grabbed his head and kissed him hard -- kissed him as though there was no tomorrow.

Because there was a real chance, there wouldn't be.

"Rage against the dying of the light," Dylan Thomas once implored.

Jesse was raging against the dawning of the day. This day that would change his life -- and he was certain it would mark the beginning of its end.

He squinted against the sun as it came into her room, just under the curtains. He watched the dust move in the peeking sunbeams and listened to the chorus of the New York street below.

He squeezed his eyes shut a moment before propping himself up just a bit. He opened them again to look at her.

She lay next to him -- asleep, spent, and exhausted -- practically passed out from the hours before. Her lips were still puffed up, and her cheeks still held a hint of rose. She looked for all the world like a woman who had spent the night before being ravaged within an inch of her sanity.

His face softened, and he let out a shuddery sigh as he watched her breathing. She'd given him everything -- absolutely everything she had. He'd done things to her that he never conjured up in his wildest dreams any woman would want him to do -- beg him to do -- as she did. And no woman had ever done to him what she had just hours before with a reckless abandon he was sure she'd never condone in any other context. It was all so primal, so carnal that for a while, it almost felt like he'd floated out of his body -- like it was some sort of intense LSD trip.

Last night she'd screamed his name, and he'd cried out hers -- again and again. He'd wanted it to stay a fantasy -- but the dream-come-true was more mind-blowing than he ever once imagined it would be.

And it was all real, and it was all Becca -- the stone-cold fox down the hall. The one he could have literally killed Keith for hurting. A friend -- one he was once convinced ever-so-briefly could potentially be so much more -- and someone he'd felt so close to, so comfortable within such a short amount of time it made his head spin.

Yet, gazing at her now, he could almost forget the sex-crazed woman who made it her job to worship him from head to toe all night. She looked like a cherub with reddened cheeks against her white skin, her raven halo falling around her pillow. She looked small, almost doll-like, and far, far too golden for the likes of him. She was an angel, he was certain of that now, and she should never have fallen to him in all her glory last night.

And he never should have given in, taken what she offered, taken the salve to his broken soul. But, God, how he'd wanted her. Since the moment he laid eyes on her, he'd wanted her. He was drawn to her like a moth to a flame. And instead of fighting it as he had been so determined to do, like he should have done, he threw gasoline on the spark and watched it burn like a wildfire.

He sighed again softly, slowly as he gently ran two fingers from her ear to her chin, then along her lips. She didn't even move. He grinned and, oh, so tenderly kissed her cheek before laying back on the bed for one more moment.

They were supposed to report for their physicals in an hour, and from there, everything was uncertain.

Liz watched as the sun came up over the city, her head on Eli's shoulder as they sat together on the platform of the fire escape. They'd gotten back to her apartment not too long before, having spent all night talking with his parents after dinner. They saw Becca's door closed, so they quietly made their way to Liz's bedroom to be together one more time before he left.

Then he wanted to watch the sunrise over New York one more time.

Everything was "one more time." Liz didn't know how she was going to make it through. She was trying to be supportive, but Eli had brought this upon himself, unlike Joe and Jesse. And she couldn't help but be angry with him and in awe of him at the same time.

With a guilty heart, she wondered, again, if they just should have gotten married at City Hall like he wanted to. And, if it really made any difference in the least where and when they got married.

But she wanted her dream wedding -- and truth be told, a small part of her wanted to punish him for leaving her in the first place, even knowing how wrong and screwed up that logic had to be.

"I'm scared," he said suddenly, softly.

She turned to him then and sat on his lap, facing him. Looking into his worried brown eyes, it truly hit her that she really did love him, and her own eyes filled with tears despite it all.

"I know," she mouthed, not trusting her voice, as he buried his head in the crook of her neck, and she pulled him to her. She closed her eyes and held him tight.

Then she opened them and froze.

She watched through the dirt-smudged window as Jesse came out of Becca's bedroom, pulling on his pants, carrying his shirt and shoes. He glanced up at the empty apartment then put his arms through the sleeves of his shirt. He turned back toward Becca's room, and even in the glare of the sun, Liz could see the look on the profile of his face, the tears in his eyes as he dropped his head for a moment.

Then he turned, walking quickly through the living room and out the door.

———

Becca's eyes shot open, and she instantly knew the space next to her was empty.

She willed her sore body to sit up as she stared at the clock. They'd already reported for their physicals. He was already gone.

Her heartbeat tripled as fear gripped her once again -- and the memories of last night came flooding back to her. She moaned softly, thinking of him, all of him. She wrapped her arms around her bent knees, coiling her naked body into a tiny ball.

Tears pooled in her eyes as she re-lived his touch, his power, their passion as she'd willingly turned herself over to him. It had been wretched and glorious, tragic, and beautiful.

She'd pulled the pain right out of him, she hoped, at least for one night -- giving him something that would make him remember what it was to live, to stay alive -- or at least something to never forget.

Oh, but a pain still lingered in her, a new pain. And now, she longed for him as her head finally caught up to what her heart had known all along. She'd never felt such a connection; she'd never felt so wanton and so worshipped in the same space. She'd never had anything like him before, and she wanted nothing but him now.

She fell heavily to her side against her pillow. She watched as a folded note on the mattress next to her bounced, fluttering slowly in the air before settling on the bed sheet once again, sliding right under her eyes.

Her name was scribbled on it in his handwriting.

She picked it up with trembling hands and read it through the tears in her eyes as she slowly sat up once again.

"Oh..." she gasped weakly after a moment, quickly pressing the note hard against her chest. She looked towards the window with a tortured face and the bright morning sun as tears fell unchecked past her chin and onto her sheets.

He'd only written two words...

Thank You

16

DAY IS DONE

Eli, Jesse, and Joe reported for duty and were told how many hours they had left as quasi-civilians before the military took over their world.

They were all scheduled to leave, at different times to various destinations, over the next two days.

It was almost worse than being shipped off right away. Going back to real life for just a little while, only to leave, again, was its own little version of hell. Though they felt like they'd gotten a taste of hell already when they showed up for their physicals.

The first thing the U.S. Army did was make all the men look uniform. They roughly slammed Jesse and Joe into two chairs, along with all the other drafted men, and quickly, forcedly shaved their heads into short crew-cuts. Jesse watched with a stone face as his longish locks hit the floor all around him. Eli, since he was an enlisted man, was treated a little differently, a little kinder. Yet, he came out of the line with just as little hair. Next, they went through the embarrassment of a physical exam. They were naked and surrounded by strangers as doctors they didn't know poked and prodded them as if they were cows being led to market -- or the slaughterhouse.

Then they, along with other draftees and enlisted men, had to go through a battery of intelligence tests and psychological exams in the 10 hours after signing their life away to the U.S. Army. Tired and bewildered, they'd made their way to get their army-issued knapsacks. It was 9 p.m. on a Thursday when they finally headed back home.

Joe was leaving on a 7 a.m. flight to Texas the following morning. Eli had to board a plane headed to California at 11 a.m. the same day.

Jesse was to board a bus bound for basic training in Georgia at 8 a.m. on Saturday, the day after Joe and Eli had already left. Since Eli had enlisted, he was told he was being sent to officers training. At the end of his training, he would be a medic. Since Jesse and Joe were both drafted, they weren't told where they would be sent after basic training. Both were relatively certain that their next stop would only punch their ticket to Vietnam.

After a brief but meaningful goodbye to Eli and Jesse, Joe headed home to Queens for the night. Eli went home to his parents' house on Long Island, where Liz, Becca, and Dr. and Mrs. Redd were waiting for him. Becca was expected to be there. She was expected to spend as much time with her brother as possible before he left...

"Darling," Wilma said as Eli walked through the Schmidt's front door that evening in army-issued fatigues.

"Mom," he said, giving her a hug and a kiss, and shaking his father's hand before Liz clutched him to her. He exchanged greetings with the Redds before noticing Becca in the corner of the living room.

"Hey," he said as she slowly walked over to him, tears in her eyes. Liz let him go a moment, and Becca held him tight as he explained the logistics for the following day to everyone. Becca hardly made a sound as she closed her eyes, water pooling under her lashes. After a moment, Liz cleared her throat.

"Joe? Jesse?" Liz finally asked, her voice thick, with a glance at her best friend. She watched as Becca's eyes squeezed closed tight at the mention of Jesse's name.

Becca didn't notice her quiet sobs and the tears that had started to fall out of her eyes onto her brother's shirt. Eli looked down at her, squeezing her shoulder and taking a deep breath.

"Joe flies out to Texas first thing tomorrow, 0700," Eli said quietly. "Jesse...Jesse has to report to Grand Central Station on, um, Saturday morning. His...he's leaving on a bus for basic in Georgia."

Saturday? Becca gasped as her pulse started to race. He'd be home another whole day? He was home now? Oh, God...

"It's OK, sis," Eli said softly, his own heart breaking as he felt her tense up. He never dreamed this was all going to play out the way it had -- that all three of them would end up joining the army at the same time. It made everything so, so much worse than if he was only going himself.

"So, is he at home?" Wilma asked, eyeing Becca carefully, though she really did feel sorry for the boy with no family.

"I think so," Eli nodded. "I told him to come out here, though. I gave him our address. I hope you don't mind..."

John assured him they did not mind.

"I doubt he'll come, but..." Eli shrugged as Becca pulled away from him and wiped the tears off her cheeks. Liz wrapped her arms around her fiancé, looking at her friend with sympathetic eyes. Becca just turned away and walked quietly back to the corner of the room again.

She couldn't breathe. By the grace of God, she had another opportunity to see him again, to touch him again, to kiss him again... but she was trapped. She couldn't dash out now. Eli was leaving in a little over 12 hours. She'd planned to stay the night at her parents' house. There was nothing she could say that would justify her leaving for her apartment right that second. Her eyes filled with tears again.

And he was alone, she thought. Alone. Again.

Her thoughts all jumbled in her mind as a myriad of feelings raced through her body. Becca took a deep, audible breath that caught the whole room's attention and paused the conversation that was taking place around her.

"Sorry," she muttered, her face turning a little pink. Her mother, clearly a tad miffed by her daughter causing a minor scene, walked over, and led her by the elbow into the kitchen.

"What is wrong with you?" Wilma asked quietly. It wasn't like Becca to break down like this, and it certainly wasn't the time for her to be pulling attention to herself.

"I'm just..." Becca started, fighting back her tears with all her might. "...tired and...worried..."

"He doesn't need to see that right now, Becca," Wilma snapped, feeling like she could lose her own cool at any moment, too. "Listen, if you can't keep it together, go to your old room until you can get it together."

It was just the release Becca needed. She nodded and bolted out of the kitchen, across the dining room and living room -- ignoring the curious and sympathetic glances being shot her way -- and raced up the stairs, closing the door hard behind her.

She leaned against it for a moment and then crawled onto her old bed. She pulled a pillow tight against her and picked up the phone. It rang his six times before she hung up and turned onto her back. Where was he?

She stared at the ceiling and could picture his face hovering over hers. She closed her eyes and moaned softly, her body heating up as she thought of the night before. She was still sore all over, and she wanted to stay that way. She wanted her body to remember what it felt like to be...loved that hard, that desperately.

She wanted to feel it so she could still feel him, even after he went away. Once again, her heart seized in her chest. She didn't want him to go away. Did he know that she wanted him to live? That she felt like she would die if he did? Did he even care? Did he have space inside his own turmoil to even think about it?

To think about her?

She let out a shuddery breath and closed her eyes. Her physically and emotionally exhausted body fell into a light sleep until she was jolted awake a while later by the sound of the doorbell. Becca blinked her eyes open and listened as her Dad greeted their visitor -- and she could have sworn she heard his voice.

She shot up in her bed. Quickly she walked across her room and opened the bedroom door, quietly making her way down the hallway.

And there he stood, at the bottom of the stairs, talking to her Dad. John welcomed him into the house and asked if he wanted a drink. Jesse nodded, and John closed the front door and walked away.

She'd slowly taken two steps down when he turned and looked up at her.

And time stopped right then and there.

She felt her heart race as she searched his clean-shaven face. His ears poked out just a little without all that hair around them. Tears sprung to her eyes as she remembered running her fingers through his silky brown strands over and over the night before. His lips were drawn into a thin smile, and his blue eyes were wide as he looked at her. She noticed the "Wanger" sewn in black, capital letters across the right front pocket of his fatigues. "U.S. Army" was sewn over the left, just like her brother -- just like so many of the men she saw in the miles of film she had to pour over at work.

Her breath caught, and she gripped the banister tighter, trying to keep herself from running into his arms.

Jesse swallowed hard when he saw her. She was in the shadows at the top of the stairs. But even in the darkness, he could see the brightness in her eyes, the surprise on her gentle, tired features. His heart slammed against his chest.

What was he doing there? In her parents' home? He should never have come. "Thank You" should have been the last contact he ever had with her, as woefully inadequate as it was. He should have left it there. He would have been fine alone. It's just, he...he didn't want to be alone. And, damn it all, he had the chance, and he wanted to see her one more time. He wanted to verify that she wasn't just a dream. He wanted to know she was real -- flesh and blood. He thought maybe the universe owed him at least that much before it did with him what it would.

He'd have one drink and leave, he told himself. He wouldn't get too close to her. He heard the rising chatter of voices in the other room. Clearly, the house was full of people that had to give them a buffer, right? Right?

Right.

"Here you are, Jesse," John said, stepping in front of him and handing over the whiskey, briefly blocking Becca's view.

"Th...thank you, sir," he said, taking the drink from him and taking a long sip. He watched her over the rim of the glass as she walked down the final few steps, the liquid burning down the back of his throat.

"Feeling better, sweetie?" John said, with a hint of concern in his voice as he looked at his daughter. She gave him a short nod, her eyes never leaving Jesse.

He felt his body twitch at the intense look on her face, and he had to fight for control. He willed himself not to think about her soft lips, her arching back, her...

Stop! He shouted to himself and looked quickly into the liquor in his glass.

Becca swallowed hard, though her mouth was suddenly dry. She licked her lips and stared at his glass. She remembered the fingers wrapped around it now making magic across her skin, gentle and demanding, then diving into her...

She gasped out, her eyes hazy as she forgot where she was and let herself get lost for just a moment.

Both men looked at her curiously.

She shook her head.

"Sorry, I..." she cleared her throat and straightened her shoulders. "Hello, Jesse."

"Becca," he said, nodding his head to her, then stealing a glance at John.

"Everyone's in the other room," John said as he turned, leading Jesse to the living room as Becca followed behind.

Eli greeted Jesse with a hug then introduced him to Liz's parents. Liz shot Becca a look, but Becca wasn't looking at her. Her focus remained where it had been since the moment he walked into the house.

"Been through a lot today, huh, boys?" Dr. Leon Redd said, taking a seat on the couch and gesturing for everyone to sit down with him. It was clear that he was anxious to start telling war stories.

Everyone obliged him and sat down, listening as John and Leon swapped stories about their time in the service. A few of the stories made everyone laugh; others caused silence to fall over the group.

Becca glanced at Jesse often. He was engaged somewhat in the conversation between the men, though not in the same spirit as Eli. He was more reserved, observational, as he always had been. But more than once, when she looked over at him, he was staring at her. She tried to follow along with the stories she'd heard many times before. She smiled at the appropriate times and answered appropriately when asked, but she could keep her mind on nothing but him.

At one point, she watched as Liz walked over to where Eli was sitting, curled up onto his lap, and softly began stroking his back. She felt a pang of jealousy. She wanted to curl up into Jesse's lap, and stroke his back, and look into his eyes...she shivered and swallowed, attempting once again to pull herself together.

Jesse nursed his drink slowly, only half paying attention to the conversation. It wasn't that he wasn't interested; he was. The army would be his new reality soon. But Becca was less than ten feet from him, and it was like fighting a magnetic pull in her direction. The more he tried to concentrate on the two war veterans, the more his mind kept returning to the night before. He felt a fine sheen of sweat under his uniform as he finally swallowed the last of his whiskey, sucking on the one small remaining ice cube left at the bottom of the glass.

He knew he really had to get out of that house before grabbing John Schmidt's daughter and taking her in the middle of the living room in front of God and everyone else.

"Want another?" John offered, seeing Jesse's glass was empty.

"No," he said, quickly standing. "Thank you, sir. I'm...I'm gonna split."

"You don't have to go, man," Eli said. "You're welcome to stay."

Everyone agreed as Becca, too, rose to her feet, her heart pounding.

Jesse shook his head.

"Thank you, but your family should be together tonight," he said quietly.

"Becca will call a cab for you," Wilma said, looking at her daughter.

"That's OK..." Jesse started.

"It's no trouble," John said, nodding in Becca's direction. "We have a company not far from here. They'll be here in no time."

Jesse nodded to John and glanced at Becca. He watched as she swallowed heavily and walked into the kitchen to the phone.

Liz reached out to Jesse and hugged him. He was surprised to see tears in her eyes when she whispered to him, "you come back to us, too."

Both Liz and Becca's parents wished him well. It felt very strange to him, being cloaked in a family circle of warmth, even for a short period of time. He didn't know how to respond to it, so he just nodded and mumbled, "thanks."

He let out a breath he didn't know he was holding as Eli finally walked over to him. Both men looked at each other a long moment before Eli clicked his heels together and raised his right hand in salute. Jesse slowly did the same as Becca, having made the call to the cab company, came out of the kitchen.

Seeing her brother and Jesse in that moment took her breath away. Her eyes filled with tears, and she felt her heart breaking in two.

Silently, both men lowered their arms, no words passing between them. Eli had tears in his eyes, Jesse a knot in his throat. Eli nodded to him, and he nodded back, then looked over Eli's shoulder at Becca. Her hands were folded, clutched to her chest, and her eyes were bright. He blinked and nodded to her, determined to keep his distance. Because if he so much as touched her...

He had to leave, right now. He turned to John.

"Thank you, again, sir," he said with a little smile.

"Godspeed, son," John said quietly, slapping him gently on the back. "Son" -- Jesse wasn't expecting that, and tears stung his eyes. He swallowed them back, reminding himself that emotions were running high for everyone. He wasn't the "son" they were praying would come home to them, so he just dropped his head and started toward the front door.

"I'll walk out with you," Becca said quickly as she walked to him. He looked back at her, surprised, then a slow smirk came over his face. She brushed past him quickly and opened the front door, closing it securely behind them.

They stood there in the dark of the front stoop, a small, orange glow from her parents' little porch light bouncing shadows against the bricks of the house. She looked at the back of his head as he moved to descend the few steps to the front pathway.

"I don't get a goodbye?" she asked with feigned innocence in her somewhat agitated voice.

He froze, then turned to her slowly, cocking an eyebrow at her. She was glaring expectantly at him.

"We said one hell of a goodbye last night," he said evenly, his heart beating so hard he was sure it was going to leap right out of his chest.

She shook her head slightly.

"We didn't say much of anything last night," she whispered, moving toward him until they were mere inches apart. She searched his face as he licked his lips. No part of their bodies touched but the electricity in the space between sent shockwaves through them both.

"I didn't come here to...continue...this...I," he said quietly.

"Then why'd you come?" she challenged.

He stood up a little straighter and shrugged, taking a step back and looking away from her.

"I was bored, and your Dad has good booze..."

"Right," she said, disbelieving, as she closed the gap he'd created between them.

He looked into her eyes again and could feel the heat coming off her body or boomeranging off his; he wasn't sure which. He flexed his fingers, fighting the urge to bury his hands in her hair and pull her to him one more time.

She wanted badly to convey to him everything she was feeling, everything she was thinking. But not there. Not now. Not tonight.

"I'll be over tomorrow night..." she said suddenly, breathlessly, feeling his eyes bore into hers in the shadows.

"Don't," he whispered, beginning to shake inside, desperately wanting another night with her, knowing it was wrong to want it.

"I work the 11 o'clock," she continued, ignoring him. "I'll come after."

"Becca..."

"I'll be there," she said, stepping even closer to him, so close she could feel his breath on her lips. She wanted to kiss him so much she ached.

"You won't be alone," she whispered, searching his eyes.

He swallowed heavily and looked into her determined face, a part of him grateful she wasn't about to take "no" for an answer. Another part of him wishing she wasn't so damn stubborn.

"I'm fine alone," he finally whispered back to her. His lips hadn't so much as brushed hers, but he could taste them just the same.

"I'll be there," she breathed.

After a moment, he nodded, glancing down the street at the taxi that was slowly heading in their direction.

She looked back toward the house, knowing by the way the drapes moved in the window that her Mom was watching them.

She gently ran her fingers down his arm just below his rolled-up sleeves and then grazed his hand. Every hair on his body stood on end.

She smiled softly at him as the cab pulled into the driveway.

"Goodnight, Jesse," she mouthed, unable to find her voice.

Then he watched her in silence as she walked back into the house and closed the door behind her, unable to tell her "goodbye."

17

ALL ALONG THE WATCHTOWER

BECCA CLASPED LIZ'S HAND JUST A LITTLE TIGHTER AS THE DOORS TO the gateway closed behind Eli. Her friend was shaking but still trying to be strong. Liz had promised Eli she wouldn't cry when he got on the plane, and she was determined to keep that promise. Fighting back the tears seemed to be a normal state of being now, Becca thought, for all of them.

It had been a stressful morning in more ways than one. John wanted his son to proudly wear his U.S. Army uniform to the airport. Becca had advised against it. She knew it would make him a mark for protestors. The war was becoming more and more unpopular with each passing day, and those in uniform were taking the brunt of the verbal abuse, if not worse.

Violent anti-war protests had recently erupted at Columbia University near Harlem. That, along with the massive "Stop the War" rally in Central Park a couple weeks ago, had put all of New York City on edge.

In the end, Eli wore his uniform. He stared down a couple of dirty looks, and "birds" flipped his way, but otherwise was mostly left alone.

A couple people applauded as he walked by, and he was saluted by a WWII veteran at the gate, but it was a mixed bag of reactions, to say the least.

Though she understood it, Becca thought the prevailing attitude just made everything even more unbearable. Her heart dropped even further as they all waited for his flight to board. She thought about Joe, already on his way to Texas, and of course, she thought of Jesse.

She never stopped thinking about Jesse.

She was so anxious to see him later after the newscast. She didn't know what she would say to him, how she would feel, or what she would do when she saw him. She didn't know what he'd say to her, how he would feel or what he would do when he saw her. Being around him was exhilarating. Being with him was intoxicating; knowing he was leaving was heartbreaking. It made chills run up and down her spine, just thinking about the hours they had left. The only thing she did know was that she was determined to make them worth his while.

"There he goes," Liz whispered finally. She let Becca's hand go, moved over to an open spot along the wall of windows, leaning up against it as she gazed at the tarmac where Eli's plane was pulling away from the gate. John and Wilma stepped back from the crowd around the glass. They weren't the only military family saying goodbye to a loved one. Liz wasn't the only fiancé or wife wanting to feel one last connection before being separated from their man for months, years, or possibly a lifetime.

Becca stood back, a few steps away from her parents, wiping the tears in her eyes. She sent up another prayer that her brother would stay safe. She studied Liz, and the heartbroken look on her face made her heart ache. It had to be difficult, so difficult to watch the person you love most in the world leave.

Once the plane had made the turn toward the runway, it was out of sight. Liz moved from the glass and stood near Becca. The women looked at each other, tears shining in their eyes.

"I'm so sorry, Lizzy," Becca whispered the childhood endearment, pulling her in for a hug, her voice catching. "I'm so, so sorry. It's so hard..."

Liz stepped back, shaking her head.

"The hard part starts now," she said softly, her voice shaking. "Waiting. Waiting for him to come home."

Becca just nodded as they clutched their hands together. Liz took a ragged breath, then looked at the floor.

"And then there was one," she finally said, almost too softly for Becca to hear, but she'd heard her.

"Yeah," she replied, her lips quivering. Liz took another deep breath, then raised her eyes to Becca and noticed her head had dropped and her eyes were closed. Neither Becca nor anyone else knew Liz had seen Jesse leave her bedroom in the morning earlier that week. Liz almost felt like she didn't need to ask her anything about it. Becca and Jesse had flirted, literally and figuratively, for months. So, the fact that they had come together at such a tense and emotional time didn't really surprise her too much. More than anything, she felt sorry for her friend -- right now was a tragic time to fall in love.

"Are you going to see him?" she asked quietly, her curiosity piqued.

Becca's head shot up, eyes questioning, but she nodded "yes."

"Tonight, after 11 o'clock," she whispered, her watery blue eyes searching Liz's.

Liz smiled sadly at her, then ran one hand over and over the side of her friend's long black hair, a lump forming in her throat. It was easy, so easy, to see that the falling in love part for Becca was over.

She was already there.

"Oh, sweetie," Liz whispered, her eyes filling with tears again. Off Becca's confused look, Liz just shook her head and squeezed her hands one more time.

"Tell him...goodbye for me," Liz said softly.

Becca nodded, a tear spilling onto her cheek as she hugged Liz.

"I will," she said softly. "I have to split. I have to go to work."

Liz nodded and watched as Becca gamely gave her a little smile before walking over to her parents to tell them goodbye. Liz let out a deep sigh. She surveyed the other women around her, tissues to their eyes or handkerchiefs clutched in their fists, knowing exactly how they were feeling. Then she glanced back at Becca.

Oh, yes, it was a tragic time to be in love.

Jesse had stacked the last box against the living room wall and had just turned out the light in Joe's empty bedroom when he heard a knock at the apartment door. He glanced at his watch. It was just past 10 p.m. He swallowed heavily, wondering briefly if Becca had somehow found a way to get off work early, though he was trying to temper his expectation that she would show up at all.

His heart was racing as he opened the door, and to his absolute shock, Penny was standing on the other side.

"Penny?" he asked dumbly, as if not believing she was there.

She barely made eye contact as she brushed past him and into the nearly vacant living room. Jesse closed the door and shoved his hands in his pockets, taking a couple steps toward her. He watched her look toward Joe's dark room, then toward his before she turned to him.

"I'm so mad at you," she said, her voice almost a yell but shaking nonetheless.

After a moment, he nodded his head, then looked toward the ground.

"How'd you know I was still...here?"

"I had the early shift in Queens this morning," she said, her eyes filling with tears. "I actually ran into Joe at 5 in the morning. He told me."

"Oh," he said, blinking in surprise. "How was..."

"Fine, he was fine," she said quickly, not wanting to think any more about her encounter with Joe. They'd barely spent two minutes together before he boarded the subway to the airport with the rest of the Ambrosio clan in tow. She wanted to stay angry with him, too, but he'd kissed her cheek before jumping onto the subway car, and she'd started to cry as she watched him pull away. She knew then that as mad as she was with Jesse, she wanted to see him before he left.

It just took all day for her to collect herself enough to do it. And now that she was standing there with him, all her anger was resurfacing -- knowing this might be the last time she would see him was tearing her apart. She took a deep breath before she launched into him, all her pent-up fears coming to the surface.

"Why didn't you apply for a deferment, Jesse? Why?!" she demanded.

"Whatcha mean?" he asked, trying to act as clueless as possible.

"I can read!" she said, her emotions getting the best of her. "If you are a citizen of another country..."

"I'm not," he said evenly.

"Your mother is Canadian!"

"So?"

"So?" she repeated, incredulous. "You can go to Canada..."

He sighed heavily.

"I can't go back there," he said, determination in his eyes as he looked pointedly at her. "You know that."

"Yes, you can!" she said, moving swiftly over to stand in front of him. "You don't have to go back...there...to that...place, but you can go to Canada and..."

"And what? What?!" he said, spreading his arms wide.

"Live!"

He waved his hands at her as if to dismiss the thought.

"Jesse!"

"I'm going into the army, Penn, alright?! I'm in the army," he shot back at her. "Just like Eli. Just like Joe. I was drafted, and that's what I'm doing. This is it; you dig? So, if you came by to give me some hippie, peace-protest, beatnik bullshit, then you're wasting more time on me than a little bit."

"So, you don't care? You don't care that you will be fighting a war our fucking country has no business being a part of?" she challenged, tears now streaming down her face. "You don't care that you might never come home? That you're probably gonna die!"

He looked at her a moment, taking a deep breath before answering quietly.

"I expected that to happen a long time ago," he said in a low voice. She was taken aback for a moment, her heart breaking.

"Oh, God, but Jesse, your life is completely different now," she said, hiccupping as she tried to calm herself down.

"That's not...don't you see?" he said earnestly, gesturing with his hands, trying to emphasize his point. "These are my cards. This is my life. If I dodge the draft and stay I...I lose any shred of respect...(he stopped and shook his head, thinking of his two friends who had already left). If I run to, to Canada...I lose...everything's gone, then, you see? Who I...was here, it's gone. If I do what...what I am supposed to do, at least then I have something...something to show for my life. And if I die, then I die."

She fiercely wiped her eyes then crossed her arms in front of her.

"And what about me?" she asked in a whisper.

Jesse's face softened as he walked to her, putting his hands on her shoulders.

"You are stronger than you know," he whispered, swallowing the lump in his throat. "You're gonna be fine."

She shook her head and looked away from him as her breath hitched. Then she stared straight into his eyes.

"You're a selfish bastard, Jesse Wanger," she said quietly, her lip quivering. "I'm never going to forgive you."

After a moment, he shrugged.

"I don't expect you to," he said quietly, dropping his hands from her shoulders. "You do what you gotta do."

She didn't move as they stared at one another. Penny had an overwhelming sense that this was the final time she would look into those blue eyes, and suddenly she turned away.

"I gotta beat feet," she said, clearing her throat and making her way towards the door. He followed and opened it for her.

She took one step into the hall before stopping to take a deep breath.

"Goodbye, Jesse," she choked out with one last glance over her shoulder before dashing onto the landing.

He had one hand in the air, waving goodbye as she swiftly turned toward the steps and disappeared from view.

"Goodbye, Penny," he whispered to the empty hallway.

He blinked a few times rapidly, then stood up straight and closed the door. He turned and glanced around the quiet apartment once again, thrusting his hands deep into his pants' pockets.

He stared at the place where he'd found his friends, where he'd forged some sort of life -- the life Penny was talking about -- and he began to feel what felt like sentimentality. It was uncomfortable. Very uncomfortable.

So, he reached back between his shoulder blades and pulled his T-shirt over his head, throwing it in his knapsack. He grabbed the clean pair of jeans and skivvies sitting next to it and made his way toward the bathroom to take a shower.

Before disappearing into the room, he took one last glance at the front doorknob -- just to make sure it remained unlocked.

Just in case...just in case...

18

LIGHT MY FIRE

Jesse was standing with his back to the apartment door in jeans and no shirt when the knob turned, and he heard her walk inside and flip the lock behind her.

When he'd left the door unlocked, he wasn't at all sure she'd really come. He thought she'd change her mind. He'd convinced himself that she had. He'd convinced himself that he'd be just fine if she did.

She silently came to him, and his breath caught as she ran her nails along his shoulder blades, then up over his shoulders and down his arms. He could feel her hot breath against him. He tilted his head to one side and moaned softly as she stepped back. He watched the shirt she must have been wearing fly in front of him and land on the floor in the living room. He began to turn his eyes to look at her, then stopped, dropping his head and inhaling sharply as her bare breasts hit his back, and her lips ran against his skin.

"Becca..." he breathed, his whole body catching fire.

"Shhh..." she whispered softly, as she ran her hands around his torso to his chest, slowly massaging and squeezing his hot flesh along the way, running his chest hair between her fingers.

She pushed her hands back down the sides of him and into the front of his jeans. Her hard breathing matching his as her hands found him already beginning to respond to her.

He put his hands on her arms to still her movements and pulled her hands out of his jeans. Slowly he turned to her. She was wearing nothing except a tight short skirt and heels. Her bare chest was heaving, her lips were dry, and her eyes were burning with a lust he knew matched the look in his.

He released his hold on her and grabbed her sides by her hips. Her arms flew up and came to rest on his, fingertips against his shoulders. Their lips barely an inch apart, their rapid breath mingling in the small space between them. Her dry lips were barely parted; she could hardly move anything now. Becca felt like her whole body had turned to molten lava when his eyes landed on hers. She was flushed from head to toe and completely at his mercy.

Jesse licked his own dry lips, then he ran his tongue thoroughly along her lips before engulfing her mouth with his and crushing her against him, turning them around to push her against the kitchen counter.

Her fingers dug into his shoulders and scraped the nap of his neck. He pushed fistfuls of her long, black hair into her back, burrowing through it until he found her soft skin.

They kissed just as they had the other night -- hard and fast until neither could breathe, and both pulled back, gasping for air. Sweat was shining on their bodies, illuminated by the only light on in the whole apartment, over the sink in the kitchen.

Becca crooked her mouth into a little grin. She swiftly hopped up on the cool linoleum, lowering her eyes and shooting him a "come get me" look as her hands moved to grip around the edge on the other side of the counter.

Jesse's eyes were a dark, midnight blue as his gaze raked over her, and the corner of his mouth lifted in a lusty grin. His hands ran up and down her sides as he lowered his head. He licked, kissed, and scraped his teeth along her stomach, unmercifully concentrating on tormenting her belly button.

Becca's head was thrown back, and her arms were shaking. She was moaning and gasping as his mouth moved from her stomach to her breasts, continuing their assault. He reached up under her skirt and peeled off her underwear, which was soaked through. Her whole body was alive for him, coiled tight and ready. If he wasn't in her soon, she was sure she would lose her mind.

Breathing hard, Jesse started to tug on her short, pink skirt.

"Leave it," she panted, desperate for him. She moved her heeled sandals to the sides of his jeans and started to push down. Jesse smirked, pushed her skirt up to her waist, and thrust two fingers inside of her.

"Ohhh!" she yelled out as she started to buck against him as he curled into her, her orgasm seeming to leap almost out of nowhere to plow through her like a hurricane.

His eyes grew wide as he watched her quickly, so quickly, fall apart in front of him. His heart was pounding relentlessly against his chest. He'd never seen anything so stunning in all his life as the woman he had at his mercy at that moment.

She was so beautiful it made his heart hurt, and suddenly he was too far away from her -- much too far.

With one hand, he pushed down his jeans and underwear. He slowly pulled his fingers from her. Her startled, hazy blue eyes tried to focus on him, and she whimpered as she continued shaking, her body still throbbing. Her sweaty palms caused her right hand to slip from the counter, and she jerked backward.

He grabbed her, his hand spreading over the small of her back, not letting her slip away. She fell forward, her orgasm subsiding only a touch, and took his head in her hands, forcing him to look at her. She looked deep into his dark blue eyes, and he was hypnotized, seeing his own eyes in hers as he moved his hands to her butt, and she breathed against his lips...

"Fuck me..." she demanded in a deep, husky whisper.

He was completely undone and let out a guttural groan as he found her entrance and thrust deep into her. She gasped sharply, and her eyes fluttered shut. Nothing, nothing had ever felt so damn good as having him inside of her.

She tightened her legs behind him, the pit of her stomach winding into a tight ball again as he moved in her. She wrapped her arms around his neck and placed clumsy, wet kisses along his forehead. Every groan, every grunt of effort from him against her chest made her kiss him harder. His temple, his short hair, everything her lips could reach as he braced his hands on the counter's edge behind her and continued pounding into her.

Their position wasn't comfortable, but he couldn't stop. He didn't want to stop. He wanted to do this to her forever. His desire for her scared the crap out of him. He'd never wanted anyone more. He'd never wanted anyone, ever...not before her. Not like this.

He felt her tighten around him and knew the tension was building again. He used all the strength he had to thrust harder, faster.

"Jesse...Jesse...Jesse...yes..." she moaned between short, little gasps for air.

He lifted his face to hers -- the intensity of her look, making him uneasy and fascinating him in the same moment. No other human being had ever looked at him like Becca was right then.

She sucked in air in a loud gasp as the tension broke in her. He moaned and reached for her lips, covering them with his as they moved wildly against each other. There was no rhythm, just carnal bursts as he came into her. They kissed hungrily as they each road out the pleasure pulsating through them.

When the rush had subsided, and Jesse could barely feel his legs beneath him, he broke their kiss with a soft pop. She fell limp, laying over his shoulder. For a moment, he held her there, tight against him, her slick body rubbing against his. She glided her hands up and down his smooth back, breathing him in, hugging him to her. His hard, fast breathing was in sync with her own, and she smiled as she felt his aftershocks twitch inside of her. When he could hold on no longer, he sat her down on the counter as gently as he could and pulled out of her.

"You sure know how to greet a man," he grunted breathlessly as he put one hand to the side of her face and pulled her mouth to his, sucking on her lips and briefly kissing her hard between gasps of air. She gnawed on his bottom lip just a moment before pulling back with a mischievous grin. Chests heaving, she pulled down her skirt, and he pulled up his jeans.

He grinned back, and she ran her finger along his lips -- wondering how they could be so soft and so forceful at the same time. She wanted more, just...more. At that moment, she forgot about the war and the fact that he was leaving in just a few hours. It wasn't hard to forget about the pain when there was so much pleasure.

Becca studied his face, then pulled his jaw to her with both hands until they were eye to eye. She kissed his lips slowly, and despite himself, Jesse whimpered into her embrace. She scooted to the edge of the counter, and he helped her to the ground, their lips never leaving each other.

Finally, she took his hand in hers, and he stepped back a little.

"You bring it out in me," she breathed as she looked seductively at him over her shoulder, pulling him to his bedroom. "Ready for round two?"

He took a deep breath and sighed shakily, following her.

"How many rounds were there the other night?"

"Six, I believe," she said as she pushed the door closed behind her and kicked off her sandals.

"That's gotta be some kinda record," he smirked, throwing his jeans and boxers in the corner, her skirt landing on top of them immediately after.

She stood naked before him and stepped into his waiting arms, gripping his shoulders, and standing on her tiptoes...

"Then let's break it," she whispered against his ear as she pushed his chest with both hands, and he fell back onto his bed.

He grinned as she straddled him, her long hair falling all around them, brushing against his arms, causing electricity to run through him with each soft stroke.

She smiled down at him, her breathing beginning to come fast once again. She brought her lips to his chest and took his nipple between her teeth.

"Oh...Jesus," he moaned, throwing his head back against the pillow and fisting the sheets next to him in his hands. She felt him come alive under her as she ran her tongue over his other nipple before softly biting down, gently rocking herself against him while doing so.

Jesse grasped her hips, his fingers digging into her flesh, as she rocked and rocked until they'd guided him into her.

"Ahhh....ohhhh," she breathed, pushing herself up from his chest as he filled her, leaving room inside her only for pleasure, for a feeling like she'd never known.

Damn, he was perfect...so damn perfect. She closed her eyes, throwing her head back, now gripping his legs behind her.

She started to move her hips quicker as he thrust up with strong, determined strokes -- his hips moving at a steady increase. She dropped her head, moaning his name, grinding into him now at every turn. This time they were in complete rhythm, moving in perfect harmony.

His eyes never left her face as she moved above him -- he watched her features change, her hair fly, her body writhe -- and he could barely breathe. She was stunning in her passion.

"Absolutely beautiful," he whispered, looking at her with awe as he moved his hands down to her thighs, pulling her harder against him. "So beautiful."

She grinned just a little and shuddered above him as he altered his pace, slowing down, wanting to make this last as long as he could. She opened her eyes to look down into his.

Her hair fell over them again as she looked down at him. He released her as she put her palms against his chest and thrust to meet his new pace. He raised his arms to push her long locks away from her face. He wanted to look at her. He needed to see her eyes.

Jesse swept her hair over one of her shoulders and looked deep into those gorgeous, dark baby blues -- and his heart slammed against his chest. He expected to see fire, lust, just a flicker of a challenge, a touch of the tease she had always been with him. All that he'd seen the other night -- when everything had been raw and rough and hazy. But that's not what he saw.

His breathing ragged, he stopped moving altogether.

"Wha..." she said, confused, both of them breathing heavily. She furrowed her brow.

He released her hair and put his hands on her shoulders, pulling her down against his chest, their bodies still locked together. He rolled her over to her back, his body nestled between her legs. She grinned at him.

"Oh, you like to be on top..." she whispered, gently teasing him.

He didn't respond; he just continued looking into her eyes with an intensity that was so strong she momentarily forgot to breathe. Her smile fell from her face, but her eyes were soft, glistening, looking adoringly into his.

She gently traced his ear with her fingertips, softly running her palm along his jawline.

"Jesse..." she whispered lovingly, tears growing at the corners of her eyes.

His heart lurched at the tenderness of her touch, her words. He searched her face, and the look he saw there made him feel like crying...and suddenly, he couldn't look at her anymore.

His lips sought hers in desperation. He kissed her so hard, so thoroughly she was sure she would pass out from the head rush, from the feel of his mouth devouring hers.

She responded in kind, never wanting their kiss to end, never wanting their bodies to separate. She wanted him to know she cared. She needed him to know...

Each of them gasped for air as their lips broke apart. He reached for her again, once, twice, with smaller, warm kisses. He wanted to remember the taste of her mouth.

He wanted to remember this last kiss.

He knew she cared for him...more than as a friend—more than as a man she was sending off to war with some unforgettable memories.

She cared about him. He could see it written all over her face.

He squeezed his eyes shut and buried his head in her shoulder as he started moving again, quickly thrusting into her. She clung to him, jarred by his sudden movement. She stroked the back of his short hair; she dug her nails into his back.

"I want you," she whispered, arching her back to meet him, tears slipping down her face. "The moment I saw you, I wanted you..."

He willed himself to shut his emotions down as he grunted and thrust harder, wanting her to crash over -- now -- because now this moment couldn't end soon enough for him.

Whatever Becca thought she was feeling would go away. It would go away when he went away. Even the people who were supposed to love him never loved him for long. She'd realize soon enough he wasn't worth the effort, and he sure as hell wasn't worth the effort now.

"Ahhh, ahhh," she cried out his name as the tension built inside of her once again and released itself in wave after wave through her. He came right after her, fighting the urge to kiss her again as he poured into her. His fingers curled around the pillow under her hair, and he slammed the top of his head into it next to her. She tried to move his face back to her -- to kiss him again -- as their orgasms finally subsided and the only sounds left were their heavy breathing.

His eyes remained closed as he shook her hands from his head, pulled out of her, and rolled onto his back, bringing his arms to rest over his stomach, breathing hard. She glanced over at him, still catching her breath, and felt a cold draft wash over her. She wanted his arms around her.

Becca rolled to her side and nudged him. He instinctively put an arm up and around her shoulders. She relaxed just a bit but couldn't shake the sudden feeling that a part of him was already gone.

19

PIECE OF MY HEART

BECCA SIGHED, HER EYES FLUTTERING SHUT, AND CURLED FURTHER into him.

He froze.

Her eyes shot back open as she felt him tense against her, and then his voice cut through the silent room.

"Don't feel too much, Becca."

"What?" she whispered after a moment, her already racing heart starting to pound.

"Don't feel...for me," he said, turning his face away and releasing his hold on her. "It's not worth it."

"What are you talking about, Jesse?" She sat up, pulling his sheet across her breasts, staring at him incredulously in the darkness.

He pulled part of the sheet across his stomach but refused to look at her.

"I'm not worth it," he mumbled.

She started to protest, but he turned to her with that distant coldness in his eyes she'd seen before. The one that pushed everyone away. The look that built the walls he always seemed to hide behind.

"You need to go home," he said so bluntly it nearly took her breath away. He reached for his cigarettes on the nightstand.

"What?" she said, hurt flashing in her eyes, her voice catching. "No!"

"Now. Go."

"Stop it, Jesse," she said, desperation creeping into her voice. "Stop pushing me away. You can't push this away, not now, not tonight."

He smirked at her, disbelieving.

"I've pushed it all my life, chick. I can push it tonight," he said, cigarette bouncing between his lips as he spoke.

He raised his lighter, she reached out, smacking the lighter and cigarette out of his hands away from his mouth.

"Hey!"

She stiffened, tucking the sheet closer under her arms.

"Don't be an ass."

"An 'emotionally unavailable ass,'" he said, looking at her and shrugging. "It's who I am."

"That's bullshit, and you know it," she said as she jumped naked out of his bed and pulled on her skirt. She crammed her feet into her heels, suddenly completely pissed off at him for doing this to her, to them. Somewhere in her brain, she knew he was saying these things to protect her somehow, but she ignored that voice as her emotions erupted unchecked inside her.

"No," he said, pulling the sheet with him as he got out of bed, too, keeping it together with his fist at his waist.

"It's better this way. Wham, bam, and I do thank you, ma'am."

She lifted her head and stared at him for a hot minute before she stomped out into the living room to retrieve her long-forgotten shirt on the floor. She pulled it on quickly, sweeping her hair out of the back as he tugged on his jeans and followed her. He could say whatever he wanted -- his eyes told her he was lying. But she was too mad and hurt for that to register in her mind at that moment.

"You can't tell me what to feel!" she said, whipping around to face him, on the verge of tears, then she flung out her arm and pointed a finger at his bedroom. "You can't tell me after...after what just happened in that bed, you don't feel anything!"

"Turn it off."

She froze and stared at him, blinking back tears, feeling like he'd just slapped her.

"Turn it off?!" she squeaked in a high-pitched voice, finally forcing herself to speak. "I can't..."

"You have to...Becca, I'm not coming home."

"Don't say that!"

"I'm not!" he said so emphatically that for just a second, she also believed it was a forgone conclusion. "Go home and...and sleep. I'll be gone in the morning..."

Her heart hammered in her ears -- no! No! No! No!

She smacked her hands on either side of her head, her eyes darting around the room, trying to keep her mind from spinning. He grabbed her elbows and forced her to look at him.

"It's a fantasy," he whispered, and she could almost swear she saw tears in the corners of his eyes. "Just like...the other...night. It's just a dream. You'll wake up, you'll forget me, you'll move on."

"No," she whispered back to him, searching his eyes. "It doesn't work that way."

"It does," he said, looking at the broken heart on her face and kicking himself for being weak -- for following her two nights earlier and beginning this white-hot affair in the first place.

He ran his hands down her arms, which had dropped to her sides, and took a ragged breath, backing away.

"Just forget about me," he said. "It won't be that hard."

She felt a pain go right to her heart. His voice sounded strained, but his face was resigned.

Forget him...*forget* him?

She swallowed hard, calming a little, and turned the tables. She stepped closer to him, and he blinked, looking like he wanted to pull away, but he stayed still.

"Will you forget me?" she asked softly, her lips drawing closer to his.

She searched his face and held her breath as she waited for his answer. His features softened ever so slightly before he put the walls up again, but he didn't say a word. She refused to move away, and they looked into each other's eyes for a long moment...

"Go home," he said dismissively, averting his eyes, exhaling loudly, and taking a step back from her.

Becca was so startled by the ice that had returned to his voice that she just stared at him until the hurt inside bubbled out in a strangled laugh. She was ready to fall apart, and she'd be damned if she was going to do it in front of him now. If he wanted to be alone, so be it.

"OK, if that's what you want, man," she said, throwing up her hands and backing away from him, pain written all over her face. "If that's what you have to tell yourself -- you go ahead and do that. You live in your fantasy world! I'm so *fuckin'* glad I got to play the part of your *goddamn* muse!"

She turned around to leave, her words hitting him harder than the punch to the jaw he'd gotten a few months back. He looked down, spotting her underwear on the floor. He picked it up.

"This is yours," he said quietly, walking with false bravado over to her.

She looked at it then screwed her face up in disgust.

"Keep it," she said, her eyes never leaving the cloth in his hand. "Hell, take it with you. It'll be a good ice breaker, 'the great fuck you had before you left.'"

With that, she walked out of his apartment and slammed the door.

His face fell, and he banged his fist on the edge of the counter, wincing a little as it began to throb, her underwear dropping back to the floor.

He breathed heavily as he looked intently at the closed door, willing himself to not chase after her again.

It was better this way. She'd hate him for a while, then she'd forget him altogether and move on with her life. Just as she should. Just as she deserved to do.

And he'd live with the pain of being so close and then going so far away until the merciful day he died.

Jesse crossed his arms as he leaned over on the edge of the counter, slamming his chin into his forearms, staring with wide watery eyes at nothing.

Then he closed his eyes and dropped his head, rubbing his forehead back and forth along his arms.

"Forget you?" he whispered, finally opening his eyes and staring at the floor. "I'll never forget you..."

She pulled harder, her scalp becoming increasingly uncomfortable as she ripped at her hair, pulling her wet, black locks tight into a long braid over her shoulder.

The fog created in the heat of her shower still hung heavy around the bathroom, clouding up the mirror. It looked just like her head felt, heavy and blurry. The pain she felt in her heart was clear enough, though, and she'd never felt anything like it before.

Becca tugged again, jerking her head, trying to push the pain away -- trying to push thoughts of him out of her mind. She snapped a band into place at the end of her braid, pinching her fingers in the process. She didn't even feel the sting.

She was so angry, so hurt that she really did want to forget him. She was almost grateful she'd never have to see him again. She'd never have to look into those blue eyes or see his slow smile...

"Umph," she exhaled shakily as a small cry broke from her lips. She gripped both sides of the vanity and hung her head, a lone tear falling into the bowl below. She gasped for air, trying hard not to throw up.

She wished for all the world she could "turn it off," but her brain kept flashing images of the war right in front of her eyes -- the images she saw every damn day. And all the young men...they were all him. They were all Jesse. They were all dying. They were all alone.

"I'm not coming home," he said. Like he knew. Like it was a certainty. And now, her mind wouldn't let that go, and her heart wasn't ready to let him go, though she had enough pride not to run back to him and beg. He'd been clear; he wanted her gone. He wanted his "fantasy" to end.

She wiped at the mirror with the sleeve of her robe and gasped when she saw her reflection. She didn't know that woman. The woman looking back at her was a wreck. Her face was drawn, her eyes were rimmed red, her face looked haunted. Her heart was completely broken.

Becca turned away in shock from her own image and sunk down onto the lid of the toilet, her whole body involuntarily beginning to convulse. She dropped her face into her hands and doubled over, beginning to sob uncontrollably.

———

She woke in her bed the next morning to the sound of the television in the other room. At some point, she'd left the bathroom, dragged herself into her bedroom, and collapsed on top of her blankets.

She blinked a few times and looked at the clock at her bedside. She swallowed the lump in her throat as she heard a knock at the door.

"Becca?" Liz's voice sounded strange on the other side. Becca fleetingly wondered when she'd come home because she hadn't been there the night before.

She cleared her throat and climbed out of bed, then opened the door a few inches.

Liz reached for her the minute she opened the door, taken aback by the look of complete devastation on Becca's face.

"You're here," Liz finally said, in a tone somewhere between confusion and relief.

Becca nodded, swallowing back the tears that had sprung to her eyes.

"That's...that's probably for the best," Liz said, glancing back at the couch. To Becca's surprise, Penny was sitting there, staring at the screen.

"Why? What's going on?" Becca croaked out, cinching her robe closer to her body.

Penny and Liz exchanged a pensive look as Becca stepped into the living room. Liz followed her. All three eyes landed on the TV.

Becca's eyes grew wide.

"They broke into local programming about 20 minutes ago," Liz said quietly. "It started at dawn."

Becca sank down on the sofa next to Penny. What looked to be at least a thousand protestors were blocking buses at Grand Central Station. That in and of itself wasn't unprecedented. Buses full of draftees had been leaving Grand Central for years, and there had always been protests. But this one seemed larger than law enforcement expected and appeared to be quickly spiraling out of control.

Becca shot Penny a look.

"Did you know?" she asked, somewhat accusingly.

"Yes," Penny nodded. "I...I was going to...be there...but...but..."

Becca's heart started to race as she stared at the screen. People were running. The protestors were pushing on one of the many buses in a long line right outside the station, and riot police were wielding batons, trying to hold people back.

Becca jumped up from the couch and ran into her bedroom, pulling on the first clothes she could find. She had no clear idea of why she was doing what she was doing. All she knew was that she had to go to Grand Central Station. The practical part of her was screaming for her to go because a big news event was unfolding, and she wanted to be there for it. She tried to ignore the other part of her, the part that knew he was there amid the chaos. The part of her that didn't want the last image from the night before to be the last image of him in her mind.

"Becca, what are you doing?!" Liz demanded, following her into her room in a panic. Penny watched her friends in confusion from her seat on the couch.

"I'm going down there," she said, buttoning up her jeans and fishing her clogs out from under her bed.

"No! You shouldn't go there!" Liz said as Becca brushed past her toward the front door, grabbing her press pass off the kitchen counter. "It's not safe!"

"It's news," Becca said dismissively as she waved a hand at Liz, who was following her into the hallway. Liz finally grabbed her arm and tugged until Becca spun around to face her.

"You'll never find him," Liz said in a desperate whisper, her concerned eyes searching Becca's.

Becca just stared at her a moment before jerking her arm away and running toward the stairs, leaving Liz and Penny behind with no real explanation.

Because she really didn't have one to give.

20

GRAND CENTRAL STATION

SHE WAS STILL A FEW BLOCKS FROM THE ONCE SPARKLING BUT NOW dilapidated Grand Central Station building when she heard the rise of voices and honking of horns, signaling the swarm of angry emotions ahead. The outside rim of onlookers was the first wave of people she encountered. They were just close enough to be nosey but not close enough to really know what was going on. Becca pushed past them just enough to spot a few of the last unmarked buses waiting in a long line. Squad cars were stopped, lights flashing, pushed as far into the raucous crowd as they could go without running over anyone.

The throng looked even bigger than when she'd seen the coverage on TV a half-hour earlier. It had swelled, as had the presence of law enforcement. It seemed all of New York City's police force was there.

People were more compact the closer Becca got to the main bus terminal, where she could now see at least 20 buses were lined up, just waiting to leave.

"Press," she yelled, pushing through a wall of people, holding up her press pass in one hand and a reporter's notebook in the other. "Press! CBS News!"

One police officer spotted her in the crowd and silently created a small path for her to push through. The officers kept the press, families, and onlookers a good 20-25 yards away from the confusion as best they could. It looked to her that the police were beginning to gain some semblance of control of the situation.

They seemed to have enough personnel now to push back most of the protestors who were out of Becca's view, on the other side of the buses. They were the people, right around her own age, who she'd seen pushing on the vehicles while she was still watching the events unfold in her apartment -- the crowd Penny would have been a part of if she'd had the heart to join the rebellion.

As Becca stood on her tiptoes, trying to look past the crowd and toward the buses, it dawned on her that all the plain-clothed people standing on the sides of the buses facing her direction were men. Young men. And the closer she got, the more she noticed the army-issued knapsacks each one of them either held or had at their feet.

It was then that she realized all the men who had been drafted. All the men heading out across the country for basic training from Grand Central Station that morning were lined up next to a bus, waiting for the order to board.

Her heart was pounding in her ears as she began scanning each face. Some were laughing, some were crying, some were disgusted, and some showed no emotion at all. She started to jog down the police barricade, getting as close as she was able, her eyes furiously looking from one bus to another, from one face to the next.

She was near tears and almost ready to give up when a figure she recognized took a step out of his line at the next bus to cast an inquisitive glance behind him, and for a moment, she froze.

It was Jesse.

She walked another 30 steps or so before stopping as close as she could get to the line he was in.

"Step back, ma'am," said an officer next to her, motioning for her to step further back into the crowd. She stepped back, but her focus never wavered.

She stared at him -- no longer seeing other people, not hearing any of the noise all around. She raked her eyes over him, from head to toe, as best she could from 20 yards away.

Every ounce of emotion she'd ever had for him tingled from the tips of her fingers to the soles of her feet. She dropped her notebook and crumbled the press pass into her fist. Taking a deep breath, her mind and her heart narrowing in on only him as she finally allowed her feelings to completely overtake her.

She let herself feel him against her once more. Her gaze traveled over his back, and she fleetingly wondered if she'd left her mark on his skin under his shirt. She crossed her arms and squeezed them as hard as she'd embraced him, watching as he threw his bag over his right shoulder, gripping it tighter in his grasp. He looked to the ground, and she closed her eyes.

A tremor that began at her shoulders spread through her chest and down her body. She started to shake. The tears she swore she would no longer shed falling freely down her face. She opened her eyes again, her gaze immediately landing on him.

How? How in God's name was she supposed to forget him?

Suddenly his head jerked in her direction. She pulled tighter into herself, trying to make herself invisible in the crowd around her. She wasn't sure she wanted him to see her -- wasn't sure he'd want to see her -- but still, she'd come and found him and couldn't turn away. The protesters got louder and started banging again on the bus as the riot police again pushed them back with batons.

None of it mattered. All she could see was him -- now looking with purpose in her direction -- seemingly sensing and searching for...something.

"Jesse," she breathed.

And a moment later, his eyes found hers, and the rest of the world fell away.

His mouth dropped open. It took a second for him to register that it was her. Her hair was pulled back tight in a braid, which fell like a black rope over her shoulder. He blinked and briefly shook his head, not really comprehending who he was seeing.

He almost couldn't believe she was there. Almost, he thought, as he felt his heart race faster at the sight of her as if it was waiting to take off from the starting gate the moment he saw her. For just a few seconds, he marveled at her determination, her stubbornness, the sheer force of her will not to break, no matter how hard he'd tried to break her. She looked tiny, far away, yet he knew she was staring right at him. He was relatively certain the entire U.S. Army could try to move her, and she wouldn't budge. She was frozen.

So was he. He closed his mouth and took a deep breath through his nose. He let it out slowly between his lips, his eyes locked with hers. He wanted to smile at her, but it felt trite. So, he just returned her stare, drinking in her beautiful face. She was a vision in the crowd, and she was the only thing he could see. He couldn't tell if she was crying but felt she might be -- because of him, and he hated himself for it.

He watched as she tightened her arms around herself, suddenly looking smaller and more vulnerable, and he felt his heart constrict. If only he'd not been so selfish three nights ago. If only he could have shut her out like everyone else, everything would have been easier -- for her and for him. He should have completely backed off when he knew he was leaving to let their little flame extinguish itself. He could have lived his whole life, never knowing the perfection that was being with Becca, moving in her and having her move in him, feeling fully alive for the only time in his life. Being numb to it would have made everything easier -- being numb always did.

He took another deep breath and watched as she did the same, her eyes never leaving his. He licked his dry lips and could still taste her kiss. He heard his heartbeat in his ears and remembered hers pounding wildly against his chest when he'd clutched her so tight against him...that final time. He blinked a few more times, trying to clear his increasingly cloudy vision.

He gripped his bag tighter and remembered her hips under his fingers the night he taught her to throw a strike, the night they danced to the blues, the other night when he'd chased her into her apartment, and they gave in to their passion the first time. He still couldn't smile at her. The moments for smiling and laughing had passed -- it was too much for him. But he couldn't tear his eyes away from hers, or keep them from watering, or keep his stomach from flipping as he gazed at the innocent and sad face looking back at him.

He forgot the heartbroken, disgusted look she so justifiably gave him as she slammed the door behind her just a few hours earlier. Instead, he remembered the softness in her bold yet delicate features. The shine in her endless blue eyes the instant all the raw sexual tension between them turned into something real and something beautiful. And something right then he deeply regretted he hadn't allowed himself to hold on to in the magic of the moment -- no matter how much better than him she so richly deserved.

Becca swallowed heavily, fighting back the sob that threatened to tear from her throat. She saw something in the way he was looking at her that caused her heart to soften just a touch, even though his face was stoic, resigned -- and if he was scared, he didn't show it.

Of course, he didn't, she thought. That was the wall, the piece of him no one was allowed to look behind. The "emotionally unavailable asshole" part that told her just a few hours ago to go home and forget him.

She realized suddenly that it was an act of defiance -- the reason she'd come. In her own way, she didn't want to listen to him. And, by God, despite everything, her heart didn't want him to be alone in the chaos and commotion, thinking it was a good thing that no one cared he was leaving.

She was carrying their night over to now, throwing herself back in his face. At the end of the day -- if she was honest with herself -- she thought doing so might, just might, start the healing process for her destroyed heart. She would either be able to watch him go, letting him go, and completely break free. Or she would, at least, be able to forget him kicking her out of his bed and remember the man he was to her less than a week ago -- when just the thought of being with him really was a fantasy. Maybe, she thought, she could go back to that and forget the rest.

So, she studied his face one more time. She took in the curve of his jaw, the point of his nose, the high pitch of his cheekbones, the thin velvet outline of his lips. And the soft, gentle slope of his eyes -- those piercing, ever-changing blues that could match the sky on a cloudless day one moment and the northern lights at midnight the next -- and that now, suddenly, squinted at her in confusion...

"Move out!"

The order had burst forth from a megaphone somewhere close to the front of the bus. The doors flew open, and the men in line started to quickly board as police did their best to hold back the protesters still swarming the buses. The man behind Jesse pushed him forward. He broke his gaze from Becca's and looked back at the man, momentarily furious, then turned and found himself quickly at the bus steps. In a matter of seconds, he was onboard and out of Becca's view.

Her face fell, and she took a step forward into the noise and chaos, still looking at the bus, scanning the windows for him, but she didn't see him. In what felt like the blink of an eye, the police escort started rolling forward, the buses trailing directly behind.

And he was gone.

For a long time, she stood motionless, looking down the road at nothing. Soon most of the protesters dispersed, having nothing more to protest. Any families or friends who had come to say goodbye were long gone, and still, she stood there on the sidewalk opposite the lane where the buses had pulled away. Eventually, she could breathe without gasping, and her heart started to beat at a normal rhythm. The tremors slowed, and her tears dried to her cheeks.

"Are you alright, missy?" said an elderly bag lady as she and her grocery cart full of junk tentatively walked a few paces toward Becca. She'd been watching the young woman for 20 minutes and didn't know if she'd even blinked the whole time.

Becca turned to her, and the hollow, heartbroken, tormented look on the young woman's face answered her question. The older woman looked at her with sympathetic eyes, having seen similar scenes play out for a very long time. Then she watched as the color slowly came back into Becca's features. She swallowed hard and stood up a little straighter, unfolding her arms and bringing them to her sides. She reached down and picked up her notebook.

"Yes, thank you," she said automatically as she stood again, a forced smile gracing her lips. The woman nodded as Becca turned and began walking away from Grand Central Station. She had an eerie feeling of déjà vu. Was it really less than a month ago she'd felt buried under a landslide when Keith had abandoned her, leaving her broken and alone? Back then, though, she'd been able to claw her way from under the rubble, with the help of Jesse's hand pulling her to comfort and safety.

If that was a landslide, this...this was an earthquake, and it was swallowing her whole; and there was no hand to hold, no hero to save her, no way out of her misery. He was gone, possibly forever, and she knew in her heart she would never be able to forget a single moment with him.

But she was alone now, buried alive in the debris he'd left in his wake...and she couldn't stop shaking.

21

GEORGIA ON MY MIND

JUNE 1968

Twenty miles.

He'd just hiked 20 miles in the humid heat of western Georgia in full gear. This wasn't something Jesse Wanger ever thought he'd do in his life, but he had. He had the blisters on his feet and five fewer pounds on his frame from the sweat to prove it.

The terrain and the temperature were brutal, but he and everyone else had been told in no uncertain terms that Vietnam was far worse.

He grabbed his canteen and slowly took a drink, learning the hard way that gulping down too much water at once after so much exertion just brought it right back up again.

Jesse grunted a heavy exhale and wiped his lips with the back of his hand as drops of perspiration trickled into his eyes. The humidity had to be more than 100 percent, and he felt like he was melting.

Truth be told, though, he'd be happy to go another 20 miles. He could get lost in the pounding of his boots or the constant shouts from the drill sergeant, and his mind would ever-so-briefly be devoid of thoughts of Becca.

Because in every spare second now entering his fifth week in the army, all he could think about was one Rebecca Schmidt. At this point, those memories brought as much pain as they did comfort.

When the buses first rolled into basic training in Georgia, everything had been such a shock he'd barely had time to think. Their training started immediately -- every man swiftly assigned quarters, ordered to perform latrine duty, kitchen duty, and other chores. The bugle sounded at 5 a.m., and roll call was at 5:05. He felt like he barely had time to breathe, let alone think beyond the task at hand.

For several nights he gave way to exhaustion. He just fell into an instant sleep on his bed at the end of the day. Waking up what felt like a minute later to start the day all over again.

Then late one night, when the day was done and everyone was minutes from "lights out," someone turned on a transistor radio. The Armed Forces Radio station was just loud enough for him to hear the opening lines of "You Make Me Feel."

That's all it took.

Most of the men yucked it up -- singing loudly to each other and mock-slow dancing between the bunk beds. Jesse smirked at them, then laid back and closed his eyes, letting his mind take him back to that night.

After that, his mind took him back to Becca every night before he fell asleep, and some nights it was all he could do not to moan out loud, breaking out into a hard sweat. He remembered every curve of her body, every time her lips crushed against his, every soft, hot breath again his skin. It was almost impossible some nights to get himself back under control. It took as much effort as any other drill he'd performed earlier that particular day. It wasn't long before "Becca" was the only place his mind wanted to wander whenever it had the chance -- day or night.

So, Jesse kept to himself those early days in Georgia, his memories of her more than enough to keep him occupied during the little downtime he had.

It was over a week before he even struck up a casual conversation with any of the other 11 men bunking in the same quarters, and he hadn't started that conversation...

"Charlie!" said the skinny, young black man with a bright upside-down smile as he hung his head from the top bunk, inches from Jesse's dozing face.

Jesse's eyes shot open.

"Where?!" he said, raising his head up quickly and nearly knocking into the other soldier in the process.

"Whoa!" Charlie said with a thick Southern accent as he swung his head back. "We still in Georgia now, brotha. They ain't no 'Charlie' here."

"Right on," Jesse said, now slowly sitting up. "Then why'd you...?"

"That's my name, man," Charlie said as he swung his legs to the side and jumped down from the top bunk, making himself comfortable on Jesse's bed. He put out a hand, and Jesse shook it.

"Jesse," he said.

"Jesse," Charlie repeated with a nod. "Like the tree?"

"Huh?" he said, confused, breaking their handshake.

"Jesse, like the Jesse Tree," Charlie said, incredulous. "Don't ya be knowin' your Bible boy?"

Jesse just shrugged.

Charlie shook his head. "I's from South Carolina."

"New York," Jesse replied with a nod.

"I figured you for a fancy Yankee man," Charlie replied with a chuckle, then looked around the room a moment. "Figured I wanted to know who I's sleepin' with. Not always somethin' I need to know if you's know what I mean, but in these here quarters..."

Jesse chuckled and shook his head. Charlie smiled at him.

"Last person I slept with, whoo, she's a fine-lookin' little lady," he said, as he reached in his pocket and pulled out a black and white photo, handing it to Jesse.

Jesse looked at the photo, then looked at Charlie, confused. The little girl clutching onto Charlie's leg in the photo couldn't have been more than 5 years old.

"That's my little Ring-A-Bella Girl," Charlie said softly. "She didn't want her Daddy to leave, ya see, she was trying to be all big. She wassa gonna cry, no sir! Gonna be a big girl."

Jesse grinned a little and looked at the photo, then back at his bunkmate. The man couldn't have been much more than 20 years old.

"Cute little girl," Jesse said, handing the photo back to him.

"Cute?!" Charlie said, clearly offended. "A basset hound laying in the sunlight after a chasin' is cute! My girl here is gorgeous!"

Jesse smiled, "Sorry. Very cute, then?"

"You got that," Charlie said, somewhat mollified. "She get that from her momma. Her momma says she gonna wait on me. She say it, I's gonna believe it."

Jesse just looked down.

"You got yourself a woman, kids back home?"

Jesse closed his eyes, and for the first time since he left New York, he had a fleeting thought of what it would be like to have Becca waiting for him to come home. The thought left his head as quickly as it had entered -- he was still certain he wasn't coming home.

Besides, he reasoned that she was already over him by this time, possibly seeing someone else. The thought of Becca with another man made him absolutely crazy, even knowing full-well that he was the one who told her to forget him and go on with her life.

He briefly squeezed his eyes shut then took a deep breath.

"No," he said, looking at Charlie again. "No one back home."

Charlie just nodded, then paused a moment.

"We's take care of each other now," he said, nodding at the other men in the room. Jesse's eyes followed his gaze. Then Charlie smiled.

"Sees, your job is to take a bullet for me, ya hear?" he said with a chuckle. "I ain't gonna be throwin' myself in front of no commie gun..."

Jesse chuckled. "You just said we gotta take care of each other..."

"Yez, I's lying, fool," he said with a gleam in his eye but a warm smile on his face. He patted Jesse on the shoulder. "Night."

"Night, Charlie...?"

"Brown," he said. "Call me Brownie."

"Charlie...Brown?" Jesse said with a laugh. "Your name is Charlie Brown?"

"Hey! I had it 'fore that bald-haired, cartoon honky kid had it!" he said, in that mock-offended way he had before.

"Man, you took a beat-down with that name," Jesse said, shaking his head.

"Better 'n bein' named after a tree ya ain't even heard no tell of," he said, putting his hands on his bunk, ready to pull himself up. "Jesse...?

Jesse sighed heavily. "Wanger."

"Wanger?" Charlie said loudly, with a laugh so infectious, even Jesse had to smile. "Wanger? Wanger! Oh, you be the fool makin' fun o' my name, oh Jesus!"

Jesse couldn't help but smile as Charlie, chuckling, climbed back into the bunk above him...

Basic training was hell, but the brotherhood he'd found in his unit was strangely comforting. The commanding officers had repeated it like a mantra -- "you protect your brother" -- and the men had taken to it. They were all strangers, 70-percent of them drafted into service. They only had each other to lean on for support, and he and Charlie had become buddies in a short amount of time.

Jesse took another slow swig from his canteen and spied Charlie coming toward him. He had a serious look on his face.

"What's happenin'?" Jesse asked as he got closer.

"Riley say he hear we leave for California in three days," Charlie said, his eyes darting around.

Jesse raised his eyebrows.

"California?"

"Yay," Charlie said, "I ain't ever been west of the Mississipp'."

Jesse grinned. California. He hadn't been to California since he was a small boy. He'd been happy in California...

"Won't be there long," Charlie continued, still looking around. "Just a pit stop."

"Yeah?" Jesse said.

"That's just a launchin' pad, brotha," Charlie said, looking at Jesse and shaking his head. "Next stop is 'Nam."

Jesse stared at Charlie just as the drill sergeant loudly ordered all the men back to formation. Then he took another quick swig from the canteen, swished the water around his mouth, and spit it into the red Georgia clay at his feet before jogging behind Charlie back to his unit.

Becca pushed the window up as far as it would go and moved the metal fan closer to it to help circulate the air in her bedroom. It was 90 degrees in the shade outside, far too hot even at this time of year, and stifling in the confines of a New York City walk-up. It seemed more humid at night, and that wasn't helping her sleep one bit. Over the last week, she'd gone from a light nightgown to a t-shirt, to her underwear, to trying to sleep in nothing at all. None of it worked.

And that was too bad because she was so exhausted during the day, she'd fallen asleep, twice, on the job in the darkroom. Malory found her both times, thankfully. The heat and the humidity always made her more lethargic. Still, the insufferable weather, coupled with her inability to sleep for more than two hours at a stretch at night, was taking a toll.

She wanted to blame her sudden insomnia completely on the heat, but she couldn't do that. She knew better than that.

Becca kicked off her heels and pulled a few bobby pins from her hair, undoing the bun but leaving in a ponytail. She tossed her belt and hose onto the chair on the side of her bedroom. She'd had the early shift this week, so she was home a good two hours before Liz was off work. Some days it was lonely. Most days, she welcomed the solitude, wanting nothing more than to be alone with her thoughts. Today was one of those days.

Becca pushed the bedspread far to the bottom of the bed and laid down on top of the cool sheets. They'd stay cool against her skin another minute or two before it didn't make much of a difference in temperature anymore, but she'd take the sparse relief. She'd take any relief she could get nowadays.

She sighed -- it was day 33, more than a month since she last saw him.

She'd had no contact with him whatsoever. He hadn't called; he hadn't written. Nothing. Not that she particularly expected to hear from him. He'd told her to forget him, and reaching out to her would be counterproductive to his edict. It would also be counterproductive to her own healing process, which honestly seemed to have stalled out before it had even begun.

It hurt. It still hurt.

Ironically, it was the memory of their one "date," the night before he was drafted, that caused the worst of her pain. She remembered wanting to take things slowly and foolishly, thinking she could shield her heart. She knew then that he was having an effect on her no one else ever had, and it had frightened her. She'd remember how he'd held her close and rocked her slowly after she'd pulled back from their kiss in the dark corner of the club. She'd felt so much promise of what was to come, so much hope, feeling his arms around her, feeling him smile into her hair.

Then it all, all of it fell apart so rapidly. Even now, most of it was a blur. From the moment he and Joe told them they'd been drafted to the moment she saw him board the unmarked bus to Georgia, it was a hazy, lust-induced, emotionally draining blur.

She wouldn't let herself think too much about their final night together -- about how her heart was exploding for him one minute then shattered in a million pieces by him the next. Those feelings were too raw, and they made her want to hate him. Sometimes she swore she did hate him. Then she'd picture the last time their eyes met at Grand Central Station or edit a long line of film containing images of body bags coming home from Vietnam, and her heart would seize in her chest. She knew she couldn't hate him.

More often than not, she wanted nothing more than to forget him because he was always, always on her mind. For a few hours here and there, she was able to pull it off until she would find herself listening to Aretha Franklin on the radio with tears in her eyes. Or she'd see a man in fatigues on the street and stop and stare. Worse yet, she'd see men his age, walking about with a normal, everyday life as they headed to work on Madison Avenue or carried "peace" signs at a war protest. And the cycle of her yearning would start all over again.

Sometimes, late at night, her craving for him was unbearable. She'd lay on her bed, covered in sweat. All she could think about then was him making love to her in that heated, carnal way they had before he went away.

She'd try to relive every touch, every kiss, every caress that made her body shudder. Once, she even cried out, bringing Liz flying into her room in the middle of the night to check on her. Luckily, she dove under the covers just in time to feign sleep and let Liz think she was dreaming instead of burying herself so thoroughly in those steamy memories it almost felt like he was in the room with her.

Becca sighed and turned on her side, bringing her pillow tight against her body, closing her eyes. Whoever came up with the phrase "time heals all wounds" had never fallen hard for one Jesse Wanger.

Knock Knock Knock

Becca furrowed her brow in confusion, craning her neck to look through the open doorway of her bedroom toward the front door. Slowly she pulled herself off the bed. She smoothed down her skirt and pushed back some loose strands in her hair as she made her way across the living room. She peered through the peephole and gasped.

Knock Knock Knock

She hesitated before opening the door. Then she swallowed hard and straightened her spine, slowly turning the doorknob.

The person on the other side looked at her pensively and gave her a small smile.

"Hi Becca," he said nervously.

She folded her hands in front of her and took a deep breath.

"Hello, Keith," she said evenly, not returning his smile.

22

LITTLE WHITE LIES

"Can, um, can I come in?"

Becca's heart was pounding hard. Keith was the last person in the world she had any desire to ever see again. He looked so different from the last time she'd seen him, too. His hair had grown longer, and he had a full, thick beard. His demeanor, though, seemed nervous yet somehow settled -- much calmer than it had ever been when they'd dated. His frantic, drug-infused energy was nowhere to be found.

Becca took a deep breath.

"What are you doing here?" she asked, now crossing her arms against her chest.

"I, ah, I need to talk to you," he said, nodding toward the living room. "Please, can I come in? I know I shouldn't be here, and I...I promise I won't stay long. You'll...and you'll never have to see me again."

After another moment's contemplation, she stepped aside and let him into the living room.

"Thank you," he murmured, taking a couple steps inside. She closed the door behind him and walked over to the far end of the couch to sit down, motioning for him to do the same.

An awkward silence fell between them until Becca finally cocked an eyebrow at him.

Keith looked down, smoothing out the knees of his jeans and clearing his throat.

"I've...I've been going to these...meetings and, and I'm learning, I mean, they're teaching us..." he said, not at all sure where to start. Becca sat motionlessly, hands folded in her lap. He sighed and looked up at her, wiping the sweat off his brow.

"I am sorry, Becca," he said, searching her face. "I was a bad boyfriend and even a...a more horrible...person. I...I was on a lot of...of stuff... then and I, I wasn't myself..."

Becca still didn't say a word, and Keith dropped his head, looking at the floor and folding his hands in front of him.

"One of the steps in my, ah, the program is to apologize to those you've hurt the most, and I know when I...I left that...night I hurt you and I'm sorry," he said quietly. "I really am."

Becca narrowed her eyes at him.

"Hurt me?" she said indignantly. "You left me alone and took my money after...after...I was completely humiliated!"

"I'm sorry, I..." Keith winced then shook his head. "I don't...I don't even remember that. I don't really remember much from that night..."

Becca was ready to lay into him and tell him exactly how the rest of that night had gone for her, but then she stopped herself. Getting into that story would only serve to remind her how wonderful Jesse had been to her then, and that was a memory she didn't dare bring to the front of her mind at this point in time. Instead, she looked at Keith for a long moment, then sighed.

"OK," she said softly.

He looked up at her then, completely taken by surprise by her reply.

"OK?"

"Yes, OK," she repeated. "You weren't 'you,' OK? I get it, so...fine, OK."

"You...you accept my apology?" he asked. She nodded, and he looked to the ceiling, relief all over his face.

"Wow," he said, disbelieving, then he reached towards her. Becca jerked back, folding her arms against her stomach.

"I'm sorry," he murmured. " I just, I didn't think it would be that easy."

"It's not easy," she corrected, eyeing him carefully, "but it is over."

They held eye contact for another minute before Keith nodded slowly.

"I get it," he said quietly. "Thank you for forgiving me. I'm, I'm trying to become a better person, through prayer and...the Lord Jesus Christ."

He crossed himself, and Becca stared at him, her face fixed in confusion. He saw her look and chuckled.

"I've been saved, Becca. Saved!" he said, earnestly as the apartment door opened behind him. "I have found Jesus, my Savior, and he has given me the strength..."

"Where'd you find him, at the end of a joint?" Penny quipped, hands on her hips and fury in her eyes. Keith whirled his head around to her as Becca smirked at her friend.

"Penny," he said with a smile and more enthusiasm than he should have. He jumped to his feet. "I'm so happy..."

"Zip it," she said sharply. "Why are you here? You're not supposed to be here."

He briefly glanced at Becca for support but seeing none, he tentatively walked over to Penny.

"I...I wanted to...to apologize to Becca..."

"Least you could do," Penny interrupted flippantly with a wave of her hand.

"...and she was gracious in her forgiveness," he said, smiling softly at Becca. She rose from the couch and bristled just a bit, sensing Penny's questioning eyes on her. Keith turned back to Penny.

"I've been sober almost two months," he said.

"Well, good for you," she said sarcastically, throwing down her bag on one of the kitchen chairs and moving to grab ice out of the freezer, dropping it into a clean glass next to the sink. "You have no idea what we've been through the last two months..."

"No, I don't," he said honestly, then nodded toward the door. "But... I'm, I'm thinking Jesse will be home soon and if he, if he can accept my apology as well as Becca, then maybe I might be able to...gain your trust and maybe...maybe become your friend again. Not right away, I know..."

"Jesse?!" Penny said after taking a long drink and setting down her glass on the counter. "Jesse doesn't live there anymore."

Keith shot a confused look to Becca, but she was looking at the floor, her arms crossed tight against herself once again.

"But...what, why?" Keith asked.

"Like I said, you just took off! You don't have a goddamn clue what's been going on around here," Penny spat out at him. "He was drafted, him and Joe. They've been gone for over a month. Management sold the apartment two weeks ago."

"Oh my...oh my God," Keith said, putting a hand to his chest. Then he looked questioningly at Penny. "Did Jesse go to Canada?"

"No," Penny said, quickly glancing at Becca and seeing her head shoot up, a confused look on her face.

"Why not? His mom's still there, right?" Keith asked. A couple weeks into recovery, when he'd had all the time in the world to think, it dawned on him why his roommate never appeared to be worried about the draft. His mother was Canadian, so of course, he could legally go back to Canada if he had to.

Becca looked back and forth between Keith and Penny.

"I thought..." she said, her head beginning to spin. "He...he told Eli his parents were dead."

"I don't think so," Keith said, furrowing his brow. "I mean, not as far as I know."

"Oh, what would you know?" Penny said, trying to protect Jesse and now worried about Becca. Her friend had turned white. "You...you've said your piece now, now beat feet, Keith."

"I'm really sorry to hear..." he started. Suddenly Becca gripped the back of a chair in the kitchen, her head spinning faster. She was sure she was about to pass out.

"Becca?" Keith said, taking a step towards her as Penny rapidly pulled out another chair and guided Becca down into it.

Becca looked at Penny, her eyes questioning. Penny pursed her lips then looked at Keith.

"You can go now."

"But..."

"I'm fine," Becca said softly; her eyes were locked with his. "I accepted your apology. Now please just go, Keith. There's no...reason...for you to be here now."

Keith hesitated, then backed up toward the door and mumbled a thank you before leaving with one last, worried look at Becca.

"I really am sorry," he said, glancing at the closed door of his old apartment across the hall before turning to face them again, "about everything."

Becca looked intensely at him a moment, then nodded. Penny looked between the two of them, a curious look on her face.

Once he left, Penny grabbed another glass and quickly filled it with water, handing it to Becca and sitting down next to her.

"Are you OK?"

"I'm fine," Becca said unconvincingly, her head in her hands. "It's just the heat. I'm probably...I haven't had enough water today."

Penny nodded but shot a disgusted look at the door.

"What'd he say?" Penny asked, convinced Becca's current state had a lot to do with her visit from Keith. "He's not trying to get back together with you, is he?!"

Becca shook her head and took a long drink of water, then she looked at Penny.

"Is his mother really alive? In Canada?" she asked.

"Who? Jesse?"

"Yes," she said wearily.

Penny studied Becca. She was surprised to see tears in her eyes. While she knew something was starting to happen between the two of them before Jesse got his notice, she now wondered exactly how much had happened. Her friend certainly had not been herself since the middle of May, but then again, none of them had been. A cloud of sadness seemed to hang over them all in one form or another.

"Becca," Penny asked, tentatively. "I know it's not my bag, but...how, how close were you and Jesse before he...he left?"

Becca pinched her eyes closed and turned her head away from Penny, taking a deep breath, her dizziness beginning to subside just a little.

"Not very," she replied in a whisper, shaking her head, and blinking back tears. She looked again at Penny. "Apparently, I didn't know him very well at all."

Penny looked as though she wanted to say something, but she didn't.

"Is his mother alive?" Becca repeated slowly.

Her friend hesitated before answering, not at all sure what Jesse would want her to reveal about his parents and his past.

"Yes," she finally said, Becca's direct, beseeching look being too much for her to take. "But it...it's complicated."

"Un-complicate it for me," she demanded softly.

"I...I can't," she said, only partially lying. "They don't get along...at all..."

Becca shook her head, then her face fell.

"Wait! Is he...is he Canadian?" she asked.

"Uh..."

"Penny?!"

"Yes, half Canadian. His father is American," she revealed hesitantly.

"Is he alive?!" Becca demanded.

"I...I think so, I don't know," Penny said, shaking her head, her own fears for Jesse coming to the front of her mind. "I tried to tell him to go to Canada so he could just live and be safe, but he wouldn't listen to me! He wouldn't do it!"

"Oh my God..."

"I tried Becca, but he...his mother..." she shuddered. Becca cut her off.

"But he could have legally avoided the military, he could have been safe, he could have...all of it, all of this, it could have been avoided?!" Becca said loudly, banging her hand on the table for emphasis.

"Becca," Penny said, reaching for her hand, but it was too late. Becca had bounced to her feet and was now pacing the room, her dizzy spell all but forgotten. Why did he lie about his parents being dead? Why didn't he go to Canada? Why didn't he tell her any of this?!

"What the hell, Penny? Why?!"

"I can't..." Penny started, getting up from her chair and walking towards her friend. "I know his life in...Canada was...bad, really bad, but I...I really can't...I don't know all the details. I didn't...I didn't know him then."

"Worse than being in Vietnam?!" Becca shouted, making Penny take a step back. "Worse than fighting in that war?!"

"I don't know, Becca, I don't know!" Penny said with just as much force. "I don't know why any of this is happening! He...he had his reasons...I..."

"This is unbelievable," she said, throwing her arms out wide, sure she was going to lose what was left of her composure at any moment. "He'd, he'd rather go...go fight in a...in that place, than stay with....than stay safe?!"

"I...I..." Penny started, but Becca threw up her hands and hurried into her bedroom, slamming and locking the door behind her.

"Becca?" Penny said, running after her. She tried the doorknob to no avail. "Becca? Talk to me, please..."

Becca was barely listening to her now, and at that moment, she really didn't care about explanations. All she could concentrate on were the facts. Jesse had definitely lied about his parents. He definitely could have legally avoided the draft; he definitely could have stayed safe and alive and possibly, possibly, somehow stayed with her.

And he chose not to do any of that.

She flopped down on her back on her bedsheets, the wind from her fan almost instantly drying the tears as they fell down the sides of her face, feeling more hurt and confused than ever.

23

WHEN A MAN LOVES A WOMAN

JESSE FLICKED THE ASH FROM HIS CIGARETTE INTO THE PLASTIC ASHTRAY then rolled the whiskey between his hands, watching as the ice cubes gently bounced off the sides of his glass.

It took a little longer than three days, but his group left the heat of Georgia 43 hours ago, landing in the chilly Bay Area in a heavy fog. They were assigned for a couple days to Travis Air Force Base in Oakland, California -- otherwise known as the "Gateway to the Pacific" for American military personnel heading In Country.

They had five hours of their 48-hour window left before they boarded a plane for Vietnam.

Jesse sat up a little straighter on his barstool, glancing at Charlie sitting to his left. The place was packed with men drinking up the last sights and sounds of freedom, lighting up everything from cigs to weed and then some. A heavy haze of smoke hovered over the buzz of the early morning hour, the bar crawling with plenty of women wanting to show the servicemen a good time before they left.

Their whole unit was shipping out at 0600, and not one of the men planned to sleep the night before, at least not alone. At least that's what they all told each other. The bar had been a target-rich environment all night, and everyone in the bar knew it. Men and women who didn't know each other just hours earlier were leaving together, or not. Make-out sessions were happening in the shadows of more than one corner.

A few guys, like Jesse and Charlie, were doing their best to ignore it all -- facing away from the throbbing masses, occasionally talking to the bartender. Initially, Jesse said he was Charlie's wingman, fighting off any temptations that came his young friend's way. It didn't take long, though, to become obvious who most of the women wanted when they made a beeline for the bar. More than one woman who had sauntered over to them in the last couple of hours was salivating over Charlie's buddy. Blonds, brunettes, redheads -- and Jesse had ignored them all.

Charlie couldn't understand why. Jesse had repeatedly told him there was no one waiting at home for him, but Charlie began to wonder if that was the case. Once in a while, he would hear Jesse moan what sounded like a woman's name in his sleep, and every so often, his friend would get a soft look on his face that Charlie knew could only mean one thing.

Charlie didn't pry, but he figured there must have been a reason the woman his buddy was clearly in love with wasn't waiting for him at home. Unrequited love was his guess, and Charlie surmised it was probably time for him to get over her.

It was clear Jesse could use some comfort, the kind only a soft woman could provide. Charlie finally decided that his presence at the bar was more than likely serving as a distraction to Jesse getting what he really needed -- and time was running out.

Suddenly he stood up from his seat, taking Jesse by surprise.

"I'm gonna split, man," Charlie said, downing the last of his alcohol and slapping Jesse on the back, eyeing the other side of the room.

"Yeah," Jesse agreed, beginning to stand himself until Charlie put a hand on his shoulder and shoved him back onto his barstool.

"No, you stay."

"What?" Jesse said, confused. "Why?"

"You don' need no fine-lookin' man like me gettin' all the eyes on 'im," Charlie said with a grin, still looking to the other side of the room. "This here's a sight better for you, brotha. No more babysittin' me... you can take a dip in the pool now..."

Jesse shot Charlie an exasperated look, then glanced over to who was holding Charlie's gaze. It was the one particular brunette who had been eyeing him all night, even though she'd been chatting up other men. She'd smiled at Jesse every time she'd caught his eye. He didn't really smile back, instead of trying to talk to any other man in the vicinity of the bartender. She was pretty, physically very attractive, and completely into him.

And in another life, knowing he was leaving never to return, he would have been all about having her in his bed for the night. No drama, no strings, just sex.

"She's been jonesin' for ya all night, brotha," Charlie said, nodding toward the woman. "Ya got yerself a good time a-comin' -- gotta tell me the details later, man."

"No, no, don't..." Jesse started as Charlie nodded the woman over to them through the crowd. She smiled brightly and sashayed over to them.

Finally, she stood in front of them, hand on her hip, cleavage bursting at the buttons of her blouse. Her sky-high skirt showed off her toned legs. Every man who wasn't otherwise occupied had watched her walk across the room.

"Little Lady, this here's my friend, Jesse," Charlie said as Jesse squirmed on the barstool. "And you are?"

"Violet," she said with a bright smile.

"Violet," Charlie nodded as Jesse narrowed his eyes at him. "Violet, honey, would ya take good care of my man here tonight? He's needin' a gentle touch..."

"Charlie..." Jesse warned through clenched teeth.

"I'll be more than happy to," Violet breathed, reaching out to slowly run her hand down the side of Jesse's hair, her fingertips grazing his neck.

Charlie smiled at Jesse, who didn't return his smile; then, with one more slap on his back, he leaned toward Jesse's ear.

"Yous gonna thank me later," he drawled quietly. "Get ya some o' that, man."

Jesse stared holes in the back of Charlie's head as he walked away until Violet came into his line of vision.

"'bout time," she cooed, moving in closer to him. "I've been trying to get your attention all night,"

"Have you?"

"Don't act like you didn't know," she said, putting her hands on his shoulders.

Jesse glanced at the hand on his right shoulder, trying to remember what it was like to flirt just for the hell of it. There was a time not too long ago when he'd been pretty decent at it, but now...he just didn't have the heart to do it anymore.

"So, what do I have to do to get your hands on me?" she whispered as she surprised him by climbing onto his lap, straddling him.

Jesse didn't move, but his heart sped up as her eyes met his. She had a seductive look on her face as she bit her lip, then her dark eyes began to search his face, landing on his mouth.

She clearly was turned on and trying her best to bring him up to speed. Jesse cleared his throat as she pressed against him, waiting for him to make the next move.

"You're the best-lookin' guy in here," Violet whispered, her lips now against his ear. "I'll show you a good time, baby. I wanna show you a good time..."

She ground her hips into him then leaned back, her mouth inches from his.

Breathing heavily, Jesse suddenly grabbed the sides of her hips -- and roughly lifted her off of him.

Violet looked at him in shock as she stumbled back, trying to catch her breath. Jesse stood up and cleared his throat again.

"Look, you're...you're very, very attractive, but...this isn't going to happen," Jesse said as evenly as he could.

She let out a mocking laugh, clearly affronted by his rejection. She put a hand on her hip, radiating cockiness.

"You know I could get any man in here I wanted," she said.

"Go to it," he smirked, gesturing to the crowd.

"I don't want any of them," she replied, walking over to meet him face-to-face. "I want you."

She reached up for him again, and this time he stopped her -- grabbing her wrists with his hands and lowering them to her sides.

Jesse looked her squarely in the eye.

"The last woman I was with is the last woman I ever want to be with," he said clearly. "You dig?"

Violet studied him a moment, then relaxed a little, no longer taking his efforts to thwart her attention personally.

"So," she asked finally, "you're in love?"

Jesse just stared at her, jarred by the question, truly not having a clue what to say. After a minute, when he didn't answer, Violet just smiled at him.

"She's a lucky girl," she said, her eyes traveling up and down his body.

Jesse shook his head.

"No, she's not," he said quietly. "I'm just an asshole."

Violet just looked at him, confused.

"I'm guessing she's a long way from Oakland," Violet said, and Jesse nodded, "and you just rejected this."

She gestured to herself, and he smirked a little. She grinned again.

"You're a rare breed, soldier, but you're not an asshole," she said, as she stepped to him and kissed his cheek.

Jesse cocked his head to the side as she pulled away, still grinning at him. She was still standing just a little too close to him for comfort.

"I...I need some air," Jesse said, turning toward the bar, smashing out his cigarette, and digging out his wallet.

"Want some company?" she asked over his shoulder. He shot a glare at her in the reflection of the mirror behind the bar.

"Hey, a girl's gotta keep warm at night in northern California," she said, with a wink, then she slowly walked away to find the second best-looking man in the room.

Jesse quickly threw some cash down then pushed his way through the crowd toward the exit.

He returned to his temporary barracks at Travis AFB to find Charlie Brown was the only other man in the room. Charlie, who was laying down on his assigned cot, watched him in silence as he made his way across to him through the maze of cots and knapsacks in the near dark.

Charlie turned his eyes back to the ceiling, briefly shaking his head in disbelief. He heard Jesse take off his boots and fall into the cot next to him. For a long time, they both stared at the ceiling in the darkened room. Just about the time Charlie thought Jesse may have fallen asleep, his friend's heavy voice broke through the quiet...

"Her name is Rebecca...Becca," Jesse said softly. Charlie turned his head to look at him in the shadows. Jesse's eyes stayed fixed above him.

"She's more beautiful than any woman at that bar tonight," he continued, "dark, black hair and bright blue eyes. Fierce, fierce eyes. Smart as a whip, strong as steel, soft as velvet, with a smile..."

He stopped, trying to get ahold of himself. He blinked a couple times.

"No one has that smile," he whispered. He took a deep breath and let it out in a long sigh. Charlie just lay still, taking in the revelation.

"By now, I'm sure she's...she's forgotten about me," Jesse was speaking in a voice Charlie didn't recognize like he was describing something happening far away. "I want her to be...to have a happy life and...and whether I live or die she...she wouldn't be happy. I'm nothing. I've got nothing. She's...everything. She's got it all."

Charlie turned on his side and leaned up on his elbow. He could see Jesse's eyes glistening in the fog-covered moonlight.

"I'm just...I'm not ready to let her go," Jesse whispered, his voice catching. "I can't lose her memory...forget that...that look in her eyes... in my mind...until I absolutely have to."

Jesse took another breath as though he would continue talking, but he suddenly stopped and closed his eyes. His mind was drowning, and his heart was thundering. It took every ounce of strength he had left in his body not to let it all go and break down. He felt the full force of being human because he *was* scared, just like every other man coping any way he could.

Lying there, he wanted more than anything to just hold her -- to clutch her to him, bury his face in her cascading dark hair, find the solace he could in her arms, letting her beauty -- both inside and out -- make him whole just one more time...

"I wasn't gonna ask," Charlie said quietly after a moment, laying back on his cot and closing his eyes, too.

"I know," Jesse replied. "But I wanted you...someone...to know...

"Her name is Becca."

Charlie swallowed hard.

"Fair 'nough," he whispered, a catch in his throat.

"Fair enough," Jesse echoed in the dark.

24

FORTUNATE SON

July 1968

Becca wadded up the paper towel in her hand and quickly wiped her mouth, trying to catch her breath. She squished up her face and flushed down the contents in the toilet on board the Redd family's small sailing yacht anchored in the middle of the Hudson River.

She glanced at herself in her compact mirror. Her sweaty face was pale in the areas that weren't splotched bright red. She shook her head, leaning up against the bathroom door. She couldn't go back up on deck for the Fourth of July fireworks extravaganza just yet. She wasn't ready to face her parents or Liz, everyone asking if she was OK.

Because there was no denying it anymore -- she was anything but OK.

Initially, she never even realized she'd missed her period. So much happened so quickly that she was just pulling herself through each day, trying to get out of bed every morning. She and the rest of the nation were still reeling from Bobby Kennedy's assassination in June, contributing to her ever-increasing workload at CBS. In addition to the national chaos, massive protest riots had broken out at Columbia University. The NYC public school teachers' union was in the midst of a months-long strike. She was in the middle of a stretch of working 12-14 hour days when Keith showed up, creating more inner strife for her and throwing her feelings for Jesse into complete turmoil.

All along, the days stretched into weeks, and eventually, she started getting sick. It was happening in the evening, at work. She thought she'd caught a summer bug, or was working too much, or wasn't eating right, or was too stressed for her own good. When it dawned on her a few days ago that she hadn't been on the rag in a really long time, she was already in full panic mode.

All the signs were there -- and they pointed to the undeniable fact that she was definitely pregnant. Once the shock wore off a bit, she came to terms with the reality -- she was single, alone, and pregnant.

Becca snatched another paper towel from the roll and ran it under some cool water, putting it to her forehead, then the back of her neck. She took a couple deep breaths and shook the tears out of her eyes, pressing the towel against them, too.

She took another glance into her small mirror. She looked calmer now, a little more settled, and not like someone who had just thrown up everything she ate the last two days. At least, she thought, she could get through the fireworks.

Taking another deep breath, she reached for the door of the little bathroom. She stopped when she heard her mom and Liz's mom, Sandy, come down the little stairwell into the tiny kitchenette just on the other side of the thin door, deep in conversation...

"Trudy is beside herself," Sandy said. "I mean, can you imagine? I don't think they'd even spoken about marriage..."

Becca could hear cabinets opening and closing and ice being put into plastic cups.

"Of course, they didn't," Wilma said in her holier-than-thou way. "That Jessica was always fast, you know. She's been dating since she was a freshman in high school!"

Sandy gasped. Becca knew exactly who they were talking about -- Jessica had been a classmate of hers and Liz's ever since primary school.

"Her father wants them to get married right away, and Jessica won't hear of it," Sandy said.

"That's exactly what Trudy told me this morning," Wilma replied. "That daughter of hers has some nerve, getting herself in the family way and expecting someone besides the father to take care of it. A child should have a married mother and father to raise it properly. All these...these tramps... getting...knocked up. It's simply disgusting."

"That's precisely what I think," Sandy said in agreement. "It would be different, I suppose, if he were serving..."

"Or if they were engaged, intending to marry," Wilma agreed. "Like our children."

"Yes," Sandy said. "Oh, yes. It would be horrid but more understandable. They just wouldn't be able to marry."

"Well, thank goodness we don't have that to worry about," Wilma said, with a nervous laugh.

"No, heavens, no!" Sandy said, with an equally nervous laugh, "at least not with Eli and Liz..."

"My daughter would tell you she's too smart for that," Wilma said. "I just hope someday she finds a husband and starts a family."

"Oh, Wilma, at least she's not dating that...that hippie she was when she first came home from school," Sandy said with disgust. "He was a cook, right? What was his name? Kim? Keith?"

"I think it was Keith," Wilma replied with equal disdain, then she giggled. "I guess she was too smart for that!"

Becca heard Sandy's fading laughter as the women made their way back up the stairwell, drinks in hand.

Becca stared at the closed door, the words she heard coming out of her mother's mouth running through her brain, confirming what she already knew.

"Fast. Tramp. Disgusting. My daughter's too smart for that..."

She put a shaking hand over her mouth. No, Mom, she wasn't too smart for that. She thought she was. She thought she'd taken plenty of precautions. She'd been on the Pill, for crying out loud, but it wasn't completely foolproof.

She crossed her arms and leaned against the door again, closing her eyes. Becca was right back where she was a couple days ago when it hit her all-of-a-sudden one night at the news station after she'd been sick. She knew then that if she was pregnant, and now there was no denying she was, she would be dealing with it on her own. Her parents, especially her mother, would disown her. And even if they didn't disown her outright, her mother would make her life a living hell -- scandalized by the gossip for eternity and unleashing her disappointment on Becca every day for the rest of her life.

She was sure Liz would do what she could to help her, but her help would have its limits. Eli would be furious, and it wouldn't be long before Liz would tell her own mother what was going on. Then there was her job. Everything she'd worked so, so hard for, her burgeoning career -- it would be over, just like that. Done. A single mother did not raise a baby alone and have a career. It just didn't happen that way.

Then there was the baby's father. He wasn't in her life anymore, and she no longer had a real relationship with him. He wouldn't be of any help, even if he wanted to be, and she wasn't sure he'd even offer to help if she told him about the pregnancy. Finally, there was the fact that she just wasn't prepared to have a baby.

She felt like she was on the verge of tears every second of the day, her emotions and hormones raging wildly as she tried to come to terms with all of it. With every passing hour, she felt more isolated and more alone than she'd ever felt in her life. Ironically, she hadn't technically spent any of those moments completely alone. She looked down at her flat stomach, wondering what in the hell she was going to do when it wasn't flat anymore. What was she going to do?!

"Becca? Are you down here?" came Liz's voice outside the bathroom door.

Becca smoothed back her hair, then turned and opened the door. She gave Liz a small smile.

"Water's been choppy out here today," Liz said, a look of concern on her face. "You OK?"

"Yeah," Becca said, putting on a braver face. "Yeah, it's...seasickness has wiped me out."

"I'd say so," Liz said, reaching for her shoulder. "Come on, the fireworks are just about to start."

She followed Liz up the few steps to the deck. People were partying all around, hopping from one boat to the next parked in the river. The older Schmidts and Redds were huddled around a couple oil lamps as small flames and cigars sparkled in the darkness over their plastic-cup brandies and casual conversation.

Liz sighed and crossed her arms as she and Becca leaned against the rail, watching the first few colorful rockets launch into the air a little further down the river.

"Freedom," Liz said, shaking her head, as the show began. They watched as someone, either drunk or high a few boats over, fell into the river to the riotous laughter of their boat companions.

"That's why Eli, Joe, Jesse, and the rest of those men are fighting -- for our freedom," Liz continued sadly, "and I wonder if anyone out here could give a damn."

Becca swallowed heavily as she looked toward the fireworks lighting up the summer sky. The show started in earnest -- more blasts and louder booms -- and involuntarily, her body jumped a little, and a vibration ran right through her each time the bombs went bursting in the air.

"Fuck, fuck, fuck, fuck..." Jesse gasped as he ran back to the relative safety of the foxhole 50 yards away. He dove in, rifle and all, and ducked down. All was quiet for a few seconds. Jesse cautiously rose, his wide eyes peeking out into the morning light under his camo military hard hat, gun cocked against his shoulder.

Then a roaring in the sky louder than thunder came over his back, so low he could almost touch the chopper's runners. The second wave of hell was unleashed as the aircraft rapidly fired round after round of ammunition into the forest just north of where his unit, and two others, were stationed to patrol. The military intelligence said the Viet Cong weren't inhabiting those woods.

The intelligence was wrong.

What started out as a routine patrol turned deadly when two men in Jesse's unit were gunned down in seconds. Before Jesse could breathe, the first wave of American military helicopters flew in -- a small contingent trying to stave off their stealthy communist enemy.

Jesse fired his first shots as a U.S. Army soldier blindly into a forest, hiding behind tree after tree, reacting to what was happening around him more than anything. The instinct to just stay alive in the mayhem taking over any conscious training he had gone through. His comrades were all doing the same. Their boots had been on the ground in Vietnam for less than three weeks, and this was the first action they had seen.

His shoulder started the throb as he shot, again, way into the forest from the foxhole. Every bullet in his weapon was released with rapid force as it pounded back against him. In training, they were told they would get used to it. Eventually, that shoulder would go numb, and a man wouldn't feel the pain anymore.

After the second wave of choppers passed, the gunfire and grenades sent from the other side slowed significantly. Jesse and others in the foxhole with him fell back into the hole to reload, breathing hard and sweating profusely. The man next to him, who was with a unit that had been in 'Nam almost a year, reloaded his weapon in what looked like the blink of an eye.

"Dammit," Jesse gasped, frustrated, as he loaded his gun slower than he should have. The man next to him was already well into firing a second-round when a small wave of U.S. soldiers came out of the far side of the tree line, sprinting back to the foxhole.

Just as Jesse got his weapon loaded and turned once again to fire, a lone explosive was launched from the trees sending a half-dozen men flying, then landing about 30 yards from the hole. Jesse's heart stopped as he watched Charlie fly and land on top of the soldier in front of him.

"Charlie!" he hollered, forgetting where he was and what he was supposed to be doing, as he began to scramble up the dirt sides of his safety zone to help his friend.

"What the fuck!" growled the man next to him as he grabbed Jesse by the shirt and threw him back into the hole. "Stay down! Son-of-a-bitch!"

Covered in dirt, Jesse scrambled to his hands and knees and made another attempt to run, his wild eyes searching the ground above him through the smoke and confusion.

"Charlie! Charlie!"

"'Charlie' is fuckin' everywhere -- goddamn!" said the soldier who threw him back into the hole. "Shut up! Shut the fuck up!"

Jesse grabbed his gun with shaking hands and laid on his stomach against the dirt, peeking just above the ground once again. After that final explosion and an intense round of gunfire from the U.S. side, all was quiet again, except for the agonizing cries of men in pain. Lots of men, including Charlie.

"What the fuck is wrong with you, man?" said the veteran soldier as he turned his head ever so briefly from its position against his gun on the edge of the foxhole to shoot an angry glare at Jesse.

"I want to help Charlie...Brown, my...my...friend Charlie..." Jesse gasped, the chaos of the last 20 minutes mixing everything up in his mind.

"Recon," the man said, his eyes never leaving the target guide on his gun. "Then rescue."

After a moment, Jesse nodded and remembered his training, nestling his gun against his shoulder and assuming the same position.

"First time?" the soldier asked after a moment.

Jesse nodded once.

"Welcome to Vietnam."

———

For 10 minutes, Becca stood on the subway platform, trying to maintain her courage as she watched Penny give one ticket after another to the passengers who came to her ticket booth during the morning rush. Becca had to ride the train to a couple different destinations before she found the booth Penny was working in that day. Finally, the morning commute began to wind down. It was never slow on the NYC public transit system, but it looked like she had a moment; she just had to take it.

"Hey, Penny," she said as she approached the window. Penny gave her a big smile.

"Becca! Hey! What brings you this far out in Brooklyn?" she said, then seeing the look on Becca's face, her smile faltered. "Is there a protest out here somewhere I don't know about?"

Becca shook her head, and Penny's face fell further.

"Jesse? Eli? Joe?" she whispered, tears springing to her eyes.

Becca's own eyes filled with tears.

"No, no, I'm sorry, no, nothing like that," she quickly assured her, blinking rapidly. Penny let out a long, shaky exhale as Becca took a couple more deep breaths. Penny glanced at the annoyed customer behind her friend and quickly motioned for him to come to the window. She watched out of the corner of her eye as Becca straightened her spine and raised her head, biting her thumbnail and clearly trying to prepare for whatever she was going to tell Penny.

"Becca, what is it?" she demanded softly as the man walked away. "What's wrong?"

She looked at Penny through watery eyes and cleared her throat.

"I'm in...trouble, and I...I need your help."

"What kind of trouble?" Penny said, furrowing her brow.

Becca gulped for air again, wringing her hands in front of her.

"Female...trouble," she said, her eyes imploring Penny to understand and not have her explain anything further.

"Oh," Penny said, gasping, her face fixed in shock. "Oh...Becca..."

Her friend cleared her throat again.

"I know you...you know...people who can...can take care of my... problem," Becca said, her voice shaking.

Penny nodded and slowly made her way out of the booth, coming to stand in front of her.

"Y...yes," she confirmed, "but Becca..."

Becca shook her head quickly from side to side.

"Please, Penny, no questions," she said, taking a deep breath again as tears fell down her cheeks. "Please, I just need to know, will you...help me?"

Penny reached out and pulled Becca to her, her own eyes filling with tears and her heart breaking for her friend.

"Of course, yes," she whispered, smoothing down her shaking friend's hair. "Yes, I'll help you."

25

WHITE RABBIT

THE RAIN CONTINUED TO FALL DOWN ONE DROP AT A TIME FROM THE large leaves in the trees above as Jesse scratched his back against the bark behind him. He'd just finished cleaning his weapon, again, and was looking over at some of the other soldiers in his unit. Makeshift stools and tables were being dried off by a few of the guys after the usual afternoon downpour, which meant a game of cards was about to commence. It was the rainy season in-country, and as wet and relatively cool as it had been the last hour or so, it would be that steamy and humid in no time at all. His shift to help man the camp's perimeter later in the day would be an oppressive one.

He'd learned that being in a warzone meant a lot of "hurry up and wait." After the "skirmish" -- as his sergeant major called it -- six days earlier, his platoon was in a holding pattern, essentially waiting for their next set of orders.

Jesse closed his eyes and leaned back against the trunk behind him.

His first experience with combat had been a shock and left him momentarily rattled. Ironically, though, his life-long experience finding ways to cope in horrible situations actually helped him. He was able to regroup and not completely lose his mind in the last few days. While most of the other men seemed to be coping just as well, some of the other guys weren't so lucky. One guy was ordered to have his mouth duct-taped shut for two days because he couldn't stop screaming. Many of the soldiers couldn't sleep.

Jesse opened his eyes again and glanced over at the card game. It was a simple activity that reminded him of home, and the few times he, Eli, Joe, and Keith played poker. He smiled a sad smile, digging a stick into the mud in the ground next to him.

He'd thought a lot about Eli and Joe over the last few days, wondering if they'd seen action already. He was sure Eli was already helping save lives, but he didn't have any idea where Joe ended up. All three of them were just getting started in this new reality of theirs, and he did miss them, though he tried hard not to linger on the thought for long. He fleetingly wondered if Keith was ever drafted but thinking about him now made him angry all over again. So, he quickly banished him once again from his mind.

At the moment, he really missed Charlie, and he knew he would have to get used to that feeling -- simply adding him to the shortlist of friendly faces who briefly came in and went out of his life.

It helped that while Charlie was badly wounded, he was still alive. He actually was in relatively good spirits when Jesse visited him in the field hospital the day before. For that, at least, Jesse was grateful...

Jesse crossed his legs as he sat on the floor at the head of Charlie's bed, a smirk on his face.

"You've given a whole new meaning to the phrase 'taking it up the ass,'" he grinned, then chuckled outright as Charlie glared at him, his head resting on his crossed arms as he laid on his stomach.

"Ain't you da funny man, now, huh?" Charlie spat back. "You'd be a fright more understandin' if yous was on dis bed here, ya son-of-a-bitch..."

Jesse put up his hand, a quiet chuckle subsiding.

"I'm sorry, I'm sorry," he said, grin still on his face. "Is it bad?"

"Hell, yeah, it's bad," Charlie said, grin coming over his face now. "I got shot all up in my dumb ass."

Jesse smiled. Charlie actually had never been shot. But the explosion from the grenade behind him fired bits and pieces of metal, shell casings, stones, sticks, and other material from the ground with such force that they embedded instantly into his skin through his uniform. His back and butt were scarred with hundreds of tiny fragments, the deepest ones requiring rows and rows of stitches on his hind side. None of the injuries from that final grenade were fatal to the men close to it, but they were no less painful.

"When do you think you'll be able to sit again?" Jesse asked.

"Don' know," Charlie sighed, "but when I do, my ass is gonna be on my rocker in the shade of the ol' magnolia at home."

Jesse cocked his head, then nodded, swallowing the lump in his throat.

"You're going home?"

"You bet your sweet, smooth ass I is," Charlie replied, and Jesse grinned.

"Good for you, man," he said softly. "I'm sure...everyone will be happy to have you back."

"Feels like I's been gone too long," Charlie said wistfully, then looked a little guilty at his friend. "I knows I only just got here..."

Jesse shrugged.

"Not a man wouldn't take a ticket home overstaying here," he said.

"You talkin' about yous, too?" Charlie asked, eyeing Jesse carefully. Jesse just shrugged again, averting his eyes.

"Lis'en," Charlie finally said quietly, casting a glance around the room before his bright eyes landed on the top of Jesse's head. Jesse was looking to the ground.

"If she feelin' ya like you feelin' her," he nodded. "She be waitin' on ya, no matter when you get home."

Jesse grinned sadly at him, then slowly rose to his feet.

"Jesse?" Charlie said, trying to crane his neck to look at him. Jesse squatted down to face him, putting a hand on his arm.

"You go home and hug your girls," he said, a catch in his throat, then he nodded. "You're a good man, Charlie Brown."

Charlie nodded, too, tears in his eyes.

"So are you," he whispered, placing a hand over Jesse's and squeezing tight. "Godspeed, brotha."

Jesse nodded one more time, then stood up and walked away -- leaving the only friend he had in Vietnam behind to go home...

"Wanger!"

Jesse looked up from his spot under the tree to see the sergeant major heading in his direction. He quickly scrambled to his feet, saluting him.

"Sir, yes, sir," he said, standing at attention. The sergeant-major saluted back.

"At ease," the man said, nodding in the direction he'd just come from. "Follow me -- lieutenant wants you."

"Yes, sir," Jesse said, furrowing his brow and following behind him in the direction of the officers' tent.

Becca's eyes darted around as Penny quickly led them to a small medical office in Harlem. Penny had it from a reliable source that the...procedures done at that office were safe, despite outside appearances. Becca wanted to have it done somewhere she'd hopefully never have to see again.

"You've got your money?" Penny asked quietly.

Becca nodded, wrapping her arms tighter around herself. She was shaking, and the pit in her stomach was getting larger and larger. Making the decision to have her little "problem" taken care of had been the most difficult thing she'd ever done in her life. But actually, going through with it was proving to be much, much harder.

Her heart was pounding hard, and she felt like she was going to be sick. It didn't help that the streets were crowded, and there was an unfriendly vibe in the air. It wasn't so long ago that Columbia University's protests had set this entire area on edge, and she wondered if what she felt was lingering tension.

Or maybe it was just the weight of her own heartbreak causing her to be filled with anxiety -- she wasn't sure. Still, all the people milling about in the Harlem business district this late in the day caught her off guard and made her even more nervous. Several sets of eyes landed on her and Penny as they made their way down the sidewalk. She wished more than anything that she was invisible. It felt like all the eyes on her were judging her.

Penny glanced at her friend, a worried look on her face. Except for asking for her help, Becca hadn't said much of anything else about the situation. She could tell by the look on her friend's face and her pensive body language that she was nervous. She also suspected Becca wasn't 100-percent sure of her decision to terminate the pregnancy. Penny was sure the baby's father had something to do with her hesitation. As much as Penny could no longer stand the sight of Keith, she did think he had a right to know Becca was expecting his child.

They finally stopped in front of a nondescript, one-story white building with a small alley running its length to a larger alley in the back.

"Becca," Penny said, facing her and placing a hand on her arm. "I hate to ask, but does...does...Keith know about...it?"

Becca, who had been staring at the building trying to find her courage, snapped her head around and stared at Penny, momentarily startled. She hesitated a moment before answering.

"No," she said. "It's none of his business."

Penny nodded.

"I understand why you feel that way," Penny said. "I do, I really do, but don't you think..."

"It's none of his business, Penny," she said more forcefully, tears stinging her eyes. "He...he has nothing to do with this. It's on me. It's no one else's...decision. It's...it's mine."

Penny nodded her head quickly, more worried about Becca's physical state than anything else at that moment. Her face was drawn, and her watery eyes looked scared.

"OK, OK," she said, rubbing her arm. "Becca, are you sure?"

Becca just nodded, taking a deep breath. Penny's heart was pounding as fast as Becca's as they walked toward the back alleyway. She couldn't shake the feeling that something was terribly wrong.

"I promise we can leave if..." Penny started as she came to the back-door entrance.

Breathing rapidly, Becca just shook her head again.

"Penny," she said, "Just..."

She gestured to the door. Sighing, Penny pulled hard to open the door, which was initially stuck. It led to a small, sparse hallway. Suddenly, a man wearing a lab coat appeared out a side doorway.

"What do you need?" he said, somewhat breathlessly as a woman who looked to be a nurse came out of the same side door.

"We need," Penny said. "My friend is in...trouble. She needs..."

"A riot's about to break out in the neighborhood, and you want help now?" he said tersely, shooting a somewhat incredulous look in Becca's direction.

The nurse stepped forward and took Becca's hand, which was shaking.

"Come with me, dear," she said sympathetically. With a backward glance at Penny, Becca followed the nurse into a small room.

"Wait here," the nurse said as she gave Becca a sad smile and closed the door. Before it shut, Becca heard Penny tell the doctor, "she can pay in cash..."

Becca stumbled back toward the exam table, swallowing the vomit that had risen in her throat. She glanced at medical instruments she didn't recognize on the tiny table next to her. She felt a wave of disgust come over her as she started to hyperventilate.

Suddenly a shadow passed outside the window's curtain in the room, closed against the bright yellow glow of the late afternoon sun. Someone was hollering angrily, and not too far away, she heard similar voices answering in kind.

She put a hand on her heaving chest and squeezed her eyes closed, her head beginning to spin -- only one question whirling around and searching for clarity in her confused mind:

What in the hell was she doing?

26

TELL ME WHY

Becca leaned against the wall as the voices outside the window grew louder. She put her hands protectively over her stomach as she continued to hyperventilate.

"He'll do one more," Penny said as she flew into the room, breathless. "We have to beat feet...once...it's...over, you dig?"

In a haze, Becca took in the nightmare around her. A fast, illegal abortion in the middle of a protest under the most questionable conditions. She'd been ready; she'd thought it necessary -- the only realistic option she had.

"Becca," Penny said as she grabbed her arms, trying to make her focus, feeling for certain that her friend was about ready to pass out. "Can you do that?!"

Slowly Becca started to shake her head as tears stung her eyes.

"I can't...I can't do it," she cried, grabbing onto Penny's arms and hanging her head. "I can't get...rrr-rid of his baby."

"But...who cares about Keith?" Penny said, trying not to panic and be supportive, forcing Becca to look at her, "He's a pathetic drug addict --

I don't care what he says about 'finding Jesus'. He left you! Like you said before, this is on you! You. Do you want this baby?"

Becca took a ragged breath before whispering fiercely through her tears.

"It's not *his*," she spat out the word like she had a nasty taste in her mouth.

"What?" Penny said quickly, completely in shock. "What do you mean 'it's not his'? Whose is it?!"

Becca lifted her tear-stained face to Penny, her eyes begging for forgiveness.

"It's Jesse's," she cried in a high-pitched voice, almost like a plea -- almost like she was asking for permission from...someone, anyone to say it was OK to want this baby. "It's Jesse's...the baby is Jesse's, and I... I want it! I want his baby!"

Penny just stared at her for a moment, trying to come to grips with what she'd just heard, her mind reeling. Suddenly she pulled Becca tight to her as her friend went to pieces on her shoulder.

Jesse's baby?! Penny had a million questions for her, but right now, all she heard was shouting and yelling and anger growing outside. She knew she had to get Becca as far away from this place as possible.

"Move," she said, pushing Becca towards the door. "We gotta get outta here. Now!"

"I'm so sorry," Becca cried, fumbling with the doorknob.

"Just go!"

Penny pulled Becca's hand as they hurried down the hallway toward the back door of the building, the doctor barely casting a glance in their direction as they ran past his office. Penny threw her body against the stuck exit door, and it flew open, slamming against the building. There were a few scary-looking stragglers in the back alley, but most of the protesters were on the main street out front.

Becca looked wide-eyed between the buildings from the alley toward the sidewalk. She'd seen this scene at work, countless times on film, at the bus depot the day he left, but right now, it was completely terrifying. The crowd had grown significantly, and it was hostile -- angry faces, homemade signs, photos of the president burning in effigy, everyone looking a half-second from pummeling the person next to them.

It was its own kind of warzone, and it was happening somewhere every night. Tonight, it was on the block of a rundown business district in Harlem.

Penny suddenly switched directions, and they slowed their pace just a touch, marching determinedly toward the subway by Columbia. Silent tears were falling from Becca's eyes -- she felt scared and disgusted with herself, and at the same time, relieved as her breathing began to even out. Penny's senses, however, were all on alert. They needed to make it to the train station before darkness completely fell. Those who heard about the riot would come looking for trouble for no other reason than they wanted to find it.

They kept their heads down, and except for two homeless vets asking for money, they were left alone.

Finally, they boarded a dirty, old subway train and started their journey back to Greenwich Village.

Becca closed her eyes and put her head in her hands, elbows spiking into her knees. She alternated between crossing her arms over her stomach and smacking her palms on her thighs.

"Stop," Penny said, grabbing her hands. "Stop it."

"Oh God," Becca moaned, so angry at herself she couldn't stand it.

"You didn't..." Penny started, her voice catching. "You're still going to have his...Jesse's...kid."

"How..." she asked, searching Penny's face, her own eyes wild and heartbroken. "How could I...even...think..."

"You're scared," Penny said, tears in her eyes, "and alone, but you're not alone, Becca. I'll be here."

"To support the baby killer's baby?" she shot back at her, then instantly she regretted it. "Oh, oh, I'm so sorry, I didn't mean that I..."

Penny cursed to herself. Until that moment, she didn't realize that while she was protesting war with blinders on, she was also shooting down the people she loved who just happened to be in the crossfire.

"To support my friend," she said softly, "and my...brother. He's like a brother and...and he...deserves to...live...somehow...if...if he..."

Becca watched as Penny began to break down. She wrapped her arms around her, and the two women held each other, crying as they made their way back home.

"Where have you been?!" Liz said worriedly as she bounced off the beaded chair in the living room when Becca and Penny walked back into the apartment.

"I'm sorry," Becca mumbled, glancing at her roommate.

"Don't sweat it, I...I was just worried, it's late..." Liz started, then stopped, noticing that both Becca and Penny looked like they'd been crying.

"What's wrong?" she asked shakily, fear creeping into her heart. While he had been at medical training in California, Eli had called her every day and written letters every week. She had only received one letter from him in the last month since he'd been shipped out to

Vietnam. Anxiety had become her constant companion now -- anxiety for all of them.

"What happened?" she said again, voice trembling.

"Everything's OK," Penny quickly assured her as they all three sat down on the sofa. "But..."

Becca put up her hand to stop Penny from saying any more, then she looked at Liz and swallowed a couple times heavily.

"I'm...I'm pregnant, Lizzy," she whispered.

"Oh," Liz gasped, briefly looking Becca up and down. "Oh my God, Becca..."

Suddenly she pulled Becca to her and held her close, finally understanding why Becca had been so out-of-sorts the last couple of months. Liz knew she was worried about her brother and Joe. But it was obvious to her that her friend's biggest heartbreak was missing the man she'd fallen in love with right before they all left for the army.

Becca hugged Liz, surprised at her friend's reaction to the news, then pulled back, preparing to take on the barrage of questions she knew would follow about the father.

"Oh, Becca," Liz whispered, tears in her eyes and a small, sad smile playing on her lips. "You're so...lucky you get to keep a part of him with you...always."

Becca looked at her, confused, and Penny was taken aback. Liz's face softened.

"I know it's Jesse's baby," Liz said quietly. "It is, isn't it?"

Becca stared at her in shock and nodded slowly.

"But...how did you know?" she asked, her voice thick.

Liz blushed a little.

"I...I saw him leaving your bedroom the morning the guys reported for their physicals," Liz explained. "I assumed you were...saying... goodbye to each other. I...I didn't want to say anything at the time..."

A fresh batch of tears stung Becca's eyes. Her heart took her back to that night -- remembering how perfectly they'd come together in that all-consuming way that had overwhelmed her -- the night the ache for him began and, despite everything, had never gone away.

"Why didn't you tell me?" Liz asked quietly, glancing at Penny and wondering why she knew Becca was pregnant first.

Becca searched Liz's face. She could see the hurt in her best friend's eyes and understood it. They'd always told each other everything, and Becca hadn't been able to tell her about Jesse or the baby. She honestly didn't know what to say or how to explain it to her when she was so unsure about her own feelings.

But now, she had to try to explain it somehow.

"I...I wasn't sure I...wanted to...keep the baby," Becca whispered miserably.

"What?" Liz exclaimed. "Why wouldn't you want to have Jesse's baby? The circumstances aren't...ideal, and...and your mom will wig--out, but..."

Suddenly she gasped.

"Becca, you weren't going to...you weren't thinking of..." she asked. Becca closed her eyes and dropped her head. Liz looked to Penny, who pursed her lips but gave no response.

"What were you thinking...I mean, it's illegal and...and so dangerous," Liz said, her voice rising. She'd heard horror stories from her father about women who had their pregnancies "taken care of" by butchers in back alleys. It sent a shiver down her spine.

"I...I don't understand, Bec," Liz said, confused. "The way you...feel about him. I don't know why...how could you even think of...not having his baby?"

"Because, Liz," Becca said, her barely controlled demeanor finally snapping apart as she began to shake. "Because he told me to forget about him! He told me to 'turn off' any feelings I had for him. He...he kicked me out of his apartment like, like nothing ever happened between us!"

Becca was breathing hard now as tears fell down her cheeks. Liz shot a sad, confused look at Penny, but the look on her face was just as bewildered.

"What?!" Liz asked breathlessly. "What are you talking about?"

"His apartment?" Penny asked, looking to Liz, "but I thought you just said..."

"We were...together the night before he left for basic," Becca said brokenly, "and...and he told me in no uncertain terms to forget him. He kept saying...he kept saying he wasn't coming home, and I just needed to move on."

"Oh no," Penny moaned, not completely surprised but becoming increasingly pissed off at Jesse with each passing minute.

"He said we...we were just a fantasy," Becca whispered, vividly reliving the pain of that moment in her heart. She took a ragged breath. "But...but it felt real. It was real...so real."

"Oh my God, I can't believe..." Liz said, her eyes filling with tears. "Oh, oh, Becca, no wonder you...I...I never would have thought...what a jerk!"

"He's not a jerk," Penny sighed quietly, shaking her head in disbelief.

"Look, I know he's your friend and all, but he makes Keith look like a saint!" Liz shot back at her.

"He's not. He's really not a jerk," Penny said adamantly, two sets of unconvinced eyes boring into her. "He...he acted like a jerk. He acted like an ass, but that's not...that's not who he is..."

"Then tell me, Penny, tell me!" Becca demanded, fiercely wiping at her tears and looking Penny straight in the eye. "Whose baby am I carrying?! Who? The man who...who was so...cold and threw me out of his bed and told me to forget him or...or..."

She paused and took another deep breath. Tears were forming in Penny's eyes as hers met Liz's, who glared back at her while quickly sniffing back her own tears.

"Or the man who was my...my friend, who made me feel...safe...who made me feel...oh," Becca whispered brokenly, dropping her head briefly and losing her battle to reign in her emotions, "who...I...I can't stop thinking about. His eyes...I can't get his...his face the...the morning he...left out of my head. I can't! I want to hate him. I want to hate him...but I...I can't!"

A sob tore from her throat as she put a hand to her mouth. Liz and Penny were unable to find any words themselves as they watched Becca completely meltdown in front of them. Liz was in shock. She'd never seen Becca like this before, and it completely broke her heart.

"How? How am I sss-supposed to fff-forget him now?" Becca whispered in broken hiccups. "I don't want to forget him! I want to have this baby. I want to have him...oh, God, I could swear...I could swear he cared about me..."

"Becca. Becca!" Penny said in earnest, taking her friend's hands in hers. "Of course, he did. He does!"

Penny shook her head in disgust.

"Damn you, Jesse!" she whispered, with tears in her angry voice.

"How do you know?!" Becca demanded. "How do you know how he feels? You didn't even know we were together..."

"I know," Penny answered hotly. "I know because this is what he does!"

"What?!" Liz spoke up now, incredulous. "Why?! Why would he treat Becca like...like...that if he really cared about her? That doesn't make sense..."

"It does to him," Penny said quietly. Then she sighed and looked at Becca's confused and heartbroken face.

"How?!" Liz said, her features filled with skepticism.

Becca squeezed Penny's hands, hanging on to any hope of an explanation she could as she cocked her head to the side.

"Explain how it would make sense to him," Becca said softly, desperately. "Please, Penny. I want so much for any of it to make sense. Please..."

After hesitating just a fraction more, Penny nodded and took a deep breath, knowing she needed to tell Becca why Jesse acted the way he did, why he pushed her away, why he thought he was protecting her from a broken heart, and not giving her one.

"I've known Jesse since he was 13," she started quietly, a tear escaping the corner of her eye as she remembered the scared, sad, skinny boy with a heart of gold she met all those years ago. She closed her eyes briefly, then lifted her head and cleared the lump in her throat.

"OK," she finally said, looking at the curious faces in front of her. "I'll...I'll tell you everything I know."

27

RIVER DEEP, MOUNTAIN HIGH

PENNY SIGHED, NOT SURE WHERE TO BEGIN. BECCA'S EYES WERE BEGGING her to say something, anything. Liz's were looking at her with thinly veiled doubt that anything she could say would make Jesse any less of an asshole.

"I grew up with my grandmother in a...a slum, really, an...an apartment building on the outskirts of the Village," Penny recalled softly. "It was a...a hole, but it was our hole, and my Grandma tried to make it as comfortable as she could. We...she worked hard as a, a seamstress, but we didn't have much. I...my parents died a long time ago...I don't remember them."

Becca reached out her hand for Penny, and she gratefully took it.

"All...kinds of people lived in that...place," Penny shuddered. "We kept to ourselves most of the time."

She swallowed hard as she continued.

"Jesse and his...his father moved into the unit down the hall during my first year of high school," she said. "At first, I didn't even know the man who moved in had a kid. Like I said, we kept to ourselves..."

She paused and closed her eyes, trying to keep her voice as even as she could.

"I...I would see this skinny little kid when I walked home from school, but I didn't know he lived in our building," she said. "He used to draw pictures and numbers with a stick in the dirt outside. I'd see him every day after school. At first, he would never look at me. Finally, after days of me saying 'hi' to him, he finally looked at me. The next day, he smiled a little."

Penny cleared her throat. Becca's eyes had already filled with tears as she pictured Jesse as that sad little boy.

"Anyway," Penny continued, her voice thick, "for a couple months, that apartment was quiet. Then...then the 'parties' started. They were always loud, and so many different people came and went at...at all times."

"In the apartment Jesse lived in?" Becca asked quietly, making sure not to miss one detail. Penny nodded.

"The only reason I knew Jesse lived there was because when it...when the parties were...were out of control, I would see him...he would curl up and try to sleep on the filthy floor in the hallway next to the door."

"Oh my God," Liz said, stunned.

Penny's eyes filled with tears.

"I tried to talk my grandmother into letting him sleep on our couch, but she didn't think it was 'right' to get involved or have a strange boy sleep on our couch," she said, shaking her head. "Until..."

Penny took a deep, ragged breath, and Liz took her other hand.

"That April, one of the boys from school followed me home," Penny said shakily. "My grandmother wasn't there, and he...he chased me into the apartment."

"Oh, Penny," Becca whispered.

"He pushed me against the couch," she said, beginning to cry. "I remember...I remember my books flying across the room...I was screaming..."

Penny looked down. Becca glanced at Liz over her shoulder; both had tears in their eyes.

"Next thing I knew, that skinny boy playing in the dirt had dragged this boy off me," Penny whispered. "He was easily twice his size, but he...Jesse was strong. He, he beat on him pretty good, but the boy was so much bigger...he really roughed Jesse up. But he left and never... never followed me again. I...I remember giving Jesse a washcloth to put on his bleeding lip, and he finally told me his name and that... that day was his birthday. My...my grandmother let him sleep on the couch sometimes after that..."

"Just like Keith," Liz whispered quietly to herself, but Becca heard her.

"What?" she asked, turning to her, confused. "What do you mean 'just like Keith?'"

Liz's eyes were as big as saucers. Eli told her about his encounter with Keith a few months back but swore her to secrecy. To hell with that, she thought.

"Eli went to track Keith down after that...that party where you two broke up," Liz explained. "When he found him at Vanhook's, he said Keith was terrified. Keith told him Jesse had...had packed all his stuff in bags and was waiting for him when he came back to our building that night. He...evidently he, Jesse, scared the crap out of him, threw him in a cab and sent him to his parents in Hoboken..."

"What?" Becca whispered miserably, her face fixed in confused surprise.

"Eli said Keith told him that Jesse ordered him to stay away from you and get help or else," Liz said, smoothing Becca's hair as her friend looked at her with tears in her eyes. "I'd forgotten all that until just now. I'm so sorry, Becca..."

"That sounds just like him," Penny interrupted quietly, nodding. "I'm sure he did just that, but as Keith's friend, he didn't just kick him out. He made sure he had a place to go. Jesse was scared to death for you that night, Becca, I remember. The party you guys were going to sounded too...familiar to him."

Becca just stared at Penny, then at Liz, who just shook her head. Her heart was pounding behind her ears, trying to take in everything Penny said about Jesse, remembering how he rescued her that night. She squeezed her eyes closed.

Penny once again began to tell them what she knew, slowly piecing together Jesse's background -- how eventually Jesse told her that his father had shown up one day at his grandmother's farmhouse in Canada and told him he was taking him to New York. She told them how he'd heard his intoxicated mother screaming that he was more of a "hindrance" than a "help" anyway, and she wasn't sorry to see him go. His father promised him a better life, but it didn't take long for Jesse to learn he'd lied. His father was a frustrated performer and started throwing those drug-fueled sex parties at his apartment to impress people he was sure would help his "career." It was clear he wanted a slave, not a son.

"Jesse told me he would hide in the closet during those parties, and then...then when the closet was...needed...he'd move to the hall," Penny said. Liz handed Becca a tissue as both wiped at their eyes, in shock over what Penny was telling them.

"He was so quiet back then," Penny said, how Jesse acted then being very vivid in her memory. "He hardly talked at all. He...it was like... like pulling teeth to get him to just speak sometimes."

She cleared her throat again.

"But here's the thing you need to know about Jesse," Penny said, looking them both in the eye. "After every...party, he would...clean up everything the best he could. He'd...he'd do everything possible to try to...he'd do what he could to help his...his father, who was always a...a mess after. He has...he has this, something ingrained in him that drives him to do...to take care of everyone...and I think, I know that's what he was trying to do with you in his...way, Becca..."

She took a deep breath again and shook her head, trying to make sure she told the whole story as best she could and not skip anything.

"He started high school that fall because the authorities found out he was 14 and not in school and made his father send him," she said. "It was his escape. For a few hours every day, he got to be a normal kid. And...and he is a whiz at math. Very smart...too smart....

"Anyway, when he was 16, his worthless father decided it was time for them to move again to Las Vegas," Penny said bitterly, remembering the screaming that had come from that apartment over those couple days before his father left for Nevada. "Jesse refused. I can't...I can't tell you the things that man said to him. 'Worthless, ungrateful bastard' were a couple of the tamer things, but Jesse stood his ground and just didn't go. His father disowned him, and...and that was that."

"You mean he, he's been on his own since he was 16?" Becca asked, her heart breaking with every new revelation about Jesse's past. Penny cracked a sad, sad smile.

"He's really been alone his whole life, Becca," she whispered. Becca swallowed hard.

"He worked his ass off, though, to keep that crappy apartment," Penny continued. "He did maintenance work in the building at night and at a couple subway stations close by. He did everything he could, and he started, well, he started coming into his own."

"How do you mean?" Liz asked.

"He started to open up a little, smile a little, he was free," Penny said, wiping her tears. "And...and when my grandmother died, he was there. I...when she died, what little money we had was gone. He even, he even got me an interview with the transit authority, and I...I got the job I have today because of him. Then I got a better apartment.

He got a job at the Pipefitters Union and met Joe. He loves Joe like a brother, and they just, they clicked from the start."

She wiped her eyes one more time, pride for her friend evident in her voice as she continued.

"He was so smart. He graduated high school despite everything and went to college," she said. "He got money from the school and earned an associate degree in accounting. And, and he grew up."

She laughed a little.

"He got taller and better looking," she said, smirking. "I used to tease him all the time that his eyes could stop a robin midflight. She'd think one of her eggs was missing from her nest and poke him in the eye with her beak to get it back."

Becca smiled through her tears, her heart feeling so heavy she thought it would burst. Liz giggled a little.

"Oh, he never thought he was much," Penny sighed quietly, then she looked at Becca. "He's never thought he deserved anything, and I...I know, never in a million years did he expect to meet someone like you. I know he doesn't feel like he's good enough for you, no matter how good he is, and I know it scares him to care, really show he cares about...anyone."

Becca crossed her arms over her stomach, a deep, aching pain written all over her face.

"Becca," Penny started brokenly, taking both her hands. "I can tell you that whatever Jesse did, he did to protect you, not to hurt you. That's what he thought he was doing, anyway. He...he used to say that his time on this Earth was short, and I think, when he was drafted, he felt that way again. And he didn't want to go back to the past. Most of all, and I know this is true, he didn't want to give you some sort of false hope that he was coming home. He...he would be the first one to sacrifice himself..."

Her voice caught, and she couldn't say any more. Becca reached out of her, tears streaming down her face. Liz reached for more tissues, keeping a couple for herself, and embraced them both.

After several minutes of muffled sniffles and soft crying, Penny leaned back from their hug and placed her palms on either side of Becca's tear-stained face.

"That's that man who is the father of your child," she whispered in a voice laced with tears, smiling a little at her. "Honest to God, Becca. He is a good man."

"Bec...how are you?" Liz asked quietly as she climbed out the window to check on her friend, whose eyes were fixed somewhere seemingly far away as she looked out over the city from her spot on the fire escape. Just a touch of pink was making its way onto the horizon as sunrise crept up over New York. Becca barely flinched at the question. The tears still swimming in her eyes for the last hour or so since Penny left for work casting sparkles in the dark dawn light.

Liz sighed.

"I've never heard such a sad story in my life," she continued softly, shaking her head and looking east. "How...how could someone treat their child like that?"

"I don't know," Becca finally said, her voice raspy and thick with tears, her arms resuming their now usual place across her belly. Twenty-four hours ago, the little person growing inside of her hardly seemed real or human -- or rather, she didn't want to think of it that way. She wasn't thinking of "it" as a person at all. But now...

She shuddered as a powerful rush of adrenaline raced through her -- an unbelievably protective vibe that came from deep inside her soul. Becca's eyes clouded over as she pushed the thought of the clinic and what she'd almost done as far out of her mind as possible.

Because now...now she'd lay down her life for his baby. For their baby. She was so afraid to think of it as a "baby" before -- Jesse had hurt her, and the thought of having an enduring reminder of him had been hard to swallow. She had those moments of deep doubt that she so deeply regretted now -- when she seriously wondered if he would even care if she was having his baby and its effect on her entire life.

But in the long hours of the night, as they sat and listened to Penny tell the heartbreaking story of Jesse's childhood -- how he took care of everyone and no one took care of him -- it all became so clear to her that she could scarcely believe she never saw it before.

He'd spent his life always tucked away in the shadows, quietly taking care of his Mom, Dad, then Penny, then Keith, even Joe, then...her. And if he knew she was carrying their child, there was no longer a doubt in her mind he'd move heaven and earth to take care of them if he could. He would do no less, and neither would she. She'd spent the last hour swearing to herself that she would make up for what she almost did the night before. She would do everything possible to have a healthy baby and raise a happy child, no matter the circumstances of the world they would grow up in.

"It is a miracle he's such a, ya know, decent man," Liz said, shaking her head again, bringing Becca out of her reverie. "I would think most people growing up like...like that would...be...so broken..."

"He is broken," Becca said fiercely, the protective feeling inside her spreading to the rapidly growing space Jesse was reclaiming in her heart. She looked at Liz, tears finally once again streaming down her face. "He's so, so broken. He's so broken, Liz, that he's...he's spent his whole adult life...No! His whole life trying to make sure no one he cared about fell apart. And...and if they did, he...he put them back together, even if they hurt him so, so deeply anyway. That's his heart...that's...I just know it is. That's why he didn't apply for a deferment. That's why he didn't run to Canada. He...he couldn't and...and he felt like he'd be letting down Eli and...and Joe, especially Joe, by not being over there. I mean, my God, that's why he was...why he pushed me away. It was...ah...his misguided way of protecting me from being hurt, from harm, from him...from...from caring about him...caring if he ever came home! Ahh..."

She pushed the palms of her hands against her eyes and took a ragged breath, then swayed just a bit, feeling dizzy and seeing stars. Liz grabbed onto her with concern.

"I'm fine," she said dismissively, trying to control her tears and her breathing. She gripped Liz's arms. The look of alarm on her face made her friend panic.

"Becca...what is it? What?!" Liz said, looking her up and down.

Becca closed her eyes and concentrated on her breathing. In, out, in, out. She finally raised her eyes to her friend.

"I have to tell him," she continued quietly, a glimmer of hope lighting up her face. "I'll...I'll write to him. I can...I can track down his address -- his unit. I...I have a...a whole team of reporters at CBS that can track it down."

The glimmer turned into a genuine smile, something Liz hadn't seen in a long time.

"He'll make it home," she continued, trying hard to convince herself as much as Liz. "He has to live to...to see his baby and then...then...if he'll let me..."

She put her hand over her mouth, then balled it into a fist and looked resolutely at her confused friend. Her blue eyes reflected the sunrise and shining with determination.

"I'll make him let me...I..."

"Let you do what?" Liz asked, at a loss and somewhat taken aback by the sheer force of will that she'd seen radiate this strongly from Becca only a few times in her life.

Becca turned her gaze from Liz and searched the sky, looking off to the east, above the sun, and into whatever of the remaining stars were left on the horizon. The stars that were making their way to Jesse thousands of miles away.

She turned again to her friend, with joy and certainty in her heart she had never felt before. Her eyes were so bright and so full that Liz felt her own eyes well up with tears. Becca took both her friend's hands in hers and held them tight, raising them to her heart. Then she smiled.

"Love him," she said, her voice thick but her smile widening. "I just want to love him, Liz. He's going to let me love him. We're going to love him, the baby, and me, and make up for all he's never had...

"We're just going to love him."

28

MAKE THE WORLD GO AWAY

LATE AUGUST 1968

Becca hurried down the sidewalk toward her building, the blazing summer sun rising steam off the pavement under her heels. Thankfully, her morning sickness had started to taper off as the dog days of summer drug on. She was beginning to feel more energetic with each day that passed. It was especially welcome this week when her alarm went off at 4 a.m. for work.

Part of her newfound energy, she knew, came from Jesse -- or at the very least the hope of hearing from Jesse -- any day now. Maybe even today, she hoped. She prayed.

After she had made up her mind that she was going to tell Jesse about the baby -- tell him why he had to do everything in his power to live through his tour and come home -- she had cautiously approached her boss, Ms. Beele, about how she could find the address for a particular soldier in a particular unit. She didn't say anything about her own baby, already wary of repercussions at work once her pregnancy was found out. Instead, she said the information was for a friend's mother who had a son who didn't tell his family where to send his mail. She gave Ms. Beele Jesse's name, and within a day, she had his address in hand.

She'd written him a short, one-page letter. She wanted to write every thought, every feeling, everything she'd been going through, but she didn't want to overwhelm him with too much. It had taken her three days to edit her letter down to one page, trying to write what she hoped were all the right things to say to him when he wasn't expecting to hear from her at all. She knew the news of her carrying his child would be a complete shock, and she wanted, in some way, to ease him into everything she was planning for them when he came home.

Because her mind had been working overtime, planning for their future -- a future she knew full-well may never come to pass, but she planned it anyway. She planned her heart out. She thought about the look on his face when he came home when he saw their baby. She had romantic fantasies of a proposal, a home to call their own, more babies, things she long ago dreamed of having someday, once her career was well established -- once she found the right man.

As she started to feel better and actually feel pregnant, Becca had gradually allowed herself to feel every ounce of love for him she had so strongly held back for so long behind a dam of hurt, fear, and devastation.

After that night with Penny and Liz, where she'd learned the reasons behind his behavior, that dam had burst and left her drowning in a sea of want, need, devotion and understanding.

Now when she remembered the night before he left, she forgot the cold sound of his voice and the harsh words he'd said, those things she had concentrated so hard on in her quest to hate then eventually forget him. Instead, she focused on what she hadn't wanted to remember -- the things that before were too painful and confusing to remember. But now, she held onto it with all her might. She remembered the tears in his eyes, the strain in his voice the last time they said any words to one another. In her mind, now his words weren't angry; they were desperate, sad, the words of a man trying to reign in his own heart and shield hers by letting her go and live a life without him.

She'd re-lived their last kiss over and over in her head so many times she was convinced she could still feel it on her lips. A man didn't kiss the breath out of a woman he didn't love.

She felt with her whole being that she was meant to find him in the middle of the confusion of Grand Central Station that day he left for Georgia. Her heart was on her sleeve then, and so was his. He'd studied her just as she'd studied him -- with pain, with worry, with adoration but most of all with love. That was the look on his face that day, the look of love. She knew that now.

Becca was certain she'd found the right man, all that had to go right was absolutely everything else in the insane world around them. She'd convinced herself of his affection, and nothing could change her mind. She refused to think otherwise or lose hope, even as days turned into weeks, and weeks had now turned into more than a month since she sent her letter, her heart, to Vietnam.

She hadn't heard a word back from him, and rationally she knew there were terrifying reasons why she had yet to hear back from him. She refused to think of any of them. Instead, she chose one reason and one reason only -- holding onto it tight like a kite in the wind.

The mail could be notoriously slow. Liz had bemoaned more than once that it took too long for Eli to receive her letters and for him to respond. Still, the longest Liz had ever waited between letters from her brother was three weeks. But Eli was stationed at a main military base, not in the infantry like Jesse. It made sense that the mail would take longer to reach an often on-the-move unit.

So, with as much patience as she could muster, she waited.

She finally opened the door to her building, only to be met with a blast of hot, stuffy air and a nod from one of her neighbors checking the mailbox next to hers. She fiddled impatiently with the keys in her hand as it seemed to take forever for the man to close his box and make way for her to open her own. Becca wiped her brow and smoothed down her kne--length skirt as he finally walked away. She put her mail key up to the slot and then promptly dropped it to the floor. Her hands were shaking. She bent down with a groan, picked up the key again, and opened the little door.

Mixed in with their other mail were two letters -- one for Liz and one for her -- both from Eli.

She moaned as she riffled through the envelopes one more time, coming to the same conclusion as she had the first time.

There was nothing from Jesse.

"Hi, Becca," Liz said behind her. Becca turned to her with a frown on her face, and Liz smiled sadly at her. "Not today, huh?"

"Not today," Becca said with a heavy sigh. "What are you doing home so early?"

"Oh, the air conditioning wasn't working at the office, and after the second secretary passed out at her desk this afternoon from the oppressive heat on the 20th floor, they told everyone to go home," she said with a flip of her hand," for all the good it'll do me here."

Becca smirked at her then handed her Eli's letter.

"We did get two letters from Eli," she said. "One for me and one of you."

"Oh," Liz said, reaching for the letter Becca was holding out for her. She laughed nervously and bit her lip. "Well, ah, that's something, huh?"

"Yeah," Becca said, smiling a little.

Liz looked at the letter, then at Becca. She cleared her throat and dropped the letter into her purse.

"Why don't we go get a drink, or dinner, somewhere that's air-conditioned," she suggested. "It's, ah, it's not good for you and, and the baby too, ah, be in this heat. It should cool down a little tonight... besides, it's Friday..."

"What about your letter?" Becca asked, raising her eyebrows. Liz usually tore those letters open right away.

"Oh, don't sweat it," Liz said, linking her arm through Becca's and leading her back outside. "I'll read it later."

Becca shot her another confused look but put the rest of their mail in her purse, her arm still linked with Liz's. They took a couple steps in the direction of an air-conditioned diner a half-dozen or so blocks away.

"Becca?"

"Yeah?"

"When, um, when we get home later, let's, ah, let's read our letters together then, OK?" Liz said.

"Um, OK," Becca said slowly. "But why?"

"Oh, it'll just be fun," Liz said nervously. "OK? Deal?"

"Sure," Becca agreed, terribly curious as to what could possibly be in those letters.

Jesse watched as mud flew off the tires of the canopied truck he was sitting in, being jostled around on rough roads paved with nothing but deep mud holes.

His meeting with the lieutenant the month before had completely changed his situation. At the meeting, he was told that he had scored in the 99th-percentile on the mathematics intelligence test he took when he reported for duty out of all the men in the armed services. After meeting with a couple more officers and following a series of what seemed to be unrelated questions, he was told to wait outside the officers' tent while they conferred. After cooling his heels for more than two hours, he was informed he would be transferred away from his unit. He would be promoted to sergeant in the next few days and be ordered to report to the main U.S. base in South Vietnam near Saigon, Tan Son Nhut, where he would be assigned to the Army Corps of Engineers -- more than likely as a surveyor.

It took almost three weeks, though, before he actually left his unit and made his way south to his new assignment. With Charlie gone home, saying goodbye to his fellow soldiers wasn't as hard as it could have been. It was a hazardous journey from the middle of Vietnam, where he had been to the base in the south, but he was floored when he finally arrived on the base. It was still a warzone, but it was more like a little city. Hundreds, if not thousands, of men were stationed there. It housed the highest levels of communications, combat operations, military police, and medical personnel In Country.

The U.S. had a stronghold in that particular region. While every soldier was still on high alert, the atmosphere had just a tad more of a relaxed feeling to it than anything else he'd been accustomed to so far in Vietnam. All branches of the armed forces used this base -- it was a hub for aircraft, tanks, artillery, and everything in-between.

Jesse was on his way back from a day of learning the tricks of the surveying trade and more about how the Army Corps of Engineers "cleared the way" for the infantry. Once his training was complete, and he was assigned to a particular unit with the engineering corps, he'd be headed back to the front lines.

Soon the truck passed through the security checkpoints and came to a stop in the same place his day had begun, not far from the large military hospital on the base. Several men, both U.S. soldiers and South Vietnamese allies, were milling about or quickly walking to and fro outside the hospital. Several medical personnel were gathering by the chopper pad behind it. Jesse knew that meant incoming wounded weren't far behind.

He strapped his weapon over his back and looked around. He was off duty for the evening and began walking back to his temporary quarters when a familiar figure coming out of the hospital caught his eye, and he stopped dead in his tracks.

Eli.

In his group, the other men passed him by as he continued to stand still and stare in Eli's direction. He was almost sure it was him. Had to be him. A smile broke across his face as he quickly made his way toward his friend, who was looking down and walking away from the hospital.

"Eli!" he shouted out, almost jogging now and waving toward him. "Eli Schmidt!"

The man turned around to see who was shouting his name and froze when he saw Jesse Wanger hurrying toward him. Of all the people in the world, Eli couldn't believe it was him.

Eli's face broke into a smile of its own for a brief moment before he remembered he wanted to pummel the man coming towards him for getting his little sister pregnant.

Jesse stood before him in a flash, then saluted him, seeing Eli was now a Second Lieutenant. Both men had changed some in appearance -- a little thinner in some areas, a little more toned and muscular in others due to their training.

Eli felt a conflicting range of emotions as he saluted back to Jesse. But despite the anger boiling up inside of him, Eli pulled him in for a hug. He was happy to see him alive.

"Hey, man," Jesse said with a smile, patting Eli on the back. Eli patted him back and then quickly pulled away, swallowing hard.

"What are you doing here?" he asked, a thin smile on his face as he folded his hands in front of him once again. Jesse watched Eli's friendly demeanor change into polite inquisitiveness, and he cleared his throat, explaining the circumstances that brought him to Tan Son Nhut.

"I've been here a little over a week," he said, finishing up his story. "Have you been stationed here the whole time?"

"Yeah, yep," Eli said, becoming increasingly incredulous that Jesse hadn't mentioned Becca or the baby.

"So, what do you do on your downtime here?" Jesse said, clapping him on the shoulder. "There's only so many games of solitaire a man can play, you dig?"

He was almost giddy to see Eli. He was grateful he was alive and well, and oh, so anxious to hear any news at all about Becca. He wasn't going to ask because he figured it might kill him if Eli told him she was with someone new. She was still so alive in his memory, moving fluidly in and out of his everyday thoughts that he was almost certain his heart couldn't handle hearing that. Yet he did want more than anything just to know she was OK, that she was living her life, that she had moved on just fine. He'd told himself all along that that alone would be enough, just to somehow know she was happy.

After he asked the question, Eli's cold stare caused Jesse to step back from him in confusion.

"I cannot believe you are just standing here, making small talk with me," Eli said evenly, after a moment, trying to keep his temper in check.

"What...what are you talking about?"

"You aren't even going to ask?" Eli said indigent. "What? You don't give a shit?!"

"About what?" Jesse asked, his heart speeding up.

"About what?!" Eli said, his temper now on full display. "About Becca! About..."

"What?!" Jesse demanded, feeling like his heart was beating out of his chest. "What about Becca? What? Is she...is she OK?"

Eli was turning several shades of red and so angry that he didn't answer right away, causing Jesse to grab his shoulders -- completely terrified.

"What?!" he shouted at him. "What? What happened to her? Eli?!"

"She's pregnant!" Eli said as clearly as he could through clenched teeth.

Jesse felt all the blood drain from his face as he stared at Becca's brother, his heart in a puddle on the ground. He gasped and stumbled back, feeling like Eli had just punched him in the gut. She was...pregnant. Pregnant?

Well...that was fast, he thought bitterly, then just as quickly chastised himself for it. Isn't that exactly what he wanted her to do -- to move on from him and get on with her life? A new life, with a new guy and now a baby on the way. Some...other...man's...baby. He took a deep breath.

"Nnn-neat. Well, ah, congratulations on...on being an uncle, Eli," Jesse said quietly, averting his eyes, his heart feeling like it was shredding in two. "I'm...I'm happy for...her. It was, ah, good to see you. I...I guess I better..."

He didn't finish as he moved to walk away, trying to turn his devastated face away from his friend.

Eli grabbed his arm, and Jesse looked at him then. Eli was taken aback by the tears swimming in Jesse's eyes. He swallowed hard. Oh my God, he thought, is it really possible he had no idea?

"Jesse," he said, trying to keep his own emotions in check, "she's pregnant with *your* baby."

With those words, all the activity around them got lost in the vacuum of Jesse's mind, and for a moment, he didn't move, then he suddenly jerked his arm out of Eli's grasp. He blinked a couple times, his mouth moving but no sound coming out, and he was white as a ghost. Eli studied him closely.

"Wh...what?" he whispered, his mouth dry, his heart hammering in his ears. "What did you say?"

"Liz...Liz said Becca...wrote you to, to tell you, I...I thought you knew," Eli said, beginning to feel sorry for Jesse, despite being completely pissed off at him. "That was...it was more than a month ago..."

Jesse swayed a little, then shook his head, trying to absorb anything Eli was telling him. She was pregnant? With his baby? With *his* baby?!

"I can't...I...no! That's not, I mean...no!" Jesse said in disbelief, putting a hand to his forehead, his head spinning. Then he whispered, desperately. "She is...she is, you mean, she's going to have a...a baby... my baby?"

"Yeah," Eli said, glaring at him with his hands on his hips. "You mean...you really didn't know?!"

"Fuck! No, Eli, I didn't know! How in the hell...? She didn't...I didn't get a letter! There was no letter! Fuck!" he turned away, angry with Eli, but oh, so much angrier with himself. If it was true, if this was true...Oh. My. God.

He hunched over and put his hands over his face, letting out a loud groan. He'd left her alone, confused, heartbroken, thinking all along he was doing the right thing by making her hate him, making it easier for her to want to forget she ever knew him.

And all along, he'd left her pregnant -- carrying his child and making it harder, if not impossible, for her to do any of that.

"Oh my God, oh my God..." Jesse gasped. "I...I have to see that letter Eli, the one from Liz! I want to see it right now!"

Eli winced and looked away.

"I don't have it anymore," he said, digging his boot into the dirt. "I was...well, I was really angry and I...I kinda took it out on the letter..."

"Jesus!" Jesse exclaimed, throwing his hands up and lacing his fingers behind his head, then he looked at Eli and took a deep breath, moving his hands to his hips. "You...you should be pissed. You should hate me. I'd...if I were you, I'd flatten me..."

"I wanted to about five minutes ago," Eli conceded.

Jesse put his hands over his face again, peeking at Eli above his fingertips. He could feel the blood as it pulsed through his veins, hearing nothing but his heartbeat in his ears. His eyes were wide, and he was suddenly desperate to talk to her. Desperate to know if she was OK. Desperate to know if the baby was OK.

Desperate to tell her he was sorry. So sorry. So very sorry. For everything.

"I have to...I have to...what? Write to her? Write her a...a letter?! Write...what? What?!" he said. Eli's anger was all but gone now as he watched Jesse pace in front of him, worry for his little sister evident in every fiber of the man's being.

"I want to...dammit! I want to talk to her. Tell her...I, God, I just wish I could talk to her...dammit!" Jesse said in a hoarse whisper, his mind and heart still reeling from what Eli had just told him, still not wholly believing it could possibly be true. He needed to hear it from her. Where in the hell was that letter?!

Eli glanced in the direction of the expansive officers' tent across the yard, then back at Jesse. What he was thinking was a long shot, but not unprecedented. And maybe, just maybe, they'd get lucky.

"I might know a way to do that," he said quietly. Jesse's head shot up.

"How?!"

Eli nodded toward the officers' tent.

"Follow me..."

29

THE GLORY OF LOVE

"Private Eugene!"

A man with short blond hair jumped out of his chair behind his desk, saluting the higher-ranking men as they approached him.

"Yes, sir!"

"At ease," Eli said, trying not to sound too nervous and glancing at the door just beyond Eugene's desk. "Is, ah, is Major Thomas in?"

"No, sir, but I expect him back soon."

"OK," Eli said, glancing back at Jesse. "We have an emergency, and we...we need you to patch a call through to the States. To New York."

The man's eyes bugged out of his head.

"Sir, I...I can't...I can't do that..."

"Listen, it's...it's an emergency," Eli said, gesturing to Jesse. "In...in regards to the Sergeant's baby."

"But sir..."

"It's...that's an order..." Eli started as Jesse stepped forward.

"If you can, man, please...call New York," Jesse said, breathlessly, pointing at the phone on the Private's desk.

"It's highly unusual..." Eugene said as Eli and Jesse both stepped closer to him, barely contained emotion radiating from each of them as they seemed to tower over him.

"Just do it," Eli said evenly. "Now."

Private Eugene sank slowly back onto his chair and picked up the phone.

"Morning, Becca," Liz said tentatively as Becca walked out of the bathroom. Her friend glared at her.

"I'm still not talking to you."

"Becca, come on, he's my fiancé..."

"He's my brother!" Becca shot back. "Did you really think...he shouldn't have known I was pregnant until after the baby was born!"

"I'm sorry..." Liz mumbled.

"Not as sorry as I'll be when he writes my mother!" Becca said miserably, sinking down on the couch, crossing her arms and her legs.

"I told him not to, I swear, Becca!" Liz said, sitting down across from her. Becca rolled her eyes just as Penny walked in the door.

"Hey!"

They both half waved, half grunted at her. She shrugged and reached into the refrigerator for some orange juice.

"I swear, I just thought you could use some...some extra support, that's all," Liz continued, imploring Becca to forgive her.

"What's going on?" Penny asked, walking over to them.

"Oh, nothing, just my friend here decided to write to my brother and tell him I'm pregnant," Becca said, waving her hand at Liz, then adding sarcastically. "The letters we received from him yesterday seem to indicate that he's just thrilled."

"What?!" Penny said, looking at Liz. "Why, why would you do that?"

Liz looked back at her, exasperated.

"I promise, Bec, I promise I won't say another word to anyone, OK? I swear, I promise," she said. Becca just stared at her, unconvinced, as the phone started to ring in the apartment.

"He...he probably has other things on his mind, Becca," Penny offered quietly as Liz moved to answer it. Becca relented a little and sighed, knowing Penny was right.

"Hello?" Liz said, then she put her hand over her other ear.

"I'm sorry, I can barely hear you. The connection is bad...oh!" Liz gasped suddenly, putting her hand over her mouth.

"Eli?! Eli, is that you?" she yelled into the phone, tears in her eyes.

Becca turned and grabbed the back of the couch, tears springing to her eyes as well. Oh my God, she thought, Eli! For a brief moment, she wondered if he called to yell at her for being pregnant, and in that same moment, she didn't care if that was exactly why he called. He was alive and talking to Liz right now, and that's all that mattered.

"No! Oh my God, oh my God, are you serious?" Liz squeaked out, turning her eyes to Becca. "Yes, yes, of course. Yes. Oh, I love you too, I love you so much, I love you..."

Penny and Becca stared at Liz, hearts pounding and breathless.

"Yes...she's right here," Liz was in tears now as she began to hand the phone receiver to Becca, her hands shaking.

"He wants to talk to me?" Becca asked, and Liz shook her head and took a deep breath.

"He's...he's with...Jesse," she whispered through her tears. "Jesse wants to talk to you."

Becca gasped and clutched a hand to her pounding heart, exchanging a startled look with Penny. She looked back at Liz, taking the receiver out of her shaking hand and holding it in her own.

Her whole body began to quiver as she put the phone to her ear.

"J...Jesse?" she said so quietly, Penny and Liz could barely hear her. She cleared her throat as tears pooled on her lashes.

"Jesse?!" she said loudly and clearly.

Jesse's sweaty palms were gripping the phone in Vietnam so tightly it almost slipped out of his hand. He put two hands on it to steady it, and himself, the sound of her voice sending adrenaline racing through his body.

"You're having my baby?!" he asked loudly over the static on the line. "Becca!"

A sob tore out of her at the sound of his voice. She took a harsh breath, trying to stop herself from collapsing into a mess of tears on the couch.

"I...Jesse..." she responded loudly, her voice trembling along with the rest of her.

"You're having my baby!?"

"Yes," she yelled back, tears spilling from her eyes as Liz took her hand.

Jesse fell back against the Private's desk, hand to his forehead, eyes squeezed shut. Eli observed him closely, a pensive look on his face, his heart breaking for them both.

"Jesse..." came Becca's distant voice. She was squeezing Liz's hand hard, watery eyes darting around the room, yet seeing nothing. "I...I am. Liz and Penny are...helping me. No one knows but you and Eli. I'm not...I'm not asking for anything...I just, I wanted you to know... did you...did you get my letter?"

"No," Jesse said, shaking hand still on his forehead. "No, Eli...Eli just told me."

Becca looked at Liz and mouthed, "Oh my God," shaking her head and gasping for air.

Jesse looked at Eli, his eyes rimmed red as he heard quiet sobs on the other end of the line. He was on the verge of tears himself, trying to control his breathing.

"Are...you...OK?" he finally asked, closing his eyes again, his heart thumping against his chest.

Becca closed her eyes, relaxing a little as she got her emotions a touch under control. She let out a shaky exhale.

"Yes," she smiled just a little bit. "Yes, I'm OK. Everything is...OK."

Jesse took a couple ragged breaths.

"Good," he said, his heart thundering as the news he'd just confirmed -- and the woman who confirmed it -- started to take over every little space in his mind and his heart.

Becca...Becca was really having his baby.

Eli looked out into the makeshift hall and saw Major Thomas slowly walking back to his office, stopping to talk to someone else along the way.

"Jesse..." Eli said, casting a nervous glance his way.

"Sir, you have to hang up. Now," said a very jittery Private Eugene.

Jesse put an arm out to stave him off and pulled away from the desk, cupping the phone cradled in his hand and moving it with him.

"Sir!" Eugene said again as Eli grabbed the Private's arm. Jesse ignored them both. He wasn't ready to hang up -- not yet.

"Becca, Becca," Jesse said quickly, desperately wanting her to know how he felt but not having a clue what to say.

"Jesse?" she cried desperately. She took her hand away from Liz's and placed it over her stomach. "Don't go..."

"I gotta," he said, then swallowed the lump in his throat as it came to him. He grimaced, thinking of that night. Thinking of how he'd wanted to push her away -- and how now, oh, now he'd give anything to hold her, to protect her, to be with her.

"Becca," he breathed, his voice thick as he looked down, knowing he'd have to slam the phone down in seconds.

"I can't...turn it off. I can't turn it off!"

On the other side of the world, she threw her head back and briefly put her palm over her mouth. Then she took a deep breath, feeling closer to him than she ever had before.

Feeling his love move in her soul.

"Oh, it doesn't work that way," she said with a watery chuckle.

He grinned through the otherwise tortured expression on his face.

"No, it doesn't," he said, slamming the bottom of the phone into his thigh while clutching the receiver in his other hand. "I'm sorry. I'm so sorry..."

"I'm not," she said, shaking her head. "To know...that our...we... created a baby out of...us. I'm not sorry...I'm not sorry, Jesse..."

"I should be there...I should take care of you...I shoulda taken you to...to Canada. I..."

Then he glanced over his shoulder to see a now panicked Eli and Eugene motioning for him to hang up the phone.

"Jesse?!"

"Becca, I have to...they're telling me to hang up..."

"I love you, Jesse," she said, firmly, loudly, so he would be sure to hear. "I love our baby...I'll protect him; I promise..."

Jesse's heart slammed against his chest as tears finally spilled from his eyes. Had he just heard what he thought he had? He took a deep breath -- and that's when the phone went dead.

He jerked his head towards Private Eugene and saw the man holding up the end of the wire he'd unplugged from the outlet.

"You asshole!" Jesse growled, livid, slamming the dead receiver back onto its cradle and walking menacingly over to Eugene.

"Jesse...Jesse!" Becca sobbed over the dead phone line. "Jesse!"

Penny took the phone from her and placed it back in the cradle as Liz, tears streaming down her face, pulled her friend to her.

"Shhh, it's alright, it's alright, honey," she said, rocking her gently from side to side and stroking her hair. "They're alive. They're both alive, and he knows...Jesse knows..."

Becca sobbed louder, her head still spinning with the sound of his voice, whirling around the caring tone in his words. He couldn't turn it off. He wanted to be with her. He wanted to take care of her. All the thoughts she had of him, all these plans she felt foolish making for their future, he wanted them, too. He wanted her.

He was still alive, and relief she didn't realize was bottled up tight inside her started to roll through her bones. He was alive, and if he could, she knew he'd be there to help her and their baby. Thank God she'd come to her senses and kept their growing child tucked safely inside of her. If she would have...oh, the guilt alone would have killed her.

"Do you really love him?" Penny suddenly asked quietly, earnestly, tears on her cheeks. Becca slowly pulled away from Liz and wiped her eyes with her palms, looking at Penny. She gave her a sad smile and a gentle nod.

"Yes," she choked out. "Yes, I do. I know...I know after...everything that's...happened, it doesn't make a lot of sense, but I can't help it, I do. I do."

Penny closed her eyes and took a deep breath. She let it out slowly and studied Becca. Then she smiled through her tears.

"I hope he heard you," she said, her voice shaking. "I don't know if...if anyone's ever said that to him. I...I should have a long time ago. I hope he heard...that."

Becca grabbed Penny's hand, a new batch of tears stinging her eyes, and pulled her into their hug.

"Jesse," Eli said, stepping between him and the Private, who was clearly all kinds of scared to death. Jesse tried to move past Becca's brother, but he stopped him. "Jesse, no! We're lucky we were able to make that call. Stop!"

Jesse looked quickly between Eli and Eugene, who shakily bent down to plug in the phone once again. His eyes searched Eli's face as he slammed the phone back down on the desk.

"Stop," Eli whispered to him. Finally, Jesse nodded and mumbled "thank you" to the Private. He wiped his eyes just as Major Thomas walked into his office.

All three men quickly stood at attention, saluting the man who outranked them.

"At ease," the officer said, clearly confused. "Can I help you, gentlemen?"

"Just, ah..." Eli said quickly. "Just came by to say 'hello' to an old friend."

He nodded at Eugene, who, after a tense, frozen moment, nodded back.

The officer surveyed each of the men, then dismissed Jesse and Eli, telling Eugene that he needed him to patch through a call to Washington, D.C.

All three saluted again, then Jesse and Eli turned on their heels and walked out.

They didn't speak as they hurriedly strode out of the officers' tent. Once outside, Eli started to motion in the direction of his barracks. But Jesse was turning his head rapidly from side to side and quickly walked over to the trees about 100 feet away. Eli followed him.

Jesse put one palm against the nearest tree he came to and hunched over, staring fiercely at the ground but not really seeing anything. He heard Eli come to a stop behind him, despite the sound of his heartbeat pounding in his ears.

Eli looked at the ground, too, putting his hands in his pockets, then up at Jesse's back as the man took a few deep breaths...in and out. The sun was blazing hot, so Eli moved over to the shade in a feeble attempt to fight off the heat. Jesse glanced sideways at him.

"I'm sorry, Eli," he said quietly. He took a step toward the tree and slowly ran his palm down the trunk, then turned to face Becca's brother.

"If I had any idea this was going to...happen, I would've, would've," he said in halted speech. "I would take care of her. I would have...found a...a way to stay and take care of her. I *will* take care of her."

Eli swallowed hard a couple times, remembering how protective Jesse was of Becca, almost since the moment they'd met. And he was truly shocked at his own naiveté -- never once thinking Jesse and Becca would have consummated the feelings between them before he left. He didn't like to think of his sister that way, but she was a grown woman, and Jesse was a grown man, and their attraction had been undeniable and obvious from the start.

Eli crossed his arms and sighed.

"I believe you," he said evenly. Jesse looked a little surprised at that, but then he nodded and looked to the ground.

"She...she said she's feeling OK," he said. Eli nodded again, relieved. Jesse leaned back heavily against the tree, his eyes seemingly fixed on the horizon.

"She said she loves me," Jesse said quietly, shaking his head in disbelief. It was one thing to think he saw love in her eyes before he left; it was another thing entirely for him to hear it from her lips.

Eli moved a little closer to him, shuffling dirt under his boot as he did so. Jesse searched his friend's face in confusion as if trying to find some trace of affirmation there.

"If she said she loves you, then she does," Eli said quietly. "She loves you."

Jesse nodded as his eyes filled with tears, then he shook his head again, still in shock over...everything.

"Why? Why does she love me?"

Despite himself, Eli smirked just a bit.

"Of that, I'm sure I don't know," he said. Jesse gave him a sad, little grin, then he took a deep breath. They were both quiet for a couple moments, each looking out over the horizon line now as the wind whistled through the leaves above and soldiers milled about all around them at the headquarters.

"I thought I'd be dead by now," Jesse said suddenly, in a matter-of-fact voice, causing Eli to whip his head around to look at him. He was still leaning against the tree, hands behind his lower back, looking at the sky.

"I never expected to live this long," he continued quietly. "I never had a reason to want to. I used to wonder why I was. Alive, I mean. Why was I living? Then, well, there's Penny...she saved me back then, really. She's like, who I imagined a sister would be like. Then...then I met Joe...even Keith, and I started to think...maybe...there was a different...way to live. Maybe my life didn't have to be the...the shithole it always had been, and I started to think...and then...then Liz moved in and because of...you, I met...her. I met Becca and... and...Becca...now she..."

His voice started filling with the pressure of unshed tears, and he looked to Eli with watery eyes. He cleared his throat a couple times.

Eli swallowed heavily, not sure exactly what Jesse was trying to say. But knowing the man had obviously been through some seriously difficult stuff in his life before they met. He turned his head away, wondering if he should stay or go.

"Can you...would you give me..." Jesse finally asked in barely a whisper.

"Sure," Eli said gently, nodding and patting him once on the shoulder. "You know where..."

Jesse just nodded and jerked away from him, turning the other way and leaning heavily against the tree trunk. Eli turned and walked several paces before he stopped and glanced back. He watched as

Jesse's shoulders started to shake, his body wracked with sobs that Eli could hear bits and pieces of on the breeze. Then he watched him slowly slide down the side of the tree and tuck his knees to his chest, his whole body shaking. Eli turned then, giving him the privacy he craved, and walked determinedly back to his quarters, tears streaming down his own face as he cursed the unfairness of it all -- the unfairness of love in war.

30

UNCHAINED MELODY

September 1968

Jesse:

Thank you for opening this letter.

I know I'm not supposed to write to you. You told me to forget you. I guess you wanted to forget me, and maybe you already have. If you've read this far, though, maybe not?

Now, you can rip this letter to shreds after you read it and forget me again, but it's important you read it. You need to know the reasons why I'm not going to forget you. When you left for basic training, I was determined to move on, to put you in my past. I can tell you right now, writing this today, that it won't happen.

I have to say this much -- I truly believe in my heart if you and I had been allowed the luxury of time, we would be together, and we would be very happy. I never felt with anyone what I felt with you. What I still feel, how I still ache, for you.

I want to remember the "us" that was taking shape before you were drafted and all the complications that came after the war took you away from me, even before you physically left New York. You should know you took a part of me with you when you left, even if your last words were harsh ones. I don't say this to guilt you or hurt you; I'm plainly stating the truth. Even if the last words we spoke to each other weren't warm, the look in your eyes the day you left was warm, at least I believe it was. I felt you as a part of me then, and I feel it now. You really are a part of me, Jesse, in more ways than one. You might not want to believe that, but it's the truth, especially now.

I know there is very little you can control there, but I'm writing to say you need to do everything you can to come home when your tour is over. There is someone who will want to meet you, and I hope you will want to meet them. Jesse, I'm pregnant. I never imagined I would be, I was on the Pill when we were together, but I am. The baby definitely is not Keith's. The baby is yours.

I am not asking for anything, nor do I expect anything from you. If you want to tear up this letter and pretend we never happened, I will find a way to accept that, and I will move on. I only wanted you to know who will be waiting for you when you come home if you want us to be waiting.

If not, then I will thank you now, in all honesty, for leaving me with a beautiful, lasting memory of us and what we could have been. It's not going to be easy, but I'll do all I can to give them the world. I promise.

I've gone through many emotions since I realized I was going to have our baby, Jesse. A lot of emotions. In the end, though, I want you to know there is nothing in the past or anything in the future that could make me hate you or wish I wasn't having your child.

Finally, if you really don't want anything to do with me or the baby, I will forgive you. I want you to know that. I know at your core, you were in pain when we were together. Honestly, we both were looking for comfort, and if nothing else, found that in each other.

If this is my last contact with you, I need you to know that I did care then, I do care about you now, and no matter what happens, that will never change.

Always, Becca

Jesse blinked once, then calmly refolded Becca's letter and placed it back in his breast pocket, where he'd carried it the last 11 days. It had finally caught up with him at the Tan Son Nhut base three days after he'd talked to her. Three days after he'd learned she was pregnant with his baby.

Three days after she said she loved him.

He'd read her words so often he didn't actually need to unfold the single--page letter again. He'd memorized every line, marveling each time at the courage it must have taken for her to write to him in the first place.

She'd given him an out -- told him he could walk away without leaving any hatred in her heart or any guilt on his soul. She wrote with no malice, no spite. The words came from her heart, and he knew she meant them. He knew she loved him. She must, he reasoned, because he certainly had given her no reason to want to hold onto him when he left.

He'd been so determined to make her go on with her life without him, so sure that was the best thing for her, that he never allowed himself to think of an alternative. He'd wanted her so badly, needed her so much before he left for Vietnam that it had never once crossed his mind that she could have gotten pregnant. And not only had he been determined to push her away, but he'd also been a complete asshole about it, leaving her alone, pregnant, and yet...and yet, he knew even if he never spoke to her again, she would still love their son or daughter, period. He was only left to wonder what kind of person had that kind of strength? But he knew. She did.

He'd heard it underneath the soft sobs and behind her elevated voice on the telephone. God, what it was like to hear her voice again... and, of course, there was the letter. A letter she'd composed knowing only the pain he'd left her with, but still, there it was in black and white in her own words, in her beautiful, even script.

In one page, she'd put any doubt he'd ever had in his mind to rest. Yes, she cared about him. Yes, she ached for him, though he couldn't conceive that it was as much as he ached for her. She said she was happy, *happy,* that she was having his baby, despite having absolutely every reason not to be. She promised to protect their child and give them "the world," calming his inner anxiety about replicating an unhappy childhood. She would do all this, with or without him. Yet, she wanted to be with him.

Jesse patted his pocket one more time and took a deep breath, letting it out slowly. He looked up at the night sky, crossing his arms over his bent knees as he sat alone on the ground outside his barracks. It was his last night at the base. Tomorrow he would be escorted back to the front by a couple men dispatched from the Army Corps of Engineers due to report to the base in the morning.

He had a whole different feeling in his gut as he headed to the front this time. Before he was willing to accept the inevitable, he'd do his job. He'd do it the best he could but really didn't care a whole lot whether he lived or was killed in action. Two weeks ago, his heart and his mind had undergone a total reversal from that way of thinking.

She wanted him to live, she wanted him to come back to her, to them, but at the same time, she understood that he might not. She was a realist, and she understood what he was up against, how he couldn't promise her he'd come home at all. She'd pushed all the right buttons, said all the right things, and at times he just couldn't understand how Becca knew exactly what to say to calm his mind and settle his soul.

Now, he couldn't wait for his damn tour to be over so he could go home to her. She was carrying his baby and his heart and was so honest in her letter that he had no choice but to be honest in return. He didn't have to hold back, try to 'turn it off,' keep her alive in only a memory anymore. It was freeing and frightening at the very same time.

If he was standing in front of her, he wasn't sure he'd know how to handle so much emotion, so much love. He'd never felt anything like it before. But being thousands of miles away, through the "protection" of a letter, he felt safe enough to empty his heart. He felt buoyed enough to bare his soul to her, holding on to her words of love like a life preserver.

He remembered gazing at her exhausted, sleeping form the morning after their first night together, knowing she'd given everything she had to him. He didn't know then just how much she'd given, how much she was willing to sacrifice, how deep her feelings really were for him. He did now, he believed wholeheartedly, and he was determined to give her no less in return.

If he was going to die in Vietnam, he wouldn't die without her knowing how he loved her. He wasn't going to die without giving something to his unborn child, even if it was only a few words on a faded piece of paper letting the little person know his old man loved him from the moment he knew he existed. That was more, he figured, than he'd ever gotten from his parents. Still, he knew it wasn't enough, not nearly enough. Yet at this moment, at this time in this place, it was all he could do.

So, he'd started writing, and he wrote until his fingertips were calloused, his heart exploding. A few times, some stray tears smudged the paper so much he'd have to start again, and he did. He hid a small flashlight under his covers. Turning it off now and again if anyone so much as stirred close to him and kept writing. He stayed awake and wrote and re-wrote all night, picturing her face in front of his eyes. Picturing him being the one to make her happy. Hoping what he was writing to her was enough.

He finally gave the letter over to be sent back to the States more than a week ago. He watched it all the way into the mail depot on the base, all the way back into the area marked 'outgoing,' silently willing it to make it to its destination. Four days ago, he'd sent another envelope.

He hoped she'd know he meant it when he told her he would take care of her.

Jesse turned his head towards his barracks and let out another sigh before pushing himself up off the damp ground and slowly making his way back into his quarters. Before lifting the flap on his tent, he caught sight of the moon hanging low against the nearby trees' broad, sparkling leaves. It cast a blue glow over the water drops, which reminded him of the tears in her eyes the last time he saw her. His breath caught, and he dropped the flap and took a couple steps toward the moon.

His watery eyes ran back and forth over the leaves. He didn't know what the next day would bring. He could only hope what he'd done, what he'd said in his letter, was really enough for now.

Jesse looked back at the bright lunar surface in the sky, and as he had every night for the last two weeks, he closed his eyes and whispered to her in the relative silence. He knew it was foolish to think it, but in some way, somehow, he hoped her heart would hear him...

"I love you," he breathed. Then he smiled. After a moment, he opened his eyes and turned toward his tent, finally making his way inside.

31

(REACH OUT) I'LL BE THERE

"Sergeant Wanger," came the voice behind Jesse as he stood with his knapsack on his back just outside the officers' tent, preparing to meet the men from the Army Corps of Engineers.

Jesse turned and saluted Eli with a smile.

"Lt. Schmidt," he nodded. Eli smirked at him as he saluted back.

"That's Uncle Lt. Schmidt to you soldier," he said, with a wink. Jesse chuckled and shook his head. He'd only seen Eli a handful of times since that memorable day they'd initially run into each other on base, both headed in different directions most of the time.

They didn't speak directly about Jesse's breakdown after he'd found out about Becca's pregnancy. Eli never asked, and Jesse never offered. But Eli had made it clear that he would support his sister, thereby Jesse. Eli knew Jesse really loved Becca and wasn't about to argue with that even if he wanted to. And he didn't want to. More immediate realities were facing each of them every day as it was.

"It's like grand central around here," Eli said, trying to break the awkward silence that seemed to fall between them and trying to stave off saying "goodbye."

"I noticed," Jesse agreed, casting a glance around the headquarters. There seemed to be more of everybody on base today -- both civilians and military personnel.

Eli shrugged.

"Guess it's expected when the big brass comes to pay a visit," he surmised. Jesse nodded in agreement. For the last few days, the base had been a buzz of excitement preparing for U.S. General Crieghton Abrams' arrival.

"You'll miss all the pomp and circumstance, huh?" Eli asked. "Headed back north today?"

"Yeah," Jesse said with a serious tenor to his voice.

Eli nodded and crossed his arms, then he cleared his throat. Jesse gave him a downward frown and nodded back.

"I don't want to see you back here, you hear me?" Eli said with a catch in his throat.

Jesse knew what he meant. Eli didn't want to see him back on base as a patient at the military hospital. Jesse swallowed hard.

"I'll do my best, Sir," he said with a little grin. "I have every intention of getting home to them in one piece."

Eli nodded again.

"Good," he said, with a little grin of his own, then he pulled Jesse in for a hug. Jesse hugged him in return and patted his back.

"Well, I'll be damned," Eli said suddenly, with surprise, looking behind Jesse. Then he added with a smile. "As I live and breathe..."

"What?" Jesse said with confusion as he turned around.

He broke into a big smile of his own as the two men from the engineering corps approached them with Major Thomas at their side.

"Why, it's Joseph Frano Ambrosio!" Jesse exclaimed as he and Eli raised their arms in salute.

Joe, who had the same Sergeant rank as Jesse, saluted Eli with a big grin on his face.

"I understand you gentlemen need no introduction?" Major Thomas said with a smile, gesturing from Joe to Eli and Jesse. "Accompanying Sergeant Ambrosio is Corporal Barry Byrd."

Eli and Jesse both shook hands with Corporal Byrd.

"They'll conduct your briefing and escort you to your new assignment with the Corps, Sergeant Wanger," Major Thomas nodded. "Godspeed."

"Thank you, Sir," Jesse said as all the men saluted the Major. He saluted back and walked away into the officer's tent.

Jesse and Joe looked at each other a moment before pulling one another into a big bear hug. Eli couldn't stop smiling. Barry just seemed amused.

"Man, it is good to see you," Joe whispered fiercely, hugging Jesse tight. Jesse hugged him just as hard.

"Likewise, man, likewise," he said, a crack in his voice as he patted Joe on the shoulder. They stepped back. Eli stuck his hand out to Joe, who took it but pulled him into a partial hug as well.

"This is unbelievable," Joe said, stepping back from Eli. "Have you guys been stationed together here the whole time?"

"I've been here," Eli said, pointing to his chest.

"I was assigned here for corps training about a month ago," Jesse said.

For a few minutes, Joe, Jesse, and Eli exchanged information about where they had been In Country as Barry looked on. All of them found the experience somewhat surreal. It almost felt normal, like they were just catching each other up on their everyday lives.

Suddenly Eli's head shot up, and in the distance, he could see several helicopters making their way toward the base. His shift at the hospital started in less than an hour. It was time to get a head start.

"Incoming," he said, with a nod to the sky. He turned to Joe.

"Stay safe, man," he said, patting him on the shoulder. He nodded to the Corporal, then turned to Jesse, not sure what to say. Jesse swallowed the lump in his throat and pushed his hands into his pockets. Eli unexpectedly felt his eyes fill with tears as he walked to him. Jesse gave him a small smile.

"You too, Wanger," he whispered. "You've got a lot to live for."

"Yes, Sir," he said quietly, looking Eli in the eye. With one last nod, Eli turned from them all and started to jog toward the hospital.

Jesse watched him for a few moments as Joe studied Jesse, curious about the exchange between him and Eli.

Finally, Jesse turned and smiled at Joe and Barry.

"So, are you ready to head to your new home?" Joe asked, dismissing his curiosity for the moment.

"Yes," Jesse said quickly, trying to concentrate on the fact that Joe was going to be there, too, and not on the fact that they were traveling to one of the deadliest regions of the country.

"OK," Joe said, with a nod to Barry, who took off toward the vehicle in which they were going to make their journey.

"Glad to have you in the engineering corps, man," Joe said, slapping Jesse on the back as they followed the Corporal.

"I'm just glad to see you," Jesse said sincerely, casting a sideways glance at his best friend. "Happy you're still around."

"You, too, man," Joe said firmly, but unbeknownst to Jesse, he swallowed hard. He'd seen a lot of destruction and death already, and, truth be told, he wasn't thrilled when he'd learned the surprising news that Jesse was the new Sergeant coming to his unit. He decided right then wasn't the time to go into the details as to why Jesse was assigned to his unit.

He'd learn soon enough that the Sergeant who he was replacing was killed, along with five other men, when their group was ambushed while trying to build a supply bridge over a swollen river in treacherous terrain at the beginning of the rainy season. Joe had barely escaped injury himself. Where they were headed, the Viet Cong were almost everywhere, and Joe really wished his friend wasn't going to be a part of it.

On the other hand, he thought, at least he'd know if Jesse was alive.

Joe looked at his friend as they walked along and noticed a calm look on his features and the almost spring in his step. He seemed more... settled than Joe literally had ever seen him.

Either war really agreed with him, which Joe doubted, or something else had caused this change in his demeanor.

They came to a stop in front of the vehicle. Barry jumped up and climbed inside in one, smooth motion. Jesse raised his eyebrows at Joe with a smirk and climbed in after him.

"Let's get it on," Joe said with a brave smile to Jesse, pulling himself up as Barry started the engine.

Becca took the steps two at a time up to her apartment, heels be damned. Once safely inside, she kicked them off, the letters she held shaking in her trembling hands. She quickly looked around. No sign of Liz yet. The sun was hanging low in the late September sky as she climbed out the window and onto the fire escape to read her precious mail.

Two letters! He'd sent her two letters. She backed up into a small, aluminum lawn chair, reaching behind her to guide her body into it, not taking her eyes off his handwriting on the envelopes. She hadn't even opened them yet, and tears were already streaming down her cheeks. She hadn't heard from him since the miraculous day he'd called her nearly four weeks prior when she'd heard his voice and felt his love flow through her. He didn't get a chance to say the words to her, but she felt it just the same. She knew it as well as she knew her own name. He loved and wanted her, and definitively knowing that only served to broaden her seemingly endless spirit.

She'd felt for weeks now like she was floating on clouds, despite the storms on the horizon. She'd have to tell her parents about the baby, and soon, and she'd have to start wearing more loose-fitting blouses to work. Not one of her skirts really fit her anymore, either. Her tiny little baby had started growing by the day, it seemed, and she wasn't going to be able to hide her pregnancy much longer. She wished she didn't have to hide it. She wanted the whole city to know she was going to have the most beautiful baby in the country come the first of February.

She took a deep breath, her heart in her ears, as she tore open the thinner of the two envelopes. Then she frowned for a moment as she studied its contents. It was a paycheck from the U.S. Treasury, made out to Jesse Wanger but signed over to her. She gasped and put a hand over her mouth, realizing what he'd done.

He'd signed over every dime he earned in Vietnam to her.

"Oh, Jesse, no," she whispered, her eyes watery as she opened the small, enclosed note...

B,

I figured since you are "on the nest," we might need a little "nest egg."

These will come directly to you in your name from now on. Don't worry about me. I have all I need.

I promise to take care of you, both.

J

Becca looked at the check again and sucked in her breath, trying to take in everything those couple sentences meant. He was planning for their future. He was trusting her with his income and was acting more like a...a husband than a man who had just had a major life-altering event thrust upon him unexpectedly. He was being responsible, and, somehow, that made perfect sense to her.

Hadn't Penny told her he'd always put others' well-being before his own? Hadn't she come to her own conclusion that he'd always taken care of everyone around him, whether they deserved it or not? Hadn't she seen that side of him in action before? This was just more proof that he really was the man she had dreamed he would actually turn out to be.

Oh, her baby couldn't have a better father...

She shuddered as she felt his protective warmth wrap around her, wrapped around them, in the glow of the evening sun. Even from so far away, she could feel him right beside her. She closed her eyes, lifting her face into the golden sunlight, a grin gracing her lips. Then her eyes popped open, and she looked down at her stomach.

"Oh!" she cried out, then she felt it again. "Oh...oh!"

She started to giggle, putting her hand over her bump. It felt like a feather was brushing the sides of her stomach in the very middle of her belly, first one side, then the other. It was as if there was a little goldfish inside of her, brushing their tailfin just hard enough against the fishbowl inside that she would know they were there.

The baby was moving around, and for the first time, she could feel it.

"What is this? What is this?" she whispered, a smile on her face, a new batch of tears lining her lashes. "You feel him too, don't you? That's from your Daddy. He loves us, you know that? Huh? He really does. He really loves us..."

She quickly unzipped her uncomfortable skirt, pushing it and her undergarments down just below her stomach, then she lifted her blouse above her belly button. Softly she ran her fingertips over her baby, as close to skin-to-skin as could be, back and forth as she kept feeling the little one brush against her. It was simply the most amazing feeling in the world.

Sitting back further in the chair, she tilted her head back and closed her eyes, savoring the moment. Then as quickly as they began, the movements stopped. She sat up again, lowering her blouse but not bothering to fix her skirt.

"You're ready for the next letter, baby doll?" she said quietly, her heartbeat quickening as she tore open the thick second envelope. His script was strong but uneven, as though what he wanted to write was pouring out in large, staggered, emotional bursts on the pages...

32

I CAN'T HELP FALLING IN LOVE
WITH YOU

Becca,

I received your letter today. I've been reassigned in the Army, and it took a while for it to catch up to me. The letter went to my former unit first. That's why I didn't get it.

I'm glad I didn't get it until now. I was able to hear your voice and your words. You love me?

I can't understand why you love me. Maybe someday it will make sense, but not today. All I know today is I sure as hell don't deserve your love. I won't ever deserve it or your forgiveness. How can you forgive me? Why would you forgive me after all that's happened? I don't know how you had the courage to write the words you did, and I still can't believe you wrote them to me.

You are amazing.

You are the bravest person I've ever known. If I could have hand-picked any woman in the world to be the mother of my child, there isn't another walking the planet I would have wanted for the job. That kid is going to have a will of steel, no doubt about it, and very blue eyes.

Becca smiled at that.

They are going to grow up strong and brave...and happy. I want our baby to be happy, Becca. I trust you'll make sure our child's happy and safe and loved. I know you will.

I should tell you why that is so important to me. I didn't tell you much about where I came from on purpose. I never tell anyone. I don't want to remember all the shit I went through, but I feel like I have to tell you at least some of it. Some of what I want to tell you not another person knows, but I want you, and our son or daughter, to know a little about me, for what it's worth.

Becca, I promise I will do everything within my limits to come home, but you, of all people, know what we're facing over here. It's an uphill climb every day, and it's only going to get steeper. I'm trying to take it day by day.

I'm just holding onto you and our baby -- Our future.

Becca paused, wiping the tears streaming down her face, overwhelmed by everything she'd already taken in, the love and pain that had already leapt off the pages and into her heart.

She gathered herself to read the rest of his letter. For so many reasons, she was grateful that Penny had told her all she could about his past. It had given her the strength to write with confidence the letter she'd sent to him. And prepared her for the heartbreaking realities of his life that she was about to read. While she knew some of his story, Becca understood it was important that Jesse be the one to tell her all of it...

I've tried very hard to forget my parents. Most of the time, I just pretend they are dead. It hurts less. From what I understand, they met in California. My mother, Ivonne, was born and grew up dirt poor on a farm in Canada. She ran away from home and came to the U.S. when she was 16 (the only action I honestly can't blame her for). My father was a good-for-nothing who couldn't hold a job. They both loved their liquor, and themselves, more than anything or anyone in the world.

I truly believe the only reason I lived into childhood was because of my grandfather. His name was Jeremiah Howard Wanger, Grandpa Jerry, and he was the kindest person I ever knew. My earliest memories are of him. He had a sparkle in his eyes that, as a kid, you think is only for you. My parents and I lived with him, more or less, but he was the one I remember taking care of me -- cooking and cleaning. We lived close to the ocean, I think. I don't remember exactly. Every day he would take me on the city bus, and we'd stop off and walk along the coast, finding seashells, talking about nothing and everything.

I can't remember a single conversation we had, though I'm sure we had hundreds of them. I wish I could remember just one. He was always nice to me. He always had a smile. He would help a stranger in need whenever we were together. He'd offer food or coin to someone who needed it. He never asked for anything in return from anyone. He just gave.

I remember he always had hard butterscotch candies in his pocket. He used to say he had "pockets full of sunshine," and I knew that meant he'd gotten more candies. I don't know why I remember that. He's the only reason I never changed my name from Wanger when I had the chance. He was a great man, and it was his last name. I wanted to honor that.

Becca stopped again. So, it was his grandfather, she thought. Jesse learned how to be kind and be the man he was today from his grandfather. Becca looked up to the sky, sniffing and swallowing back her tears, picturing the little boy picking up seashells by the ocean -- such a sharp contrast to the skinny kid playing in the dirt outside a rundown slum in New York. She took a deep, shaky breath, then tucked her feet under her on the chair...

He and my father were opposites, and they constantly fought, mostly over me, I think, and my mother. Grandpa couldn't tolerate her. Then, when I was almost 8, Grandpa Jerry was hit by a car as he crossed the street in front of our house, and he died. So, did I, I think, a little bit.

The fighting between my parents after he was gone was intense. My mother left, taking me with her. I was too small to know what was happening. I just wanted Grandpa Jerry back. She took me to her "home" in Canada. I don't even remember traveling there. All I remember is arriving at this farm, in the middle of nowhere, with this old woman who disliked my mother and hated the sight of me from the start, I guess. I think my mother assumed her mother would take care of me like Grandpa Jerry did. She didn't want to. My mother was drunk all the time. My grandmother would work me hard, yelling at her and me. She was a cold woman, as cold as the weather there in January. I hated it there.

Whenever my mother had a man in her life, it was worse. If they were nice to me at all, she got rid of them fast. I don't think she liked sharing their attention. Soon I stopped talking to them. I pretty much stopped talking to anybody.

I didn't see my father again until I was 13. One day he just showed up at the farm and told me we were going back to the U.S. He wasn't right. He was probably drunk or high; I don't know which. I didn't want to leave with him, but I didn't want to stay. I remember just wanting to die. I was 13, and I hated my life.

My father took me to New York. He said things would be different there. They were different, just a different kind of awful. He thought he was an "entertainer," but he was a user and a bum, a drunk and a bum. He had "friends" that were just as bad as he was, and they used him badly. I know that now. I didn't then. He would throw very wild parties in that cramped shack of a place, and I couldn't stand it. I couldn't stand him. I still can't. He never gave a damn about having a kid. I was just there to keep the apartment livable.

He left New York when I was 16. I didn't. I haven't spoken to him since.

I stayed in high school and worked and went to college. I have an associate degree in accounting. I really like math. I wonder if our child will. Maybe she'll be a trailblazer instead, like her Mom.

Becca grinned through her tears, marveling at him calling their baby a "her," making it all the more real for him -- and her. His sad, sad life was flashing before her eyes as he poured out all he'd held so deep inside of him for so long. She wished at that moment more than ever that he could be right there with her and she could make all that pain from his past just disappear...

I hated New York until I met Penny. She was the first person I'd met since Grandpa Jerry that was always nice to me. She's like a sister to me, Becca; she really is. She hates the war, but she's a really good person. I'm glad you are friends. I wouldn't have survived in New York without her.

I met Joe when I started working for the Pipefitter's Union. He's like a brother to me, and I couldn't let him go alone...

Through her own tears, Becca could see the smudges on the page. There was a break in his writing. And she couldn't read the words very clearly. She could tell he had wiped off the pages, guessing what he'd wiped off were his own tears. Sighing heavily, she blinked several times, trying to refocus her eyes, his words breaking her heart. She knew he meant he couldn't let him go to Vietnam alone...

The last couple of years, I started to feel like I had a "normal" life. I had found a couple good friends, even Keith (before he hurt you). Then Liz moved into the building, and I met Eli. I almost felt like I'd found a sort of new family.

Then I met you, Becca.

I never believed in love at first sight, but I swear I think I loved you from the first moment I saw you. I don't know if I've stopped thinking about you since February. I haven't stopped thinking about you since the day I left for basic. I still remember your face at Grand Central, your eyes. I still see you so clearly, like you're branded on my brain. You are branded on my heart, Becca. I swear you are.

I regret our last night more than you'll ever know. I regret what I said and how I acted after we were together. I felt like my whole damn world was crashing down again, and I didn't want to pull you down with me, but that's no excuse. There is no excuse for the way I treated you. I'm sorry. I'm so sorry...

"Stop..." Becca whispered, shaking her head as she continued reading. "Just stop..."

I wanted you to forget me and go on with your life because I had convinced myself it was the best thing for you. I never asked you. How asinine is that? I just thought you'd find someone there better for you than me. I thought it would be easy, and I figured I'd have my memories of you, and that would be enough.

They're not enough. They will never be enough, but I have nothing to offer you. Nothing, except my love. That you will have until the day I die.

I never thought I'd make it impossible for you to forget me by leaving you with a baby. You with a baby. Damn, how beautiful you must look right now. I wish I could see you. I wish I could see our baby changing you.

Becca stopped as the words got smudgy again, but she couldn't tell if it was because of his dried tears or her new ones. She glanced down at her disheveled skirt as a lock of her long hair fell out of her up-do. She hadn't felt attractive in weeks, but his words had just made her feel like she was the most beautiful woman on Earth...

I met this soldier in basic named Charlie Brown (yes, actually Charlie Brown). He was injured shortly after we arrived In Country and is home now. He pretty much quietly harassed me until I told him about you, the little shit.

Despite everything, Becca giggled, picturing the crooked grin on his face when she read those words. She was glad he'd found a confidant...

He told me once that if you were "feeling me," the way I was "feeling you," you would be waiting for me. I didn't believe him, but he always seemed wise beyond his years.

I never imagined that you wouldn't want to forget me, and now I'm begging you not to. I know you told me you won't, but I still can't believe you love me. I don't understand it, but I know it, I feel it, and that is the biggest miracle of all. The other miracle will serve as a pretty strong reminder of me, too, I guess.

I never once dreamed a woman like you would fall for a guy like me. You're so beautiful and smart and strong. You have a fire in you that takes my breath away. Knowing you love me, knowing you're going to have our little baby, knowing you are waiting for me has made me happier than I ever imagined I could be.

I'm thousands of miles away, in the middle of a jungle, in the middle of a fucking war zone, and I am happier than I have ever been in my entire life. Ain't that a goddamn kick in the head?

Becca, I love you. I love you and our baby already more than I ever could have believed it was possible to love, and I'll do all I can to come home to you both.

Always,

Jesse

P.S. I guess there is one tangible thing I can give you. I will send it along when I have it. I promised Eli I'd take care of you, and now I promise you. I'll do the best I can.

Becca gulped for air, half-sobbing, half-laughing. She gripped his letter in both hands, reading his final lines over and over again so many times. She didn't even notice the fading sunlight turn on the shadows stretching against the building.

She couldn't get enough of him, from him, in those words. She read it all again, devouring every line as best she could. He loved her, and he was happy. Happy?! She'd made him happy...oh God, that made her feel like she could rocket to the moon all by herself. She was giddy, as happy tears endlessly flowed down her face.

"Becca?" Liz said, poking her head out the window. "Becca, are you OK?! Sweetie..."

Liz quickly climbed through the opening and squatted down in front of her, worry etched on her face. Every day she grew more and more concerned about her friend. She'd finally convinced Becca to go to a "female" doctor a week ago to make sure everything was OK after Becca mentioned a few times about getting headaches again, just like she had when she was younger. The stress of worrying about Jesse, the demands of her job, and her life changes were taking a toll.

To the relief of them both, everything checked out fine, except for a slight elevation in Becca's blood pressure. The doctor chalked it up to nothing more than Becca being nervous about the pregnancy and coming to the doctor. Becca accepted that.

Liz wasn't so sure, so she called her father. Liz didn't mention Becca's name, saying she was calling for a colleague. Her father gave her an earful about the complications, especially to a mother with high blood pressure during pregnancy. He'd scared her to death, and now all she wanted was to make sure Becca was as calm as could be at all times, which was not easy or, frankly, realistic. So, she worried. The very last thing Becca needed was something to upset her, something to cause her more stress and anxiety than she was already experiencing.

"Becca?" she asked gently, her hands on her arm. She noticed that her skirt was undone around the waist, and she was holding military mail in her hands.

But when Becca turned to face her, she gave Liz a brilliant smile behind her tears.

"He wrote to me," she whispered, trying to control her breathing, holding her long letter to her chest. "He wrote to me the most...most beautiful...heartbreaking things..."

"Ohhhh," Liz said, her own voice shaking as she began to smile herself.

"He loves me, Liz," she said, a catch in her throat. "He said...he said he's loved me the whole time..."

"Of course, he has!" Liz said, full smile on her face. Becca couldn't wipe the smile off her face as she picked up the other envelope resting on her lap.

"Look...look," she said, gesturing for Liz to look inside. Liz opened it up, then her eyes got wide as her head shot back up, and she met Becca's eyes.

"He's already taking care of the baby, Lizzy," Becca said, her voice still tinged with awe. "He wants to take care of us..."

Liz closed her eyes, relief flowing through her as a stray tear fell on her cheek. This would make everything so much easier. Jesse had no idea. She handed the envelope back to her.

"I'm so happy for you, Becca," she said, sincerity in her voice. "This is...it's just perfect."

"I know!" she said, shaking her head again and giggling now, overcome with happiness in her heart, making Liz giggle in surprise. "Somehow, everything is perfect."

Then Becca let out a big laugh.

"Ain't that a goddamn kick in the head?!"

At that, Liz laughed too and pulled her friend in for a hug, both laughing and crying on the fire escape as the bright sun descended over New York City. Becca hugged her back tight, standing up when their embrace broke, then she noticed her skirt was still undone.

"Oh," she said, beginning to wrestle with the zipper while still holding onto her letters. Liz put her hand over both of Becca's.

"You know what we need to do tonight?"

"What?" Becca said, raising her eyebrows.

"Go shopping!" Liz said, with a wink and a gesture to Becca's skirt. "Somebody's telling Momma she needs some new clothes!"

Becca laughed again as she nodded, folding her treasured words from Jesse and putting them back in their envelopes. She held them close to her heart in one hand as she somewhat clumsily, but very happily, made her way back through the window.

33

ONLY THING THAT I KNOW

OCTOBER 1968

"Becca, why don't you let me do that?" Malory said, standing behind her colleague in the low light of the film strip in the darkroom.

Becca looked back at her and gave her a small smile.

"You sure?"

"Yeah," Malory nodded, taking over the seat Becca immediately and willingly vacated. "You don't need to see...this."

Becca nodded and smiled again, grateful that Malory had been so supportive as a coworker and a friend. She was almost as invested in Becca's little bundle of joy as her closest friends were. She'd covered for Becca months ago when her morning sickness and fatigue got the best of her. She was covering for her now, especially on the days Becca's head was pounding. Anytime they worked in tandem, or more recently together, Malory kept an eye out for her. The woman had already been through so much that Malory's heart went out to her. She wanted Becca to stay healthy, have a healthy baby, and, if possible, keep her job.

They'd talked about it many times. Becca had told Malory about Jesse's financial support. However, Malory understood she still wanted to keep her career if she could. She'd worked hard and had been catching the eye of the higher-ups because of her keen instincts when it came to finding the right footage to tell a story. She was wearing looser clothing to work and had convinced almost everyone that she was just putting on weight. Malory wasn't sure their boss was buying it, though. She'd cast a few sharp glances Becca's way for the last couple of weeks, and Becca hadn't failed to notice them -- neither had Malory.

"Why don't you go through the stills?" Malory suggested, handing over a huge stack of photographs that had come in over the last week. Most were from entertainer Bob Hope's USO tours and other non-combat events happening In Country.

Becca shrugged.

"There's usually nothing there, but I should make myself useful," she said, walking across the room and taking a seat under a low light at the other end. The darkened space caused her to have to squint to see the photos clearly, and that did nothing to help the dull headache that seemed to be coming on more and more frequently.

Becca placed the pictures on her lap after a moment, squeezed her eyes closed, and tilted her head back against the wall behind her. She let out a deep breath. No, she didn't need to look through combat photos from Vietnam. Not today.

Some days she could handle it better than others, somehow knowing in her heart he was safe. It helped that she knew from his latest letter he was serving with Joe now. That gave her some measure of comfort.

Logically she knew she just didn't want to believe anything bad would happen to him. She wanted so desperately for him to come home, but still...she felt that connection. She felt as if some invisible line between her heart and Jesse's had snapped right back into place when she knew without a doubt, he loved her, and he knew she loved him.

Every day that imaginary thread, which was strengthened each time the material evidence kicked her or rolled from one side of her stomach to the other, sustained her.

But today was one of those days when she felt particularly fragile, and she knew exactly why.

And even though she knew it had to be done, she wished she'd never gone to her parents' house the night before...

"And just what are you going to do?" Wilma said, hands calmly folded in front of her in the darkened kitchen on Long Island. Her chin was up as she gazed down at her daughter, her posture of superiority and disappointment stifling the already suffocating air around the three of them. Becca glanced at her father, who just sat at the kitchen table, staring at the completed meal on top of it.

Becca lifted her chin, running her hand along her belly.

"I'm going to have a baby."

"Yes, you've mentioned that."

"What else do you want to know?" she said, attempting to match her mother's attitude for attitude. Still, Wilma always had a talent for deflating that effort.

"What about your lofty 'career'?" Wilma said, mildly disgusted. It had never completely suited her that her fiercely independent daughter had decided on such an unladylike and unusual profession for a woman.

"I plan to keep working, if that's what you mean," she swallowed hard, feeling the full force of the confrontation before her. Her mother scoffed at her words.

"Really? And how is that?" she asked. "You can't have a...a baby one day and return to work the next. You'll never be able to keep working..."

Becca smiled a little. Here was her ace-in-the-hole, the one thing her mother would never have suspected.

"He...Jesse has been sending me his Army paycheck, every month, to cover expenses," she said proudly. "He's, he's already planning...taking care of us."

John's head shot up at that, and he dared to look approvingly at his daughter.

"See, that's something..." John started, nodding to Becca, allowing her to relax just a little. Wilma crossed her arms, barely containing her anger and fear at the situation, at her daughter.

"It's all fine and good that he wants to take care of his bastard child now..."

"Wilma!" John said hotly, as Becca gasped.

"...what if...if he's killed Becca, what then?" Wilma continued, standing and losing any semblance of control. "You're not married to him! You can't prove to anyone it's...this is his baby! The money train stops then, sister, it stops! Then what are you going to do? What?!"

Becca started to tremble as her headache got stronger. This is precisely how she knew this conversation would go, no matter how much she wanted it to unfold otherwise. Now she just wanted it to be over. She wanted to be out of that house. She looked up at the fury on her mother's face with tears in her eyes.

"You're not moving back here," her mother said emphatically, backing away from the table, the tears in her eyes mirroring her daughter's. "No unmarried daughter of mine..."

Becca had had enough. She stood and pushed in her chair, the force of it smacking against the metal around the linoleum with a sharp crack.

"You're having a grandchild, the only grandchild you may ever have," she hollered, tears streaming down her face. "That's all I came to tell you. I don't need a goddamn thing from you!"

She glanced more painfully at her shocked and saddened father.

"Or you!" she whispered hotly. She narrowed her eyes at Wilma.

"He's coming home!" she cried as she grabbed her purse from the kitchen counter and started walking toward the front door, both parents now on her heels. "He loves me, and he loves our baby, and...and he's going to come home!"

She slammed the front door in their faces and walked quickly down the sidewalk toward the cab company in her neighborhood, crying harder with each step. She heard her father call out to her from the front stoop, but she never so much as glanced back in his direction...

"I'm going to the powder room," Malory said, shaking Becca out of her thoughts. Becca opened her eyes and nodded as Malory gave her a grin and left the room.

Becca sighed and got back to work, trying to push the night before away from her mind. She began flipping through one photo of Bob Hope and some Hollywood starlet after another for a couple minutes, seeing nothing of particular interest. The next group of stills was from General Abram's visit to a couple of the main bases In Country.

She smiled as she quickly leafed through the photos, seeing a few shots of servicemen looking relaxed on the base, talking, and even laughing together. She rubbed her eyes as she looked at the next photo in the stack. Then she blinked.

"Oh God!" she gasped, sharply sucking in her breath and jumping out of her seat, the stack of stills falling to her feet. She clutched the one black and white photo of the three men in fatigues firmly in her hands.

In the dim light, she could barely see them, but there was Eli, on the right, hands on his hips with a grin on his face, looking at Joe and Jesse. Standing between the two, Joe had his hand on Jesse's shoulder, a big smile on his face as he looked at his friend. Jesse, on the left with his knapsack on his back, had his right hand on his hip, the other presumably behind Joe. He was digging the toe of his right boot into the dirt, his head dropped with a smile as big as Joe's on his face. But his eyes were wide and bright as they peeked up at Eli.

They looked happy. They looked healthy.

He looked beautiful.

"Oh, my God!" Becca shouted, tears stinging her eyes as she reached for the darkroom door and pulled it open. "Malory...Malory!"

"What?!" said a surprised Malory, who was standing just on the other side.

"It's him! It's them," she said, eyes shining and voice squeaking. Her heart was racing, and the baby started kicking, making sure to make his presence known, too. She held the photo up to the hall light for Malory to see and pointed a shaky finger.

"It's Jesse," she breathed, with the brightest smile Malory had ever seen on her face, "and Eli and Joe! It's them! It's him!"

"When does it end?" Jesse yelled, frustrated and miserable.

"What?!" Joe answered, in as irritated a voice.

"The goddamn 'rainy season'?"

"Fucking January, if we're lucky," Joe said with disgust, looking hopelessly up at what was left of the seemingly relentless, dark late afternoon sky. Jesse wiped the sweat and rain from his forehead as he, Joe, and several other men sloshed their way back to the relative, very relative, safety of the makeshift base they all now called home.

If Jesse's first foray into combat experience in Vietnam had been unnerving, the last month had frayed what nerves he had left. Not only was there gunfire every day, but he constantly had to redo numbers he'd done just hours before in his surveying work in this new assignment with the engineering corps. Mainly because of the never-ending rain, the landscape was in a constant state of flux. Where there was a tree one day, there wasn't the next. A stream became a river overnight, throwing off all calculations done by him and the men who worked under him.

Joe's job was to put together the bridges or runways or pipelines that needed to be built according to those calculations with his fellow soldiers. Time was never on their side, and neither was the weather. And the Army higher-ups wanted to be on the move, and they wanted to be on the move yesterday.

The hard rain shower had finally turned to a light drizzle once the men reached their tents. Jesse and Joe took off their parkas and changed into the least damp socks they could find. Joe tried to start a small fire just outside as Jesse sat on a makeshift bench and reached for whatever was left of the coffee rations that had been sitting cold in a pot since mid-morning.

He grimaced as he swallowed what could only be described as brown gunk. He put down his tin cup on the ground, groaning as he folded his grimy hands together. He put his forehead in his hands between his knees, numbers swimming through his brain.

"Sir," said Corporal Byrd as he lifted the tent flap.

"Yes?" Jesse said curtly, not bothering to look up.

"Mail call, Sir," Barry said, smiling a little as he handed Jesse a letter from home.

Jesse's head shot up, and for the first time in what felt like days, he smiled.

"Thank you," he croaked out, earning a smirk from Joe outside as Barry exited the tent. The sun was trying to make a comeback against the drizzle now, as Jesse tried not to tear open the envelope before the tent flap fell closed again.

The instant the flap closed, his filthy fingers tore it open. He pulled out a very short note from Becca, which momentarily puzzled him.

Jesse,

They say a picture is worth a thousand words. One of these left me with no words, only the happiest of tears. I hope the other one is worth a thousand kisses for you.

We love you so much, my love, so much, and we can't wait for you to come home.

Always,

Becca and Baby

P.S. Turnabout is fair play...

Jesse fumbled with the other contents of the envelope, wondering why she'd signed "Baby" too for the first time, a new excitement growing in his pounding heart. Slowly he pulled out two small black and white prints. One was stamped "CBS News copy." He grinned, completely surprised. It was a photo from the day he, Joe, and Eli had run into each other at Tan Son Nhut base. It was the day of the General's visit, and he now remembered there had been a lot of reporters there. But he never knew anyone had taken their picture.

She must have seen at work, he reasoned.

"Wow," he said, a chuckle in his voice as he swiped at a rogue tear in the corner of his eye, then called out. "Hey, Joe!"

"Yeah?" Joe said a moment later when he came back into the tent. Jesse was holding out the picture to him as he entered and added, "fire's almost ready..."

But Jesse wasn't paying attention to him anymore. Joe watched as his friend's jaw dropped, and his bright blue eyes filled with tears. Joe quietly took the one photo from him, grinning in confusion as he glanced at it.

The hand that once held the picture from CBS News was now balled into a fist against Jesse's mouth, and he was breathing heavily against it, clearly trying to keep himself together.

"What, man?" Joe said, quickly grabbing a stool and setting it next to him. He looked at the picture Jesse was holding.

"Oh, my God," Jesse breathed, his eyes never leaving the photo in his hands. Looking back at him was the most beautiful image he swore he'd ever seen.

Becca was leaning against the outside of what looked to be their apartment building. Her body was turned just a touch away from the wall and toward the camera, both arms and hands flat against the bricks behind her. Her long, straight hair cascading down over her left shoulder that, along with her bent left leg covered in a knee-high boot, served to frame her baby bump, which lay bare between her pushed-up pilgrim blouse and the low-hanging waistband of her long skirt.

Her smile was dazzling, her dimples deep surrounding it, and even in the tiny black and white photo, Jesse could see her eyes were sparkling.

Jesse's heart was hammering in his ears as he pushed his fist against his lips. He gasped loudly behind it a couple times, trying to fight back his tears. There she was, more gorgeous than he even remembered, and there was their baby. Their child was growing inside of her, and she couldn't have looked happier.

Her radiance seemed almost to beam right into his soul.

Joe took a long moment to look at the photo, pursing his lips together, then smirked at Jesse.

"As God as my witness, I don't know how you managed to get a fox like that, man," he said, letting out a low whistle, earning an elbow in the ribs in return.

"Hey, that's the mother of my child you're talking about, you dig?" Jesse chastened, though he couldn't hide the smile that quickly crept onto his lips.

"Right on, right on," Joe said, putting his hands up in a surrender gesture with a matching smile of his own. They both stared at the photo, another couple of moments as the sun outside got brighter.

"You're going to be a father," Joe finally said, softly breaking the silence. He looked seriously at his friend.

"Yeah," Jesse replied quietly, running his fingers over her figure in the photo. "Yeah, I sure am."

"You're going to be a Dad," Joe said, placing a hand on Jesse's arm, causing Jesse to finally turn his face to him.

He was looking at him so intently that fresh tears sprang to Jesse's eyes. Big Joe had been dead for years, yet Jesse knew Joe thought of him every day. Even through the horror of the war, Joe kept the man at the forefront of his thoughts. His motivation in life was to make his father proud. Jesse found himself greatly respecting a man he never knew because of the son he'd left behind.

He put one hand over Joe's and swallowed hard, looking into his friend's deep, brown eyes in dim sunlight now barely beaming its way through the tent.

"If I live through this," Jesse said, his voice raspy and low. "If I live to see...my...baby, I...I hope I'm half the father your Dad was, Joe. I hope I'm half the man he must have been."

Joe inhaled sharply, eyes filling with tears, as Jesse gently smiled at him.

After a moment, he nodded, squeezed Jesse's arm, stood, and quickly walked back outside to the small campfire without another word.

Jesse turned back to the picture in his hand, tears finally spilling onto his cheeks as he swept his dirty, calloused fingers over his mouth.

He sniffed once, twice, gazing at the photo through watery eyes and wondered, just as Joe had, what he'd ever done to deserve her.

What he'd ever done to deserve them.

And praying he'd make it home.

34

STAND BY ME

MID-OCTOBER 1968

Becca put a hand to the side of her growing belly and moaned. It was the "witching hour," that time in the middle of the night when little Baby Wanger decided it was time to throw a party in her uterus.

"Come on, kiddo," she implored quietly, putting just a little pressure on her stomach as she rubbed her hand back and forth. "Mommy's got a big day tomorrow."

The kicking only increased, and despite her tired state, she smiled. She'd actually felt relatively good the last couple of days. The cooler weather of autumn started to take a bit of a foothold in the city during the week. The fall colors were at their peak. If it wasn't for the daunting task before her the next day, she might have felt what could only be mistaken as "relaxed."

She sighed as she laid back on the stack of pillows behind her. She couldn't blame the baby for keeping her awake this night.

The next day was her day off, but her boss had ordered her to report to her desk at 9 a.m., and Becca was almost certain as to why. There was no use denying it. Her slight frame was making it impossible for her to hide her growing belly. Now at almost 24 weeks along, she had started to "pop" in only two areas -- her stomach and her breasts. She couldn't camouflage it as "weight gain" anymore. So, she was preparing to lose her job, and possibly her career, in the morning. She was certain she would be fired.

It was a very thinly veiled secret in the newsroom that she was pregnant -- unmarried and pregnant. Only Malory knew the whole story and truly understood that she felt married to Jesse. Not that it would have mattered to anyone she worked for, but it mattered to her.

He hadn't proposed, of course, and she hadn't planned a big wedding shindig, but that didn't matter much to her anymore. She really only needed his love, and she had his love. At this point, the piece of paper was just a formality. In Becca's mind, he was hers, and she was his. She'd honestly been "his" since her eyes first met his baby blues. She'd definitely been "his" since the moment she gave herself to him before he left. Despite all the heartache and misery that followed, she'd always remained "his."

Becca closed her eyes and pictured his face, shuddering as the phrase "til death do us part" briefly flew through her mind. What a crock, she thought. It wasn't until "death do us part" for them, not when "death" loomed daily for him. No, this was it. She didn't care if she was only 24 years old. If, God forbid, she was left a "widow," she'd be one for the rest of her life.

He was her "forever."

She turned to her side, willing Little Mr. Kicky to calm himself again. He paused momentarily when she moved, then started rolling.

"Geez, you are a busy bee tonight," she sighed as she reached for her notebook and pen on the bedside table and flipped on the table lamp. "I know, let's write to Daddy."

She sat up again and stared at the blank paper, putting the end of the pen against her lips. Writing to him and shielding him from some of the harsher aspects of her life and pregnancy was becoming more difficult. She didn't want to worry him, so she fought hard to stay positive in her letters. She wanted him to know everything was fine. She was fine, the baby was fine, work was fine -- they were just waiting for him to come back to them.

Her reality, at times, overwhelmed her, though. She'd come to terms with losing her job. She wasn't happy about it, but she'd sacrifice it willingly to have a healthy baby. Even if she didn't lose her job, she thought she may quit anyway. Jesse's income made that possible, and she was grateful for it.

And she wasn't oblivious to her own condition. She knew something wasn't completely right. She'd written off the headaches as stress before, but they had been getting increasingly stronger. Liz and Penny had been like Mother Hens, one or both of them checking on her morning, noon, and night. It was rather annoying, but comforting, too. Outside of Jesse, they were the only "family" support she had.

Liz kept suggesting she go back to the doctor or have her father over to "make sure everything was OK." Becca vetoed the idea each time. The baby was moving and kicking, and she was holding her own. She just needed to keep it up for 16 more weeks.

Becca put her pen to the paper as the baby started to kick again. She sent a letter to Jesse as often as possible, sending what encouragement and comfort she could. About once every 10 days to two weeks, she received a letter from him in return. She literally lived for those days. In those letters, she felt like they were having an ongoing conversation, and it kept his presence vivid in her mind and in her heart. It kept her spirits up in those long days in-between.

She took a deep breath and smiled to herself as she began to tell him the latest news from Baby Wanger...

...I swear he kicks all night. I think he wants to be awake when his Daddy is awake. Our baby must know you're working hard. He wants to make sure I know, too, so I don't forget all you are doing for us. Sometimes I whisper to him to settle down so I can sleep, but he doesn't listen. Does that sound like anyone you know? I'm so happy he's kicking, though. I'm glad I can feel him moving and growing. That means he's healthy, and every kick, every move just reminds me of you. He wants to make sure I don't forget why he's here! I can't wait to see his little face...

Late October 1968

...You're convinced we're having a boy, then? I don't know. She sounds pretty stubborn to me. Does that sound like anyone you know? She sounds pretty strong and determined, just like her Momma.

What does it feel like? Does it hurt when the baby kicks? I'm glad she's moving around. That is a good sign. Do you think I could feel her if I was there? I wish I was there. I wish I could hold your hand and kiss your lips and try to calm you down when they take you to delivery. I wish I could see her beautiful baby face the moment she's born. God willing, she'll look just like you...

Early November 1968

...Penny wanted to make an afghan for the baby, and I asked her to make it blue. Yes, I'm stubbornly convinced we're going to have a boy on the first of February. I want a boy. I want a little "you." Whether we have a boy or girl, I want our baby to look like you. I want our friends to take one look at our baby and say, "that's Jesse Wanger's baby."

I want him to be a miniature version of you in every way. I want him to have more than your features, though, Jesse. I want him to have your good heart. I want him to have your strength, your loyalty, your capacity to give love. You wonder why I love you? That's why I love you. It's not just your dreamy eyes, or your infectious grin, or your strong body, or the way I ache for you to make love to me again. It's you, the best man I've ever known. I love you. All of you...

Mid-November 1968

...If I'm the best man you know, maybe you should get out more?

If I'm the best, Becca, it's only because of you. Any strength I have now comes directly from you, do you know that? I read your letters over and over. I carry your picture in my shirt pocket. I look at it every chance I get and wonder how much you've changed since it was taken. You and the baby, you're my light at the end of this godforsaken tunnel. It's shitty over here. There's no other way to describe it, but you keep me going. You keep me sane, and I refuse to let you down.

I cannot wait to see our son or daughter. I cannot wait, but I want to live through this hell just to get back to you. I want you in my arms again. I want to make love to you the right way. We never made love. Can't deny we had amazing sex, but we never made love. I want to kiss you and hold you and make you feel more loved and wanted than any woman in recorded history. I owe you that. I need to give you that. That last time can't be our last time...

Late November 1968

...I pretend. I pretend all the time. I pretend you're here. I hold a pillow to me and pretend you're laying here beside us. Sometimes my skin crawls. I want to feel your touch so badly. I'm trying to be as strong as you think I am. Some days it's easier than others. I miss you so much, Jesse, and I worry about you. I have to admit it, I do, and I don't feel strong at those times. I just feel lost. I worry that you're safe, and I know there is nothing I can do about it if you're not. There's nothing I can do to make you safe. There's nothing I can do to bring you home. I have no control. I don't like having no control. The only thing I can do is keep our baby safely growing inside me until it is time for him to be born. I'm doing all I can to give you that much. I refuse to let you down...

Becca put her pen down on the secretary table, wiping a tear from her eye as she watched snow start to fall through the gray sky just outside the big picture window. It looked calm, peaceful. She dropped her head and ran a hand along her large stomach.

Ten weeks. She had to keep him safe inside for 10 more weeks.

Groaning, she pushed herself up off her chair and gingerly made her way over to the kitchen, trying not to sway too much in the process.

"Becca," Liz said in a worried voice, hurrying from her bedroom to her friend in the kitchen. "What are you doing?"

Becca grasped the sink tightly with both hands and glanced back at Liz, the movement making her head spin just a little.

"I'm getting some water," she replied, with a hint of agitation. "It's really strenuous."

"Honey, you don't look so good," Liz said, dismissing her last statement and grabbing a glass from the open cabinet to fill up. "You need to lie down..."

"I'm sick of lying down," Becca mumbled miserably, and she was. She'd felt like she'd been on bed rest for months. The last four weeks had been almost unbearable but necessary. Earlier in the month, Liz had found her passed out in her bed and, in a panic, immediately called her father. He was stunned to find out the patient his daughter was so upset about was John and Wilma's Rebecca.

Becca's blood pressure had skyrocketed, and Dr. Redd told her in no uncertain terms that she needed to stay in bed. If it didn't go down, he'd make her go to the hospital and deliver the baby, the only sure way to cure "preeclampsia." That thought absolutely terrified her. Thankfully, her blood pressure had fallen in the following 24 hours and remained steady. So, she was on bed rest.

It made her crazy, but she knew it was worth it when she felt the baby move.

Liz handed her the water.

"You can come with me," she suggested, tentatively. Becca narrowed her eyes at her.

"No, thank you," she said, taking a long drink.

"Becca, it's Thanksgiving," Liz said quietly. "Eli isn't here, and...and my Mom and Dad will be there. He'll make sure you're OK...and, and your parents..."

"Liz, I said 'no,'" Becca said, pulling out a kitchen chair and taking a seat. "I don't want to see them."

"Becca..."

"Listen, you don't want to upset me, right?" Becca challenged. Liz nodded, sitting beside her. "Then you understand I cannot take even one night with my mother."

"I'm sure she's worried about you..." Liz started.

"No, see, no," she said, starting to get animated. "That would mean she cared, and she doesn't care."

"Of course, she does."

"No, Liz," Becca said, tears in her eyes. "She made it very clear that I would get no support from them, and I won't. I'm never stepping in that house again."

Liz sighed and shook her head.

"Fine, then what do you want me to tell them?"

"Just tell them I'm working tonight," Becca said with a sad little smirk.

"But..."

"They won't know any different," she said, worry suddenly replacing the sadness in her eyes. "Your Dad didn't say anything..."

"No," Liz said, certain he hadn't. "Doctor, patient privilege."

Liz studied Becca as she acknowledged her with a weak nod. There were circles under her friend's eyes, and she was pale. Despite her pregnancy, she even looked thin in her features, but her eyes were still as determined as ever. Liz knew better than to fight with her.

"OK, then," she said in resignation, with a nod of her own. "I'll be home early, but I called Penny..."

"You didn't have to..."

"She's coming over after her shift," Liz continued, ignoring Becca's interruption. "You won't be alone for long."

"I'm never alone," Becca said, with a real smile this time, patting her stomach. She reached over and pulled Liz's hand, placing it just above her belly button, where Baby Wanger was blissfully kicking away.

Liz gave her a sad smile and let her hand linger there a moment, fighting the worried tears in her eyes as she felt the baby kick.

"OK, Momma," Liz said, standing, trying to make her voice sound as positive as she could muster. "Then let's get you back to bed before I leave."

35

IN DREAMS

...I have no control. I don't like having no control. The only thing I can do is keep our baby safely growing inside me until it is time for him to be born. I'm doing all I can to give you that much. I refuse to let you down...

Jesse furrowed his brow again; just as he had the first half-dozen times, he'd read Becca's latest letter.

What in the hell was wrong? Something was, he could feel it. Her words were desperate. It looked as though she'd written them quickly like she'd wanted to get them on the paper before she lost her nerve to write them at all.

He ran one hand along the base of his skull and closed his eyes, straining his head back to loosen his stiff neck. What sleep he'd been able to grab lately came in the form of awkward positions -- against the side of a fox hole, on top of a crate while sitting on the ground, and sometimes lying directly on the uneven Earth itself. It felt like a million years since he'd been where he was now, in his tent on a cot in his temporary home.

The engineers were close, so close, to completing the necessary work to begin the construction of a makeshift airstrip that could land large, heavy freight planes loaded with supplies.

Securing enough land around the perimeter had been daunting for his comrades. The Army Corps had a small window to get the work done while the infantry held back the enemy.

It was almost a blessing that he'd had so much work and so much distraction recently. He hadn't heard from Becca in a month. It was really only a week or so longer than usual, but it was almost too long. He lived on her letters as his fuel to survive, and he was running on fumes.

He glanced down at her words again.

I refuse to let you down.

How could she possibly let him down? She'd done nothing but give him the world, promise him the moon, since they'd finally come clean with their feelings for one another. What could she possibly think could happen that he would be upset about?

He fumbled in his breast pocket and pulled out her picture again. A slow smile crept across his face, as it did every time he looked at her photograph. She looked so beautiful -- young, healthy, happy -- so full of life. He sighed. This was what he'd initially wanted to avoid -- causing her any worry or pain because of him. Instead, here she was, pregnant with his baby -- worried about him and worrying about the baby.

"Dammit," he whispered, slowly lying down on his back on the cot and holding her picture up in the dim light. He studied her face for a short while until his tired eyes turned blurry, and he fell into a restless sleep...

Jesse clutched her to him, as he had 100 times before, feeling her naked body against him as they lay together in his bed in his apartment. Slowly he ran his fingertips up her arm and over her shoulders, gently tugging on her, urging her to turn to him. She sighed, turned to face him, and smiled that brilliant smile of hers.

"Are you OK?" he whispered.

"Yes," she said, still smiling, her eyes searching his.

"Are you sure?" he asked again, not convinced, as his fingers lightly traced her jawline.

"Yes," she said softly, reaching up to bury her hand in his hair and pulling his mouth to hers. They kissed long, slow, and deep like they did ever so briefly the first time they'd kissed. Not with the fast, hard, unbridled passion when they'd been together before. This was languid, just soft enough, as though they had all the time in the world. And as it always was, it was as amazing as he dreamed it would be.

He smiled against her mouth as his left hand roamed lower, searching for the bump that housed their baby. He gently ran his hand over her round, smooth stomach.

She put her hand over his, and they smiled into each other's eyes for a moment. Then she scooted out of his embrace.

"I have to go," she whispered, still smiling, but her eyes were beginning to water. Suddenly she wasn't naked anymore. Rather she was standing by the bed in a simple, pale blue dress.

He jerked to a sitting position, covers over his naked waist, his heart suddenly thundering in his ears.

"Go? Where?" he asked, fear creeping into his voice. "Where are you going?"

"I have to go," she repeated, tears in her eyes. "The baby needs me."

"The baby? What?" he asked, wanting to move but somehow frozen in place. He watched her as she started to somehow...fade away. "But...the baby's not here yet. Where are you going?! Becca?!"

"I love you," she whispered, tears in her voice as her form faded further from his sight.

"Becca, no!" he said, reaching out to the empty room, feeling as though his heart was bleeding out around him. "Don't leave! Becca!"

Jesse tossed around on the cot, kicking to free himself from whatever imaginary force was trying to hold him in place. He was gasping for air, his eyes trying to force themselves open and free his mind from the nightmare he had fallen asleep into. He was kicking hard, and in his sleep, his hand found the metal side of the cot. Gripping it, he pulled hard and flipped his body right out of the tough green canvas and onto the dirt floor below with a hard thud.

"Becca!" he gasped as he scrambled to his elbows and knees in the dark, eyes now wide open.

His breathing was ragged, shaky as he frantically attempted to take in his familiar surroundings, blinking rapidly to clear his vision. His heart was pounding.

Jesse took a few more deep, ragged, audible breaths in an attempt to move past the hellish dream and reestablish an even heart rate. He closed his eyes. God, he could actually feel his arms around her, then just as clearly, he could see her walking, no...fading away.

His whole body shuddered as he shook his head, opening his eyes just enough to glance at her latest letter sitting on the crate next to his cot. He folded it and put it back in his nap sack, where he kept almost all of her letters. He patted his shirt pocket and frowned.

Where was her photo?

"Fuck! No, no, no..." he whispered fiercely, fumbling around in the dim light, still on his hands and knees on the ground. His heart was speeding up again. He ran his hands over the top of the cot, over the crate, almost knocking the barely lit oil lamp off the top of it. After a couple of panicked moments, his fingers felt the matte paper's familiar texture in the shadows far under his cot. He grabbed the picture, falling back on his knees as he pulled it out from the dirt under him. He quickly brushed it off and checked for tears or scratches. Thankfully, he found none.

Jesse slapped the photo against his chest and hung his head, feeling like he was losing his mind. Of course, it had just fallen off him in his sleep. He hadn't lost it. He hadn't lost it, and he hadn't lost her. He hadn't lost her. He wasn't going to lose her. She was fine. The baby was fine. Everything back home was fine.

"She's fine, man," he said quietly to himself, trying to convince himself. "Don't sweat it. Don't sweat it..."

After a moment or two, his breathing evened out, and he tucked the photo safely back in his pocket, right next to that first letter she wrote to him. Going back to sleep now, though, was a lost cause.

He heaved himself into a standing position and took a deep breath, straightening his arms, palms down, trying to pull himself together. He exited the tent, hoping to find some solitude and peace in the moonlight hanging over the endless cluster of trees surrounding their makeshift base.

Jesse looked to his left and saw a familiar figure standing alone, not 50 paces from him. A thin trail of smoke was dancing in the reflection of the lunar light next to Joe as he looked heavenward.

"No sleeping tonight?" Jesse said quietly as he came to stand by his friend.

"Hey," Joe said, glancing at him, then he nodded to the moon.

"Think they'll make it up there?"

Jesse's eyes followed his. The ongoing NASA Apollo missions that were attempting to orbit the moon were a good distraction on Armed Forces Radio for the soldiers every once in a while. There was another mission planned for the end of the month.

"Dunno," Jesse said, with a little shrug, not having given it a whole lot of thought.

"If they finally get their shit together, we'll never hear the end of it from the Air Force guys," Joe said with a small smile, putting his cigarette to his lips then quickly pulling it away again.

Jesse smirked then nodded as he raised his eyebrows at Joe, his eyes shifting from his friend's profile to the cigarette in his hands.

"When did you start smoking?" he said, with a nod toward the smoke rising next to him.

"Right now," he said, smirking, lifting his hand as he looked at Jesse. "This is my first. Want one? Looks like you need it..."

"Hell, yes," he said, as Joe offered the brand-new pack of cigs to him. Jesse dug one out, then dug out his lighter in his pants pocket, lighting up the cig and taking a deep drag. He let it out slowly.

"Why can't you sleep?" Joe asked, looking to the sky again. He was confident he knew the answer. What kept any of them up at night in the middle of a war?

Jesse took another drag before answering. He wasn't about to go into details about his dream, a wonderful dream he'd had countless times since he'd found out she was pregnant but had never once ended in the horrible way it just had. Yet, he thought he might just be able to talk to Joe about what he thought may have triggered it.

"I...I got a letter from Becca," he said pensively, making his friend worriedly whip his head around to face him. Then Joe grinned.

"Finally came to her senses and dumped you, did she?" he said, earning a shoulder shove from Jesse.

"No," he said, with a little grin, appreciating Joe's attempt at humor. "But something's...off. I mean, she's more...worried...she's usually pretty strong, but she just...something's bothering her."

Joe looked at him like he was crazy.

"Love of her life's In Country, and she's carrying his baby?" Joe said in a matter-of-fact voice. "You're wondering why she's stressed?"

Jesse sighed as he shuffled his feet.

"I know, but..."

"Jesse, she's pregnant," Joe said, taking a small, almost non-drag on his own cigarette. "I've got a ton of sisters, and they've all been pregnant. It ain't pretty. Look, I know she's your Wonder Woman, but she's probably a hormonal wreck right now."

Jesse looked at Joe, somewhat dumbfounded but very appreciative. The man had a point. That was probably all it was -- and he was overreacting.

"Yeah," he said with a nod, flicking the end of his cigarette to the ground, taking his frustration over not being with her right then out on the butt, grinding it under his boot. "Yeah, you're probably right."

"Believe me, I'm right," Joe nodded, then turned and offered Jesse the rest of his cig. "These are disgusting, by the way."

"Nah, you're just not doing it right," Jesse said, taking it from him. Joe grinned, then his face turned serious again.

"We've got a job to do," he said quietly, clapping Jesse on the shoulder. "Gotta focus on that. Day-by-day, remember?"

Jesse swallowed and nodded in understanding. He gave Joe a little grin as the smoke from his exhale drifted back across the moonlight in the sky.

36

LET IT BE

LIZ STOOD UP FROM THE BEADED CHAIR AND WALKED ACROSS THE ROOM, snapping off the TV. She glanced at Becca dozing on the couch, then walked over to the big picture window, looking up at the moon. They'd made it. Apollo 8 had orbited the moon, the first humans in history to accomplish that feat. It was a great day in the American space program.

The much-anticipated Christmas Eve broadcast from the spacecraft had just ended, leaving Penny and Liz with tears in their eyes. Becca had laid on her side, on the couch. She watched one of the biggest news events of the year unfold from the confines of her living room with half-closed eyes. She remembered what a buzz there had been in the newsroom when NASA had decided a few months back to orbit the satellite a few months earlier than expected.

She didn't think then that she would be anywhere other than the CBS studios, watching it all play out, being in the middle of history.

Instead, she was barely awake most days. Sluggish didn't begin to describe how she felt. The baby was moving around, taking in the nutrients from whatever food she could force herself to eat. She lived with a dull ache in her head all the time. Yet she kept willing her body to cooperate, and some days, she felt like it was listening to her. She'd have good days -- days when she could walk around the apartment a little and even fix herself some breakfast or lunch if Penny and Liz would let her.

She hadn't been out of the apartment in weeks, though. Even she knew she'd never make it back up the six flights of stairs again if she tried in her current condition.

Still, she wasn't about to give up. Their baby needed about six more weeks. He needed his Momma to hold her own for six more weeks, then he would be ready to make his debut. And she would be fine. She was young and, until now, healthy. She'd bounce back. She knew she would. Her body would have no choice. The baby would need her. Jesse. Jesse would need her. They'd need her as much as she needed them.

She'd push her body to do what it needed to do, come hell or high water, because the alternative just tore her heart apart. The thought of losing their little baby to preterm birth then possibly losing Jesse to the war was completely unbearable.

Becca knew she'd never survive that, so she controlled what she *thought* she could -- she could keep their baby safe, no matter how hard it was. She reasoned that it was nothing compared to what Jesse was facing every day. If he could be a warrior for them, she could be, too.

She opened her eyes as she heard the familiar sound of Penny at the sink cleaning up the dishes. She sighed. She knew Penny and Liz cared about her, and she loved them for it, but the worry in their eyes each time they looked at her was beginning to weigh on her. In some ways, she really wished they'd leave her alone.

Becca took as deep a breath as she could and pushed herself up to a sitting position as Liz turned from the window and rushed to her side. She smiled weakly at her.

"I have to use the bathroom."

"OK, " Liz said, tucking her arm under Becca's and lifting her off the couch. Her eyes widened as she looked at Becca's feet. The swelling around her ankles was getting worse.

She swallowed hard.

"There ya go," she whispered, holding Becca's hand as she stepped up the one step to the bathroom. She watched her closely as she disappeared inside and closed the door.

Liz picked up the remaining popcorn bowls off the coffee table and walked over to Penny, dropping them in the kitchen sink's soapy water. She stole another glance at the closed bathroom door.

"I swear she's going to give me a heart attack," Liz whispered, putting the unopened bottles of Coca-Cola back in the refrigerator. "She won't go to the doctor, she won't go to the hospital, she won't even let my father take a blood pressure reading!"

Penny nodded.

"She's just scared..." she said quietly.

"I know she's scared!" Liz whispered harshly, her eyes watering. "But Penny, she's sick. She's really sick..."

"I can see that!" Penny snapped quietly, drying her hands on the dish towel, and turning to her distraught friend, her own fears coming to the surface. "But as long as the baby is still moving, she's not going to budge, you know that. She's stubborn as a damn mule, that one."

Liz cast another glance behind her at the bathroom door.

"We have to make her, Penny!"

"But how...."

"She's trying, but she's barely eating or even drinking anything; her ankles are swollen," Liz interrupted in a quick, hard whisper, crossing her arms. "I know her head hurts, but she won't tell me. She sleeps all the time. Eventually her...her kidneys will shut down, or she's...she's gonna have a stroke..."

"What?!" Penny said, more loudly than she meant to. "What are you talking about?"

"She's killing herself," Liz gasped quietly, tears now falling down her cheeks as the worry and stress she'd tried to hold back for weeks came spilling out of her, finally saying out loud what she hadn't even written to Eli or told her future in-laws. "She's killing herself to keep her baby alive. The only sure way to cure preeclampsia is for the baby to be born. If she stays too...stubborn for too long, she could die!"

"Oh, my God!" Penny said, putting her hand over her mouth. She'd been worried. She knew Becca's body wasn't handling the pregnancy well, but she had no idea she was in such bad shape -- and she knew Jesse would be insane if he knew.

"I don't know how," Liz said earnestly, grabbing onto Penny's arm, "but we've got to find a way to make her go to the hospital and deliver the baby and...and get better. You've got to help me."

Penny nodded, then glanced past Liz's shoulder and froze.

Becca was leaning against the wall outside the bathroom, staring daggers at them both with hurt in her eyes.

"My baby will be born when he is ready to be born," she said evenly. Liz jumped at her words, then turned and took a deep breath.

"Becca, will you please listen to me," Liz said as she slowly walked toward her friend. "You...you are not well at all..."

"I'm fine," Becca said quickly, raising her head.

"You're not fine!" Liz pleaded. Throwing her hands in the air and then putting them over her mouth to stop herself from saying any more.

"Liz's right, you're making yourself sick," Penny said as calmly as she could as she walked over to Becca, really examining her for the first time. She looked ashen, her forehead fixed in a permanent pinch. She was thin where she wasn't swollen, but her eyes were bright. They seemed to be the only remainder of the ball-of-fire of a woman Penny had met earlier in the year. Becca looked like a shadow of her former self. A very pregnant shadow.

"Look, Jesse...Jesse wouldn't want you to sacrifice yourself..." Penny started before choking on her words. She put her hands on Becca's arms and watched her eyes fill with tears.

With watery eyes, Becca searched Penny's face. This was the woman who saved her from herself, who helped her escape the clinic when she found out she was carrying Jesse's baby.

And even she didn't understand.

"He deserves to live on," Becca croaked out after a moment, her voice thick. "You said it yourself. Don't you remember? This is how he lives."

"But Becca..." Penny whispered.

"Penny, we have lost so much," she whispered, her cracking voice pleading with them both as her eyes darted between her two friends. "I've lost my job, I've lost my parents, Eli is gone, and Joe and...and Jesse. Don't you see if I lose Jesse? If I lose him and...and the baby... oh, no...no, no. no..."

She took a deep breath and shook her aching head, trying to forget even the thought of losing Jesse. Trying to forgive herself for even saying the words. She swallowed heavily.

"I will...I'll be fine," she said as confidently as she could, trying to straighten her spine. "The baby is...is going to be healthy and...and I...I will be, too."

Penny and Liz looked at each other, tear tracks lining their faces.

"The only way to make sure that happens..." Liz started.

"No!" Becca said, taking a small step back from them both. "He's...he's not ready yet. I will not put him in jeopardy; I just won't! No! If...if you can't handle that then, then I don't need you. I...I..."

Becca wrapped her arms around her stomach and began to cry in earnest. Both Liz and Penny reached out for her, their hearts breaking, not wanting to upset her anymore. They looked at each other, each with fear written all over their faces.

"OK, OK," Liz said quietly as Becca leaned against her; she looked at Penny on Becca's other side. "We'll do whatever...whatever you need us to do."

Becca took a couple deep breaths, trying to find her voice again.

"Just be my friends," she whispered, suddenly very, very tired. "Help me through the next six weeks. Please, just promise me you'll help me keep him safe until then. Please."

Penny pursed her lips and looked at Liz, who closed her eyes and whispered "OK" as they helped Becca back to her bed.

Jesse walked along a trench that ran the length of the airstrip the Army Corps was currently constructing, shuffling the final blueprints between his hands.

The project was a day or two away from completion, and the weather had, miraculously, cooperated. Though the sky was overcast, it seemed that the rainy season was drawing to a close.

He passed by Joe and his group doing the physical work of linking the pieces of the airstrip together. Their eyes met briefly. Joe gave him a thumbs up, which Jesse returned, not breaking stride. There were at least a hundred soldiers working in and around the site today, everyone working double-time. It was Christmas Day, and many of the men were just trying to keep their minds off of the fact that they weren't back home with their families.

As Jesse walked along, he meticulously looked over the work being done and compared it to the blueprints in his hand.

Everything was going damn near perfectly, but he couldn't fight the feeling that something wasn't right. It had been hanging over him for days now, and he couldn't shake it. He chalked it up to just being where he was and doing his job in the middle of a war. He tried to remember Joe's mantra -- "day-by-day" and maintain his focus.

Though Becca and the worry he read in her latest letter was never far from his mind.

He'd sent her a letter in return just six days earlier, trying to calm her worries and cheer her as she had always cheered him. After a sleepless night mulling over her last words to him, he finally accepted somewhat reluctantly that Joe was probably right. She was emotional and needed his support. So, he did all he could do, hoping his letter would make her smile a bit, letting her relax as much as their current situation would allow.

And make her realize that no matter what surprises come their way in the future, he'd always, always love her.

"Sir?" he heard Corporal Byrd say behind him. Jesse turned to him.

"Here are those last prints you wanted, Sir," Barry said, handing the papers to Jesse just as big drops of rain began to fall down all around them.

"Thank you," Jesse said, squinting up at the sky. "Looks like we haven't escaped the damn rain yet."

"No, Sir," Barry said with a chuckle, as the rain started to fall harder. Jesse swore he could hear thunder in the distance, but it wasn't thunder.

Jesse jerked around and looked at the sky as a small brigade of American choppers came screaming over the construction site, shooting into the tree line, not 50 yards from where he and Barry were standing. Then, out of nowhere, gunfire and grenades sprang from the trees next to them.

And all hell broke loose. Screams, curses, and bullets were flying -- everywhere.

Men were scurrying from their position on the airstrip and reaching for their weapons. Many of the men were carrying little weaponry on their bodies. Most had to run to get their guns, having been assured the large perimeter around the construction zone had been safely secured. It hadn't. They'd been sitting ducks.

Jesse dropped the blueprints and swiftly brought his rifle from its sling on his back and into his hands. His eyes were wide as he tried to look through the rain and shoot into the forest.

He fired one round and watched in horror as Barry, not 10 feet from him, was shot through the neck and collapsed face-first into the trench below. Jesse barely had time to react when a pain like he'd never felt before ripped into his left shoulder, knocking him and his rifle back and twisting his feet around themselves on the edge of the trench. He heard a loud crack as if lightning had bolted through the trunk of a sturdy tree.

Then everything went black.

Liz knocked quietly on Becca's bedroom door.

When she received no response, she slowly opened it up and walked across the room to push back the curtains and let in Christmas Day's morning light.

"Becca?" she said quietly as she turned around and walked back towards the bed. Becca was lying on her side, away from the window. Liz gave her shoulder a little shake.

"Becca? Honey? We have some milk and toast..."

Penny came into the doorway and gasped, dropping the tray she was holding to the floor.

"Liz!" she gasped, hurrying to Becca's side and kneeling down. "Liz! Call for an ambulance. Now!"

"What? What?!" Liz said, hurrying now to the other side of the bed where Penny was.

Becca didn't stir even a little bit. Her breathing was shallow, and she was as white as a ghost, but with a fine sheen of sweat covering her body.

Liz raced out to the living room and picked up the phone. Penny took Becca's wrist in her hand to check her pulse. It was racing.

"They're on their way," Liz said a moment later, her voice shaking as she stood at the bedroom door.

"Call her parents," Penny said quickly. "Call everyone you can."

Liz briefly stared at Becca, then squeaked out a sob and ran back into the living room.

"Wilma?" Penny heard Liz say brokenly a minute later. "Wilma, it's... it's Liz..."

Becca remained motionless as Penny stroked her hair with one hand, placing the other hand on Becca's stomach. She could feel the baby moving.

A tear ran down her nose as she cocked her head to the side and studied her friend's face.

"Hang on," she whispered to her, her voice thick. "Please, just hang on."

37

FOR WHAT IT'S WORTH

"COME ON, BUDDY, COME ON! GODDAMMIT! COME ON!"

Joe had hooked his arm under Jesse's right arm and across his chest, slapping his hand down in a seeping pool of blood on the left side of Jesse's shirt. Joe's eyes were wide, despite the mud that flew up into them as he tried to crawl out of the trench, dragging his best friend moaning in agony behind him.

Men were lying everywhere -- dead or dying. The second wave of choppers slowed the onslaught from the trees considerably, but not completely, and Joe knew another wave wouldn't come until the relentless rain slowed down.

When Joe spotted Jesse lying broken and bleeding at the bottom of the trench, his heart stopped. The hole had been built for drainage, and the rapidly draining sky was quickly filling it up with a murky flash flood.

Instinctively, he knew the only way Jesse, or any of the men, would eventually get immediate help from the medical personnel would be out in the open field, not in a trench. They had to be seen to be heard.

And Jesse had to be seen. Joe didn't hesitate to move him, but he couldn't look at his foot -- now contorted at a grotesque angle, and he really wished his hand wasn't currently buried in Jesse's blood.

The Viet Cong seemed to have fallen back and become deceptively quiet in the downpour. Retreating? Regrouping? It was impossible to tell, but Joe had a window, and he was going to take it. He called out to a couple of the uninjured men in his unit and ordered them to help move the injured men out of the trench. Though stunned and shaken, they jumped into action.

Joe finally scrambled to the top of the trench, then, putting his other arm under Jesse's knees. He hoisted himself into a hunched position. Jesse almost rhythmically cried out in pain as Joe started jogging as fast as he could toward the clearing on the far end of the airstrip, as far from the trees as he could get.

Jesse's head lolled to the side, his whole broken body screaming from being jostled around in Joe's arms. His eyes were blurry slits, and he couldn't focus on any one thing as he drifted in and out of consciousness.

He could hear someone yelling. Joe. Joe was yelling. Joe was screaming; why was he screaming right in his ear? Didn't he know his head hurt so bad, so bad? He wanted Joe to stop yelling. Just stop!

But instead of anything stopping, Jesse started flying. He was taking off in the air one minute, bounced like a pinball against something or someone in the next, and then landed, flat on his back, in the middle of a pool of muddy water.

He couldn't hear Joe yelling anymore. All he could hear were indistinguishable noises around him and the thunderous pounding of his own heart before it all started to fade away from him once again.

Becca rolled her head to the left, her blurry vision soaking in only the bright light above her. She blinked a couple times as the stark white uniforms worn by two women she didn't know slowly came into focus.

One of the women came closer to her and smiled gently.

"Miss Schmidt?" she said softly, taking her hand. "Miss Schmidt, my name is Monica. Do you know where you are?"

Becca stared at the red cross on the woman's nurse's hat, and her eyes grew wide. She reached for her stomach.

"It's OK, dear," Monica said, as another nurse came to her side. "Your baby is fine."

"Why am I here?" Becca said in a loud, hoarse whisper. "What's happening?"

The second nurse stepped forward.

"You are severely dehydrated," she said with a hint of disgust in her voice. "You clearly haven't been taking in enough fluid. Haven't you been taking care of yourself?"

"I...yes," Becca said meekly, still trying to understand what was going on. Where were Liz and Penny?

The nurse snorted, and Monica shot her a disgusted look.

"No husband in the picture, I presume?" she said, judgment in her voice as she adjusted the sheets around Becca as Monica switched out her IV bag.

"Gladys!" Monica scolded.

"He's in Vietnam," Becca said, feeling stronger and not at all caring for the nurse's attitude. "The baby's father was dr...drafted into the Army."

"I see," Gladys said, pursing her lips together and shifting her gaze. Becca could have sworn she heard her mumble "another bab-killer bastard" under her breath, and anger sprang to her eyes.

"Our patient is awake, Gladys," Monica said, crossing her arms and glaring at her colleague. "Will you please go inquire after Dr. Goldman? He wanted to assess Miss Schmidt's condition as soon as she woke up."

With that, Gladys turned on her heels and left the room.

Monica picked up a blood pressure cuff and started to put it on Becca's arm.

"I feel better, much better," Becca said, putting her arm above her head and away from the nurse. Monica smiled softly as she lowered Becca's arm and put on the cuff. Becca nervously licked her lips.

"That's because of the fluid," the nurse said as she put on the cuff and started to tighten it around her arm. Monica's expression didn't reveal anything as she took the reading and wrote it down in her chart.

"H...how is it?" Becca asked, her voice shaky.

Monica gave her a downward frown.

"The doctor will be right in," she said just as Penny and Liz walked in the door.

"Becca!" Liz said, rushing to her bedside, Penny right behind her. "You're awake -- oh, thank God!"

Becca narrowed her eyes at them both.

"Why am I here?" she asked, searching their faces with a sad and confused expression on her face.

"We couldn't wake you up," Penny said somewhat sternly. "What were we supposed to do?"

"I would've, would've..." Becca started.

"No, you wouldn't have," Liz said, taking her hand. "You need to be here."

"Miss Schmidt?" said Dr. Goldman interrupted as he walked into the room, clipboard in hand.

"Yes," Becca said weakly, her scared eyes still on her friends, who began to back up toward the door to make room for the doctor.

"I'm Dr. Goldman," he said, introducing himself. "You gave your friends quite a scare."

Becca just closed her eyes and nodded once.

Dr. Goldman then examined her pregnant belly, measuring it with a tape measure, and then checked to see if she was at all dilated. He looked into her eyes and listened to her heart, then he picked up the chart he placed at the end of her bed. Monica, who was standing close by, looked at him expectantly.

"It says you're almost at 34 weeks," the doctor said, furrowing his brow. "You're measuring at 32...small. BP is 168 over 119..."

Becca's eyes grew wide. Was the baby small? What did that mean?

"He's...he's too small to be born now, then, right?" Becca said as if the thought of her baby being born anytime soon was completely absurd. "We need more time. He needs more time..."

Dr. Goldman glanced at his patient as she trailed off, her eyes pleading with him. She was young, scared, and completely exhausted -- and had no idea how sick she was. He was surprised she hadn't started seizing already. He shook his head and looked to the nurse, nodding to the other side of the room. He knew if this baby wasn't born today, this mother was in serious trouble.

"Give us a minute," Monica said as she patted Becca's arm, trying to be reassuring as she walked away.

"I'm fine," Becca said quickly, desperately, her eyes darting to Penny and Liz standing just outside the door. She watched as the rude nurse reentered the room and joined the conversation -- a conversation that would change the course of her life, their lives, yet didn't involve her in the slightest.

Becca placed both hands on her stomach and started to panic in earnest.

"He's...he's fine," she said as loudly as possible, trying to get the attention of anyone she could, her heart sinking and her strength beginning to ebb.

"Can we go home?" she whispered, tears filling her eyes. "Please?"

Jesse's body had started to go into shock, and somehow that startled him into an uneasy consciousness. He didn't know where he was or what he was doing, but he felt like he was drowning...because it was raining.

Rain.

He was vaguely aware that it was raining, pouring in fact.

Wave after wave of water fell off the trees above him, crashing down onto him in a relentless onslaught. He tried to open his eyes; actually, he believed his eyes were open, but he couldn't see anything. As he lay flat on his back in a pool of mud and puddles of slime, all he could do was feel. He could feel pain, a sharp, searing pain radiating throughout the top of his body. The pain seemed to be coming straight from his heart.

Jesse used all the strength he had left to raise his right hand, weakly attempting to swat at the rain. His stark white face was fixed in a pinched grimace. Giving up on making the rain go away, he tried to roll over from his back, trying to push himself up with his right hand.

But he couldn't find the ground under him, and soon, with a sound somewhere between a sob and a primal moan, he gave up and let his hand slide back to the ground with a gentle thud.

Between the rain and the pain, he couldn't breathe. Taking a deep breath was impossible. Small, shallow breaths were all he could muster. He was waiting for the darkness to come, almost welcoming the numbness ahead. Almost.

Then he remembered that he had legs. If only his legs...

"Move," he whispered weakly to no one, willing his body to do anything, anything he asked it to do. "Move..."

In that lucid moment, he realized the agony he felt from his chest up seemed to stop at his waist. He couldn't feel his legs. The numbness had started to creep up his body.

And an overwhelming feeling of sadness and loss he had never once associated with this moment in his life crushed against him. His tears started to mix with the downpour as both rolled down the sides of his face.

As he lay there for several minutes, body and soul broken, the rain started to let up, though Jesse didn't realize it. What thoughts he could piece together all swirled around Becca -- knowing deep down that he'd never see her again. He yelled out more from emotional wreckage than physical pain, and yet the darkness still stubbornly refused to come.

Suddenly a wave of strength washed through him, and he forced his eyes open a crack. He could see trees and sun through the rain and felt a swift, strong wind that seemed to drown out all other noise. The numbness started to seep into this chest as he raised his right hand again and slowly, clumsily fumbled with the drenched pocket of his shirt. After several attempts, he pulled out the soaked contents inside with shaking fingers.

Jesse tried to focus on the faded photo, but his eyes wouldn't cooperate, and the small amount of strength he had seemed to run away as quickly as it had come.

His hand dropped with the picture against his chest, and his eyes fell closed once again as his body finally began to shut out the pain.

All she could clearly make out was the word "die."

She watched through a haze all the flurry of activity around her. She was there, but she wasn't there at the same time. Doctors, nurses, all of them running around, not listening to her. Not letting her tell them what needed to happen. They weren't listening.

The nurse, the one who had been so kind, moved in front of her and took her hand and gave her a gentle, sad smile. Becca began to panic in earnest.

"What?!" she demanded, her blue eyes wide and watery and her heart pounding so hard and loud in her ears she was certain everyone could hear it.

"It's time," Monica said quietly.

"No!" Becca yelled, trying to jerk her hand away, but the nurse held firm. "No, it's not time!"

"Miss Schmidt..."

"No!" she whispered fiercely, now gripping the nurse's hands in both of hers, squeezing her fingers so tight her knuckles turned white. "It can't be...not now!"

The other nurse came over, the one who had been so rude before. She had a syringe in her hand. She was waiting for the first nurse to give her the order.

"Should we sedate her?" she asked in a cold, matter-of-fact voice.

"Wait, Gladys," the first nurse said, somewhat exasperated at her colleague, but her gaze never left Becca's.

"Miss Schmidt," she said, her heart breaking for the young woman before her. "I know this is...difficult...but..."

"You don't understand," Becca said desperately, searching the woman's eyes with a crazed look on her face. "He needs me...I...I need him..."

Gladys took another step toward Becca before Monica put up her hand in a "stop" gesture to halt her, and then she motioned to the side of the room.

Becca could see Liz and Penny come into view through her tears, tears streaming down each of their faces. She vaguely thought she caught a glimpse of her mother, too, but knew at that point she must have been hallucinating.

"Becca...Rebecca," Liz whispered softly as she took her hand, and the nurse stepped back a moment.

"Don't let them do it," Becca begged, imploring first Liz, then Penny. "Don't let them take him away from me..."

"Becca," Penny choked out, stroking her hair. "He...he wouldn't want...it...this way. We have to let the doctors...do what's best..."

Liz nodded and cried harder as Becca's fingers clamped down on hers.

Becca started to tremble as she looked at her best friends, her last rays of hope...and the betrayal and despair she felt ran deep.

"How could you..." she said miserably, looking right at Penny, her breathing deep and ragged. With enormous strength, she grabbed Liz's hand and jerked her until they were face to face, causing Liz to gasp in pain.

"*How could you?!*" she growled at her, sweat beading around her temples now.

"Rebecca," Liz said sternly, tears spilling unchecked down her cheeks, trying to disengage her hand from Becca's. "I'm sorry...I'm so sorry, Becca."

Becca's nails scraped against her hand as Liz made one more attempt to pull away.

"Let go," she said a little more forcefully. "Becca, you have to let go..."

Liz snatched her hand away and started massaging it, both she and Penny sobbing now.

"I won't let you do it," Becca said, trying to move away from them. "I won't! I swear to God, I won't!"

"Gladys," Monica said, quickly coming to Becca's side and grabbing her arm, struggling to hold her still.

"Now!"

38

PAINT IT BLACK

JANUARY 1969

Eli hurried across the field, almost jogging to the officers' tent.

He'd just finished his rotation at the Tan Son Nhut base hospital at dawn and was about to fall into an exhausted sleep when Major Thomas summoned him and another lieutenant to his office "on the double." He quickly threw his boots on and took off, his heartbeat racing a mile a minute.

"He's waiting for you, Sir," Eugene said, with a little glare as Eli entered the office. He nodded to the Private and took a deep breath before he opened the door.

Lt. Paul Becker rose from his seat as Eli saluted Major Thomas, then shook Becker's hand. The Major gestured for them to sit down.

"You are both being reassigned with two teams of medical support personnel to the military hospital at Da Nang base in Quang Nam Province," Thomas explained. "The following surgeons are on their way. 'Charlie' is fierce in the region. The base hospital needs reinforcements."

He handed them both a short stack of papers, including a list of doctors already on their way to the northern province in South Vietnam.

Paul and Eli looked at the list, then at each other.

"That's a lot of people," Paul mumbled, eyes back on the paper in front of him.

"A fourth of our personnel," Thomas said with a nod. "The supply team will be ready at 0700. Your group will move out no later."

Eli swallowed hard, a new fear taking precedence in his mind. He knew Quang Nam Province was where Joe and Jesse were stationed with the Army Corps of Engineers.

"Losses have been great, casualties worse," Thomas said, eyeing Eli carefully. He cleared his throat, and Eli looked up from the list and locked eyes with the Major. "The engineering corps was...hit particularly hard a couple weeks ago. Ambush..."

Eli's face fell as Thomas trailed off and sat back in his chair, not willing to share more unless his lieutenant asked.

"How hard?" Eli finally asked evenly, quietly. Thomas hesitated just a moment.

"Twenty-one dead, 47 wounded, three missing," Thomas said, a veiled sadness in his voice. Eli just stared at him, unable to comprehend his friends being in the middle of such a massacre.

"Who...?" Eli croaked out.

"I only have numbers," Thomas said, standing as Paul looked back and forth between the two and also stood. Thomas looked at them both before he dismissed them. "You have your orders. Godspeed, gentlemen."

They both raised their hands in a return salute, Eli's slightly shaking at his forehead, and turned to go. The Major stepped out from behind his desk.

"Schmidt?" Thomas called before Eli was completely out of his office.

"Sir?" Eli asked as he turned back to him.

"Remember, you have a job to do," he said sternly after a brief, sympathetic look crossed his features.

Eli stood up a little straighter and nodded.

"Yes, sir."

Major Thomas made a little nod of his own and turned back to his desk as Eli walked past Eugene and out of the officers' tent.

Lt. Becker was waiting for him outside.

"Sounds bad," he said as he hurried to match Eli's determined stride back to their quarters.

"I know," Eli snapped, looking around at the hustle and bustle of early morning on the base. They walked further together, both lost in their own thoughts. Eli had gotten a telegram from Liz right before the new year. Later another from his mother, telling him he'd become an uncle earlier than anticipated. There wasn't much more detail than that. All he knew was the baby was early, and Becca was "better," whatever that meant. He was waiting, impatiently, for a letter from someone, anyone, at home to tell him what had happened to his sister and her baby to cause the little one to be born on Christmas Day.

And now this. Not only were Becca and the baby apparently in some kind of emergency medical situation two weeks ago, but Jesse and Joe were also in the middle of an ambush at just about the same time.

"See you at 0700," Becker said as he broke off towards his quarters to look over his orders. Eli nodded vaguely toward him and pulled out his paperwork, scanning it quickly. The words began to blur on the paper, and he tossed his head back with a deep sigh.

"You better fucking be OK, Jesse!" he said to the sky, "and Joe...dammit!"

He shook his head and looked back at the papers in his hand.

"I gotta get up there. Now," he muttered to himself, finally beginning to read his orders.

Becca pushed her fingertips against the glass of the hospital nursery.

Her eyes never left the incubator against the wall to her right. Her little baby boy was there, as he had been every moment of his young life, lying on his back with his little eyes closed tight against the harsh light of the room and the heat lamp above him.

She'd watched there for hours every day, observing as nurses scurried about, often paying more attention to other, sicker babies in the room instead of her son. She'd thrown an absolute fit just a week ago as she'd watched her son's chest once again rise and fall as rapid as a hummingbird's wings. He was in distress, and no one was coming to his aid. She'd heaved her sore body from her wheelchair and used all the strength she had to practically break the door down, trying to get to him. It was only seconds before a nurse and doctor examined him. Eventually, his breathing slowed, but it felt like forever to her.

They'd sedated her and made her stay in her room for the rest of the day.

Today he seemed calm, peaceful, breathing in a somewhat normal rhythm. He'd have days like this, then he'd have days when he was teetering or seemed to be getting worse instead of better. Becca was sure those days were the ones that were making her lose her mind. Those days and the fact that she had yet to hear from his Daddy.

Liz had sent a telegram to Jesse's unit a day after their baby was born via an emergency C-section. He was small, only three pounds, one ounce, and didn't make a sound as he came into the world. Becca didn't know if he'd lived or died until the next day when she came out of the anesthetic crying out for Jesse, then their baby. She burst into painful, uncontrollable tears when she learned he was alive. He was undersized, but the bigger issue was the development of his lungs. Were they ready for life outside of his mother?

That was 17 days ago. He was fighting the odds every day, but it seemed recently that more days than not, he was winning.

Every day she put every ounce of will, thought, and feeling she could into that nursery, begging him to keep winning. She needed him to live like she needed to breathe. She needed to hear from Jesse more than she could bear.

And she hoped, beyond hope, that they would both find it in their hearts someday to forgive her.

Becca grinned a little as she watched her boy sleep. He was absolutely beautiful. Small, yes, but completely perfect. He had little wisps of wavy brown hair and perfect, tiny features.

She longed, with an ache she had never felt before, to hold him in her arms. She'd been able to touch his little fingers and toes in the incubator, she'd brushed her finger along his little velvety cheek, but she had yet to be able to hold him.

She was completely in love with him already.

"Becca?" came her mother's quiet voice at the corner of the hallway.

Becca froze, then closed her eyes. She opened them and glanced briefly at her mother before returning her gaze to her son. While Wilma had been there almost every day since her grandson was born, the two had barely spoken more than pleasantries to each other and periodic reports on the baby's health. Wilma was afraid of upsetting her daughter. Becca wasn't ready to hear her mother's warranted criticism, so each kept the other at arm's length, and there was a definitive tension in the air.

Wilma pulled one of the chairs lining the wall up to the glass and next to Becca. She glanced into the nursery, smiling as her eyes landed on her grandson.

"Sleeping away," she said softly as she watched a doctor go from one baby's incubator to another's. "How is he?"

Becca tried to sit up a little straighter before her shoulders slumped again.

"I...they haven't told me anything today...yet," she said, her eyes briefly leaving her son's face to cast an impatient glare at the doctor.

Wilma cast a sideways glance at her daughter.

"You're being released tomorrow?"

Becca felt her eyes fill with tears. She was recovering well from surgery. Her blood pressure had almost immediately returned to normal after her baby was born. Her appetite was back, and she was, of course, no longer dehydrated.

She was steadily on the road to recovery. Her body was bouncing back as she suspected it would, and they were going to send her home -- and the guilt that caused her was so immense it almost overwhelmed her. At that moment, with her mother by her side and all the tension in the air, it finally did.

"Yes," she almost hissed, trying to keep her tears in check and failing. "It seems I'm just fine. My baby is fighting for his life. His Da...daddy could very well be fighting for his life, too, for all I know, but yep, I'm just fine! Fine and dandy!"

Becca started shaking, putting her hands over her face, as her tears started to come faster.

"Becca!" Wilma whispered, her heart breaking for her daughter. She reached out to pull her into a hug, and Becca immediately pulled away from her.

"No! Don't!" Becca cried brokenly. "I don't deserve sympathy...just... just say it. Just say what you...you want to say!"

"I don't...I..."

"Just say it!" Becca whispered fiercely, turning her tear-stained face to her mother. "I brought this on myself. I...I didn't, I couldn't...I couldn't even carry my baby to term! And now he's...he's...and his father... Jesse...my Jesse...I...I..."

"Rebecca, stop!" her mother said firmly, once again reaching out for Becca and this time not letting her back away.

"You stop it now!" Wilma said sternly, but with tears falling from her lashes. She held her tightly until she felt Becca relax in her arms as her daughter's tears soaked her blouse.

Finally, she pulled back and put her hands on her shoulders.

"Look at me," Wilma whispered. When Becca finally calmed enough to look up, she saw an expression on her mother's face that she had never seen before. Wilma took a deep breath.

"I know exactly how you feel," she started. Becca looked at her skeptically, but she continued. "I have spent the last few months not speaking to my pregnant daughter, who unbeknownst to me was so sick she almost died and worrying about a son who may or may not come home from war. I know what it is like to worry about your children. I know what it's like to watch your children...suffer or, or be in, in pain and not...and all you can do is hope they will be OK..."

"But I did this to him," she whispered miserably, glancing back at the nursery. The doctor was with her baby now. "How can I...how can he ever forgive me? How can Jesse forgive me?"

"What are you talking about?!"

"If I hadn't...let myself get dehydrated, Penny and Liz wouldn't have... have panicked, and he...he would have had more time..."

"Becca! If you hadn't been dehydrated, you would have both died!" Wilma gasped out. "Don't you dare blame yourself! I'm your mother, I should have been there! I...the only thing you can be accused of is being incredibly, incredibly stubborn, and *that* you get honestly. Oh, heaven help Jesse when he comes home!"

Surprised by that comment, Becca grinned just a little at her mother, then her eyes clouded over, and she took a ragged breath.

"I haven't heard from him," she admitted quietly, tears filling her eyes again. Wilma closed her eyes for a moment, then watched as fear came over Becca's features.

"If he's...he's at the front, it could be...difficult..." Wilma started, then stopped on Becca's look.

"It's been more than two weeks," she whispered as she shuddered and wrapped her arms around herself. "If he was...able...I know he'd move Heaven and Earth..."

Suddenly the nurse they hadn't noticed standing at the nursery door cleared her throat.

"Miss Schmidt? Mrs. Schmidt?" she said with a smile. "Would you like to come in?"

Becca rose as quickly as she could to her feet, with Wilma's help, and they both made their way inside the nursery, putting on facemasks the nurse handed to them. The doctor was still standing with his back to her next to her son's incubator. When he turned, he was holding Baby Wanger in his arms.

"I think this little one would like to properly meet his mother," the doctor said, smiling from behind his mask.

Behind her own mask, Becca's face broke into a bright smile as tears ran unchecked down her cheeks.

"Is he...is...?" she started, stumbling slightly back into the rocking chair the nurse had pulled over to her.

"He's doing very well and has been gaining stamina for a few days now," the nurse said as the doctor gently placed her baby into Becca's waiting arms. "He's a fighter, this little guy."

"Oh, oh!" Becca cried softly as she felt his light, little body lay in her arms for the first time. She looked up at the doctor.

"Just for a few minutes, Miss Schmidt," he said, with a nod. "I want to keep him here until his gestational age is 40 weeks, but I'm cautiously optimistic. In the last few days, his lungs have started functioning well on much less forced oxygen, and he's gained three ounces."

"Oh, baby boy!" Becca breathed as she looked down at him in wonder, rapidly blinking back her tears so she could see him clearly. Her heart was pounding hard, and her very soul was filling once again with a joy that she hadn't felt for a long, long time.

"I love you," she whispered softly to him, tracing his little forehead with her fingertip. "Oh, I love you, I love you. I'm sorry, I'm so sorry. Mommy's sorry..."

She felt Wilma's hand on her shoulder and a gentle "shhh" from behind her. Becca gasped a couple times, trying to take in the moment and maintain her composure. He was going to be OK. She was all but certain now that he was going to be OK!

"Oh, oh, your Daddy's gonna love you," Becca said softly, almost laughing as much as crying now. "He can't wait to see you. I know...he wants to see you. He...he has to...meet you..."

She briefly closed her eyes, trying to push the pain and anxiety of not knowing if Jesse was safe out of her mind and her heart for just a moment. Just long enough to hold their son -- their strong little baby boy.

She found two small, little sky-blue eyes looking right back at her when she opened them again. It was the first time she'd seen her son with his eyes open, and his eyes were exactly his father's. Becca stifled back a sob.

"What gorgeous eyes," Wilma whispered, bending down and lightly running her fingers through her grandson's hair. The baby's direct gaze never left his mother's.

"Now that's a look," Wilma chuckled softly as she heard Becca gasp and cuddle him closer. "He's telling you he...he's saying 'Mommy, don't give up on me, don't give up on my Daddy...'"

———

Eli walked quietly through the dimly lit corridor where the patients with the most serious injuries were housed at the hospital's far end.

He'd been on the base 25 hours, working the first 24 of them until he was able to inquire after his friends.

He stopped in front of a white curtain surrounding one bed and took a deep breath, trying to prepare himself for what he would see on the other side. It was hard enough to see random patients in horrible conditions. It was another thing entirely to see a friend that way.

He pulled back the curtain and was startled to see someone else sitting by the bedside.

"I'm...sorry," Eli mumbled out, though he made no attempt to step away. The man in black turned, and Eli could see he was an Army chaplain, not very much older than himself.

"No, no, please, come in," the man said softly with a sad smile. "Do you know him?"

Eli just nodded as his eyes ran over the man lying in bed. He hardly recognized him. His head, arm, and leg were wrapped, his face was bruised and swollen. He was as broken a patient as Eli had ever seen.

Eli had to look away before he broke down. He cleared his throat and reached for the chart at the end of the bed, blinking back tears as he read his way through it.

"Oh, my God," he murmured, reading the details about one injury after another, shaking his head.

The Chaplain watched him closely with sympathetic eyes.

"He's a friend of yours?" he asked quietly.

"Yeah," Eli said in a hoarse whisper, putting the chart back. He wiped his eyes and looked back at the bed.

"Lt. Schmidt, what's your first name?" the Chaplain asked after a moment.

"Eli," he said in barely a whisper, then he turned to the man and said in a clearer voice, offering his hand to the Chaplain. "It's Eli."

"Eli," he said as he nodded, shaking his hand. "I'm Chaplain Matthew 'Matty' Cochran. Would you...like for me to pray with you?"

At that, Eli nodded his head and took the seat next to the bed. Matty pulled over a chair. He took Eli's hand and placed it on the soldier's hand, then covered it with his own.

"Heavenly Father," Matty began as Eli's head dropped, tears spilling out of his eyes. "Eli and I pray together tonight for your son, Jesse..."

39

THE TWELFTH OF NEVER

FEBRUARY 1969

...so, Joe thinks the Air Force pilots will give us loads of crap if Apollo 8 makes its orbit around the moon. Guess Army guys would, too, if we were astronauts. Too bad I wasn't drafted into the Air Force. How do you think I'd look in one of those flight suits?

I bet you're excited about Dec. 21st. I can see your face lit up right now. That'll be far out. You'll have a front-row seat to history in the newsroom. Just don't let them work you too hard.

Is it snowing yet in New York? I can't believe I'm going to admit this, but I miss snow. I miss the seasons. There is one season here -- rain. Well, humidity and rain. I've been told it gets better in January. I'll believe that if it happens.

When I come home, can we live somewhere it never rains? San Diego? New Mexico? Can you work at CBS in New Mexico? Not that I expect you to work. I don't. I mean, you will be working, we'll have our little baby then, and I know that will be a hard job. Of course, if you want to keep working at CBS, you can. I didn't mean to imply you couldn't.

Boy, I've stepped in it now, haven't I? Dammit.

Changing subjects, before I dig myself a deeper hole, did you know Joe could sing? He's actually got a nice baritone. He broke out into Christmas songs tonight and made all of us sing a verse. It was 90-degrees after sundown and spitting rain, but here we all were singing "White Christmas" at the top of our lungs. It was ridiculous, but I'll be damned if it didn't feel good.

I wasn't dreaming of a white Christmas, though. Not this year. This year doesn't count. But next year? Next year will be our little one's first Christmas. Or maybe Hanukkah? I don't know. What do you celebrate? I should have asked you. I just never thought of it. I've ignored the holiday season for 25 years, but I know next year will be absolutely amazing. I hope my tour is over and I can be with you to celebrate whatever you want to celebrate, everything you want to celebrate. Hell, I know a random day in May will be amazing with you and our baby to spend it with.

As of this moment, you have, by my calculations, 44 days -- and since I'm a day ahead, it's really 43 days my time. See what I did there?

How are you feeling? I got the impression from your last letter you might not be feeling swell. That was idiotic; of course, you're not! You've got a perfect little parasite growing inside of you. It's natural for you to be more worried as the due date gets closer, but don't be.

I worry about you because I love you, and I want you to be healthy and happy. But I'm not worried. I have no doubt, zero doubt, in my mind that our baby will be anything other than happy and healthy.

You are a remarkable woman, and our child is lucky to have you as their Mom. I mean that, Becca. Please don't ever doubt yourself or ever think that I doubt you. I will always be in your corner. I will always be on your side, no matter what happens. No. Matter. What. Happens. I will always be with you. I will always love you. Nothing will change that. Nothing, do you hear (read) me? Nothing.

Please relax. Put your perfect little feet up, wrap your arms around our little bun in the oven, and squeeze. You're in the home stretch now, babe...

Becca's head jerked around at the shrill ring of the telephone in her parents' kitchen. She looked down at her baby, checking to make sure he was still sound asleep in her arms. She couldn't help but smile. Every day he was getting bigger; every day, he was becoming more alert.

Every second she held onto the light he shed in their lives like a lighthouse in the dark. This little man had a lot to carry on his tiny shoulders. It seemed he was everyone's port in this storm of the unknown.

Careful not to wake him, she ran her fingers over Jesse's signature then folded his last letter in line with the well-worn creases it already contained. She slipped it into the folds of her boy's soft blue blanket. She made sure it was never far from her reach.

The letter, dated Dec. 19, was the last correspondence she'd received from him or about him of any kind. She was past panic; she was past pain. She just existed, floating in and out of a fog both day and night. Her luminous little baby was the only heartbeat keeping her going.

Her own heart was one beat away from being completely broken.

She stared towards the winter sun hanging low out the Schmidt's front window, where a light, fresh coating of snow graced the ground. It would probably melt away, she thought absently. Quietly, without fanfare, it would slowly disappear...

...No. Matter. What. Happens. I will always be with you. I will always love you. Nothing will change that...

Becca's eyes shifted back to their baby. She cupped the side of his little head and slowly ran her palm along with his soft baby hair, lightly over the skin of his ear, his cheek, and his tiny chin. She didn't have tears to blink back anymore. For weeks she'd awaken every day, and she'd immediately start blinking back tears -- all day, every day. Waiting to hear from him. Waiting to hear any word at all. Still, nothing.

She was still receiving his monthly paycheck, but she knew that could simply be a lag in the Army's clerical work. It meant nothing, yet it meant everything. She truly didn't know if the Army would contact her if they had to. Yes, she received his paycheck, but she seriously doubted she was ever listed as his "next of kin" when he was drafted. Considering the mental state he was in, they both were in, when he left, she wouldn't have been surprised if he'd left that question unanswered.

Becca laid her forehead gently against her baby as she heard her mother's muted voice on one end of the line in the kitchen. Wilma and John had insisted their daughter and grandson come live with them when first she, then he, was released from the hospital. Wilma had said it wasn't practical for Becca to live in a six-story walk-up, after major surgery, with a fragile newborn.

Liz agreed and asked Penny to move in with her. Penny, whose lease ran out at the end of 1968, readily agreed. Still, Becca saw one or both of them every day -- they'd "ooh" and "ahh" over the baby and tried to keep Becca's spirits as high as possible.

She knew they thought she'd given up on Jesse. She hadn't; she wouldn't as long as she held out hope there was breath left in his body. The worst part, what caused her the most anxiety, was just not knowing.

She heard Wilma hang up the telephone and walk toward the living room. Becca turned her head from her perch next to the bay window. It offered a perfect view of the front stoop and sidewalk. She'd had her mail forwarded from the apartment, so she would sit and watch for it to come every morning. Her eyes briefly fell on the photo of Jesse, Joe, and Eli together at the military base that sat on the small table beside her as her mother walked into the room.

"That was Gracia," Wilma said softly. "She wanted to know if it would be alright for her to stop by this afternoon after the snow melted."

Becca gave her mother a sad smile.

"Of course," she said.

"That's what I told her," Wilma nodded, pulling the blanket a little tighter over her grandson's chest. Becca looked out the window again.

"Can I get you anything, darling?" Wilma said, putting her hand on Becca's shoulder.

Becca shook her head "no" as her eyes scanned the sidewalk, seeing only the vanishing snow.

"Thank you," she whispered, still looking through the window.

Wilma's eyes filled with tears, but she held them back as she ran her hand down her daughter's hair and nodded. She turned and walked back to the kitchen before she let any of her own tears fall.

"X-rays show his ankle is healing well," the doctor said, turning to Eli. "It was a nasty but clean break. His chest and shoulder wounds have stopped seeping, but we'll have to keep an eye out for infection."

Eli nodded.

"And...?"

"There's no change," the doctor sighed. "We still are not detecting an involuntary reaction to stimuli in tests. He may have some feeling. We just won't know..."

"...until he wakes up, I know," Eli said, throwing a frustrated glance at a comatose Jesse.

"Lt. Schmidt," the doctor said, now standing directly in front of Eli. He crossed his arms. "It is a good sign that X-rays continue to show no breaks in the spinal column. His body is actually healing itself quite well, but..."

"None of that matters if he never wakes up," Eli said sharply. "Does it?"

"I'm afraid not, no," he replied. "The same trauma that injured his back caused swelling in his brain. As you know, it's gone down now, but we just don't know how much damage it may have caused."

Eli closed his eyes, crossed his arms, and nodded. The doctor patted him on the shoulder.

"I have four more to see," he said with a little frown. "See you tomorrow?"

"I start 24-on in a half--hour," Eli replied. "Won't be until later tomorrow night."

The doctor nodded again and left the room.

Eli put his hands on his hips and looked at the small, curtained space around him. Finally, he jerked a chair and moved it next to Jesse's bed. His friend was much less bruised and less swollen than he was almost a month ago, his face looking much more like he was just sleeping off a bad hangover.

If he'd been awake, Eli thought he may have punched him. He was at war with himself, and he'd finally had enough. For weeks he'd prayed with Chaplain Cochran, talked soothingly to his friend about Becca, about his baby boy, about the people who were counting on him to come home.

But now, now he'd had enough. His anxiety had hit a breaking point. It was all too much, and, fairly or unfairly, he was ready to take it out on someone.

"You listen to me, you son-of-a-bitch," he said hotly to the motionless body on the bed. "That's enough of this shit, do you hear me? Do you hear me, Jesse Wanger? You know what today is? Do you? It's February 15. It's the day you met my sister. One year ago, today! You know how I know that? Huh? It was the last day Liz and I had that apartment to ourselves, that's why, and we'd had one hell of a Valentine's Day night. One hell of a night! Then my baby sister moved in, and she met you!"

Eli sucked in his breath and leaned back in his chair before quickly lurching forward again, hot tears burning his eyes.

"She's been crazy about you since then, do you know that?! Even when she was dating Asshole, Liz said she talked about you all the fucking time! She fell for you. She fell for you hard, Wanger and... and here you are. Here you are, and I...I don't know if...if I should tell her you're alive, only to have you die before the message gets to her. False hope, man? Should I give her false hope? If I did, would you wake up? Would you?!"

He jumped up from the chair and started pacing the floor. With a beet-red face, he pointed a shaky, angry finger at Jesse.

"I trusted you," he whispered fiercely. "I thought you were different -- that you were good enough for my Rebecca! You fought for her, you saved her, you adored her. You loved her. You love her, you ass, you love her, and now, what? What?! You're not gonna put up a fight?! You're not gonna fight to be with her? To see your baby. Jesus, Jesse, your son! She's been through hell; do you know that? Hell! But she came through. She came through it with your baby boy! My nephew! They need you...dammit, they need you to fight and wake up and... and be with them! It's your turn, man. It's your turn! Come on! Wake the fuck up!"

Eli stared angrily at Jesse a few moments more before he slumped down into the chair again, covering his face with his hands and slamming his elbows into his knees. He took deep breaths, trying to calm himself enough to have some composure before starting his shift at the hospital. After a couple minutes, his blurry eyes glanced at his watch. With a heavy sigh, he cocked his head to the side and looked at his friend. He blinked as his vision cleared, and then he gasped and quickly clasped Jesse's hand.

As he roughly wiped his eyes, he could see, very clearly, a single tear escape the corner of Jesse's closed right eye and slowly make its way down his temple and toward the pillow under his head.

"Jesse?!" Eli said as loud as he dared, his eyes wide. "Jesse? Do you hear me? That's it...that's it! You fight, you fight right now!"

A small, disbelieving smile broke over Eli's face as he took a deep breath.

"You fight to get home to Becca!"

"March first," Liz said, shaking her head as she handed Rebecca's son back to her. "I can't believe how big he's gotten since he's been home, Becca."

"I know," Becca said as she cuddled her son to her and looked into his little face. His bright blue eyes were staring right back at her. "He's been so alert the past few days. If he sees anything shiny, he just stares at it."

Liz patted his forehead, and he shifted his focus to her. She swallowed heavily.

"My God, he has his eyes," she whispered.

"I know," Becca whispered back, with that sorrow in her voice that Liz was sad she was used to hearing by now. "I know. Even the doctor couldn't believe how bright they are."

Liz smiled sadly and watched Becca walk back to the window and look out. It had snowed heavily overnight, but the roads were clear this morning. March was truly coming "in like a lion."

It had been a harsh, harsh winter for all of them. Becca and Jesse's baby was really the only bright spot, and his life had begun under a cloud of uncertainty. Liz was grateful beyond belief that Eli was OK. In January, he'd written to her asking her all kinds of questions about Becca and the baby and letting her know his new address, telling her he'd been transferred to another base. She'd only heard from him one other time, about three weeks ago, to let her know he was working a lot of hours. He told her he loved her and asked her to keep a close eye on his sister.

Liz walked over to sit next to Becca as John and Wilma came down the stairs and made their way into the living room.

"We're headed into town," Wilma said with a small smile and a soft brush along her grandson's arm. "Do you need anything?"

"No, I don't think so," Becca said with a small smile of her own.

"OK, then," Wilma said. "Oh, we may go crib shopping, too."

"Mom," Becca started to protest.

"He is growing like a weed!" Wilma said firmly, tolerating no resistance. "He'll be out of the bassinet in no time."

"My boy needs room to grow," nodded her father, with a twinkle in his eye. He was completely enamored of his little grandson.

Becca shook her head and rolled her eyes a little at Liz, who stifled a giggle.

It was painful, so painful, to be planning the next, even small steps of her son's life without Jesse by her side. But she truly appreciated her parents' support. Finally, she nodded and sighed.

"Oh, alright," she whispered.

Liz, still amused, looked out the window and then frowned. A currier was quickly making his way up the Schmidt's walkway. Before she had a chance to say a word, there was a hard, brisk knock on the door.

Becca's heart leapt into her throat as John and Wilma exchanged a pensive look. John opened the door.

"Can I help you?" he asked, his voice shaky.

"Is this the Schmidt residence?" the young man asked.

"Yes, I'm John Schmidt."

"Telegram for you, sir, Western-Union," he said, handing John a yellow piece of paper and a clipboard.

John hastily signed the paper on the clipboard then fumbled with the change in his pocket for a tip. He handed him a few coins, and the young man turned to go.

Becca and Liz were on their feet in the entryway, their expressions anxious. Becca's heart was pounding in her chest, tears shining in her eyes. She swallowed hard and pulled her baby closer against her breast, trying to rapidly prepare herself for whatever the message might say. It wasn't delivered by the military, though. Maybe that was a good sign?

Liz wrapped her arm around Becca's waist and reached out to grab Wilma's hand.

John put on his glasses and scanned the telegram.

"It's from Eli," he said, his voice thick. Liz squeezed Wilma's hand and stole a glance at Becca. Her friend's watery eyes were wide. She looked at the baby, who had turned his face at the sound of his grandfather's voice and wore a similar expression...

Becca, Mom, Dad -- STOP -- At the base hospital in the northern province -- STOP -- I'm fine -- STOP -- Jesse injured in December -- STOP -- Was in seriously critical condition -- STOP -- Corner turned now he's healing -- STOP -- Sends his love Becca -- STOP -- Can't wait to meet his son -- STOP -- He's coming home -- STOP -- Details to follow -- STOP -- Love Eli -- STOP

"Ohh! Ah...ah," Becca gasped, tears spilling onto her son's blanket as her knees gave way. Liz and Wilma rushed to steady her as her father joyously wrapped them all in a warm, big hug.

"He's OK, Rebecca, he's OK!" Liz shrieked as she buried her huge smile in her friend's hair.

Becca swayed, her head spinning. The cloak of worry and grief and pain seemed to fall effortlessly from her shoulders as hope and light made way and banished them in an instant. When their family hug finally broke, only a mess of tears and smiles was left in their little circle.

Becca looked at her parents, their eyes bright with tears and warm smiles. At that moment, she was more grateful for her family than she had ever been. It seemed Eli had looked after her Jesse and her parents, once she'd let them in, had looked after her and her baby.

Becca held him close to her cheek, her heart bursting. Jesse was alive! He was broken, he was in pain, he was close to death, and that knowledge made her heart hurt, but he was alive! She didn't give a damn what shape he was in when he came home, as long as he was alive. That's all that mattered now. That's all that ever mattered. He was alive; he was going to meet his baby. He was going to come home to her.

He was going to come home to them all.

"Oh, did you hear that?" she whispered in her son's little ear, her voice so thick with tears he probably couldn't have understood her even if he was able to. "Did you hear that, Baby Boy? Your Daddy's OK. Your Daddy's coming home. He's coming home!"

40

AIN'T NO MOUNTAIN HIGH ENOUGH

APRIL 1969

...and he's gaining weight at the speed of light. The doctor said he's right in line with babies that would be about two months old. Of course, he's almost three months old now, but he's growing very well since he was born early. He's healthy.

He's just learned how to smile. It is the cutest thing! He will melt your heart, Jesse. He's completely beautiful. He looks just like you. He has your eyes, everyone says it, and it's true. The picture doesn't do him justice. He's all wrapped up, and his eyes are closed, but I wanted you to see him. He's small, but despite that, he is perfect...

Jesse's eyes glanced over, again, at the small black and white photo in his palm. His baby. His little boy was wrapped up tight in a baby blanket in a hospital crib. He was tiny, incredibly tiny, but Jesse really had no frame of reference when it came to the size of a baby, having never been around them much. To him, he looked perfect -- a little tuft of hair, a button nose. He didn't see how he looked like him, but if Becca said their son looked like him, then he did.

His son. He had a son. He had a son with the most beautiful, loving woman he had ever known. It was nearly incomprehensible to him. Every time he thought about it, which was nearly every second of the day, he almost couldn't believe it. Some days it just felt like a dream.

He was wild and more frustrated than ever to get home to them both. He never expected their baby to be born on Christmas Day. Eli had told him what little he knew. Becca had endured some type of medical emergency that made it necessary for the baby to be born early. His son's life had been touch and go for weeks before he was cleared to come home. Becca was living with her parents, and she wasn't working anymore.

She'd been through her own Hell, and he couldn't help but feel guilty about it. He wished she'd shared her struggle with him but understood why she hadn't. He knew that they'd each been careful to shield the other, wanting nothing more than to feel safe in the world they created when they wrote to one another. Yet, if anything had happened to them -- to either of them. He shuddered. He felt damn guilty for not being there when she needed him the most but unbelievably relieved they were well. He smiled once more at his little boy, then tucked his son's photograph into the pocket of his shirt...

I can't wait for you to meet him. I can't wait for you to come home. It is impossible for me to tell you how much I love him. I can't even comprehend it myself. And when we received Eli's telegram, it was as if the whole shattered world came back together again. I know it's not the same. We've all been through so much, and we have lost so, so much.

I guess it wasn't fair to him how much I relied on him to keep me going during that time. He's a little, sweet, innocent child I want to protect with every fiber of my being, but he's been my strength. I won't let him out of my sight. It's making my mother crazy, but I just won't. He's my physical connection to you, and I just don't want to be away from him.

My love, my precious, precious Jesse, how I want to touch you again. I want to hold your hands, I want to touch your face, I want to look into your eyes. Sometimes I look into Jay's eyes, and I swear it is you looking back at me. Of course, it's not the same, but soon, blessedly soon, it will be you.

I thank God it will be you. Every day I love you more than I did the day before. My feelings come over me, so suddenly, they take my breath away. In those moments, even holding our son isn't enough. Nothing eases my longing for you. I love you so, so much...

Jesse's breath caught, and he looked up from her letter, blinking his eyes as the breeze blew through the trees outside the military hospital where he was seated. He grasped her letter in both hands to steady it against the wind. He shook his head quickly. He'd been wallowing too long in the sad, in the hard, in the pain of recovery. Not today -- not when he had her love, her words in his hands. Not on the day when his baby boy's picture was lying against his pounding heart. Today was a day to let himself get lost in the love that was leaping off the pages at him, in the hope that was waiting for him at home. Today he didn't want to feel any pain, any hurt.

He needed to feel her love cascade over him, coating him in comfort and warmth he was in no way yet totally accustomed to but was desperate to feel. He needed to feel her and, in the way only she could, wash away the physical and emotional pain he'd lived with since he finally woke up to his new reality almost six weeks ago...

I have so much to tell you, so much you don't know that I need to share with you. You have showered me with unconditional love and understanding, no questions asked. I don't know if you have any idea how incredible that is, how incredible you are. You are everything to me, and our son is so blessed to have you as his father. You will love him. I know you already do...

"I do," he whispered softly, with a nod. "I do."

Jesse, I know you, and I know you want to take care of both of us, and you have. Sweetheart, you have, but all I want you to concentrate on is healing. Please understand that I know it will take a while for us to find our center. I don't know yet where we'll live or exactly how we're going to build our future, but it's enough to know we have one. I don't want you to feel pressured or rushed in any way because the only future I need is one with you and Jay in it. That's all. That's everything, and the rest will take care of itself in time. Eli wrote and told me how badly you were injured. When I think of how close we were to losing you, I can't breathe. You're coming back to me, to us, and that is all that matters.

Just let me take care of both my boys. My desire to spoil you two is unstoppable, so don't try to deter me. You won't win. I have made up my mind that you will be the two most loved people in the whole world...

"Sgt. Wanger?"

With tears in his eyes, Jesse glared momentarily at the orderly who'd interrupted him.

"Sir?" the Private said, "It's time for your therapy, Sir."

Jesse closed his eyes and nodded, folding Becca's letter and placing it in his pocket beside his son's picture.

He frowned a moment and then folded his hands on his lap, looking straight ahead. The Private walked behind him and grabbed the handlebars. He backed up the chair, turned it, and then pushed Jesse back into the hospital.

––––––––

Becca tucked her legs under her and spread the newspaper out onto the lawn. It was a beautiful, dry spring day with low humidity, and she'd brought her boy outside for some much-needed fresh air. After a fair number of smiles and giggles, he'd fallen asleep on a blanket under the big oak tree in the Schmidt's back yard. Becca had wrapped a smaller, lighter blanket around him. After staring at him with hearts in her eyes for a good long while, she let him sleep undisturbed in the shade of the afternoon sun.

Her eyes half-heartedly scanned the "want ads," not at all sure what she was hoping to find. She'd kept in touch with Malory, who had encouraged her to call Ms. Beele and ask for her old job back, or any job, at CBS headquarters, but she wasn't sure she wanted to do that. She glanced at Jay, softly snoring next to her, and smiled. When she'd chosen her child over the grueling commitment of her job in November, she had every intention of finding a way back to it someday. Working in TV news had been her dream for so long, but there was no doubt her dreams and priorities had shifted. The long hours in the newsroom were hard ones, and she didn't know if she wanted to be away from her baby for 12 hours a day or more.

And she didn't know what kind of care Jesse would need. When Eli finally detailed the extent of his injuries, she'd almost fainted. She'd cried for an hour, thinking about how much pain he must have been in. He'd been in a coma for weeks. He'd had shrapnel embedded in his chest and shoulder and a compound fracture of his ankle. Most importantly, though, his spinal column had suffered severe trauma, and he was paralyzed from mid-back down.

In his last letter, Eli assured her that the Army neurologist at the base believed the paralysis was temporary. Jesse did have some feeling in his feet and one leg, but he had a long, painful road ahead of him.

Becca was preparing to go down that road with him. She knew it would be difficult, but she was determined to let him know she loved him and wanted him, no matter what condition he was in when he came home. He was alive, and she would never, ever take that miracle for granted.

Suddenly her other miracle sneezed a couple times, little sweet baby sneezes. She smiled as he settled again without so much as a whimper. She glanced quickly through the apartment listings, then back to the employment ads. One ad piqued her interest. The very newspaper she was reading was looking for a local government reporter.

The back door creaked open, and Becca looked up to see both her parents walking out into the backyard.

"Isn't the breeze a bit too much for him out here?" Wilma said, pulling her light sweater tighter around her and throwing a worried glance at her grandson.

"Mom, he's fine," Becca said, with an amused look on her face. Her father slowly made his way to sit beside her and glanced at the paper.

"What's this?" he asked.

"Oh," Becca said, neatly folding the newspaper back into place. She wasn't sure how much she wanted to share with her parents about her sparse plans before mapping them out in her own mind.

"I'm just thinking about our future," Becca shrugged as she glanced at her slumbering baby, then back at her parents. "Look, I know you're going to say we can stay here as long as we need, and I appreciate that, but at some point, we have to find a place to live and a way to support ourselves."

"Well, when you get married…" Wilma started.

"Mom, stop," Becca insisted, forcefully. She took a deep breath and closed her eyes. "I can't keep having this conversation with you…"

"Rebecca," Wilma interrupted.

"Ladies," John said quickly as he shot a warning look to his wife and gestured to the sleeping baby on the blanket in the grass. Wilma pursed her lips, crossing her arms in front of her, but she said no more. John cleared his throat.

"As for supporting yourselves, Jesse will get checks from the Army," John said.

"I know, but I don't think it will be enough," Becca said, shaking her head. "And if...if he needs special care...and we need to find a place to live, with no steps..."

John sighed and frowned a little, then he looked up at his wife and raised his eyebrows. She sighed, then nodded.

"I think we may have a solution for you, at least for the time being..." Wilma started, first glancing at her grandson then looking at her daughter's curious expression with just a hint of a smile.

———

"You have a stop in Europe, right?" Eli asked.

"That's what they've told me," Jesse nodded. "Then it's on to Andrews AFB then..."

He trailed off, swallowing the lump in his throat.

"Then New York," Eli said quietly.

"Yeah," he nodded, his voice thick.

Eli nodded, his eyes wandering over to the neatly folded uniform and shoes on Jesse's bed, his knapsack lying next to it. He looked back at Jesse. His shoulders were shifting uncomfortably in his wheelchair as he ran his palm over his chin.

Eli folded his hands between his knees and leaned up on the edge of his seat.

"Give it some time," he said softly.

"It's been two months," Jesse said, shooting Eli an exasperated look.

"It might take two more," Eli said. "Maybe six more, but it will come back."

Jesse looked away quickly, tears burning his eyes, then sighed and looked down.

"I don't want to be half a man," he whispered. "I want to take care of her, of them, and I...I don't want to do it from this fucking chair!"

He slapped his hands hard on the armrests. Eli sat back and sighed.

"Jesse, you'll get there," Eli said evenly. "She...doesn't care..."

"I care," Jesse said hotly, then he stopped speaking. He knew he should be grateful. He was going home alive to the woman he loved. He knew oh-so-well that the opportunity to do that wasn't granted to everyone. Flying off the handle wasn't going to make anything better either. He looked back at Eli and shook his head. His friend had three more years left in the Army, and here he was going home.

"I'm sorry, man," he said. "It's just frustrating, you dig?"

"I dig," Eli said with a little smirk. "Listen, it's going to take time, but you will walk again."

Jesse smirked back at him and cleared his throat enough to at least feign confidence.

"Damn straight," he said, with a nod, then his face turned serious, and he reached a hand out, which Eli took.

"Thank you, man," Jesse said, with a handshake, his voice low but sincere. "I'm...I'm glad you've been here."

Eli swallowed heavily, then smiled.

"Give everyone my love," he said thickly, then added. "You scared the shit outta me, Wanger. I thought you were gonna bail on my little sister."

Jesse gave him a sad smile.

"She's stuck with me," he said, shaking his head, "whether she likes it or not."

Eli squeezed his hand.

"She loves you, man," he said. "Don't ever forget that."

Jesse looked at Becca's brother and at the tears in his eyes. No, he would never forget that.

"She loves you, too," he said quietly. "So does Liz. Cast of thousands, man, don't *you* forget *that*. You come back home in one piece; you hear me?"

Jesse's eyes searched Eli's with a quiet desperation in them that Eli understood.

"Roger that," Eli said, then he nodded. With one more shake, they dropped hands. Eli cleared his throat and stood to leave. He stopped at the edge of the curtain and turned back to Jesse.

"See you in Hawaii?" he asked. Jesse gave him a crooked grin.

"I'll wear my hula shoes," Jesse said with a wink.

Eli smiled, then raised his right hand in a salute, a tear threatening to escape his eye.

Jesse pushed up on the armrests of his chair with great effort and hoisted himself into a standing position as a tear ran unchecked down Eli's cheek. Sweating and shaking on his unsteady legs, he raised his right hand in salute.

"You've served well, Sergeant," Eli said. "Godspeed."

"Godspeed, Lieutenant," Jesse said as evenly as he could. Eli gave him an upside-down smile, lowered his hand, and finally turned to go.

Jesse let out a small gasp as his hands found the armrests again. Groaning, he gingerly sat back down in his chair. He ran his hands down his wet cheeks and wiped away his tears, then he looked over at his bed. He let out a heavy sigh.

In three hours, he'd be leaving Vietnam for good. In time he'd leave Europe and head for home.

And before summer began, God willing, he'd see her face again.

41

THE FIRST TIME EVER I SAW YOUR FACE

MAY 1969

Liz placed her hands on Becca's shoulders and looked at her friend in the reflection of the mirror in the airport restroom lounge.

"You look beautiful," she reassured her as Becca, for at least the fourth time, smoothed down the front of her light blue pleated skirt that was just a shade darker than her simple silk blouse.

"Do I?" she asked absently, her stomach doing flip-flops as she glanced at her watch.

Twenty minutes. His plane was scheduled to land in New York in 20 minutes. He was flying home on a smaller plane from Andrews Air Force Base, a special transport that brought home soldiers who weren't going to be able to walk the corridor from the airplane to the gate. They would meet him on the tarmac at the foot of the plane.

In some ways, she was relieved he wouldn't have to come through the gate. The war was no more popular now than it had been a year ago when they all left for the Army. She knew she wouldn't be able to control herself if someone threw so much as a disapproving glance his way.

Liz turned Becca around to face her and smiled.

"Are you ready?" she asked softly.

"Yes," Becca said. Off Liz's cocked eyebrow, she smiled. "Yes. I'm just... anxious...I...I can't wait to see him. Then, then it will be real. He's... he's...it just doesn't feel real...yet."

Liz smoothed down Becca's hair and grinned a little sadly at her.

"I know," she said softly. "But it is, Becca. He's...he's alive, and he's coming home. Just a little while longer, alright?"

Becca nodded and swallowed the lump in her throat.

"Right on," she said, then added in a whisper, "just a little while longer."

Finally, she smiled at Liz as her friend looped her arm through hers and led her out of the restroom, back to Jay, Penny, and everyone else.

Jesse pulled on the lapel of his Army green dress jacket and straightened the knot on his tie. The uniform was crisp and new. He looked down at the patch on his arm. Before he left Washington, D.C., he'd been promoted to Master Sergeant, awarded a Purple Heart and a medal for bravery.

He didn't feel brave at the moment, as his eyes scanned the runways at JFK as his plane came in for a landing. "Excited" didn't exactly describe his feelings either. He was...nervous.

As much as he was desperate to see Becca, as much as he longed to meet his son, he wasn't sure exactly what to expect when he disembarked and was "home" again.

For many reasons, "home" wasn't the same place he left -- and he was sorrowful and grateful for that at the same time.

"How are you doing, Soldier?" Matty said with a soft smile as the plane landed.

Jesse's gaze left the window and met the Chaplain's sitting across from him. He smiled at the man who'd become a good friend. Not only his friend, Jesse thought, but his confidant, almost his therapist. After spending hours and hours together over several months, Matty knew just about as much as Becca did about Jesse's childhood, about his fears of being a good father, about the tremendous relief and guilt he felt at being able to come home from war.

When Matty knew he was leaving Vietnam at the same time as Jesse, he volunteered to be the chaperone who brought him back to his family. At the end of his second tour of duty In Country, Matty was assigned to West Point for the foreseeable future. He was happy to be making the voyage to New York with Jesse, and Jesse, in turn, was grateful for his company.

"OK, I think," Jesse replied, then he took a deep, shaky breath.

"That well, huh?" Matty said with a grin. He reached out and patted Jesse's arm. "It's going to be fine. You're almost home."

Jesse nodded and looked out the window again as the runway passed quickly under the wing of the airplane. The airport itself was outside the window on the opposite side of the aisle. Jesse closed his eyes and laid his head against the wall as the taxing plane came to a stop.

He heard the unbuckling of seatbelts and opened his eyes. Matty gestured to the equipment hold at the end of the aisle.

"Do you want me to get it?" he said, gesturing to the back of the plane.

After a moment, Jesse sighed.

"Yeah, I'll need it," he said.

Matty nodded and made his way down the aisle as Jesse ran his palm over his face, his eyes wide as he attempted to prepare for the emotions that awaited him beyond the confines of the aircraft.

After a minute, Matty stood before him again.

"Are you ready?" he said with a small smile.

Jesse took one more deep breath.

"Yes, Sir," he said with a little grin. "Let's go."

———

Becca ran her palm over Jay's blue blanket as he lay sleeping in Penny's arms, lulled to slumber by the ebb and flow of planes taxiing to and fro on the tarmac by the airport gates. Penny pulled the little blue crocheted cap she'd made for him over his ears as she caught Becca's eye, and they smiled softly at each other. Becca looked just beyond Penny to Liz and her parents, and Liz's parents. All wore encouraging grins on their faces, her mother dabbing at the tears in her eyes.

Becca knew these people loved her, they loved Jay, and they were all waiting to show love and support to Jesse.

She turned back and took a step forward and faced his airplane, which had come to a stop less than 40 yards away from them. The air draft gusted around them, whipping her shorter locks all around her face. Her hair was shoulder-length now, a much more manageable length for a new mother. She unsuccessfully tried to smooth it back, momentarily tucking some behind her ears before the wind made it fly right back out again.

Her heart raced as she watched the ramp being lowered down one side of the small aircraft as steps were lowered down the other. She swallowed hard. Again, she went over what she wanted to say when she first saw him, rehearsing words she'd thought about for days --

words of welcome, encouragement, comfort, and love. She braced herself for the sight of him in a wheelchair, determined to smile through whatever tears would fall. She felt like she was ready.

She sucked in her breath as first the pilot and co-pilot made their way down the steps, then plastered a smile on her face as she saw him being rolled down the ramp by another soldier on the far side of the plane. She took a step forward, then abruptly stopped when the chair turned around, and a family a ways away from hers began to run out to the soldier in the wheelchair, their cries welcoming him home.

Becca looked back to the empty ramp, her heart in her throat. She failed to hear the collective gasp behind her when out of the corner of her eye, she saw two men slowly descending the steps on the side of the plane closest to her. One of them was gripping the handrail and bracing each step with a cane at his side.

When he reached the bottom step, he looked up at her with those brilliant blue eyes that matched her baby boy's, and her heart slammed so hard she thought it might leap straight out of her chest. His lips were turned up ever so slightly at the corners, and suddenly she swooned as her mind took her back to the first moment she'd ever laid eyes on him...

...she could tell his eyes were blue.

"It's so nice to meet you," she said, smiling and extending a hand to him. "Everyone's been giving me the low down on you."

A slow, sweet, crooked grin came over his face as he put his hand out for hers.

"Have they?" he said, his warm hand fitting snugly into her grasp.

Then he smiled at her, and her breath nearly caught. Those eyes and...my God, that smile...

Seeing him made every word she wanted to say to him disappear from her mind. Her planned speech dropped with a silent thud on the ground at her feet as she made her way to him as slowly as he made his way to her, her eyes never leaving his.

It didn't even immediately register with her that he was walking, somewhat gingerly, toward her, too. Her hand was in a fist at her chest, her mouth slightly agape, her eyes searching his, one simple phrase on a continuous, soft loop in her brain -- *"I love you, I love you, I love you..."*

Jesse's labored breath caught more than once as she came closer to him, her shorter hair blowing all around her delicate face. She was a vision. She was a dream, and he could swear she fell directly out of the white, puffy clouds above him. With every move he made towards her, the struggle of putting one foot in front of the other seemed to lessen, as though the chains holding him back were breaking link-by-link, step by step.

He could see no one else but her. He could hear nothing but his heart pounding away in his ears. She was as angelic and perfect as the day he left, but with no sadness fixed to her features now, only wonder and, as she walked closer to him, endless pools of love in those deep blue eyes that had entranced him since they first met his...

...Her smile deepened as she took his hand and gazed boldly into his eyes. He thought her hands were soft, but her grip was strong. Her smile was adorned with little dimples on each side of her cheeks as she looked up at him.

But...it was her eyes. Her eyes were completely mesmerizing, hypnotic almost, and the deepest yet brightest blue he'd ever seen...

They slowed to a stop only a foot or so away from one another, each drinking in the sight of the other. It was then that Becca realized he had walked to her, and she gasped in surprise as the tears pooling in her eyes spilled to her cheeks. She began to cry as Jesse's cane dropped to the ground next to them, and he cupped her face in his hands, gently pushing her blowing hair away from her eyes.

Becca's soft, quiet sobs grew as she felt his palms on her cheeks, her tears soaking them as she searched his eyes. They were full of such intense feeling, intense love that no words would ever be able to describe it well enough. Slowly she fell crying into his embrace, her trembling lips finding his.

He took a small step closer to her, his mouth tasting her tears, which had begun mingling with his own. He felt her trembling hands reach his shoulders then move, her fingertips feeling like fluttering butterfly wings against his cheek, his ear, and the nape of his neck. She was shaking from head to toe as he deepened the soft, slow, wet, loving kiss they'd each dreamed about for such a long, long time.

Finally, he felt her fingers digging through his short hair as she moved to circle her arms around his neck, pressing her body flush against his. He moved his hands slowly across the silk against her back, holding her close in his embrace, steadying himself against the spinning in his head and the unsteadiness of his legs. He could feel her thundering heart in sync with his own.

Gently, slowly their lips parted as they caught their breath, still staring into each other's eyes and clinging to one another. Becca opened her mouth to speak but had no voice.

"I love you," she mouthed softly, one hand clutching him, the other caressing his cheek. Then she smiled brightly, blinking back a new wave of tears as her emotions overwhelmed her. She fisted the back of his uniform jacket, determined she was never going to let him go.

He smiled back at her, his watery eyes never leaving her face. He took a ragged breath as Penny slowly stepped forward, tears streaming down her face. It was only then that he noticed the small army of family standing behind Becca.

Becca broke their gaze first as she turned her head and grinned at Penny, her eyes landing on the bundle in her friend's arms. Jesse looked into the face of his oldest friend, trying to sustain a faltering smile as he looked at her. She slowly nodded as more tears filled her eyes. Years of shared experiences and raw emotions instantly passed between them. Then Penny took another step forward, and Jesse's eyes fell to his son.

He froze, his mouth slightly open, staring at the sleeping baby in his friend's arms. Instinctively he reached out his right arm, Becca still securely being held in his left. Gently, Penny moved to place Jay's head into the bend at Jesse's elbow as his hand slipped perfectly under his bottom, his fingers wrapping securely around his little legs under his blanket. Jesse briefly closed his eyes as Penny reached up and kissed his cheek.

"Welcome home, Daddy," she whispered as she smiled and stepped back, grinning softly at the smiling man standing back behind Jesse, who was now holding his cane, then walking back to join a crying Liz and the rest of Jay's family.

Becca watched as Jesse studied his son, who was now squirming just a bit in his father's embrace. Jesse pulled him a little closer against his body as Becca wrapped one arm under his, helping him cradle their baby.

Jesse watched in awe as this oblivious little person yawned then smacked his little lips together, causing Jesse to chuckle. He opened his sleepy eyes and looked at his father.

"Ohhh..." As his teary eyes shifted from Jay to Becca, Jesse shuddered, a look of complete adoration on his face. He looked back at Jay. His son's piercing, bright eyes sent shockwaves through Jesse. He held him closer still, feeling a power come over him, unlike any force he'd ever known. Slowly he raised Jay up to his face and placed a soft kiss against his forehead, silently vowing to be the strong, loving father his son deserved.

With a small, muted cry, Becca pulled both of them closer to her, her brilliant smile finally breaking once again through her tears as she looked into Jesse's face. He grinned, unable to speak as he moved his free hand into her hair, pulling her to him. He closed his eyes and pressed a kiss to her forehead, then looked down into her eyes and took a deep, shaky breath.

"I love you, Becca," he said in a whisper, his voice quivering. "I love him. I love you. Thank you..."

Becca started to cry in earnest again as she pressed her lips once more to his. After a moment, she broke away, and in a shaking voice, full of love mixed with profound relief, she whispered, "thank you for coming home to me."

He nodded with a whimper, then laid his forehead to hers as they closed their eyes, holding on tight to their baby boy and each other.

42

UNFORGETTABLE

JUNE 1969

"Tuck your fingers there..."

"Like this?"

"Right on. Do you have the pin?"

"Yes."

"Great, now just fasten it through..."

Jesse froze, and Becca glanced at him, a slow smile forming on her face.

"You're not going to hurt him, Jesse," she said, rubbing his shoulder reassuringly.

"What if I poke him?" he asked, unconvinced.

"That's why your fingers are there," she said. "You'll poke you, not him."

Jesse shrugged a little, then carefully slid the safety pin through the front of his son's cloth diaper as Jay started to squirm.

"Oh, hold still, buddy. Daddy isn't good at this yet, you dig?" Jesse said, furrowing his brow as he safely closed the pin. "There!"

He stepped back slightly, feeling relatively triumphant. Becca gave him a bemused look as Jay started pushing his feet against her grandmother's quilt, the diaper beginning to slide down over his bottom. In one quick motion, she reached over and refastened the safety pin, keeping the diaper securely in place.

Jesse ran his tongue along the inside of his cheek, then cocked his head to the side as Becca picked their baby up off the bed and turned to him with a bedazzling smile.

"I'm never gonna get it," he said, shaking his head slightly.

"Sure, you will," Becca replied, picking up the bottle that was waiting on the nightstand, then reaching up to give Jesse a peck on the cheek. "Most Dads wouldn't even try."

"Oh, I'll keep trying," he said with a lopsided grin, running his hand over his son's hair as he sat against his mother's arm. Jay bounced his arms and fists up and down a couple times, giving his Dad a gummy smile before his little fists found his eyes, and he rubbed them, burying his face in Becca's chest.

"Someone's ready for night-night," she whispered, kissing his baby hair and closing her eyes, briefly resting her cheek against his head.

A wave of warmth washed over Jesse as he looked at the two of them, momentarily cuddled up together, both looking like cherubs. He moved his hand to Becca's hair, lightly running his fingers through it as she peeked up at him over Jay's head. He took a step closer to them, the warmth turning into the familiar heat it always had whenever their eyes met. Suddenly Becca's mouth went dry as she lifted her head and licked her lips. Since he'd been home, the look in his eyes when he held her gaze rocked her very soul. Despite all they'd been through in the past year, both together and apart, she almost couldn't believe there was ever a time she'd doubted his love.

Jay started to whimper, and Jesse cleared his throat, breaking the spell between them.

Becca blinked, then smiled with a slight blush on her cheeks.

"I'll put him down," she said, then she gestured to the bed. "Why don't you rest? You've been on your feet a lot today."

"I'm alright," he said, though his legs said otherwise. She smiled softly at him before disappearing with Jay to the other bedroom. He readily sunk down onto the bed, took a deep breath, and let it out slowly, kicking off his shoes and socks to free his throbbing feet. His legs were aching badly. He opened the drawer of the nightstand and pulled out some aspirin tablets, quickly swallowing them down.

He'd regained almost all the feeling he'd lost less than 10 days after landing in West Germany in early April on his prolonged trip home. By the time he'd landed in New York in late May, all the feeling was back from his temporary paralysis, but his muscles were weak. He'd been in intense physical therapy for six weeks at both the base in West Germany and again in Washington, D.C., painfully building his strength up again.

He turned toward the screened window as the breeze moved through his hair. Not 50 steps beyond the covered east porch outside lay the ocean, slowly taking on a golden glow as the sun began its descent in the west. He breathed in the salty air through his nose as he looked around the bedroom of their new "home," a somewhat secluded small, two-bedroom, beachfront cottage about a half-hour's drive from Becca's parents' house on Long Island. Becca's grandmother, Agnes, had lived there almost year-round until she passed two years prior.

The sturdy, one-story wooden house didn't have much. A small but serviceable kitchen flowed into a living room area. There were two small bedrooms and, thankfully, an indoor bathroom. Agnes had loved the place so much she'd had it as insulated as possible to protect it from the harsh beachfront winters. The Schmidts had talked about selling it in the spring, but those plans changed. Instead, John spent every weekend in April putting new screens in all the windows, cleaning and airing the place out for Becca, Jesse, and Jay.

They'd spent the last two days moving in, though, in truth, there wasn't much to move -- clothes, baby supplies, a few furniture pieces. Wilma had gone grocery shopping for them that morning and bought so much that they probably wouldn't have to leave the place for a month. To top it all off, there was already a small crib in one bedroom, an heirloom that had been in Wilma's family for generations. Every baby born in the family had slept there at least once, and for now, the crib was Jay's.

Wilma and John kept the fancy new crib she'd bought at their house for when her grandson would pay a visit. Becca knew living apart from Jay wouldn't be easy for her parents, but it was beyond time for it to happen. Her mother's well-intentioned yet constant clucking around Jay was beginning to wear on the closer relationship she'd established with her since he was born. In order to sustain it, they both needed space. Wilma sensed it too, and so the beach house solution was born.

Of course, Jesse knew he and Becca wanted and needed that space as well. They both needed to learn how to be together as a couple, which they hadn't had the chance to be, and as a family with their baby boy. So far, it had flowed naturally, both of them having matured and changed in the past year. They still had much to share and feel through together, and yet the connection that had been between them since the moment they met remained. Being secure in their love for one another had only made it stronger.

Jesse could hear the creaking of the rocking chair against the hardwood in Jay's room; it was in rhythm with the light pats on his back as Becca tried to get him to burp before laying him down. He dropped his head and grinned to himself. What an incredible mother she was, he thought, exactly as he knew she would be.

His head popped up as Jay let out a little wail, a sure sign that his son was having a little trouble going to sleep in his new surroundings. Jesse heaved himself up off the bed. After steadying his legs, he slowly walked into the living room, having earlier spotted an old turntable and wire files full of records in the corner. He remembered Becca telling him that music sometimes helped Jay sleep, so he blew the dust off the cover and opened it up. He checked the arm for a needle then plugged it in, hoping the old record player still worked. The familiar pop sound that followed assured him the electricity was flowing, so he picked up several albums in the middle of the stack.

He chuckled to himself as he looked through the first few covers, now knowing where Becca learned to love the blues. He pulled one record out of its sleeve and placed it gently on the turntable, putting the needle down and adjusting the volume just as Becca walked out of Jay's bedroom.

"I thought you were going to rest," she said as she pulled the door closed behind her.

He turned and shook his head, a smile playing on his lips.

"Is he down?"

"Yeah," she said, her breath catching a little as she looked at him in the evening light, barefoot in old blue jeans and a faded green Army t-shirt. Her heart started to pound heavily.

"Good," he grinned, then he held out his hand. "Then come dance with me."

She grinned as she swallowed hard, slipping off her slip-on canvas shoes and placing them neatly between the bedroom doors. She was wearing a light, short-sleeved red sweater which cuffed around her shoulders, leaving them bare, and khaki pedal pushers. As she slowly walked over to him and placed her hand in his, he was quickly reminded of the effect she had on him when she moved this way, her eyes not leaving his, a small smile and blush on her cheeks.

He pulled her to him, his free hand landing on the small of her back, her free hand doing the same to him as she started to make slow circles against his t-shirt with her palm. Soon her other hand wrapped around him, and both tracked up and down the muscles in his back as he locked his hands behind her waist, her head resting against his chest securely underneath his chin.

They swayed gently, eyes closed, reveling in being close and being alone as one song faded into another. As golden light came in like the tide across the hardwood floor, the smooth vocals of Nat King Cole's "Unforgettable" softly filled the small cottage.

Jesse's arms crossed around her back as he pulled her closer, tighter against him. As the song's final lines began to fade away, she shifted her head and kissed his chest through his shirt. She didn't see the slight grimace that came over Jesse's face despite the thundering of his heart. She leaned back and looked up at him. He smiled down at her, drinking in the love on her face and the lust in her eyes, then captured her lips with a pent-up tension that had no choice but to be released.

She gasped against his mouth as she moved her hands to his hair, feeling her body being crushed against him. This was the passion she'd dreamt of, longed for, all those lonely nights over the past 12 months. All the worry, ache, and sorrow was lost in the head rush she could barely describe to herself. And she drank it up, feeling his tongue against hers, sucking on his bottom lip...kissing, just kissing him. Trying to make up for all they'd missed.

They'd kissed long, they'd kissed deep and slow in the few weeks he'd been home again, but the opportunity for more just wasn't there in the Schmidt's crowded suburban house. They'd both felt the vibe, the desire to be together nearly overwhelming them at times. But Jesse was still recovering and was sleeping in Eli's old bedroom while Jay was sleeping in the room with Becca.

But now, now was the time.

Breathing heavily, Jesse lifted his lips from her mouth, desperate to taste her. His lips massaged her neck as she moaned, her rapid breath hot against his ear, a look of pain and pleasure mixing on her face. She gripped his shoulders, every inch of her crying out for his touch as he gently began to suck the skin on her shoulder.

"Jesse..." she whispered in a shuddery breath. He pulled back and gave her a small smile, but his face was red, and his breathing very labored. It was then that she realized his legs were shaking.

"Jesse!" she cried softly as she pulled him against her, trying to steady him as his unsteady weight made her sway back a step.

"Dammit!" she heard him whisper harshly against her hair. Tears immediately stung her eyes.

"It's OK," she said softly, stroking his hair, holding him close to her as his body started to shake. "We don't have to..."

"No," he breathed, stopping her. He pulled back just enough to lay his forehead to hers, his hands holding on hard at the tops of her hips. "I want you. I want you now. I need you now."

"I know..." she choked out, her voice full of tears; she pulled his head into her neck. "I know...I know, oh, God, how I know."

She gulped to fight back the tears, then straightened up as he began to pull back. She searched his eyes; they were blazing with desire and determination.

"I'm going to make love to you," he whispered, his shaky hands now running once, twice over her bare shoulders. "We're going to make love. Tonight, Becca. We've waited long enough."

She clicked the top of her mouth with her tongue in an attempt to keep the water in her eyes at bay and nodded. Her gaze locked with his. Feeling him against her, being so close, alone, in the light of the sunset, she needed him more than she'd needed anything or anyone in her life.

She craved him, too, and she was done waiting.

Becca took a deep breath and licked her lips, her determination matching his.

"I need you to make love to me, Jesse," she whispered, pulling him closer, one hand now bracing his back, the other gripping the top of the back of his leg.

He looked at her, surprised for a moment, then turned himself over to her as the words he needed to hear rolled like hypnotic caresses off her tongue.

"You promised me," she whispered, pressing her lips against his sweaty jawline. "You promised to make love to me. I need you so much. I want you so much, Jesse. I've waited. I've waited to feel you inside of me again. I want you. I need you. I want your strong body on top of mine."

He moaned as she kept speaking, blood loudly pulsating through him, the excruciating pain in his legs becoming a little more tolerable with each gentle, firm word she spoke. She kissed his neck, and his head dropped. She kissed his mouth, running her tongue along his lips.

"You're strong, Jesse," she whispered hotly against him as she continued to brush his lips with hers. "Your body is strong; your heart is strong. You make me strong; your love makes me strong..."

He kissed her hard and deep for a moment as he began walking backward, making stilted movements towards the bedroom. She grabbed his forearms, making him turn to walk forward as she slowly backed into the room, the pain on his face breaking her heart.

"Lay down," she said softly, and he groaned as loudly as he dared as his back hit the mattress and his head hit the pillow. He put one hand over his eyes.

"I'm sorry," he whispered hoarsely. She gently crawled over him, her heart beating wildly, and pulled his hand away from his face. There were tears in his eyes.

She smiled softly, studying him. Then she kissed him gently while she undid the button and let down the zipper of his jeans. His breath caught as she gently ran her hand along the hard length of him through his underwear, fighting the urge to move faster, to wrap herself around him right then. Jesse just lay there, watching her, completely captivated by the concentration on her face -- and silently giving thanks for being able to feel again.

Slowly Becca dragged his jeans out from under him and down his legs, dropping them on the floor. Jesse propped himself up on his elbows, breathing heavily.

"Are you alright?" she asked, her breathless voice the only external giveaway of how excited she felt. She ran her hands up and down the sides of his thighs.

"Yes."

"Good," she said as, much to his confusion, she scooted back off the bed. Then she picked up his left foot and started to massage it with a strong grip, working her way up, kneading the muscles in his calf.

"Ohhhh..." Jesse moaned, throwing his head back, mouth wide open. "Oh, God..."

She smiled and worked the muscles and tendons around his knee, finally digging into his thigh and hamstring.

"Feel good?" she smirked.

"So good," he breathed, pain and pleasure mixing on his face. "A little painful, but good. So...so good. God, Becca..."

"See, better than sex," she teased as she moved to his other leg. She watched his mouth twitch up into a crooked smile.

"Let's not get loony," he said, and she giggled. He dropped flat on his back as she worked on his other leg. She'd almost reached the top of his thigh when he reached out and grabbed her upper arms. Becca let out a little squeal as he pulled her on top of him and kissed her.

"Thank you, Florence Nightingale," he whispered when their kiss broke. All Becca could muster was a brilliant smile back at him. He remained hard, now against her thigh, and she could hardly breathe.

She pushed herself up by her arms just above his shoulders, her mouth finding his again, as he ran his hands under the bottom of her sweater, slowly lifting it to her breast line. His fingers were leaving trails of fire on her skin. They maneuvered her sweater over her head, and he reached for the hinge of her strapless bra. She kissed the top of his head as he undid the hook, and it fell to his chest. She moaned into his hair as she felt him teasing her nipple with his tongue, kneading her other breast in his hand, before wrapping his mouth fully around her, sucking like he was starving.

"Jesse!" she half-gasped, half-moaned, need coursing through her as he moved back and forth between her breasts, lavishing endless attention on both of them as she ground her hips into him, feeling him against the fabric between her legs.

She sucked in her breath as his mouth released her, his hands taking their place, and pushed her body down to face him and kiss him. His mouth was warm and wet as their lips glided together, tasting each other.

His hands reached the waistline of her pants just as hers reached the hemline of his t-shirt. He grunted, breathing hard as he pulled them and her underwear down at the same time, and she shimmied out of both. She lay naked, flush against him. He slowly ran his hands over her backside and up the sides of her torso, sending shivers down her spine. Then he cupped her face.

"You are so beautiful," he breathed, placing small kisses all along her cheekbones against her chin. "You are an angel. My angel. I love you,

Becca. I'll love you 'til I die."

"Oh, baby," she whispered, her voice shaking. "Oh, Jesse, I love you. I'll always love you...."

He captured her lips again as she slowly began to slide her hands up the inside of his t-shirt. When her fingertips reached the skin near his left shoulder, she momentarily froze, tears stinging her eyes. Jesse winced, then pushed himself up against the pillows behind him and pulled off his shirt. His pensive eyes searched her face.

Becca's hands flew to her mouth as she sat up and straddled his legs. She reached out a shaking hand and gently, so gently ran her fingers over the spray of dozens of scars, some small on the surface, some large and deep, that started just above his heart and shot out all over his chest, stopping just below his armpit.

She looked at him, pain on her face, with watery eyes.

"The...bullet hit some...thing else before it...hit...me," he said softly, swallowing hard. He cleared his throat. "It's designed to, to rip through on impact..."

A look of horror crossed Becca's face as tears fell on her cheeks. She gulped for air -- how close she'd come to losing him rushing back to her in an instant.

"It's nasty, I..." Jesse started, grimacing.

"No," Becca whispered, shaking her head vigorously. "No."

Her breath caught, and he reached out to wipe her tears away. She caught his hand and kissed his palm. She held onto his hand, and he whimpered as she leaned over and kissed his field of scars, slowly resting her forehead against him. He dropped his head on her shoulder as she quietly cried into his skin. They held onto each other, bathed in the orange light that filtered into the bedroom. The only other sound was coming from the waves crashing against the shore outside their window.

Finally, she raised her head up and took a deep breath, looking into his eyes. She gave him a sad smile as she moved the hand she was holding and placed it against the bottom of her stomach.

"We both have scars, Jesse," she said softly, running her hands over his cheeks. "Those we can see, and those we can't. Some will heal, and some..."

His tear-filled eyes searched hers as her voice caught.

"Some will never...fade away," she choked out, and he nodded, understanding.

He gently ran his fingers over her stomach, feeling her vertical c-section scar under them. He sucked in his breath through closed teeth and buried his other hand in her hair, pulling her against him and kissing her temple. She whimpered against his neck. He closed his eyes and cradled her against him. Then slowly, gently rolled her onto her back and tenderly kissed his way down from her neck, to her chest, over her stomach, pressing light kisses over the length of her scar.

She started to squirm against him as he kissed his way back up her body, gently pushing her legs apart. Feeling little pain now, he peeled off his underwear, then reached over and grabbed a condom out of the nightstand drawer. He rolled it into place as she waited for him, short breaths passing through her parted lips.

He hovered over her once again, love shining in his eyes, and gently kissed her.

"We have Jay," he whispered, and she nodded, tears slipping down her temples as he ran his hand along her arm, linking his fingers with hers above the pillow. "We have us. We have this..."

She gasped and threw her head back as he sank into her. He brought his lips to her neck as their shadows began their slow dance against the far wall of their bedroom, their baby sleeping soundly on the other side.

43

AT LAST

Light from a full moon that was brightest just before daybreak filtered into the beach house as Becca's eyes fluttered open and landed on his sleeping face.

His breathing was deep, heavy, rhythmic. So relaxed and perfect, she momentarily wondered if he'd ever had as good a night's sleep in his entire life.

Her foot was still wrapped around his, their naked bodies brushing each other under the sheets, the fingers of her right hand still entwined with his left against her breast.

They'd fallen asleep facing one another, looking into each other's eyes until exhaustion overtook him. His eyes grew heavy first, and she'd kissed them closed, then watched him sleep, almost afraid to close her own eyes.

But it wasn't a dream, after all. So often, she'd prayed to wake up with him by her side just one time. She smiled softly, now knowing this was but the first of many times he'd really be next to her when she opened her eyes.

Becca searched his sleeping face, seeing traces of Jay in his features. She'd watched her baby sleep so many times she'd memorized every little detail. Now she wanted to memorize him, this man who had swept into her heart like a hurricane and never departed from it, despite every storm that passed, despite the fires of hell they both went through.

Her eyes started to water as a thought struck her heart, as it sometimes did when she awoke for no particular reason in the dead of night. What would have become of her if she'd lost him -- if she'd lost them both? If she'd made one decision instead of another?

Becca tried to push the ugly thoughts from her mind, but it pulled on her heart as he peacefully dozed beside her. She still had that fear, that anxiety, and she truly wondered if it was one of those many scars that just would never go away.

Her eyes shifted from Jesse's face as her ears perked up. She could hear Jay in the other room, moving around in his crib, and she guessed that was the noise that jostled her awake. He let out a squeak and a baby sigh. Becca grinned, waiting for what might happen once he realized he wasn't in his crib at Grandma Wilma and Grandpa John's house. It didn't take long for her question to be answered as the soft squeaks turned into little panicked cries.

She untangled herself from Jesse just as he shot up out of his sound sleep beside her, eyes wide and looking around, completely startling her.

"It's OK," she said quietly, her heart suddenly racing.

"What's wrong?!" Jesse said, a little louder than he meant to, his heart pounding heavily.

"It's Jay," Becca said, pulling the sheet over her breasts and leaning back a bit from him. "He's just feeling a little lost."

Jesse blinked, then looked into her startled face.

"I'm sorry," he said hoarsely. "I...I didn't mean to scare you. I...it's a...reflex...I guess...I..."

He swallowed hard, willing his heart to slow down, his eyes glancing at the bedroom wall as Jay's cries grew louder.

"What can I do to help?" he asked as Becca took his hand in hers.

"I've got it," she smiled as she squeezed his hand and climbed naked out of bed. "Go back to sleep."

Jesse swallowed again, watching her body bathed in the moonlight as she grabbed a new pair of underwear out of a drawer. She then picked up his green Army T-shirt off the floor, shook it out, and pulled it over her head.

She grinned at the slack-jawed look on his face, then walked over to her son's bedroom.

Jesse shook his head a little, then threw the sheets off himself and swung his legs to the side of the bed, standing slowly. His legs were stiff but not as painful as he thought they'd be. He stretched and shook them out a little, too, as he heard Becca's soothing tone in the other room. He grinned to himself and grabbed his jeans off the chair in the corner as Becca, with a more-settled Jay in her arms, walked back into their bedroom.

She stopped in her tracks. He was facing away from her, completely naked, as he stepped into his jeans. The muscles under the smooth skin of his back were rippling in the moonlight. She watched as he pulled his jeans up over his bottom, somehow completely mesmerized by every move he made.

Finally, he turned to her and grinned as he actually heard her swallow hard.

"Maybe Jay would have been OK staying with Grandma and Grandpa a day or two," she mumbled, her eyes running up and down his body.

He smirked.

"We've got time for plenty more of that," he said, walking slowly over to them. He kissed his son's head then gently, firmly kissed Becca's lips. She sighed shakily as he pulled away.

"And they'll be plenty more of that," he promised in a whisper, then he ran his hand over Jay's hair.

"What's happenin' with this little guy?"

"He woke up, and I don't think he knew where he was," she frowned a little. "He might be hungry. I think he may be going through a growth spurt. He definitely needs a new diaper."

Jesse recoiled a little.

"I'll get the bottle if you get the diaper," he offered.

"Are you sure?" she asked, a little unsure.

"Becca, I can boil water," he said with a wink as he turned toward the kitchen. She smiled to herself and went back into the bedroom.

"You're a natural, you know that?" she said, her arms and legs crossed, elbow on one knee and chin resting on her fist. Becca was sitting on a stool across from Jesse as he slowly rocked Jay back and forth and fed him, an adoring look on her face.

"Oh, I don't know about that," he said, pulling back the bottle just a little bit to see how much was left. He didn't know much about babies, but he was pretty sure this one was in no mood to go back to sleep. His eyes were wide open.

"He's almost done," Jesse frowned, not entirely sure that was true. It was hard to tell when the formula in the bag inside the bottle was truly empty.

"Almost," Becca whispered, reaching out to run her finger along Jay's cheek. Jesse smiled at her, but her eyes had misted over and were filled with tears.

"Becca?" he asked gently. "What is it?"

She shook her head, trying to fight back her emotions, her feelings of guilt.

"What if...we didn't have him?" she asked, her voice thick. "What if...?"

"Becca. Don't..." he said softly, slowly taking the empty bottle out of Jay's mouth, putting it down on the floor next to him. He moved him against the thin blanket laying across his bare, scarred shoulder, softly patting his back.

"What would we do without him?" she asked, tears finally spilling onto her cheeks.

"Rebecca, please stop," he said, his eyes imploring her. "Please don't keep beating yourself up over...things that never happened."

"But, Jesse, what if I'd gone through with it? I...I wouldn't have him or you...I," she said, asking him the same questions she'd asked a few panicked times before. While she'd told him all about her pregnancy complications and Jay's birth in her letters, she'd never mentioned Harlem, the clinic, all the initial, conflicting emotions she'd had about being pregnant until he'd been home a few days. Becca suddenly brought it up one day when Penny and Matty both happened to be at the Schmidt's visiting with them.

At least that's how she felt about it; her confession left the four of them in tears. Matty tried to talk her through her guilt. Penny held her hand while Jesse held her close. He never judged her; he only felt rage at himself for leaving her so hurt and confused in the first place.

Now here she sat, her arms crossed over her stomach, rocking back and forth.

"Becca," he said calmly, knowing exactly how it felt to carry around misplaced guilt in your soul. His heart broke for her. And he felt guilty, too, for in no way being there when she needed him. So, yes, there was plenty of guilt to go around.

"Becca, look at me, please," he said firmly. She raised her teary face to him. "He's here. He's right here. He's healthy. He has two parents who love him. He has a...a bunch of people who would do anything for him..."

"I know," she whispered. "I know that, but..."

"No, no 'buts,'" he said, shaking his head as Jay let out a loud burp, causing them both to grin through the tears in their eyes.

"I will keep telling you this until you hear me until you believe it," he said, turning serious again as he looked into her eyes. "There is nothing for me to forgive. Nothing, OK? There is no blame here, you dig? I was the one...I made...bad choices..."

"Jesse..." she reached out, then pulled back, an apprehensive look on her face.

"You forgave me," he said quietly, and it hit him all of a sudden. A blank look came upon him as he realized right then that even though she'd done nothing to be forgiven for, she needed him to forgive her anyway.

He cleared his throat and blinked back tears, looking into her confused and expectant face.

"OK," he whispered, still patting his son on the back. "OK. You need to hear it, don't you?"

She sucked in her breath and slowly nodded.

"OK," he said, taking a deep breath. "I forgive you. I forgive you for... almost terminating...the pregnancy."

She closed her eyes.

"And...?" she asked quietly.

"And that's all I'll forgive you for," he said quietly. Her eyes shot open, questioning him.

"Becca, you can't help that you were sick. You quit your job; you did everything you...."

He shuddered.

"You nearly killed yourself to bring him into this world," he whispered, earnestly looking into her eyes. "No, I won't forgive you for that. I won't let you do that to yourself again, but there is no need for you to feel guilty about that, OK? Please, I beg of you, don't."

She swallowed and wiped her eyes, nodding once, the look of pure love on his face strengthening her.

Finally, she smiled at him, and he smiled back.

"I love you so much, Becca," he said softly. "Don't let this weigh you down anymore."

She looked at him, both knowing how often she'd repeated those very same words to him over the last several weeks, and his face turned a little pink.

"I know you love me, and I love you," she said, standing as he stilled the rocking chair and she kneeled in front of him. Jay turned his head around and looked at his mother.

She grinned, cocking her head to the side, and looking back at her son's toothless grin.

"'Don't let the sins of the past drag down the promise of the future,'" she whispered, and Jesse nodded.

"Chaplain Matty would be so proud," he said, his lopsided grin coming over his face.

Becca smiled at him.

"You're my angel," she whispered, watery eyes searching his as she nodded to their son. "And he's our promise."

Jesse looked back at her with equally watery eyes and nodded.

"Right on."

Jesse was right in guessing that Jay was up for the day before the dawn, even though a very tired Becca tried to convince him -- and herself -- otherwise.

"Sometimes he just likes to cuddle," she said with a yawn as she climbed back into their bed, a not-so-sleepy Jay tucked in her arms. Still clad in just his jeans, Jesse crawled back into bed behind her, wrapping his arms around them both, his lips brushing Becca's hair.

About five minutes later, he'd propped himself up on his right elbow as Jay reached out and poked Becca's nose and grabbed a strand of her hair, clearly trying to make his point that he wasn't tired, and his Mommy should wake up. Jesse had gently untangled Becca's hair from his little fist, holding his son's gaze for a few moments, conceding that they had, indeed, conceived the most beautiful baby on the planet.

Quietly Jesse backed away from Becca, who was deep in sleep, and threw the thin blanket back over his scarred shoulder, walking to the other side of the bed.

"Come on, Little Man," he said, picking him up. "Let's let Mommy sleep."

Jay didn't so much as whimper as his Daddy slowly, quietly walked through the living room and opened the screened door to the covered porch. Light was just peeking over the ocean as Jesse sat down in an old, wooden Adirondack chair just under the outside of the kitchen window. The sunrise wouldn't be too far behind.

Jay immediately turned his little head towards the sound of the waves, so Jesse sat his son on his lap, facing the water. He smiled as he wrapped both his hands around his tiny torso, and Jay leaned back against him, completely spellbound by the water and the breeze coming off the ocean.

Jesse took a deep breath, and the two sat there in silence for a few moments, soaking in daybreak. Then Jesse looked down at Jay, still seemingly captivated by his surroundings, and chuckled.

"Buddy, when you can walk, we'll go down there at low tide, and we'll collect all kinds of seashells, whatcha think?" he asked softly. "I used to do that with your great-grandpa when I was a little boy, you know."

Jesse blinked a couple times, then kissed the top of Jay's head.

"Boy, he woulda thought you were the peaches and the cream, I tell ya," he whispered, shaking his head a little bit, following his son's gaze. "He would have loved you. He would have loved your Mommy. He was a good man, Jay, and he was good to your Daddy. That's why your sweet Mommy gave you his name."

Jay looked back at Jesse as if to say, "you're interrupting my ocean sounds," and Jesse couldn't help but grin at the Becca-like glare. Jay's head turned back toward the ocean again when his Daddy was quiet.

Jesse swallowed hard and closed his eyes, thinking of his grandfather as he listened to the peaceful sounds of the waves crashing against the shore. Then he opened his eyes as they began to fill with tears -- and he thought about the first time he met the other good man his son was named after...

...Jesse leaned up against the bar and signaled for another drink. It was his first social event with the Pipefitters Union, and he didn't know a soul, except for the man who hired him. He'd conveniently decided not to show. Jesse knew he'd need to down a few more before he felt relaxed enough to make casual conversation with complete strangers.

"You're new," he heard someone say behind him.

When he turned around to see who was addressing him, he came face-to-face with Union legend Big Joe's son, Joe Ambrosio.

"Y...yes, Sir," he stammered, just a bit, tugging on his sports coat. "Yes, I'm Jesse Wanger, the new bookkeeper in, um, accounting."

"Yeah, yeah, that's right, yeah, I heard they hired a new one," Joe said with a nod. Jesse smiled a little, extending his hand.

Joe shook it, then gestured toward the bar.

"Want another?"

"I have one on the way, Sir, thanks."

"Sir? Dude, don't call me 'sir.' My Dad was 'sir.' I'm just Joe," he said with a shake of his head and a smile.

Jesse grinned back.

"Yes, Sir...er, Joe," he said as the bartender brought him another Jack and Coke and put a beer in front of Joe, with a nod.

They were silent for a moment as they both took a sip of their drinks.

"You know what pisses me off?" Joe said suddenly. Jesse shook his head, having absolutely no clue.

"California baseball," Joe said with disgust. "I still can't fuckin' believe the goddamn Dodgers and Giants moved, now the Boston Braves are in Atlanta? What the hell is in Atlanta, Georgia?"

Jesse chuckled, and they spent the next hour talking about anything and everything, from baseball to women to the Union. Joe told him of his newfound love for bowling and his mom's famous Queens cannolis -- both laughing at turns and settling into one of the most comfortable conversations of their young lives.

"Well, I've put in my time," Joe finally said, looking around and downing the remainder of his latest beer. Jesse felt a little disappointed but sat up a little straighter and nodded.

"It was good to meet you, Joe," Jesse said, extending his hand. Joe looked at it in confusion.

"You're coming with me," Joe said as if it was a foregone conclusion. "You don't want to stay here with the stiffs, do ya?"

A surprised but grateful look came over Jesse's face.

"Well, I..." he said, looking around. "I don't know how long I'm supposed to stay, you dig?"

"Man, you're with Big Joe's kid," Joe said with a wink and a smirk. He slapped one hand down around Jesse's shoulders as he stood up off the barstool, giving it a little squeeze. "I'll take care of ya."

Jesse smiled and nodded as he followed "Big Joe's" son out of the bar...

Jesse squinted through his tears as the sun started to shine brighter on the horizon.

He looked down at Jay, who'd apparently become bored enough with the sunrise to fall peacefully asleep on his father's lap. He lifted him up and turned him away from the light, laying him softly on his stomach against the blanket on his shoulder. He began to smooth tiny circles on his back as Jay curled against him, sound asleep.

Laying his head against the chair, Jesse closed his eyes. He could feel his son's soft breath against his neck as tears slipped down his temples...

...Eli dropped his head.

"You're lying," Jesse whispered, looking from Eli to Matty and back again from the confines of his military hospital bed.

Eli shook his head.

"Eli, tell me you're lying to me, I swear to God..." he started, beginning to panic, beginning to think...no, it couldn't be true.

He'd been awake for three days before he realized Joe hadn't come to visit him, and no one had said a word about him. He finally asked.

Now he wished he hadn't.

"I'm sorry, Sergeant," Matty interjected softly, taking a step forward when he saw Eli wasn't going to be able to continue. "Sgt. Ambrosio and several others saved a lot of men before...they pulled a number of men out of the drainage trench and into the chopper field, but..."

"Stop," Jesse begged, closing his eyes, his aching head swimming. He remembered voices. He remembered Joe's voice. He remembered Joe yelling.

After a tense silence, Eli finally took a deep breath.

"He...was...buried in New York about three weeks ago," Eli said quietly, his voice breaking, tears streaming down his face, "next to his Dad."

Jesse grunted out a sob, quickly bringing his fist to his mouth. He nodded, fully crying now.

"I'm so sorry," Matty whispered with tears in his eyes.

Jesse gulped for air a couple times, causing Matty and Eli to look at each other, momentarily panicked. Finally, he put up his palm then looked Eli straight in the eyes, his breathing heavy and ragged.

"My s...son was born too soon and fought for his life," he said in a hoarse whisper. "Bec...my....Becca almost died before he was born. I'm...I'm paralyzed and...and my...my best...fr...friend is...d...dead. KIA? Right? Do I have it all fucking right?!"

Eli nodded and whispered, "yes."

Jesse turned his cold stare to Matty.

"I thought you had to die to fuckin' go to Hell, Reverend," he seethed, on the verge of breaking down again. Matty closed his eyes.

"Not always," he whispered apologetically.

Jesse stared at him blankly for just a moment before slapping the base of his palms against his eyes and rubbing hard, trying to make the nightmare go away...

His face filled with pain. Jesse hugged his son tighter against his chest as he heard the music begin to play inside the house, signaling that Becca was awake.

"If you are anything like your namesakes, son, you'll be golden," he said brokenly as he wiped away his tears.

"And his father," Becca said as she stepped out onto the porch and walked over to where they were sitting. He turned his face to her, and she smiled sadly at him, seeing he'd been crying.

"If he's anything like his namesakes and his father, he'll be golden," she said softly, a catch in her voice, as she ran her fingers through Jesse's hair. He dropped his head a moment, closed his eyes, and grinned.

"Etta James?" he asked, lifting his head again and nodding toward the inside of the house, trying to change the subject. He patted his right knee, gesturing for her to sit down with them.

"Yeah," she smiled, sliding onto his knee as his arm wrapped around her.

"What are you boys doing out here?" she asked quietly, running her hand over the top of Jay's sleeping head.

Jesse gave her a sad grin, then a brief chuckle.

"Thinking about past pain," he said quietly, shaking his head a little. "Just what I told you not to do."

"Hum..." she hummed for a moment, laying her forehead against his cheek.

"It's unrealistic to think we won't think about it, but we shouldn't... dwell on it," she conceded softly. Jesse sucked in a hard breath and nodded.

"The past makes who we are now," she continued, placing her hand over his on Jay's back and closing her eyes against the bright sunrise. "It...it makes us appreciate what...who we lost but also what we still have. Maybe...maybe that's how, someway, someday, we'll find our own kind of peace."

Jesse smirked a little.

"At last?" he asked.

Becca smiled against his shoulder.

"At last," she whispered.

Jesse took a deep breath and laid his head back against the chair once again, closing his eyes and soaking up the quiet dawn of the new day, holding his whole world in the palm of his hands.

44

WHAT A WONDERFUL WORLD
(EPILOGUE)

NOVEMBER 1982

Becca felt her husband's hand clasp hers a bit tighter as they walked closer to the Wall. She looked up at his pensive profile and squeezed his hand reassuringly in return.

Jesse, Eli, and Matty had all marched through Washington, D.C., to the Vietnam Veterans War Memorial with thousands upon thousands of other Vietnam vets two days before, at the dedication ceremony. The memorial itself was controversial, many not liking the simple design of names in white letters carved into a shining black stone. But, what, or rather who, it represented, wasn't controversial to anyone. Each letter spelling out the name of an American killed in or missing from the war, and there were more than 58,000 names on the Wall.

Knowing the dedication ceremony would be very crowded, Jesse, Eli, and Matty went to D.C. first for the somber event. The families arrived the next day, and today was the day they wanted to find Joe's name and pay their respects.

Jesse's eyes scanned the scores of people looking for the names of loved ones as he walked closer. It was less crowded, but several hundred people were still milling about, some crying, some talking in hushed tones. The grounds had already taken on a spiritual atmosphere that seemed to resonate with everyone.

Jesse stopped walking about 100 feet from the Wall and swallowed the lump in his throat.

"You OK?" Becca asked, rubbing his arm.

"Yeah," he croaked out with a nod, a brief smile coming over his face as he looked down at her. She smiled back at him then looked toward the Wall again, taking a deep breath.

"What do you think?" she gestured toward the memorial.

Jesse took a good, long look, this having been as close as he'd been able to be to the memorial itself. He took a deep breath through his nose, and let it out slowly, the cold November air floating around in his exhale.

"I think it's perfect," he said quietly. "It's bold but simple. Black and white, just like...him. I think he'd approve."

Becca nodded sadly.

"Me, too," she agreed softly. "Are you ready?"

He nodded, then looked to Jay, who was walking just a couple paces ahead of them. He was almost 14 years old now and was a lanky and slightly shorter image of his father. However, he had his piercing blue eyes and crooked smile, which he turned and gave to his Dad before he walked ahead of them again. Becca and Jesse started walking again, too, catching up to the rest of the large family that had come together to honor Joe and all the veterans.

Everyone spread out to look in the section where Joe's name was supposed to be. Eli was looking in the column next to Jay when the teen suddenly stopped and dropped on one knee.

"Uncle Eli?" he said, turning his face to his uncle. "Here he is."

Eli knelt down by his nephew and read the name next to a small diamond...

"JOSEPH F AMBROSIO"

Eli ran his fingers over the name, and his eyes filled with tears.

"Yeah," he whispered, catch in his throat. "Yes, that's him."

Jay nodded and pulled out the folded, plain white paper and pencil from his coat pocket. As many others were doing, he scratched the pencil on the page over Joe's name. Becca and Jesse approached them, leaving a perfect tracing of the name on his paper.

When Jay was finished, he stood, locking eyes with his father. Tears pooled in Jesse's eyes as he knelt in his son's place, Jay putting his hand on his shoulder briefly before walking back to his mother. A silent look passed between Eli and Jesse as they both reached out to run their fingertips over their friend's name.

'Hey, man," Jesse whispered as tears rolled down his cheeks.

"We're here," Eli added quietly, laying one hand flat against the smooth stone, using the other to wipe his eyes.

They both froze in time at the base of the Wall for several minutes. Then, finally, Matty came up to them, putting his hand on Jesse's shoulder. After a moment, Jesse swallowed the lump in his throat and reached inside his breast pocket. He pulled out a small, plastic frame. A copy of the picture of him, Eli, and Joe smiling together at the base In Country rested inside. Almost reverently, he placed it on the ground below Joe's name.

"Haven't forgotten you, buddy," he whispered. "Never will."

Eli nodded as they lingered a few moments more. Eventually, John walked up behind the three of them and wrapped his arms around them all. Jesse looked back, and John nodded to him. Jesse and Eli both slowly rose to their feet and moved back as Joe's mother, Gracia, stepped forward. She looked up at Jesse and smiled through the tears in her eyes. She took his hand, then ran her other palm down the side of his cheek.

Jesse smiled softly at her, then silently pointed out her son's name. She squeezed his hand before letting go, then took a couple steps closer to the memorial. He watched as she bent down, ran her fingers over the letters, then bowed her head to pray for her son...

He stared at the front window. Two gold-star flags hung there, one faded by time, the other shiny and new.

Jesse swallowed the lump in his throat, rooted to the sidewalk, leaning on his cane. He'd been home 10 days and today was Memorial Day, a new federal holiday officially remembering those who died in service to their country. It seemed an appropriate day to go to Queens, and he told Becca he needed to go alone.

After dinner one evening, Wilma and Liz had quietly shared with him the details of Joe's funeral as Becca put Jay down for the night. Hundreds of people had packed the church, a Catholic parish not too far from the Ambrosio home. There were so many people there that several mingled outside because they couldn't get in. Liz noted that family, friends, and union representatives were everywhere, including Felicia, her father, and her new Park Avenue husband. She mentioned Keith was there too, having never been drafted in the military.

Jesse had listened, pain in his heart, as they told him how they all tried to talk Becca into staying home from the funeral. She'd only been out of the hospital a couple weeks, and Jay was still there. At that point, they hadn't heard any news about him, and everyone worried that sitting through Joe's funeral would be far too difficult for her. Becca, being Becca, steadfastly refused. She said she owed it to Joe to be there. She owed it to Jesse to be there. So, she went and sat stoically throughout the entire Mass until the bagpipers played "Amazing Grace" as a closing hymn.

"She lost it then," a teary Liz had softy told him. "She sobbed the rest of the day..."

Jesse stood up a little straighter and squared his shoulders, now looking at his best friend's childhood home. He took a step forward just as a small stampede of 6- or 7-year-old boys came charging from the back of the simple two-story brick house to the front, racing up the stone steps with their canvas cowboy hats and plastic guns. The front door flew open.

"No running in the house!" said the stern voice.

"Yes, Nonna," came the chorus of young responses. Gracia smiled a little and took a step out onto the porch, looking at the young man on the sidewalk she'd spotted a minute earlier through the window, trying to summon the courage to walk up to her door.

"Hello, Jesse," Gracia said with a soft smile as she closed the front door behind her.

Jesse nodded, slowly making his way up the stone steps.

"Hello, Mrs. Ambrosio," he said as he reached the top step.

She smiled again and gestured to the empty chairs on the porch.

"I'd invite you inside, but there is a fort in the middle of my living room and no place to sit," she said, with a little smile as they both took a seat. "Marie-Alice had her fourth yesterday, and I have the boys until tomorrow."

"Congratulations," he said, smiling a little.

"Thank you," she nodded, folding her hands in her lap. "She got her girl, Isabella Rose."

"Beautiful name," Jesse nodded. He cleared his throat to speak but couldn't find the words to say. He glanced at Joe's mother, then at the ground. Gracia smiled sadly at him.

"I'm glad you're home, Jesse," she said softly. He squeezed his eyes closed as they filled with tears.

"I'm sorry, J...Joe...isn't..." he started, trying to clear his voice a few more times.

Gracia reached out her hand and covered his shaking one. He took a deep, ragged breath and looked at Gracia as tears fell out of his eyes.

"He was there," Jesse whispered. "He was with me. I think he dragged me...I don't know...I don't know, but he was there. I remember. I heard him. I know I heard him..."

Gracia's eyes filled with tears as she squeezed Jesse's hand. He breathed deeply again and swallowed down his tears, trying to calm his emotions.

"I loved him like a brother," he said clearly, looking into Gracia's face, placing his other hand over hers. "He is one of the best men I've ever known, and I miss him. I know it can't possibly be the same as how you miss him, but I miss him. I'm sorry, Mrs. Ambrosio. I'm so sorry I couldn't...I couldn't...I was..."

She shook her head and took a deep breath.

"You're a good boy, Jesse," she said, a smile behind her tears. "My Joe was always a good boy, but I always felt a little sorry for him."

She looked away a moment as Jesse raised his eyebrows.

"He idolized his father, for good reason," she continued, "but his Dad wasn't around anymore. He grew up with all us women clucking around him all the time..."

She chuckled a little, and Jesse grinned.

"He stepped out of his father's shadow; he stopped being the 'little brother' and became his own man when he met you," she said softly, a loving glow in her eyes. "He loved you like a brother, too, I can tell you that for certain."

Jesse smiled sadly and nodded, looking back to the ground once again.

"You had to come home," Gracia said after a moment. Jesse's head shot up, his eyes searching hers. "You had a beautiful little boy and his mother

waiting for you here. And as much as I wanted my baby boy home with me, God had other plans."

Jesse looked at her, confused and awed at the same time. She smiled again and wiped her tears with a handkerchief she pulled out of her skirt pocket.

"God puts you where you need to be until your job is done," Gracia said, nodding firmly, that belief fully alive in her heart even as her voice shook. "My Joe's job was done. If I can forgive the Holy Father for taking both my husband and my son Home on His time, you can forgive yourself for coming back to Jeremiah and Becca and all the people who love you. Your job isn't done, Jesse. It's just beginning."

Jesse nodded to her just as a crash was heard inside the house. It seemed the cowboys and Indians were getting a little out of control. She turned her head toward the house, and slowly they both stood. Jesse swallowed heavily as Gracia smiled up at him.

"Joseph Jeremiah," Jesse said, a catch in his voice. "His name is now Joseph Jeremiah Wanger. We, Becca and I, can't quite call him 'Joe,' but..."

Gracia's hand clutched her chest, a fresh batch of tears in her eyes.

"I'm honored," she said with a nod, patting Jesse's cheek as he gave her a relieved smile. "I know you'll raise him right. You better. I'll be keeping an eye on you."

She smiled at him and winked before turning to walk back into the house...

Jesse walked away from the Wall and straight to Becca, reaching out for her. She fell into his embrace and ran her hand over and over the back of his head as he buried his face in her shoulder.

"It's OK," she said quietly, her eyes closed. "It's OK. Everything is going to be OK."

She felt him nod against her, then clear his throat. He moved back a touch to look into her watery eyes, both gaining strength from each other, as they always had. Becca's eyes flicked behind him.

"How's Nonna Gracia holding up?" she said. He shook his head in disbelief.

"Strong as ever," he said. "She's one tough Italian lady."

Becca smiled and nodded, then turned to look behind her when she heard someone call her husband's name.

"Jesse Wanger?" came a voice in the crowd behind them. "Dat yous, Wanger?!"

"Oh my God," Jesse whispered, looking over the top of Becca's head, a big smile breaking over his face. "Charlie? It's Charlie Brown..."

Jesse stepped back from Becca, taking her hand and turning her around. Her sad tears turned into happy ones as her husband stepped from her to wrap a lanky black man in his arms in a big bear hug.

"Lordy, all mighty, it's good to see you again, boy!" Charlie said, megawatt smile firmly in place as he patted Jesse on the shoulder. Jesse didn't think he'd aged much since the last time he'd seen him.

"Here, here's," Charlie said, gesturing for his family to join him, "this here's my wife, Rita, and our girls, Bella, Bea, and Bonnie."

Becca shook Rita's hand as Jesse called his children to him.

"This is Jay," he said, introducing his son to Charlie. Just then, an impish little10-year-old girl popped up under Jesse's arm and pulled a butterscotch candy out of his coat pocket. She smiled, black pigtails bouncing and a gleam in her dark blue eyes, "and this is Hope. I gotta keep an eye on this one."

The adults chuckled as Becca and Jesse's daughter waved to Charlie's family, immediately catching Bonnie's eye. They looked to be about the same age. She pulled more candies out of Jesse's pockets and offered some to Charlie's daughters.

"And this," Jesse said, putting his arm around his wife, "is Rebecca."

"Rebecca," Charlie repeated, smiling warmly at her and taking her hand in his. "Well, well...you're his Becca. I's never forgot yer name."

"It's so good to finally meet you, Charlie Brown," Becca said, her smile just as bright.

"Yous look kinda familiar," he said, furrowing his brow. Rita nodded.

"Hey, you're on the news!" Charlie said as he suddenly remembered where he knew her from. "That...what's it called? CNN?"

Becca blushed.

"Yep, that's me," she nodded.

"She's a reporter in their New York bureau," Jesse said proudly, smiling at her. Becca had worked as a newspaper reporter and editor at the local Long Island paper for a couple years when they lived at the beach house. Soon they needed a larger place and moved to a three-bedroom home not too far from John and Wilma.

At that time, Becca took a job at a local TV news affiliate. She kept in touch with Malory all those years. When Malory became a producer at the fledgling 24-hour cable news channel, she talked Becca into coming in for an interview. She was hired almost immediately, and it didn't take long for her to become a lead reporter in their new New York newsroom.

"That's the cat's meow right there," Charlie said with a chuckle, "And what about you, man? Whatcha do when your tour is over?"

Jesse smiled softly.

"It hasn't ended yet," he said. Charlie looked at him in surprise.

"He didn't wear his uniform today," Becca explained, looking up at him with equal pride in her eyes, "but he's Major Jesse Wanger now."

Jesse nodded.

"I'm an instructor with the Army Corps of Engineers," he said. "I travel around the country some, but my base is West Point."

"I'll be damned," Charlie said, shaking his head. "Didn't peg you for career military."

"Neither did I," Jesse chuckled, "but it just felt right. My job's not done yet."

He smiled softly at Becca, and she smiled, too.

"What about you?" Jesse asked.

"I's a State Senator now in South Carolina," he said, puffing out his chest a bit. Jesse's jaw dropped.

"Really?!" he asked, looking to Rita for confirmation that Charlie wasn't pulling his leg.

"After I made an honest man outta him, he goes and becomes a politician," Rita said, with a smile and a nod. "Can you believe it?"

Jesse laughed.

"I sure can, ma'am," he said.

"Yeah, after we got married..." Charlie started.

"Where'd you get married?" Hope interrupted, breathless. She loved to talk about weddings.

"Hope, honey, that's rude," Becca said sternly.

"Nah, it's OK," Charlie said, answering the little girl who was the image of her mother. "We got married in the oldest church in Charleston."

"My Mom and Dad got married on a beach -- in Hawaii!" Hope exclaimed, having just heard the story in full not too long ago.

"Oh!" said Bonnie, excited to hear all about a wedding at such an exotic location.

Hope quickly launched into the story of the double wedding in Honolulu -- where her Mom and Dad and Uncle Eli and Aunt Liz were married by Uncle Matty on the beach. Only Uncle Matty wasn't Uncle Matty then, she explained. But she was told, he spent as much time dancing on the sand with Aunt Penny as both newlywed couples did, and it wasn't too long after that he became Uncle Matty.

She giggled as she talked about watching her 1-year-old brother Jay dancing in a little grass skirt with her parents in the home movie they'd just viewed together not a month earlier. Everyone giggled right along with her, except Jay, who rolled his eyes at his little sister and shook his head.

Becca caught Jesse's eye and smiled. Jesse smiled back at her, only the two of them knowing when they truly became husband and wife...

"We need a new birth certificate," Becca told the confused clerk at City Hall.

"Excuse me?" the clerk answered, lowering her specs and looking at the somewhat furious woman before her.

"Look," Becca said, not about to take "no" for an answer. "My little boy's name is not 'Baby Boy Schmidt,' and 'blank' is not his father."

When the copy of Jay's birth certificate finally arrived in the mail in September, Becca went through the roof. She just knew it was the "devil nurse" who probably filled out the paperwork.

She handed the copy of the certificate over to the clerk.

"Let me ask," the woman mumbled, slowly rising out of her desk chair and disappearing into the back.

"They'll take care of it, honey," Jesse said, shifting 9-month-old Jay from one arm to the other. They really needed a stroller, he decided. The kid was getting heavy.

"They better," Becca said, shooting a glare at the closed door beyond the clerk's desk. Then she smiled sweetly at Jay, who was looking at her blankly.

"Your name is Joseph Jeremiah Wanger," she said, tickling his tummy, eliciting little giggles from him. "Yes, it is, yes, it is."

Jesse smiled. He loved hearing his son laugh and seeing Becca's smile, even if it was only temporarily masking her anger.

"If they don't take care of it now, we'll make sure it's taken care of later, Becca," he offered.

"No," she shook her head adamantly. "No, he's a Wanger, and his father is a Wanger, and I want that fixed right now. I want you to be known as his father in the eyes of the law. I want him to legally have your name, your grandfather's name."

"OK, OK," Jesse said, running his free hand down her arm, trying to calm her down as she became more animated. "OK, we'll get it fixed today."

Suddenly Becca's head shot up, and she searched his eyes.

"I want your name," she said. "I want Jeremiah's name."

"What?" Jesse said, a puzzled look on his face. Becca looked from him to Jay, who was wearing the same confused look. She grinned.

"I want your name," she repeated, softer this time. "I want us to get married. Today."

"What?" Jesse said again, still confused. "Um, Hawaii? Double wedding? January? Ring a bell? Dr. Redd is paying for us all to..."

"Yeah, I know," Becca said with a wave of her hand. "We'll still do that, but I want to be Mrs. Jesse Wanger today. I want us to become the Wanger family officially, legally. Today."

"I, uh..." Jesse stammered as the clerk came back to her desk with another paper.

"You'll have to fill out a new form..." she started.

"Can you give us a marriage license form, too?" Becca asked, being much sweeter now.

The clerk looked to Jesse, who just shrugged and smiled a little, then he cleared his throat.

"Yes, we need a marriage license, too, oh wait," he said. He turned to Becca and took her hand in his, then slowly knelt down on one knee, balancing Jay on the other.

"Rebecca Schmidt," he said, smiling up at her. "Will you marry me? Right now?!"

"Yes," she said, giggling and pulling him up to kiss him, hugging them both to her.

"Yes, I will marry you right now!"

They both turned to face the clerk, who was looking at them like they were a little crazy, smiling like fools in love.

"Ah...can someone do that, I mean, marry us, right now?" Jesse asked.

Not taking her eyes off the trio in front of her, the clerk picked up her telephone.

"Denise, it's Janet. Is the magistrate finished with his lunch yet?" she asked as she finally cracked a smile. "We've got a couple of live ones here."

Twenty minutes later, Jesse and Becca, all paperwork complete and marriage license in hand, became husband and wife under the watchful eye of Denise, Janet, and Jay, who stayed in his father's arms through the whole, short ceremony in the magistrate's office.

"You may now kiss the bride," the magistrate said as he smiled. Jesse bent down and gave Becca a soft kiss, then they both kissed Jay's head. The judge and the two clerks began to clap, and much to everyone's delight in the room, Jay smiled and clapped right along with them...

Hope Francis Wanger, who had finally finished telling her version of the Hawaiian wedding story, was born in 1972. Despite the complications with her first pregnancy Becca really wanted another child. Jesse finally relented, and they conceived easily, but he watched her like a hawk. They loved being able to share the experience together this time. But her body didn't like being pregnant the second time any more than it liked it the first time. Yet this time, her stress level was much lower, scores of family and friends checked up on her regularly, and Jesse was by her side. She carried Hope 36 weeks before it became necessary for her to be born via c-section.

Their baby girl was completely healthy and didn't require a stay in the NICU, but Becca's doctor advised her not to have any more children. Jesse and Becca agreed that their family was complete and focused all their parenting energy on raising their little boy and his baby sister.

After the story was over, the Browns and the Wangers exchanged contact information and hugs, vowing to stay in touch.

As they waved goodbye, Eli slapped Jesse on the shoulder, and he turned around.

"Boys are getting a little restless," Eli nodded toward his three sons -- Levi and John, who was holding a soccer ball, and little Leo. "We're going to head over to the Mall."

"Yeah, OK," Jesse said.

"We'll take Jay and Hope with us, if you want to stay here longer," Liz offered, walking over to them, holding 3-year-old Leo in her arms.

"We can all go," Jesse said.

"You sure?" Becca asked.

"Yeah, yeah, that's fine," Jesse nodded, then glanced toward the Wall again. "Where's Gracia?"

"Marie-Alice took her back to the hotel," Penny said as she, Matty, Wilma, and John, and all the kids walked up to the group. "She's OK, just a bit tired."

"I can imagine," Becca said, putting her arm around her daughter and nodding to Penny and Matty's twin girls - Samantha and Danielle. "You girls going to play soccer with the boys?"

"Yep," Samantha nodded. "All of us are going to play!"

"The whole gang?" Becca asked. All the kids nodded. "That's two full teams."

"I know!" Hope said excitedly as she started to weave through the crowd, her cousins, Joe's nieces, nephews, and almost all of their parents following close behind.

Hats and gloves were quickly piled into makeshift goalposts. The group found some open grass just beyond the Reflecting Pool, not far from the Washington Monument. Soon the game was underway, under the watchful eyes of the adults.

Jesse smiled as he scanned the faces of the big family in front of him. That's what they'd all become, a big family, supporting each other through thick and thin, good and bad. He shook his head, having never imagined any future, let alone this future, in his wildest dreams.

Becca wrapped her arms around his waist, laying her head against his chest.

"This is a good day," she said quietly, with a little nod.

"Strangely enough, it is," he agreed, wrapping his arms around her. "By the way, where's our son?"

Becca smiled up at him and nodded toward the Reflecting Pool. He looked over just in time to see Jay shyly take Isabella's hand in his as they sat down on a bench at the edge of the water.

A look of surprise came over his face. "When did that happen?" he asked, completely dumbfounded.

"When we weren't looking," Becca shrugged. "They're growing up together, so you never know. You know that's how it happened for Eli and Liz. They were friends for years before they fell in love. It could be a match made in Heaven."

"Hum," Jesse murmured, smiling to himself, not at all unhappy to see his son holding hands with Joe's niece. "Time will tell. I guess sometimes love happens that way."

Becca stepped in front of him and smiled, wrapping her arms around his neck and pushing her body against his.

"And sometimes it strikes you like a lightning bolt, and nearly 15 years later, you're still wondering what hit ya," she whispered, softly kissing his cold lips. He wrapped his arms around her tighter, deepening the kiss until she pulled back, breathless, her eyes bright and looking adoringly into his.

"Either way," he whispered against her lips, his loving eyes searching her face. "It's worth it."

"Completely worth it," she agreed, capturing his lips with hers once again.

THE END

CPSIA information can be obtained
at www.ICGtesting.com
Printed in the USA
BVHW071423250122
627118BV00007B/68